Celestial Sailors, Chasing Sunsets

Michel Forlini (450) 965-1186
oracle@caribcoms.net

Celestial Sailors, Chasing Sunsets

Michel Orlando Forlini

ISBN: Softcover 978-1-4363-3159-3

This is a work of fiction. Names, characters, places and incidents either are the product of the author's imagination or are used fictitiously, and any resemblance to any actual persons, living or dead, events, or locales is entirely coincidental.

This book was printed in the United States of America.

To order additional copies of this book, contact:
Xlibris Corporation
1-888-795-4274
www.Xlibris.com
Orders@Xlibris.com
48380

Contents

"All that is given with love is added to the soul."

Michel Orlando Forlini

I wish to thank the following people:

To my wife Sotiria and my two boys, Matteo and Dantes, thank you for the support.

Special thanks to Nellie Corsi and Melpa Kamateros, for their creative input and editing skills.

Cover picture, map from Davidrumsey.com, design by Michael J. Hanlon of Inzinc

Part one

The Essence of Reality

Signs

The noises slipped into my office through invisible crevices. I rose to my feet, stared everywhere. Inch by inch a trail of unseen footsteps unfolded beneath the beam of morning sunlight plunging through the window.

"Not again," I muttered. Distressed, I sat down, and listened as they creaked their way around my desk. I observed, intently, the pocket of air not three feet away from me. Something moved. Deeper into the air I peered, when the contour of a translucent silhouette surfaced from the void.

Whispers began addressing me. The language itself was indiscernible, though the tone suggested an urgency to communicate. And as it dangled in the air awaiting God knows what, I remained uncertain if this appearance was an illusion, or something more. Something freed from the grave!

This proved too much for me and I screamed. Immediately the ghost melted away into the void. But soon, I feared, this *thing* would return. In silence, I waited, wishing it would never come back. Yet there it was, I knew. Out there.

Cruelty has an enormous power, especially when combined with cunning, in which case it becomes merciless.

"Please," I cried. "Tell me what or who you are."

Noises, emerging here and there around me, poisoned what little sanity I possessed. The mysterious unknown had come to visit. Screaming for help was pointless, for this had been tried before, unfortunately resulting in colleagues whispering behind my back:

"Look! Look how pale Thomas is this morning. Some say he's losing his mind."

The noises slowly exited through the wall. I exhaled profoundly, searched everywhere, and finally realized that even emptiness concealed secrets. I felt doomed. Lost to whispers I couldn't translate.

With one hand supporting my chin, I pondered. These manifestations had started on Father's Day, ten months ago. That day I had gone alone to the cemetery, laid a flower on my father's grave, and came back home. But that was also the day I slapped my eldest son Nicholas, just because he hadn't mowed the lawn. The one and only time I ever hit any of my children, I might add.

I wondered why these manifestations persecuted me at work and home. Curiously, no other witness was ever present when they arose. Unable to make sense of any of this, I got up, walked to the large window, and gazed at the Manhattan skyline.

"Will these hallucinations ever stop?" I grumbled.

Minutes later, a faint knock on the door interrupted my thoughts. Joyce, my assistant, came in, and informed me of an important meeting about to take place.

"Really?" I replied. I slipped my arms through my jacket sleeves, when abruptly she came forward, looking quite distressed.

She pressed her hand on my forearm. "You're not invited, Thomas," she announced.

"Ah? And who exactly is invited?"

"The executives," she noted, in a faint whisper.

Such news did not sit well with me, for an impromptu meeting in this investment firm, with all of the executives except me, meant I no longer orbited close to the center.

"All of this because of a few cries," I said.

I discreetly opened the door, peeked down the corridor, and stared at the men and women about to enter the conference room.

"By the way, I haven't been able to find a store that carries the toy your son asked for," Joyce said.

"Who?"

"Your son," Joyce sighed, showing her exasperation. "You know, Michael, the one whose sixth birthday is in two days."

"Ah, yes. What was that about a toy?"

"I haven't found a store that carries it."

"Don't worry about it," I said. My lack of disappointment seemed to puzzle her. I stepped outside my office, and casually strolled down the corridor.

As I neared the conference room, I glanced inside and noticed Christopher, a colleague I faintly knew and who wasn't an executive.

"Oh, you guys are great," I remarked, in a low voice. "A few troubling episodes, and I'm excluded."

Back inside my office, as I wondered how I could salvage my situation, to my great despair, the noises again creaked their way around the room. This was unbearable. With nerves ready to collapse, I rushed out of my office and ran down the hall to the water cooler.

Breathing heavily, I managed to regain my composure as two persons approached—Chris, who I had seen earlier in the conference room, and

Travis, a take-charge colleague I had always found a bit too sneaky. Greetings were exchanged, and I soon perceived, through their humorous voices, that a frivolous subject was being discussed.

"All I'm saying," Travis said, "is that the age difference between men and women matters less if the oldest one possesses a sufficient amount of money to compensate. Here, let's ask our friend Thomas about what he thinks."

"Someone mentioned my name?" I asked, casually.

"Chris and I would appreciate your input," Travis said.

"Go on."

"Well," began Christopher, delicately, "one only needs to look at Mister Robbins and his bride-to-be to dispel your theory. She's fifteen years younger than him and he seems very committed on keeping her happy. I believe the key is not money, but commitment."

Chris had spoken to me as though he had known me for years, with a warm smile and his hand on my shoulder. This man knew how to be pleasant. Curiously, I realized I had underestimated him and saw why he had been invited at the meeting—even though he wasn't yet an executive.

These past months had cost me dearly. My reflections stopped shortly after, for as soon as Chris left, Travis, himself excluded from the inner circle, proposed to form an alliance, one that would have us inform Mister Robbins, a chief executive officer, about the words spilled by Chris.

"He didn't say anything bad," I countered.

"That depends on your interpretation, not what he said."

Sordid thoughts flooded my mind. Then, just as suddenly as they had surged, something stirred my conscience and swept them aside like grains of sand under a mighty desert wind. Shame and concern could be seen on my face.

"I don't think so," I said, hesitantly.

"Oh, spare me the theatrics," Travis scoffed.

With his hand on my shoulder, Travis insistently led me away, and talked very convincingly about my overseen merits.

"Let's have a confidential meeting of our own," he proposed.

* * *

The seven o'clock traffic was lighter than usual that Thursday night, and in less than an hour, I was home. I parked the car in the driveway and remained there, just for a few minutes, looking at my house. Sitting on a corner of a quiet suburb, the house had an enormous well-lit living room, a den, a large dining room with patio doors leading to the huge terrace, four bedrooms and three bathrooms.

Jane, my wife of fourteen years, through careful and artistic taste had handpicked the selection of shrubs, flowers, bright interior colors, gaily patterned tapestry and furniture—details that grace a house with personality and transform it into a lively home.

"You did well," I said to myself, with a faint smile, acknowledging the house's worth. "You did well, Tommy Boy, but you can do better."

I stepped out of the car, and saw Michael's bicycle, carelessly left outside our two-car garage. Gazing at the sky, I beheld the moon's silvery smile. How nice. But it was after opening the door that true beauty greeted my eyes, for I had not taken more than a few steps inside that Michael excitedly rushed towards me.

"Daddy!" he shrieked, running with outstretched arms. I welcomed his magic like a breath of fresh air. I indulged completely in the soothing impact of his little body, my two arms wrapped mightily around him, and in that frozen moment the smell of his hair was perfume that sweetened my existence. Everything about him was so genuine and loving. A golden smile that everybody thought compelling, and his embrace that melted my soul.

He looked at me, blue eyes filled with such bliss that I wondered how God had managed to create such sunshine. Yet his purity also distressed me, for I feared such an enchanted child, who brought happiness with his twinkling smile, would be an easy prey in today's cruel world. With wild abandon, he flung his arms around my legs, squeezed me, and erased those thoughts.

"Michael," I said, seriously, wishing his full attention. "I told you a many times not to leave your bicycle outside. You have to put it in the garage the next time." I took off my jacket, laid it on the couch, and loosened my tie. When I turned around, I saw him standing there. A cloud lined his face.

"Are you mad at me?" he asked, his eyes the color of rain.

"No, it's just that I want you to be careful with your stuff, which reminds me; I'd like to get you something else for your birthday, since I can't find the toy you asked for."

Meeting my eyes, his stare quizzed me. "You promised," he said.

What could I do in front of such sorrow? I knelt and put my hand on his heart. "You know what sound daddy cannot stand? The sound of your heart breaking. That is worse than all the volcanoes in the world erupting at once. You're right . . . I did promise."

The sparkle in his eyes returned.

There is something profoundly sacred between a father and his son. A bond that is unique.

I was glad Michael's words had struck a chord, forcing me to change my position, since I knew all too well the impact of broken promises.

Extending his hand, Michael touched the golden pendant I wore around my neck.

"What's that?" he asked, wanting to strike a conversation, since the answer was known to him.

"You know what this is. It's my crucifix."

"How come you wear one and I don't."

"I'll get you one next week."

"Promise?"

"Promise."

With a big smile on his face, he jumped in my arms with such unpredictability that I lost balance and fell backwards on the floor, with him on top of me. He said that he loved me, and that, warmed my heart. His eyes bore into mine. Somehow, he knew what remedy to apply and grinned mischievously, as if we both shared a secret. Putting both of his hands on my cheeks, he giggled. A giggle I enhanced when I tickled his ribcage for a few seconds. Then I stopped. For no reason.

I stood up and looked at Nicholas, slumped on the couch, unmoved by my presence, his eyes riveted on the television. Deep inside of me, a voice kept repeating, '*Go to him.*'

Though Nicholas still ignored me, I approached him and brushed my hand against his shoulder.

"Nicholas, did you have a nice day?" I asked. Receiving no answer, I moved into the kitchen where I found Jane waiting for me to come to the table.

"Have you tried talking to him?" she asked, anxiously.

"Yes, and with the same result," I answered. Knowing the hurt she felt when disruptions invaded our home, I curled an arm around her shoulder. "Everything is going to be fine," I assured.

We sat at the kitchen table, ate dinner, all the while exchanging very few words. Suddenly, to my left, a flash of light caught my attention. Curious, I turned around.

"Dear God!" I whispered, my eyes widening. On the front page of the newspaper lying on the table was the picture of a sailboat, rising above the ink, or so it seemed, dazzling and inspiring, like a polished dream. I seized the newspaper, lifted it to my eyes, somewhat impressed by the sailboat's puffed sails and elegant lines but, mostly, for what I felt its capacity to cover great distances in this great world.

I began to read the ad which promoted a free family cruise aboard a sailing yacht in the Caribbean when quite unexpectedly, I saw myself standing behind the helm, amid blue waves, golden sunshine and reggae music. Reading further down, the ad specified the urgency to call.

What spell did this article cast over me? I felt bewitched by the proposed adventure of an exalted life that demanded wages in courage and sweat, yet rewarded with spectacular sunsets and the deep blue seas. What was happening to me? Where were these thoughts coming from? This ad was assuredly a ploy, wasn't it? Something this valuable? For free? It had to be a trap!

Just then the picture darkened. Then the winds died, mysteriously, until the sails uselessly fluttered. And the ship, which had valiantly plowed through the waves, now barely floated on a sea the color of doubts.

Struck by such magic, I wondered; could I be responsible for turning a diamond into coal? Nonsense, I finally concluded.

Further down the page, an article caught my attention; that of an invisible little boy heard crying in a cemetery by many people. In the article, a prominent psychic detailed the fate of souls having crossed over before their time—'Lost Spirits', he called them, stranded between worlds, unable to find the Light and with no other spirits close by to guide them.

"Oh! That article simply brought me to tears," Jane confessed, obviously affected. "Poor little boy. Stuck all alone, and no one to guide him into the Light. How awful this little soul must feel, seeing people coming and going everyday and never stopping to help."

Of course, one of the theories I had envisioned for my affliction was the presence of spirits. It was a frightful prospect. One that scared me to death. I wondered how much longer I would suffer if this was the case. I opted not to pursue the riddle, considering the possibility too gloomy.

Later that evening, while my family slept, I retired to the den. Shortly after, while seated at my desk, an unknown manifestation disrupted my solitude.

"Oh, no!" I whispered. I tried to remain calm, but the dimness of the room, suddenly filled with invisible footsteps circling around me, brought me to the edge of insanity.

I shuddered and wanted to scream for help. Then I remembered what kind of help Jane would suggest. Though weary of all these noises, I nonetheless stared into the emptiness and was able to discern the contours of a turban-clad man.

With a surreal and vaporous ease, the phantom approached, so manifestly intent on establishing contact that his airy flight froze me. Peaceful and solemn, the phantom started opening its mouth. Far from welcoming this materializing ghost, I wished for the end of this madness, and suddenly it disappeared.

Having witnessed this unknown entity's dissolution, I nervously waited to see it again. Perhaps the time had come to face my demons after all. Nothing, however, surfaced from the void. Discouraged, I went to bed.

Shortly after, while sound asleep, vivid images of my father paraded in my dreams. With a desert warrior of some kind by his side, my father pleaded that I might listen to his urgent message. Great lamentations and spectral limbs made me wish for the end of this nightmare until I noticed that, indeed, I was awake!

Unable to move, I remained in bed, vulnerable and scared, while my father and the desert warrior, standing not ten feet away from me, claimed all of my attention. With his face harboring a grave expression, my father floated a bit closer, this under the agreeing and watchful eyes of the desert warrior. The weight of years gone by had spared my father's appearance, as he stood there just as I last remembered him. With a measured tone, he expressed grief and agony over choices he and I had made.

"By what I have seen beyond the grave," he announced, "and by all that I am allowed to say, you must listen to your conscience. That is where we wield our influence. The covenant forbids more instructions."

He paused, and stared at me with the clear objective of telling me something. A secret. To make me understand! Great sorrow emanated from eyes burning like fire yet colorless as water.

"Pinch yourself before you think we're only a nightmare!" he pleaded gravely, showing the disappointment raging within. "Accept our presence as proof that we exist. Oh! If you only knew what needed to be surmounted just to be perceived!"

His voice took a more commanding tone and, sensing an opening, he used his fatherly influence, which to my surprise still existed. "Great fortunes are not what I thought." He shook his head. "Wealth," he added. "I used to see it in things that don't cross over to the other side."

A look of pain swept across his face. My silence gave him strength.

"There are messengers in one's life," he insisted, "and you must pay close attention to them. They secretly glide beside you, wait for the opportunity to enter and once given access, slip into the mind and touch the heart, so as to provide illumination where darkness rules. They insure one's Original Design."

Those words appeared to have lifted away some of his pain. His face softened, and he continued with extreme care. "The earthy body is meant to be used in a manner that will enhance your soul." He paused, as his searching gaze probed my thoughts. With the litheness of a shadow he glided forward, stretched out his hand and waved his translucent hand at the top of my head. Immediately a cold whisper ran through my body. Unable to endure this madness any longer I screamed, with such vigor that the ghosts dissolved into the darkness. I could not lie still any longer. I leaped out of bed and screamed at the top of my lungs.

"What is it?" Jane asked, rubbing her eyes after lighting her night table lamp. "My God, you're soaked!"

My body quivered. I hurriedly slipped underneath the sheets. Seconds later, in a trembling voice, I explained that I had dreamt of my father, in such vivid details that the sheer recollection chilled my body. She detected my distress, and thoughtfully asked me to share my dream.

"It was my father," I answered, clearly aggravated. "He was trying to talk to me. His eyes were puffy, like he had been crying, only there were no tears. He was reaching out to me, from the edge of our bed!"

I shook my head, and added, angrily: "And why am I lately assailed by visions of desert warriors and sand dunes? What is it that they want from me?"

"Just relax, Thomas," Jane said.

"Relax? Let me tell you something. If it was my father trying to relay some message, he can just go back inside his coffin, because I sure as hell have nothing to say to him."

"Shhh! Don't talk like that," Jane cautioned. "You don't know what he was trying to tell you?"

"I haven't the faintest idea," I retorted. "But the mere fact he was trying to talk to me makes it an unbelievable dream altogether, like all the others I've been having for months."

Suddenly the alarm clock rang loudly on my night table. Puzzled, I picked it up, observed that the programmed settings had not suffered any alterations, then stopped the ringing. I carefully submitted it to another quick inquiry and, finding nothing wrong, set it back on the night table.

"Maybe you should see a doctor."

"I'm not sick."

"I'm talking about a psychologist, or a psychiatrist."

"I'm not crazy," I answered, curtly.

"I never said that," Jane consoled. "But these dreams must have a meaning. Maybe you should pay more attention to them. A specialist might help you unlock their secrets and, who knows, maybe they're more than dreams."

"What do you mean by that?"

"I'm not sure," she replied, in a strange voice. "Maybe it's something you unconsciously wished so hard in your mind that dreams have become something more."

Lying down, my silence and discouraged face enticed Jane to adopt a more soothing tone. "Maybe you just need a vacation," she said, pressing my hand. "You spend less and less time with your children since your last promotion. You barely talk when you're home, and when not immersed in your laptop, you're simply too tired for anything."

"Oh, yeah," I replied, sarcastically. "I see us now, sailing on this free cruise in the Caribbean."

"What do you mean?"

"I'm talking about the newspaper ad."

"In which newspaper did you see this?" she asked, narrowing her eyes.

"Jane, for God's sake! I snapped. "It's on the same page as the article about the little boy's soul unable to go into the Light."

I leaped out of bed, went downstairs, making certain I flipped all available light switches on the way, took the newspaper and rushed back upstairs. There I searched the paper through and through, easily finding the article about the little boy's trapped soul. But the ship being a mysterious entity from the start, instead of surrendering its magic, was sailing somewhere outside my grasp—eager, perhaps, to stir someone else's dream.

Jane looked at me with a face both surprised and suspicious. I shook my head, and waited for the sailboat to rise above the dried ink. Minutes later, I threw aside the paper and curled under the blanket. Could things possibly get worse?

I awoke that Friday morning feeling depressed. Sleepless nights generate such emotions, and as I shaved in the bathroom, the door burst open and in walked Nicholas. Without a word, keeping his distance from me, he dug his hand into the pantry, grabbed a towel, then exited. I remained there, motionless, contemplating my lathered face in the mirror like a sad, frozen clown.

Nicholas, now in his teens, was a stranger to me. My mind pondered. I remembered pressing my father for details about himself, his thoughts, anything. Simple things. Like his favorite color, most fearsome nightmare. Any answer would have entered my childhood's sacred shrine.

I recalled a hot summer evening, when I was ten years old, sitting on the balcony of our New Jersey home, watching the sky with my father. I asked him about the stars, hoping to steer the conversation towards other topics. Things like his past, his dreams.

"Thomas, what do you want me to say?" he sighed, his eyes made weary from my insistence. 'Anything!' I pleaded in my head. 'Anything!' He shook his head, not at me, I realized much later, but at the silence he was unable to shatter. Was he annoyed at his ineptitude to converse? I'm sure of it. Did his weariness show? Absolutely. Did he break the curse? Sadly, he never did. Shortly after, he promised to be more open, but he broke that promise, along with my heart, for his words had once carried hope.

My father died shortly after Michael's birth. My father; a man I barely knew. Incredibly, no tears ever formed in my eyes.

Last week, after being awakened by unusual noises from Michael's bedroom, I rushed in and found Michael propped up in bed, talking to no one. He asked me questions about ghosts and phantoms. I quickly deflected those questions, covered him with the blanket, kissed him goodnight and exited the room.

As I hastened down the corridor, something parted the darkness that blinded me. Then it hit me; how easily we become what we despise. Struck by the similarity with my father, I hurried back to Michael's room and held him tightly. But as no words escaped my lips, I sobbed uncontrollably. "You can't go on like this," I whispered to myself. "You have to change."

That was a week ago. And I was still the same.

I finished shaving, put on a suit, and heard Michael bid me goodbye from downstairs.

"Bye Thomas," Jane also shouted before closing the door. I rushed to the bedroom window just in time to see Jane backing up the SUV, with Nicholas and Michael in it. I gazed at them in wonder. What good deeds had I performed to merit such bliss? Searching vividly, I came up empty. God must love me, I told myself.

I rushed downstairs, ate a quick breakfast, then searched all of Manhattan for Michael's toy. At the last store I visited, a clerk, seeing how discouraged I appeared and sensitive to my situation, ordered the toy and told me it would arrive in a few hours.

"The trouble is I have no time to get it tonight. What time is your store opened till on Saturday?

"Five o'clock."

"I'll be here tomorrow."

* * *

Shortly after six o'clock, I accompanied Mr. Robbins and Travis to a restaurant. With Mr. Robbins nudged between Travis and me, we followed the hostess to our booth. Looking around, I noticed that this restaurant quickly filled with patrons wearing expensive clothes and sparkling jewelry on their wrists and fingers. Somehow, as I subjected this place to a deeper scrutiny, I believed that this place lent itself perfectly to the birth of secret alliances and covert tactics.

It was then, just after ordering cocktails, that Travis, who knew the underside of the business world and understood wealthy people with enormous egos, dropped the first words of contempt. Playing a man's fragile ego, none more fragile when alluding to his masculinity, Travis casually inquired about our companion's bride-to-be.

"You know her?" Mr. Robbins asked, surprised.

"Not really. Chris told me about her."

"Who?"

"Christopher Moyers."

"Ah, and what did he tell you?" Mr. Robins curiously pursued. I knew by his suspicious stare that Travis had sparked his interest.

"Not much, really," Travis replied, half-jokingly. "Chris doesn't fashion himself as the kind of person who talks behind one's back. He just mentioned that she was quite a bit younger than yourself and hoped you had it in you to make her happy, or something like that."

The ghastly plan had been set into motion. I innocently looked around, while Travis, feigning vague boredom, took a menu. Flipping the pages, he examined it, his voice softly inquiring on what to eat. I perceived in this detached behavior, a clever subterfuge supporting the fact that he had uttered such gossip without any intended self-profit.

The tense silence came to an end.

"Is that all he said?" Mr. Robbins asked. The beads of perspiration on his upper lip and words spoken through his parched throat clearly betrayed the embarrassment he felt.

"I think so," Travis replied. "Although I really can't be sure. Perhaps Thomas remembers." Travis had pronounced the statement in a solemn fashion, expecting me to go along.

The waitress came by, put our drinks on the table, and quietly walked away, her footsteps sinking into the thick carpet.

Mr. Robbins took a sip of his vodka martini, breathed deeply, and nervously tapped his foot. Of course, now and then, remorse for resorting to such a hideous plot nibbled at my conscience. Unfortunately, reentering the circle had become an obsession.

"Did you witness this discussion, Thomas?" he finally asked me.

I tried to appear credible. I knew such an act would spell my curse, and as I pondered on my reply, I was assaulted by images, no doubt generated by the remorse gnawing at my heart. Images of a desert warrior waving his hands and clearly determined to stop me from speaking.

"Not again," I whispered. To exterminate this vision, I imagined a terrifying sand storm. Nearer and nearer it came, and though the desert warrior wildly agitated his arms and fought for survival, the next instant the storm invaded, leaving nothing behind.

"Yes, I did," I finally answered, concealing my disgust. We both stared at each other, unflinchingly, reading thoughts through camouflaged emotions. Through the crowd's informal chatter and soft music playing in the background, a deep silence fell and isolated us in an invisible pocket.

"Anybody else in the office made such comments?" Mr. Robbins asked a few seconds later. There was a threatening calm to his tone.

"I'm not sure."

"Bullshit! he roared. "There's never only one that talks. Never!

He glanced around, satisfied himself that no one else cared for the outburst of just another man in a suit, then looked at Travis and me with a faint, devious smile.

"You both know I have a lot of pull in the firm," he informed. He was eyeing me quite intensely, much more than Travis. He called the waitress, ordered three more drinks, and smiled at me.

* * *

Later that evening, as I sat in the kitchen, angry at myself, Jane interrupted my thoughts.

"Honey, do you mind taking Michael to soccer tomorrow? I have to visit my sister in the morning. She's not feeling well."

"What time?"

"One o'clock."

"I can't. I want to finish some work and get Michael's toy in the afternoon."

"But I have to see my sister," she pressed.

"What's wrong with her? Is she depressed again?" My tone of voice, rather than ending the argument, had just fuelled it.

"What if she is?" Jane countered. "It's not easy being divorced with two kids, especially with her ex-husband not doing his share."

"She's the one who filed for divorce."

"He used to hit her and—".

"I have work to do," I interrupted abruptly. "Besides, haven't you done enough for her in the past few months?" She looked at me in disbelief, but that didn't affect me. "Furthermore," I added, "can you not, in light of your sister's choice, appreciate your husband's sacrifice at providing money, therefore having to occasionally submit myself to wicked work schedules?"

"Occasionally?" she remonstrated, raising her tone. "You're always working! You're so conceited and self-centered, it's unbelievable."

"You mean because I earn money for all of this!" I opened my arms, inviting her eyes to admire our luxurious surroundings.

"We don't need more money. We need you here more."

"Next week things will change."

"How can you be sure?" she vehemently protested. "Thomas, don't you get it? The business world only wants masters it can enslave."

"And since when is making money a sin?"

There was an awkward silence. Jane offered no reply, vaguely drummed the cloth with her fingernails, and looked at me pensively. I had been so absorbed in winning the argument that consoling gestures had never entered my mind. What was wrong with me? Everybody I spoke to in this household had a sad look, save for Michael.

I gave in. "Okay, I'll go," I nodded. "I'll bring him to the toy store in the morning, give him his gift, then bring him to the game."

"Perfect. Just make sure to be here for three o'clock. That's when the other kids will be arriving for his birthday party."

"We will," I said, smiling.

She rose from her chair, opened her arms, and hugged me.

The following morning, as I ate breakfast, I admired the sight of Michael in the living room as he jumped with joy and played frivolous games with the beam of sunlight streaming through the living room windows.

He twirled as though he and the sunlight formed but a single entity, and the appealing sparkle in his eyes, with its blend of gold and blue, enticed visions of heavenly shades, mysterious emotions, and inestimable treasures. It was fantastic! Unexpected! It promoted a place of disregarded wealth. A kingdom filled with everything I tried to achieve or obtain elsewhere. A place where one feels safe, appreciated and loved. A place so close and yet, for many like myself, so far. Suddenly I realized the emptiness of my life. Emptiness I had expanded every year, for I had missed all of his few birthdays.

Outside, spring was in full bloom. Inhaling profusely, I filled my lungs with fresh air, looked at my lawn, and smiled as the damp grass, which bore traces of the night's dew, shimmered in the sunlight.

I looked up. Hardly a cloud strode across the clear blue sky. I strapped Michael in the backseat, rustled his sunny hair, and closed the door. I drove along. The traffic was light, and we made our way towards the bridge.

Life was beautiful, for when I looked at Michael, he smiled at me. A smile dappled with wisdom, which totally surprised me, for such an expression is usually surrounded by wrinkles. I asked myself; 'What else could anyone need?'

As if caught in some spell, it seemed that my true fortune was being revealed. From the confines of my heart I felt what could only be Michael's magic. He seemed too perfect for this world, yet too magnificent and valuable to belong anywhere else.

I stopped at a red light and, just as it turned green, proceeded along. That's when a speeding car changed my life. I saw it coming. I turned the steering wheel, pulled it all the way to the left, hit the brakes. The distance separating us vanished, and the next moment my car ripped open under the impact.

For a moment, even the simplest gesture of moving my fingers seemed impossible. Gradually I recollected what had happened, just as I regained some physical capabilities. I looked around. Twisted metal surrounded me on all sides. I pushed with my hands, elbows and legs. The curved metal seemed to move away. And as I turned around I saw Michael, his chest pressed against the jagged edge of the caved-in door, lying in blood I knew was not mine.

Tragedy

"Daddy, I'm scared," Michael whispered. His face grew paler and paler, this while the sunlight streaming into the wreckage intensified the redness of his blood. After holding my stare for a few seconds, Michael, frightened by his injuries, seemed to realize the somber reality.

"Daddy, I'm scared," he repeated.

I worked my way into the backseat, and noticed that the door had been pushed way inside the car—way inside his ribs.

Relentlessly, my hands pressed against his body, and reluctantly, I observed his blood seeping between my fingers. Harder and harder I pressed.

"It's okay," I tried comforting. "You'll be fine. I promise."

I felt his troubled breathing on my face. His blood seemed to be getting colder. "And you know," I said, painfully mustering a smile, "that there's one sound daddy cannot stand, and that's the sound of your heart breaking."

He coughed, and his eyes questioned mine through a veil of tears. Feeling the scope of their scrutiny, I further concealed my agony, noticing how, all of a sudden, his animated blue eyes protested with vigor. He looked thoughtfully at me. In those wonderful eyes, his incomprehension dissipated. Then, as if some unknown voice had smoothed his agony, he smiled and closed his eyes. For the last time.

For what seemed like an eternity, I gazed, speechless, before the first word escaped my parched throat.

"No," I whispered. I dutifully extricated his body from the twisted metal, cradling him once done. Kneeling on the sidewalk, I buried his head in my chest. I felt numb. With a bloodied hand, I wiped away my tears. This couldn't be happening.

"Oh . . . my God!" I muttered. For the second time in my life, all in the same week, and always with Michael in my arms, I cried. Running my hand through his hair, I tried to understand. But how can one understand madness?

I stared into a tiny opened slice of his eyelids—into lifeless eyes. In shock, no rescue maneuver ever entered my mind.

Trembling uncontrollably, I looked around at the growing crowd. My life was over. Finished! Lunacy and delirium seemed logical extensions of this tragedy.

I grabbed the golden chain around my neck, tightly closed my fingers around it, and vigorously snapped it free. It was under great hope that I held the pendant. Under greater hope that I stared at it, convinced that something exceptional was going to happen. For one never knows the blissful gift such a religious object may grant.

Crucifix between thumb and forefinger, I pressed the divine symbol on Michael's forehead, and prayed.

"Dear God, please don't take my little Michael," I implored.

I pressed harder, prayed louder, yet Michael's lungs did not inflate. Burning tears rolled down my clenched jaw. I uttered another cry. "Please, sweet Jesus, not him. Take me instead."

The sight of Michael's still limbs positively rendered me mad. Infuriated, I screamed:

"How dare you take him?"

I pressed the crucifix with such force that droplets of Michael's lifeless blood escaped the new cut on his forehead and trickled down to his cheeks.

Quite unexpectedly, I found myself shunned by all that I implored, while Michael, the joyful soul with honeyed laughter, inherited the attributes of rigidity through which death solidifies its ghastly hold. Faced with such cruelty, my faith shriveled.

I threw away the crucifix, tightly hugged Michael's body, and rocked him while muttering a litany of blasphemies. Then in the tumult of my fury, as I willingly sank into this hell, there surged a voice of reason, resilient and full of hope, one meant to void my despair. Yet no matter what that voice encouraged, I was a prisoner of emotions and, as such, beyond the realm of reason.

Not without tremendous effort I tossed aside this unsought voice when, out of the corner of my eye, I caught sight of two paramedics pushing vigorously through the crowd. At last they arrived, pried Michael from my arms, and gently laid him on the ground.

As they began their examination, I tried to regain my breath, inhaling profoundly the still air while getting up.

I nervously observed the two paramedics working on my little boy, expertly running their hands over his ribcage for signs of internal injuries. One of the paramedics bent over Michael's face and gave him mouth-to-mouth resuscitation.

But life would not enter.

A sentiment of detachment took over. This wasn't happening. In a couple of seconds, I would wake up, in bed, next to Jane, and tell her about this atrocious nightmare.

I felt a tap on my shoulder. "Sir, can you hear me?" a policeman asked.

A sense of reality slipped into me, unfortunately, since reality was the last thing I wanted. I looked down at the paramedics working on Michael, whose shirt had just been ripped open. A deep gash across his ribs proved so horrific that I choked and nearly vomited.

I would never forgive myself. Never! Then a crazy thought entered my mind. Why didn't I tickle him more the other day? I could have tickled him more. Why didn't I?

It was under such a thought that I watched the two paramedics stop their maneuvers. Under such a thought that I watched one of them furtively glance at his watch. They grimly shook their heads, and seconds later, looked at me with revealing eyes.

The death of a son is an abomination.

Parents are not meant to bury their children. It is an unnatural act of unspeakable proportions. Becoming widowed or orphaned are undoubtedly among life's greatest tragedies. But no words can describe the intolerable pain caused by the death of your child. That kind of suffering is beyond words.

I didn't feel abandoned by God. It was much worse. I felt betrayed and cheated by Him.

"No!" I yelled. "No, please no!"

I fell on my knees, sobbed uncontrollably. Wave after wave of guilt came crashing over me. A horrible desire, of being swallowed by the earth and never spat out, came upon me.

Just then a million things raced through my mind. And out of the lunacy of this moment, one of them made sense. It appeared under the recollection of Michael's last words, of him being scared, combined with the newspaper article of a little boy's spirit stranded between two worlds and unable to go into the Light, that my destiny unfolded. My spirit, thrashed and battered, refuted a Higher Power, for I knew my traditional beliefs had proven futile. In my eyes Heaven was nothing more than a mirage, and the crucifix laying on the ground an object made of metal—a useless thing!

Things needed to be done. And fast.

"I want to touch him," I told the policeman. Holding my left arm so as to make sure that I didn't crumble, the policeman knelt beside me. I gently stroked Michael's hair. He remained there. Bloodied. So young and innocent. Motionless, under my touch, his angel-like face never to smile again.

I felt more determined than ever. I turned to my left, and observed the policeman, whose eyes grieved so genuinely I briefly regretted the actions about to take place.

Discreetly, my eyes traveled down to his hip. There, in a leather holster, was the object capable of granting my wish. I inhaled profoundly. Then, I shifted my body to the right, causing the policeman to stumble, and with my right fist tightly clenched I hit him square in the jaw. He fell back, limp and unconscious. I bent down and hastily tried to unsnap his holster. But the holster would not surrender the weapon.

I madly pulled the pistol's grip, no doubt encountering problems with what I believed to be the holster's safety device. Yet a closer inspection revealed no such thing. It was as if my muscles were counteracted by an invisible force.

Encountering such resistance, I willed with all my might and found strength where somber thoughts are to be found—in darkness.

The policeman's faint moans compelled me to pull harder, when deep within me emerged a voice of reason which sounded, all of a sudden, so familiar. Perhaps too familiar.

There was a great struggle within me. But the darkness I sought was overwhelming. Then, something gave.

At long last, I held the pistol. It briefly glinted in the fading sun; this passport to a world where Michael aimlessly wandered. I had to get to him. Holding up the pistol, I waved it and heard the loud gasps of shocked onlookers.

The crowd took a step back, and stood silently, as their eyes followed my every movement with a morbid fascination.

Suddenly, I felt something. A presence inside of me. It rose and brandished the Light I wished to extinguish. Nothing mattered. Already the sun seemed less bright, and the air I breathed unkind. This only strengthened my resolve.

I turned and looked at Michael.

There is something profoundly sacred between a father and his son. A bond that is unique.

I knelt and whispered in his ear:

"It's okay. Don't be scared. Daddy will soon be with you. I promise!"

Caressing his cheeks with one hand, I put the cold, comforting steel canon in my mouth, closed my eyes, smiled, and pulled the trigger.

After Life

I floated in total obscurity, and though weightless, there seemed to be a force tugging me downward, like quicksand. A faint light blinked before me. Just then, noises outside this mysterious abyss resonated. I listened, attentively, and as the light intensified and chased away the darkness, I discerned the shape of two bodies lying on a street, motionless and unrecognizable.

"Daddy?"

The anxiety I felt evaporated. I turned around and beheld two glittering blue eyes over an endearing smile. I approached Michael, knelt to hold his body in my arms, yet for some unknown reason felt nothing. Quite frankly, each footstep carried a strangeness not yet understood.

I looked at Michael. "Your presence feels like gold," I softly told him, "and I long to hold you, yet my body receives no warmth from yours during this embrace."

Standing there, peaceful and serene, he offered no reply. I gazed at our surroundings; at this crowd massed around a car wreck. Michael pointed down. I scrutinized the two bloody faces before me. My God! Was I dreaming?

Suddenly to my left a policeman approached, one who neither looked at me nor stopped. I braced for the impact when, aghast, I dissolved into him. This scene repeated itself, as Michael and I left the bustling corner.

In this manner we travelled, from one street corner to the next, melting through the crowd. And nervously I noticed that as we did so, nothing stirred my body—nothing save the illusion of a draft, the anguish of the impact, and the astonishment that there wasn't any!

Confused as to whether I was dreaming or not, I decided to solve this riddle. I looked at my hands and, consciously trying to join them together, beheld spectral inter-penetration instead of contact. This confirmed it! I was neither dreaming nor physically alive. I remembered everything. My plan on joining Michael in the after life had worked!

Just then, I perceived a glimmer, mysterious and penetrating. Michael and I walked towards it without any sort of physical effort. Within a lighted dome I discerned a man in his eighties with sparkling blue eyes, wearing a robe of sublime whiteness which softly fluttered with each waving gestures.

Once close to the dome, a whirlwind of clouds erased the streets, and the silence was broken only by my deep gasps of astonishment. Seconds later, I saw a turban-clad man making his way towards us, walking while floating. Of course, at once I recognized the wanderer of my dreams, the desert warrior I had persistently chased away.

Once near us, the desert warrior smiled at Michael and me, then bowed with deference to the old man. "I am sorry, Master," he said. "I tried to prevent it, and failed."

He turned around. "I am sorry, Thomas," he told me. "I have failed you."

And before I could ask what incident had prompted his apology, the Master addressed him in a voice filled with grace. "Your soul summoned all the powers you possess, and for this we are grateful," he assured. "You are a loyal disciple and there is no need for apologies, for these greater powers that could have curbed such dreadful events belong to Heavenly Beings other than Spiritual Guides."

Spiritual Guides? Heavenly Beings of greater powers? What kind of world was this?

The desert warrior bowed his head.

"I suggest you proceed with your next assignment," the Master indicated. "But before going to the Council, please extend our gratitude to the one who tried helping you."

Proud and noble, the desert warrior acknowledged the instructions. Once more he bowed to the Master, closed his eyes, and made no sound as he dissolved into the clouds.

In a soothing voice, the Master welcomed us. Then, he looked solely at me. "Even though grim emotions clouded your mind and contributed to your regrettable gesture, Thomas, the taking of a life is a most serious matter." His voice was clear, solemn, with a trace of judgment.

Having claimed all of my attention, he continued. "Suicide and murder are never part of the Original Design."

"The Original Design?" I asked.

"The series of trials meant for your spiritual growth," the Master answered. "As mentioned, murder and suicide are not sanctioned."

"But they do happen," I protested.

"They do," he assented. "But even then, the trials are meant for the soul's elevation, not its abandon."

I contemplated the barrier I had erected.

"You are to dwell on a plane different than Michael's," he resumed, sternly. "Different, in fact, than all the souls who previously held family ties with you in the material world. There you will find yourself unable to communicate with beings on a higher plane, though they, if they wish, are capable of coming to you. You will discover more as you journey for answers. But on that plane you will remain, this until a final decision is taken on your fate."

"Is that it?" I asked, bewildered. "Is my whole future compromised by a single act?"

"Impeding the Original Design carries a penalty," the Master replied. "Serious consequences follow serious transgressions. Death is meant, in some cases, for others to draw strength and faith, to draw inspiration for greater things."

It was then that my voice turned cold and severe. Yes, I had committed a grave sin, and though I argued I had acted out of compassion for Michael, the Master shook his head.

The end only made me wish for a new beginning, one with Michael, Jane and Nicholas. Unwilling to give up, I vehemently restated that compassion had proven to be my sole motivation.

"So, you committed this transgression out of compassion?" the Master gravely observed. "Did compassion for your wife and other child enter your mind prior to pulling the trigger?"

Nothing could be shielded from this being. He stared at me, his eyes filled with the brilliance of a thousand stars, an intense and guiding look.

"I pray you closely examine the motives that led to your downfall," he said. "This so you may hasten your soul's healing."

Sensing my despair, Michael moved forward and proposed that since my future seemed uncertain, then why couldn't the both of us return to the physical world while awaiting the final decision regarding my fate?

The Master pondered my son's request. I anxiously waited, pleasantly surprised and impressed by Michael. I looked at the Master. His eyes sparkled with instructions that magically hopped into my mind. Then, the Master smiled, just as his luminous core shone like the blazing sun before he vanished in a burst of light.

From those instructions, I gathered that my nature enabled me to float, to hover, to fly through the air, to ride the winds, if I chose to, to dissolve into objects or people, quite naturally.

With the reflex of walking still fresh in my mind, I could move my ethereal essence accordingly, although no effort was required. I could also manifest myself to others, but in order to do so, a combination of desires, thoughts, abilities and Heaven's permission were required.

Finally, only through some form of spiritual growth was I to gain powers approaching those of Spiritual Guides, who remain with an earthly host the duration of their physical lives and are amongst the entities who muster the necessary influence to try and curb events outside the Original Design.

* * *

A slight trick of the will sufficed to seep through the walls, and in this manner Michael and I entered our home. Soundlessly, we hovered and wandered, unnoticed, when I discovered a sad reality—that invisibility had not spared me from grief or torment.

The house felt cold. I looked around, expecting to see some traces of my earthly passage. But as of yet, none were visible. As usual, Nicholas sat in front of the television, endlessly changing channels. Was this to be expected so soon after our deaths? Noises flowing from the kitchen beckoned my attention.

There I found Jane, keeping herself busy by cooking. She roasted something in the oven, and carelessly sliced vegetables while keeping a weary eye on a picture of Michael set on the counter.

I approached the picture, one Jane had brought down from our bedroom. It showed Michael laughing as he held between his little hands a newly unwrapped Christmas gift.

Every so often Jane extended her fingers, which slightly trembled, and caressed the picture in hope of soothing her grief.

With a deep sigh, she would then wipe her eyes. I felt cheated by this display. Was I being selfish to expect my wife and son shredded in sobs so soon after my death?

I dropped my eyes in shame. As expected in the natural laws of the world, death had removed my body, but scarce memories of me had erased everything else. I felt as if I had never existed.

I wasn't even a ghost.

Because of my misplaced obsession, I was deprived of the most endearing currency a departed one relishes—that of a treasured imprint of his passage. I was disgusted with myself.

Michael, however, wishing to alleviate his mother's pain, smiled, as if some instructions had been revealed.

"Michael," I whispered, immediately feeling silly for whispering. "Michael," I repeated, hoping to get his attention, but to no avail.

He approached his mother, his footsteps surprisingly spilling noises, finding himself exposed to the physical world. He stopped a few feet from her.

Unexpectedly, the air stirred, as Michael, silent and focused, began to step out of the void.

Alerted by the creaking noises, Jane by now had turned fully around and stared, open-mouthed, at the strange phenomenon taking place in front of her.

She shook her head. Particles and molecules of air twisted all around Michael. She focused deeply at the source of the air disturbance when, through the blurry threshold, he visibly emerged.

Michael flashed a rejoicing smile, opened his palms, and beckoned her embrace. His dazzling features enticed a deep fascination. He was the wish turned into reality, but, also, the sight validating an appalling past. Thoughts of his demise forbade enjoyment of any kind, even if his wispy shell appeared magnificent in the light of day.

Then Michael's shell vibrated and enveloped the kitchen in a whirlwind of flashes.

Jane's eyes widened. "Michael!" she shrieked.

The scream startled Michael. He instantly vanished from the premises. Next moment I heard Nicholas' rushing footsteps before he burst into the kitchen, finding his terrified mother clutching her body with trembling hands.

I closed my eyes, concentrated, and condensed all of my being. Again I was hurled into a vortex, and ended up next to Michael.

"I scared her," Michael said. "I never meant to."

"Light, at times, dims a star's sparkle," I comforted.

He considered my words, looked at me, as though he knew something, and smiled, as though he was about to share it. He embodied these surroundings, the life-force behind all that moves.

Michael looked up. He had perceived something. Then the clouds enveloped us. High above, bolts of lightning exploded. And beyond the lightning, nestled in the mystical shades of the unknown, I beheld a mysterious and enticing glimmer pulling me closer and closer.

A Mystical Vessel

I was hurled into vortex. To be honest, the sinking sensation that accompanied all of my travels, both for physical destinations as well as time zones (this I was soon to experience) felt quite pleasurable.

Sights began to appear out of the blinding flash. The form of a tropical island took shape below Michael and I. Then, I was able to distinguish long desert strips of white sand caressed by the undulating embrace of crystal blue waters. As we floated closer, I spotted a quaint town, with a sign identifying it as Port Lucaya, in the Bahamas.

What a delightful place to start my journey. We wandered into the town, where I discovered a languid rhythm filling the atmosphere. An old Bahamian woman, putting on display the many straw hats for sale outside her shop, hummed calypso tunes. Not fifty yards away, a group of workers sat on rickety chairs, eating hearty breakfasts on a terrace. And at the center of all this commercial activity, a marina, with its long wooden docks stretched before us like bony fingers, offered berths to ships of all sizes.

As for Michael, he had quickly mastered the subtle art of walking on air, his little legs amusingly moving a few feet above the ground. But something else about him proved of interest. There seemed to be a formal and dignified allure fused in with that of a buoyant child, which promptly set forth the enlightenment of one not belonging in so young a body.

He turned his face to the East, and the way he looked at the sea was quite beautiful. Moving towards me with airy steps, he smiled, hands in the air as if to catch the rays of sunshine in which he melted.

"Oh, daddy!" he exclaimed, joyfully. "How marvelous for us to be together." I told him I agreed, all the while contemplating his gleaming ethereal shell, whereas mine paled in comparison. I grieved at the paleness of my core, and wondered if I could ever atone for my shameful sin.

Then a great force wished to be heard. I listened, and progressively, there emerged a message regarding our situation. Assuredly, even though we were together, Michael and I were to embrace different paths.

We ventured onto the docks, unnoticed, as you may well imagine, using that cloak of secrecy which only spirits possess. I paused next to a well-synchronized crew working the teak decks of a one hundred foot yacht, all adorned in blue and white horizontal striped t-shirts and beige Bermuda shorts. They polished the steel, hosed and scrubbed and oiled different mechanical parts when a boisterous laughter begged my attention.

Having located the source, I hovered twenty feet above the wooden docks and eavesdropped on two well-dressed middle-aged yachtsmen, silvery hair and tanned wrinkled faces, leisurely drinking coffee on the flybridge.

"You think there's any truth to this island?" one asked, as he put the cup to his lips.

The other man shook his head, and offered a crooked smile. "Bah!" he grunted. "All I know is that nobody else ever visited it."

"You'd have a better chance of finding a *chickarnie* than that island."

"Or the Loch Ness Monster," the other mocked.

"What I still have trouble understanding is his obstinacy to serve as Senator. There's no place in the U.S. Senate for believers of spirits and other nonsense."

They burst out laughing.

I remained for a while, observed their office-like manner and penchant for lavishness, and noticed that their soft, polished, pristine hands appeared unacquainted with the handling of ropes. I saw how the sun's warmth and salty air only tinged the outer layers of their being. They exuded no sense of adventure.

I promptly left these men and searched for characters that breathed true seamanship. Quite naturally, I made my way where the sailboats were docked.

How wonderful the difference a few feet can make. For what I saw in that secluded area was more than a tightly-knit community, it was a parallel world, inhabited by people with their own language.

Groups of sailors met everywhere, barefoot. This world was made all the more enchanting by the exhilarating passion of the sea that filled every sentence, as each mariner carried an air of mystery, trading tips from crossings made glorious by howling winds and towering waves. They reminded me of astronauts in the final phase of preparations, moments before being launched into space.

It was something I had dreamed of long ago. A dream of being one of them. Money had then become an issue. Then time killed all that was wild. I've heard of numerous stories like mine, of putting out dreams just for the necessary time to gather financial independence. A stage never reached by most no matter how thick the billfold. I know I'm not alone, yet the burning regret in my soul cannot be redeemed by the similarity of others.

As I listened to the sailors' coded language, where every rope possessed a name of its own, I noticed their lively eyes and gentle persuasion. These men and women, inhabited by an alert and refreshed spirit, had welcomed the sea into their hearts.

I was a child exploring.

I devoured these new words and nautical expressions; bear away, closehauled, bowline and sundowner.

I was a child exploring outer space.

Then I saw it for the first time! A sailboat unlike all others. Anchored out there in the bay, floating and inviting, like some magnificent space craft, undoubtedly capable of great odysseys.

I swiftly covered the distance separating me from the sailboat, and the manner with which I accomplished that space travel amused me. All it had required was a simple thought.

I absorbed this sailboat's every detail, especially its name, 'Thairica', which appeared in bold letters on both sides of its hull and on the transom. The furled sails, large blue canvas awning, wind generators and solar panels seemed to convey, in this particular instance, a spirited force.

Somehow, this craft did not only entice a dream—it revealed the dreamer. I savored this thought, wondering about this vessel's master when a slight disturbance broke both the sea's surface and Thairica's spell over me.

As my attention progressively returned to my immediate surroundings, I perceived, quite near where I hovered, a man rising and swaying in the blue waves from crests to troughs. The way he lazily bobbed in the ocean, his bronzed face and the muscles rippling under his sun protective shirt convinced me that he was in his element.

Surprisingly, it was also then that I noticed another sailboat anchored not twenty yards away from Thairica. I dutifully observed the man swim towards Thairica and vigorously pull himself up the transom ladder.

He emerged from the sea with fluid ease—a deftly manner suggesting great physical skills. Once out of the water, I was able to contemplate the man from the sea more thoroughly. He was tall, in his mid-thirties, with long brown hair, a slim waist, and the broad shoulders of a fighter. His chiseled face exuded confidence, and his eyes shone bluer than the azure sky, lively and fierce, while his precise and subtle movements reminded me those of a jaguar ready to pounce at any given moment. All of these observations I had made while watching the man from the sea inspect his vessel's lifelines and stanchions. Having completed that task, he entered the cockpit where, with perfected gestures, he lit a cigarillo.

"Is the anchor dug in securely?" a feminine voice called out from inside the cabin.

"Yes, even dove just to make sure, although I'm not so sure about the boat next to us."

"Are you going to advise them?"

"In a little bit," he calmly answered.

Moments after finishing his cigarillo he dove back into the water, reached the other boat, and knocked on the hull. Seconds later a man with a sunburned face and big stomach climbed out of the companionway, careful not to drop the bottle of beer he carried. He looked at the man from the sea with a puzzled look on his face.

"I beg your pardon," the man from the sea said, "but I fear your anchor might drag."

"What's he saying?" another man said, just as he emerged from the sailboat's cabin.

"He says the anchor's not properly set," the first one repeated, with a smirk.

"I can always verify a second time for you," the man from the sea offered, and before receiving an answer he promptly kicked up his feet and slipped under the surface like a knife.

Although both men on the sailboat shared the same exasperated grin, they nonetheless kept glancing at their expensive waterproof watches.

"He's been under for over two minutes," the man with the sunburned face muttered.

More time elapsed.

"He's been under more three minutes!" the other one exclaimed. Then, just as they leaned over and curiously peeked into the water, the man from the sea surfaced.

"You were under for nearly four minutes!"

"Bah! That's nothing," the man boasted with pride, catching his breath. "I once held my breath for six minutes."

The two men exchanged glances.

"Six minutes?" they inquired, suspiciously.

"Six minutes ten seconds to be exact," stated the man from the sea. For the next minutes he tried convincing them, and seemed gravely disappointed that they didn't believe him.

"Why would I lie about something like this?" the man from the sea insisted. "I suppose you probably won't believe that I once retrieved a weight belt of more than thirty pounds."

"Thirty pounds?" the man with the sunburned face asked.

"That's by far my most prized feat, since I did it without fins and at a depth of no less than fifty feet."

"Thirty pounds, fifty feet, and without fins?"

"That's what I said, thirty pounds, without fins. I imagine that in depths of, say, thirty feet, like we are now, I could raise the load and make it to the surface with forty pounds." He smiled, and remained lazily afloat, like some languid sea creature, barely moving from his relaxed and polished swimming skills. He looked back towards Thairica, seemed refreshed by the sight, then turned back around, his clever eyes fully probing the two men's fanciful expressions. I found it odd he chose not to climb back aboard his vessel.

He narrowed his eyes upon hearing a burst of laughter, and slowly swam closer to the sailboat.

"Did I miss something?" he asked, noticing the two men's covert sneers.

"We're just debating whether your mind suffers from oxygen depravation or sun exposure."

"Ah, non-believers," he replied. "I wish I could change your mind."

"You could."

"Aha! A challenge!"

"Prove it to us at once," sunburned face shouted, as he sprang to his feet. He made his way to the foredeck where, with a prolonged stare he tried appraising the physical capabilities of the man from the sea, who had remained immersed from the neck down.

"Would you care to wager a couple of beers?" asked the man from the sea.

"No problem," answered sunburned face who, having re-entered the cockpit, lifted one seat and produced from a concealed cavity a weight belt. He at once proceeded to add the required weight, then with a cavalier motion, he tossed it into the sea.

The man from the sea dove, and resurfaced shortly after, empty-handed.

"We knew it! Now hand us our beers."

"It is what we agreed upon, gentlemen," the man from the sea gasped. "If only that hammerhead shark had not appeared so suddenly."

"A hammerhead?"

"Yes, it frightened me and forced me to resurface," he said in a most unusual, calm voice. Almost like he wished to be doubted.

"And you expect us to believe this? Please, put on a hat or stay out of the sun for the remainder of the day."

"I could try again, double or nothing."

"You're a persistent devil, but we're not interested. Now go and fetch us our beers, like we agreed."

"By the way, I noticed, while down there, that you don't have the proper anchor."

"Can you repeat that?"

"You don't have the proper anchor," the man from the sea restated. "You see, we're anchored in a grassy bottom, and your anchor is a Danforth. Now, in such conditions, the CQR does hold better, as long as you verify that the plow's tip is firmly imbedded."

"Is that right?"

"Yes, and you also didn't let out enough scope," he replied. "Really!" he chuckled. "Sixty feet of chain in thirty feet of water! Altogether, you made two important mistakes, but, hey, that's okay, a lot of armchair sailors make them."

I found it strange that this man demonstrated such insolence. Frustration swept over the two men's faces. They whispered to each other, through clenched jaws and gritted teeth. Eyes red with anger, sunburned face slammed his bottle on the seat. "It's a bet!" he blurted.

"Excellent," the man from the sea acknowledged, with a smile that revealed a set of sparkling white teeth. "But it would be sad to try again for just a few beers. Why not raise the stakes? I'll give you five cases of Budweiser if I can't do it, but if I succeed . . ."

"Name your price!"

"A box of Partagas cigars. The special Robusto edition. And don't be stingy. I want the box of twenty-five."

"Those are Cubans cigars, aren't they?"

"Yes, very hard to come by," he confirmed, nonchalantly.

"How exactly are we supposed to get them?"

"There's a Canadian by the name of Ronald, who has aboard his sailboat a box of such delicacies. Luckily for us, he so happens to be docked at the marina. Just find him and trade the bottles of delicious red wine you scammed off the restaurant owner in the Spanish Virgin Islands."

The man with the sunburned face looked gravely embarrassed. "That's absurd," he hesitantly said. "What the hell are you talking about?"

"I'm talking about your little scam at the Blue Bay restaurant, on the island of Vieques."

"What do you know about this?"

"Oh, just that you approached the owner with what you claimed were Mayan artifacts that came from an illegal dig in Guatemala. Now, I also heard that those extremely valuable collectibles were, in fact, cheap souvenirs bought in Cancun. Am I correct until now?"

The mute expression of the two men held the validation of a resounding affirmation.

The man from the sea resumed. "Since the owner didn't have a lot of cash, you traded your crap for four dozens bottles of Italian wine."

"How did you find out?"

"It's a very tightly-knit community we live in," the man from the sea confirmed. "Something you hadn't learned before buying into your ten-week partnership program in Tortola. If you wish, just to make the bet more interesting, drop another belt with ten pounds and I'll return with both."

"Here!" sunburned face retorted, throwing another weight belt into the water. "Fetch those two and you have a deal!"

Delight and sweet jubilation flashed across the man from the sea's face. Very swiftly he kicked his legs upright and disappeared in a flash of subtle foam.

* * *

Some people naturally yield to their wildest desires. And the man from the sea, surfacing with a big grin and two weight belts in his hands, obviously belonged to that breed. After handing over the two weight belts to the sour-faced losers, he swam back to Thairica and sat down in the cockpit. For the next minutes, he delightfully sipped a glass of red wine while watching the falling sun.

"What have you been up to?" a woman called out.

"I was engaged in the pursuit of reacquiring stolen goods, my love."

"What did you say?"

"Righting the wrongs, my dear."

"A bit more details would be helpful. Which stolen goods are you referring to?"

"Remember the old man in Vieques? The one swindled by a couple of sneaky boaters?"

"Is this why you insisted on anchoring here?"

The cooling breeze picked up a few knots and brushed against his face.

"Absolutely," he boasted cheerfully. "As we speak, the scoundrels are bringing the bottles to our new recruit, Ronald, the Canadian heading for Puerto Rico in two days."

He gazed at the golden sparkles dancing on the wrinkled surface of the Caribbean, with eyes showing a unique kind of exaltation, a subtle worship, the recognition of a greater force that gives this world its existence. Astonishingly, he seemed to feed off the sun's immortality, while traces of bravado echoed in each furrow of his conquering smile.

I was intrigued. Here. A few feet away from me. A man on a quest. Mysterious like the sea, vibrant and unpredictable, like life!

I rose, reached the top of the mast, and spotted Michael, joyfully darting in and out of boats. I yelled out to Michael, who stopped. He smiled at me, before resuming his games, his mind an endless garden of secrets, no doubt filled with tales of pirates, desert islands, legends and treasures.

When I looked down, I noticed that the man had gone inside the cabin, and just as I descended he emerged from the companionway, this time sporting a white, unbuttoned shirt that revealed nasty scars that snaked across his tanned, muscular torso. Undoubtedly, the severe scars forged his appearance and expanded, I believed, the scope of his capabilities. And judging by the vessel he commanded, one yearning to be launched far away, I just knew this man's domain stretched way beyond land or water.

Sinking into one of the striped cushions, the man from the sea lit a cigarillo. It was then, once conveniently slumped, his eyes closed, that he softly uttered the words: "Welcome to Thairica."

Struck by those words, I looked all around. Had this man actually addressed me? Besides a feminine voice singing in the cabin and the lone Captain in the cockpit, nobody else was here. For a moment, I actually believed those words had been intended for me. I minutely examined his closed eyes, and shortly after rejected this possibility. But just then, the man from the sea strengthened my disbelief with a growing smile that vivaciously lit his face!

Everything about this moment was both suspicious and reassuring. I searched the playful lines of his face, hoping somehow they would surrender the key to this mystery. I was a spirit, a being of ethereal substance. No device or elaborate schemes were required to conceal me. I floated, tucked inside the air's transparency. Why then all this confusion?

A disguised conversation took place between the two of us. A conversation made up of smiles and frowns, played out by actors from different worlds, actors who yet enjoyed the same dazzling waters of the Caribbean. And as if it wasn't enough that this coded dialogue had enhanced my confusion, on the man's face emerged a devious smile, discreet, yet possessed with that hooked curl that men find at times very threatening.

I moved closer, hovered mere inches above him, taking advantage of my weightlessness. Suddenly the man opened his eyes, shriveled his face, and turned his rugged features into a monstrous grimace!

Baffled, I looked behind, and confirmed yet again that no other being stood behind me.

"My name is John Corto," the Captain said. "We've been expecting you."

"You can see me?" I attempted.

"See you, and hear you," he boasted, laughing.

From the custody of invisibility, I had been thrust into unexpected intimacy.

"I channel spirits on occasion," Corto went on. "I can see and hear you, same for your precious little one."

That confession flooded my mind, just as Michael approached. I immediately confessed to Michael what had happened when out of the companionway a woman emerged. She was tall, slim, and looked very healthy. A puff of wind teased her hair, which was long and dark, and her green eyes mirrored the sea's golden sparkles. A quiet strength lived in those eyes, a disarming and startling strength, and her smile was honest and pure.

With fluttering fingers, she groomed Michael's hair. That gesture indicated that she possessed Corto's gift. How fantastic Michael's smile became under that airy touch.

Such a sight pleased the woman, who affectionately gazed at Michael. "Sunshine and happiness, what a delightful combination," she said. "My name is Paris, and my husband John and I welcome your presence."

"Paris," I murmured.

"It's short for Paraskevi, named after my Greek grandmother."

Wishing to satisfy my curiosity as to what I had earlier witnessed, I looked at Corto. "I saw the way you regained a man's lost bottles of wine," I told him.

Far from embarrassment, Corto let out a thunderous laugh, and briskly slapped his knee. "I'm a 'channeled one,' Thomas, not an angel!"

They looked to the West. Blazing streaks of orange, amber and purple interlaced one another. Just then the sun winked its last flicker, and Paris and Corto toasted this magical sight:

"To chasing sunsets."

"To sunset chasers."

Then our hosts told Michael and me about their two sons. A seven-year-old named Matthew, and a five-year-old, Danny, both bundled down below in their cabin, asleep.

"You'll notice that my sons cannot see either of you," Paris said, "although they may demonstrate some sensitivity to Michael, much like an imaginary friend. Children's spirits are more perceived by mortal children, and my sons know that no harm will come to them from Michael. Tomorrow night, I will make the introductions."

Hearing this, Michael beamed with joy.

Then Paris bade us to join her inside. We followed. A dozen candles burning here and there brightened the whole interior, while plenty of hatches and bronze portholes insured great ventilation. As I admired the spacious layout, the salon large enough to sit twelve people at the table, an unknown energy seized me. I looked everywhere. Nothing out of the ordinary caught my eyes, and as I kept wondering about the vibrations surrounding me on all sides, Paris noticed my baffled look.

"My dear Thomas," she said, smiling. "There's no need to be shy. I will happily answer your questions."

"You read my mind," I said, half-jokingly, not even concerned with that probability.

She laughed, and answered in the affirmative without a hint of teasing in her eyes. "What you feel is the result of forbidding any bad thoughts or emotions from entering this cabin."

"This simple rule permits such soothing vibrations?" I asked.

"Everything is energy," she insisted. "What you see and what you hear, what you love and what you fear. Your thoughts, your emotions, life and the after life—everything! To surround yourself with positive energy should be your first priority. It is this sensitivity to the energy flowing from this world to the next, the force that inhabits every living thing, the vibrations that have been transferred from the dawn of Time that enables us mortals to contact beings such as you. But more must be done! To establish contact is only the first step. Soon, the contacts are going to yield immense knowledge; knowledge concerning The Eternal Energy."

She paused. A tense eagerness was expressed in her glittering eyes, as she observed with great interest the two specters in the cabin.

She then explained how important it was for someone to discover his true-self, thus fulfilling his Original Design.

"You're the second, euh, soul I meet that mentions the Original Design," I said.

She smiled. "What have you been told?"

"That it's a series of trials meant for the soul's elevation," I replied. "A path guarded by Spiritual Guides and other entities."

"You were well informed. Spiritual Guides try to encourage their host during difficult times."

"What happens when the signs are ignored?"

"More powerful beings, which I call Heavenly Beings, are at times called into action. They are supremely powerful and wise."

"And what if that doesn't work? Surely, there must be some failures, I mean, since murder, suicide and a lot of other ugly things keep happening."

"Then the universe realigns itself," she replied.

She spoke quietly, filling the salon with such a soothing tone that even the candles wavered harmoniously.

For a few seconds nobody spoke. Then, curious about The Eternal Energy, I asked her to elaborate on the subject.

"The Eternal Energy is the link between our two worlds," she answered. "Let's take levitation, for example. This skill is feasible to those with the proper mind attributes, bestowed at birth to all, yet only acquired after years of meditation. For others, a gifted mind will enable them to read minds, read auras, or contact spirits. The portal I mentioned, the one leading to The Eternal Energy, lies just beyond the abilities previously mentioned. But I'm getting ahead of myself. You'll learn more as we sail, for no journey is more profitable than one dappled with the charm of the unknown."

She was mindful, as she relayed just enough to satisfy my curiosity, to remain within the limits of her awareness. Suddenly, Paris stood within my ethereal shell, then exited through my back. Cries filled the salon. The sound of a knob rattled, as Corto emerged from the forward cabin with both of his children in his arms.

She put her hands on their heads. "What is it?" she asked Corto, who delicately laid down his children in the salon's seats.

"Both are complaining of stomach aches."

"Oh, well, let's see what's wrong with my two boys." Paris dutifully asked about their aches, in the soothing, motherly tone that conveys to a child all of the reassurances in the world. She placed her hands on their stomachs, closed her eyes, and breathed deeply. Turning around, I observed traces of concern rising in Michael's eyes, as he was no doubt inquisitive about the state of his two future friends.

All attention focused on Paris, eyes closed, immersed in deep meditation.

"You've heard of healing through the quantum touch?" Corto asked me. I told him I had, and asked if they proceeded like that with all of their illnesses.

"No, let me assure you, we don't advocate an utter withdrawal from conventional medicine."

Progressively the hurt and saddened look of Matthew and Danny turned to an expression of relief.

"But their recovery could also be the result of natural comfort," I pointed out.

"Yes, it very well could be," she admitted. "If you mean that their minds created an energy capable of soothing pain, a sort of healing vibration, then yes, you are right. All I demonstrated to you was how emotions are linked to thoughts."

Later that night, while our hosts slept, I joined Michael near what was to become his favorite place; at the top of the mast. Recollecting my discussion with Paris, I wondered how a mortal could possess such knowledge. The Original Design, beings mightier than Spiritual Guides—these had been mentioned by the Master upon my arrival in the after life. Talks about The Eternal Energy and of ways to gain, through the mind's development, access to this force of creation only enhanced my astonishment towards my hosts.

* * *

I shall forever remember the following morning, when all of us went sailing. A brisk crackling sound, a bloated piece of canvas, its freshened expansion, and the ship charged forth.

With Paris steering a downwind course, Thairica progressed admirably. In the midst of this pleasant motion, Corto went inside the cabin and returned shortly after sporting a straw Stetson, which shaded his eyes from the glaring sun.

"Can you feel the spray on your face?" Paris asked me. Her eyes blazed with wild delight. I told her no, and she quickly added, "You will, one day."

I wanted to reply, but chose not to, and just kept looking at her. She moved her hips and bent her knees, undulating to the rhythm with feline grace, and the sound of her wealthy laugh never failed to amaze me.

This family lived surrounded by vibrant colors and vivid emotions. They were enjoined with Mother Nature. Companions in this agitated pursuit which appears harsh yet is the spark of life, filled with the essence of the soul. An essence that routine and comfort so often pollute and cripple.

As for their splendid sailboat, which I sensed they treated as though it lived and breathed as they did, it magically rolled under their swaying limbs. There existed, as the many discussions about their sailing craft indicated, a profound affection between my hosts and their vessel. This is why many sailors refer to their vessels as 'she'. Indeed, objects seemed meaningless for Paris and Corto, yet Thairica meant so much more than a mere assembly of steel, fiberglass and wood.

"Did you inspect Thairica's rigging this morning?" Paris asked Corto.

"All is well. There's nothing holding her from another circle, if we keep loving her." Corto was undoubtedly respectful in his praise. His fingers grazed the shrouds, while Paris, staring at the distant, elusive layer where ocean and sky met, rested her hand on the helm like one would do to a friend.

"She will take us much, much farther," she said.

Just then, as if 'she' had heard those words, Thairica clipped herself to the winds and leaped forward. The winds stiffened. Streams of froth lathered the sea. I studied Corto's admiration when Thairica united her will with nature's mood.

"Behold how magnificently Thairica handles herself," he offered in a soft tone. "She's not just a ship, but a body, much like the one given to us when coming into the physical life. Can you imagine the dreams made possible by a vessel designed to explore the far shores of this world? For that's exactly what she is. What she was designed for. An opportunity to serve one's life. You see, dreams are productive if they are realized, or, compel you to act. Beliefs are one thing, but nothing is built solely out of our thoughts. In the end, we become the sum of our actions, and nothing else."

Moments later, gustier winds stirred dreams in their eyes while the coast dipped below the horizon.

"Where's your voice, Thomas?" Corto shouted, visibly excited. "Don't you know each scream of joy lifts your spirit and adds years to your life?"

Meanwhile Paris turned the helm and Thairica embraced her new course. They praised their synchronism, gybing and tacking, when with a vibrant gesture, Corto removed his straw Stetson and whirled it as if he was riding a bull in a rodeo.

Close by, Paris also screamed aloud her joy, followed suddenly by Michael's laughter. It was true, the day was splendid. Clear skies, enchanting seas, and yet, albeit in the presence of all of this, I only mustered a smile.

After relinquishing the helm over to her husband, Paris sat next to her children.

"You have intelligent and calculating eyes, Thomas," she began. "To make this journey as meaningful as possible, try not to worry so much. Nobody ever added a second to their life by worrying."

"Perhaps," I replied. "But my recent visit at my house makes me feel so empty," I sadly confided. "My reality was a gigantic illusion."

"All that's left," she said, under a hint of caution, "is for you to accept that the utter surrender to the Universe is the only path to choose. Quite simply put, you have to let go."

She again spoke of the signs set forth to guide us, and I told her of the time I had read an ad promoting a free-sailing adventure.

"Unfortunately, the ad proved to be an illusion," I relayed to her. "Curiously, now that I think about it, the sailboat did bear a strange likeness to Thairica."

"Your eyes did not deceive you," replied Paris. "The ad wasn't an illusion. It did exist at that precise moment, printed in bold letters in the newspaper held by your two hands. For years we have sailed with people unknowingly sent to us by their Spiritual Guides. Know this; the Original Design is not one without pain, it's one conceived for the soul's elevation in the face of pain. If the Original Design is threatened, Spiritual Guides emerge from the hushed murmurs of your conscience to try and sway it back on course—the course favored for your soul. It is in the course of their journey at sea with us that these people are introduced to certain concepts and practices that enhance the mind's power. But such signs are temporary, for the Universe encourages those who quickly pursue their intuition."

"How does this work?"

She plunged her eyes into the liquid domain from which she drew her inspiring smile.

"Soon you will witness the arrival of three souls who answered such an ad," she said. "It is through their trials that you will witness the five stages that we believe lead to the ascending path, to The Eternal Energy. Through their trials, you will inherit invaluable insight. Now why don't you, for the rest of the day, succumb to the sweet intoxication that only sailing can provide."

Noticing I had no intention of enjoying myself, she sighed deeply. "Very well then, I suppose I could allow a few questions, so long as it's not about the five stages—those I want you to experience with our future guests."

"What if I wanted to learn about your supernatural abilities?"

Paris answered my query, and told me stories about herself at a young age, a time when she discovered a particular sensitivity to spirits, of seeing and talking to them.

"At such a young age, how did you handle being visited by the remnants of the underworld?" I joked.

She laughed. "With the secrecy they commanded, Thomas."

"Your parents must have been thrilled."

"I never knew my father," she said, calmly. "As for my mother, let's just say she never seemed surprised with the things I could do."

"And are you certain you can't tell me how people will one day access The Eternal Energy?" I pursued.

"Ah, you're a persistent and curious one."

"I've been told that."

"Very well then; how is it you held the ad promoting the sailing adventure, yet failed to satisfy this great curiosity of yours? Take your time. Your spiritual growth lies in the answer."

Her question forced me to understand why my curiosity had not probed further soundings, especially with a prize of such value. I suddenly realized how the wisdom of her question so underlined the scope of all my problems.

"I had lost faith," I sheepishly announced.

"Yes, you had lost faith."

The spiritual path had just unfolded.

* * *

Of the many sights that charmed me that day, the one of Michael communicating with Matthew and Danny proved the most endearing.

On a sailboat's deck, under a full moon, two mortal children playfully indulged a soul of another dimension, much like an imaginary friend. The secrets confessed by Matthew and Danny touched Michael, who gleamed in the dark like a torchlight. His feelings for those boys aroused the wings of his soul and enticed him to perform a swift aerial ballet that astounded Paris and Corto, who relayed the performance to their children. A loop. A dive. A twirl. The trail following Michael's shape sparkled, lofty and pure, on the dark celestial canvas.

Though my journey had just begun, an important lesson had been provided by Michael, whose exuberant display taught me that happiness is to be shared. For at that moment, all Michael had wished for was to extend his feelings to all, and this, by the only means available to him.

Moments later, beaming and radiant, having dazzled the cheering crowd, Michael retreated near the top of the mast.

"Ah, my celestial voyagers," Corto said, outstretching his arm and pointing to the sky. "How many stars can you name tonight?"

They peered into a world whose vastness inspires humility.

"Look, over there, Rigel," Corto indicated.

"Yes, I see," Paris acknowledged, before raising her finger. "And there's Betelgeuse, the red super giant."

"Where?" Danny asked.

"Directly above the three stars which make up Orion's belt."

"Over there," Matthew shouted, pointing a finger. "Aldeb-"

"Oh, look," Paris interrupted. "Castor and Pollux."

"And over there, mommy, Aldeba-"

"And there," she interrupted yet again, while looking over to Corto, who bit his lips as he gazed at her. "The star that shines as much as my love for all of you, Sirius."

Later that night, while Matthew and Danny slept in their cabin, I asked Corto about his past. He told me he had served as a Lieutenant in the Navy SEALs, and after his discharge had spent a few years investigating war crimes in Bosnia and Rwanda for the United Nations.

A silence filled with secrets enfolded him. There he was, on the foredeck, lying dreamily and pensive in the sultry darkness of the tropical night when I interrupted his reveries and asked if some experiences with spirits had shaped his quest for The Eternal Energy.

"Ah, yes," he answered. "There was this vision, years ago when, true to my Navajo bloodline, I entered the world of spirits."

"You have Native American blood in your veins?" I asked.

"I do. You see, we're all children of God, enabled, with the proper will, to wander the lands of The Great Spirit, but few master this gift like the Navajo. It is in the lands of The Great Spirit that I venture next to sorcerers without fear. My spirit explores shores my body encounters years afterwards, and through those astral voyages and spiritual encounters an understanding of the after life is gained."

It was then that the Captain of Thairica seemed invaded by memories. His eyes sparkled, and the sparkle came with a truth. A truth able to part all darkness.

"Everyday and everywhere the Universe parades before you sights which are meant to inspire you," he declared. "You asked about experiences with spirits and of their influences in my quest. I will answer with a sight of this world, one which shaped my resolve. And though it dwells in the horror of world indifference, it underlines something so rare in this world."

"Which is?" I asked.

"Courage!" He slapped his hand on deck and sprang abruptly to his feet. "I'm talking about courage, and faith." Corto sat down slowly, and resumed. "In December, nineteen ninety-six, thousands and thousands of Rwandan refugees, under military escort, marched their way back to their homeland through the Tanzanian border."

His mood darkened. He raised his head and gazed at the stars, which burned in the reflective pools of his eyes. I knew from his stare that the recollection of this event would never go away, could never go away. He wiped his eyes.

"Amid all the tragedy," he said, "I beheld, in a child's eyes, the hopes of mankind. Yes, the hopes of mankind, I assure you. I saw this boy while I was driving a Jeep along a dirt road that linked Tanzania to Rwanda, with a colleague by my side always in need of sleep due to his frequent visits to this club in Kigali—"The Cadillac," yes . . . that was the name of the nightclub. Well, this man fell asleep every two seconds while I, purposely, drove into every crevice and bump on the road, just to shake him up. But he got accustomed to my driving and was able to fall into a deep sleep. Irritated, I then resorted to a more drastic approach, one which combined the rough contact of my right elbow with his left shoulder. 'What happened?' cried my colleague. In pain, he nursed his shoulder, glaring at me. 'Sorry about that,' I answered, 'but I had to swerve and my hand slipped.' You must understand that during those moments, some uncontrollable urge came over me. I had to hit something, strike someone. I just had to! To this day I never felt sorry for hitting him, that imbecile. But I, on the other hand, just had to look. I had to look at the shuffling of thousands of feet, like an endless dusty river, with soldiers overseeing the rigid order. That's when I saw it! A sight amid torn clothing and emaciated faces. One of a child illuminating a trail. I dare say that in order to perceive Light, one must first be kindled from within. That's why Light is dimmed by many, because even if it rises from the blood of Man, it's also shadowed by apathy. I asked myself, 'Why this child? Why any child?' There was the child, walking, carrying in a makeshift harness made of torn cloth an infant no more than a few months old."

Corto paused, nodded his head in dismay, and continued. "The child proceeded along. I observed this symbol of misery, tiny bare feet, dark face and exhausted limbs trudging along under the watchful stare of armed soldiers positioned every fifteen feet. Head bowed, the child walked, mile after mile, this while his voice neither cried nor professed anger or contempt. This was absolute madness. 'Look at this child!' I cried, pointing at him. 'Who?' my colleague answered, half-asleep. 'The young boy carrying the baby,' I hastily added. He searched, more to stop me from bothering him, I surmised. At that moment, I understood why such abomination happens and keeps happening, since indifference sat not two feet away from me. But then, even though we were surrounded by misery and despair, this idiot next to me starts eating a sandwich. This I couldn't allow. Was I being over-sensitive? Can one be such a thing when children are involved? 'Put that away you fucking moron!' I shouted aloud. My colleague narrowed his eyes, shoved his club sandwich in his backpack, and dozed off again. As I slowed the Jeep to maintain visual contact with the child, the heavy scent of human agony filled the air. A revelation can come in a thousand disguises. This one came from the deep wells of two dark eyes, just as we made our way up a long slope. Thank God the child leveled his eyes into mine. I felt the power of his stare cross the road, like suspended, energized molecules that plunged into my eternity."

Corto fell silent, and looked up at the sky, at a particular star, or planet, at the full moon, his mind perhaps wandering the vast lands way beyond.

"It's been years since that stare, yet its imprint did not dry," he said, in a tone no louder than a murmur. "I knew from that stare that mankind, though cruel at times, would survive. It was in his eyes that God revealed to me this secret. Don't you see why I'm telling you this story? You are, at every moment of the day, exactly where you ought to be. The sights you witness are meant to inspire you."

I stared at Corto. He embodied the clashing of swords, distant campaigns, the toil of victories achieved under impossible odds. In his world, he soared freely, like the Eagle, fierce and romantic.

After another brief silence, I asked my hosts about the circumstances surrounding their first meeting.

"Indeed, this would offer more clues as to the inner workings of the Universe," Paris answered. This led Corto to confide that after working in Rwanda, he had travelled to Thailand, where one day he saw Paris' picture in a Bangkok newspaper. The article described Paris' work in the northern town of Mai Sai as she provided care to Thai and Burmese girls who had been sold into prostitution, but luckily, managed to escape the slavery ring.

"There was a secret design at work," Corto stated. "A merciless, unrelenting, vibrant message filled with electrifying energy. A constant pounding of my heart which hammered and screamed and drove me insane. 'Go to Mai Sai, you fool', a voice whispered in my heart. 'She needs you as you need her.' I always follow these instructions, because one must never silence the voice of the heart, for if ignored, it will cease to beat. Such instructions that stir your core are clever disguises worn by Spiritual Guides and other Heavenly Beings. They come through murmurs of the heart, dreams and secret desires. They come concealed in articles you have read yet cannot find again, as you now know so well. Many signs had come to me before, but this one embodied a formidable appeal. The kind which cannot be ignored, must not be ignored."

Corto looked at the tender green eyes near him. A great desire invaded Corto's gaze. A desire filled with love and commitment for this woman, the desire to share everything.

"I knew on our first evening together that something extraordinary was happening," he resumed. "You see, I first met Paris in a Mai Sai hospital, where she was recuperating from a horrible horseback accident she had suffered a few days before. When her condition improved, she insisted that we go to the temples. Once there, as our first sunset gave way to the stars, Aldebaran, which is never the first star one sees in the night sky, never, revealed itself before all the others. In fact, it even outshined Venus and Sirius put together. A sort of celestial confirmation. One that came with a revelation."

All of this displayed the magical realm of their lives. Reaching out for her husband's hand, which she lightly pressed, Paris spoke of the revelation that came to her.

"That revelation," she noted, "whose finer details remain unknown to John, paved the way for our union and mission."

Her body stretched out on the foredeck, leaning on one elbow, she observed the night sky with an expression I perceived somewhat strange.

Corto looked at her lovingly.

"We got engaged at the Royal Palace in Bangkok," he said, wishing to fill the uneasy silence. "And that explains the name Thairica, a mixture of Thailand and Africa, two places that shaped our destinies."

"Following our engagement," Paris added, her eyes now exuding a beautiful clarity, "we both traveled back to Mai Sai for a few weeks so I could insure my work's continuity, while my dear fiancé waited around doing God knows what."

At that moment, Corto looked at her intensely, as if she meant the world to him, devoted and loving. This was a love found in great sagas, so vivid, so pure, with the glow of passion attracting dangers, inspiring hope.

Not wanting to intrude on their privacy, I waited for them to look at me before inquiring about the cost associated to these free journeys at sea.

"The money is supplied through an entrepreneurial philanthropic organization," answered Corto, "whose head is none other than Senator Williams."

"Really?" I replied. "I believe I heard two yachtsmen speak of him yesterday."

"I'm not surprised. The Senator has been the subject of many talks since rumors have linked him to the mystical quest for The Eternal Energy."

"And how, if I may ask, was he introduced to this mystical quest?"

"During a sailing trip, when his vessel sank off the coast of South America. Luckily for him, he was rescued after a couple of hours and brought to this island where research on The Eternal Energy is still being conducted. You see, once opened, the mind of Man has the power to surpass the body's physical restrictions. Having witnessed great feats before his eyes, the Senator asked in what capacity he could help the research. The influence of Heavenly Beings quickly followed, and before you know it a movement was created. A movement made up of channeled beings with certain gifts, sailing the seas and coming to the aid of those not attuned to their Original Design."

"What's the name of this fraternity of sailors?"

"One you'll discover as you journey with us," Corto answered with a smile.

"One last thing," I insisted. "You said The Eternal Energy is a link between our two worlds, and can be reached through the mind's development."

"Correct," Corto assented.

"The mind of someone already capable of levitation or other great feats."

"Go on."

"Then, what mystical application awaits someone capable of harnessing that power?"

Paris and Corto stared at each other without exchanging any words. I had already asked that question, hoping this time to have an answer.

Raising her eyes, Paris longingly gazed at the unfathomable boundaries of the universe. Sensing her fascination for this subject and not wanting to break the spell, it was Corto who answered.

"Know that you are proof of this energy and already possess a sample of its power," he said in a low voice. "You are a soul without a material body to curb your magic, and as such can melt through people or walls, cover great distances with a simple thought. What we believe is that this energy, once harnessed, will enable a soul having achieved the highest level of enlightenment on Earth, that of Ascended Master, to perform great feats."

"But these gifts I possess are useless in your world," I retorted.

"Perhaps for you, at this precise moment, because your pilgrimage is incomplete. But not to Spiritual Guides, not to Heavenly Beings, and especially not to an Ascended Master on Earth. Once a soul reaches that level of enlightenment, we believe great healings can be performed, healings beyond anything imaginable."

"You mean . . ." I left the sentence hanging.

"I mean miracles."

"Just like . . ."

"Yes!" he exulted, raising his voice. "Just like the greatest of all Masters. The one whose legacy inspires billions of hearts, two thousand years after his departure. The only one ever to have been seen walking on water—the Son of God, Jesus Christ!"

Part Two

Awareness

A Magical Path

Wearing a colorful shirt, Bermuda shorts and sandals, Corto patiently waited for his three future guests set to arrive at different times at the Freeport airport. He lounged smoothly against one of the palm trees dotting the area.

Newly arrived tourists with bulging suitcases squeezing into colorful taxis made him smile when, after stealing a glance at his watch, he jogged into the thinning crowd.

Shortly afterwards, he exited the terminal accompanied by a black woman who I gathered to be in her early thirties, and a young man about fourteen years old, who was her son. Corto escorted them to a wooden bench, then went back inside to await the arrival of another guest.

I casually moved next to the woman and young man Corto had picked up. The woman, whose name was Esmeralda, had a pretty face, well-rounded hips, and neatly brushed black hair.

As for her son, Emilio, slumped on the bench and taking space for three, he was dressed in black and red oversized clothes. Moments later Corto emerged from the terminal accompanied by Jared; an expensively dressed tall man in his mid thirties, with clear eyes, dark curly hair, and walking as if unconcerned about anything.

Once they reached the marina by taxi, the guests immediately embraced, with an eager stride, the maze of wooden docks. Just then, a wave of mystery swept through them. A new world opened its gate, so raw, so alluring. Tall masts greeted their curious attention. These were ocean crossing machines, some made of old wood some gleaming like a polished gem, all of them alight with the everlasting appeal of discoveries.

Caught amid the rising excitement of this marine environment, Esmeralda cast her dark brown eyes at the sailboats tied securely to the docks, resting in peaceful idleness. Emilio, however, seemed unimpressed. Perhaps in his world, hiding one's emotions was a necessary tool for self-preservation. I suspected adolescence had set its many traps and wished dearly that Nicholas be spared.

Moments later, comfortably seated in the cockpit, the guests ate a sumptuous conch salad, all the while listening, enthralled, to sea stories.

"Where did this rescue occur?" Jared asked, upon hearing of the time Paris and Corto had taken aboard a couple whose yacht had been sent to the depths by a half-submerged container.

"Off the coast of Madagascar," Corto replied.

At the sight of everybody enjoying themselves, Paris asked why they had decided to experience a sea journey. After being told, quite naturally, that they had won a contest, Paris informed, quite unexpectedly, that the ads had been placed by Spiritual Guides.

"An unfulfilled life reaps no benefits," explained Paris, standing up to capture their attention. "Your stay among us is meant for you to achieve your true-selves. I know that to be seated here and told that messengers from Heaven magically concocted the newspaper ad may appear as pure lunacy, but I swear to you that it's true."

Once finished, faced with a tense silence, Paris waited. Her words, tinged with mysteries, had caught everyone off guard. Wondering what sort of witchcraft inhabited Paris' world, the guests experienced that unavoidable suspicion the mind so often feels towards the unknown.

"You might want to repeat what you said," Jared said. "Perhaps my Bahamas Mama was stronger than I thought."

"Spiritual Guides, messengers from Heaven, what is this?" Emilio snickered. He rolled his eyes and twirled his index finger next to his temple. "This is crazy."

"Let them speak, Emilio," his mother interrupted calmly, yet authoritatively.

"John and I are telling the truth," Paris resumed. "This voyage, as specified by the ad, is an all expense paid journey. This doesn't change, and there is no catch. The Universe saw fit that all of you, at this point in your lives, come to benefit from the teachings aboard this ship. Rest assured, we will neither preach nor entice you to join any religious movement. What we suggest, and in no way oblige you to follow, are exercises in meditation and in other fields we feel will bring happiness and help define your true-selves. So, the question you really should be asking yourselves is this one; 'Could I benefit from a little bit of happiness at this point in my life?'"

The guests looked intently at their hosts, switching back and forth from a set of green eyes to a set of blue ones.

However foolish the statement appeared, Paris' appeal benefitted from the sudden interruption of Matthew and Danny who, after entering the cockpit, dutifully began examining the fine seashells gathered from their many treasure hunts. As they stumbled upon a rare specimen, they pressed their father, again and again, for the name of such a precious and valuable find.

Under this family image, unbounded magic whisked through the cockpit. Fear of demons being raised from the darkness evaporated. And in the minds of those watching, the seduction of a wild and eccentric adventure materialized.

"Sure, why not," Jared said. "I mean, what's the worst that could happen? If I don't like it, I leave, right?" He seemed to wait for a confirmation, which Paris gladly gave.

"Yes, of course," she agreed. "Nobody is held against their will. We're not some sort of cult, just curious people intent on using God's greatest gift to mankind, which is the mind, to pry open secret doors." She went into the cabin, returned shortly after with a lime pie, and proceeded to serve it.

Then, she looked straight at Emilio. "I notice that you still seem unconvinced," she told him.

"Be serious," Emilio said to his mother. "You've never believed in this sort of thing, not since being left alone with me."

"Perhaps the message was always there," she answered. "Only I could neither hear it nor see it."

"But this is crazy," he objected, shaking his head skeptically.

"Shh! Listen to me." She touched his cheeks with gentle strokes, yet he appeared resolved on staying outside the realm of her influence.

"Let's try this and make up our minds together," she insisted. Taking hold of her son's hands, she tightened her grip. This new force sparked confusion in his eyes. Her resolute stare reached him, urging him to be bold and flamboyant and seal this defining moment with the appropriate decision. Conscious of the importance of this decision, Esmeralda waited, when moments later, upon seeing her son's slightly curbed lips, upon feeling the gentle tremor of his fingers faintly clasping back, she flashed a radiant smile.

* * *

The next day, the guests were introduced to Thairica's equipment.

"I agree that it does seem like a lot," Corto said to the guests assembled in the cockpit.

"Which is why attending the Bahamian parade tonight will offer a nice distraction," Paris assured.

A few hours later, as the whole group neared Port Lucaya Marketplace, I noticed a vibrant sense of madness enveloping the streets. Here and there, throngs of people ran towards the parade. Just then, the sight of a guitar playing woman interrupted Paris' stride.

Seated cross legged on the sidewalk, she exuded the boiling features of a Gypsy woman, with mysterious eyes, sensuous lips, and a white gardenia weaved in her dark hair. Leaning against a lamppost, she tickled the strings in a subtle, nonchalant manner. She wore tan shorts and a slightly unbuttoned white shirt that showed parts of her generous cleavage.

Two young men, both with olive skin and slick black hair, sat next to her. Once in a while, they would risk a question, but the Gypsy woman's only response consisted of polite smiles. Sovereign of her seduction, she unscrupulously wielded hope and lust, pleasure and frustration, and though her skin was a shade of copper, her demeanor was of steel.

"Excuse me," Paris said, as she fell under the umbrella of light.

The Gypsy woman arched an eyebrow. "Yes," she said.

"Can you play 'Into the Mystic,' it's my husband's favorite."

"I'm sorry, I don't know this song."

A few feet away, Jared, persistently staring at the Gypsy woman, seemed spellbound by her charms. Seeing this, Esmeralda's eyes turned downward.

Shortly thereafter we arrived at Count Basie square, filled with people that danced and jumped and threw their arms up in the air. Michael and I hovered twenty feet above the parade, enjoying a prized vantage view while still close enough to Thairica's crew to share their exultation.

The music wafted across the square. The crowd rocked to the riveting rhythm, mesmerized by the chaos of disguises. Some revelers, adorned with cowbells and horns, sounded loud noises. I observed Michael, waving his hands, charmed by the eccentric looking dark aliens covered in gold.

Suddenly a force took complete possession of Michael. I saw a mighty soul in the making, with sparkling eyes and a silvery mist that linked his gleaming core to a place high in the sky. Michael's gaze, travelled to the far corners of the galaxy. Michael nodded. Then the silvery mist dissipated. The message had been communicated. And for the rest of the evening Michael hovered above the square not like a child bewildered by the colorful costumes, but rather like a king beholding his domain.

* * *

Wishing to learn more about Jared and Emilio, Corto arranged a spearfishing expedition the following day.

"The island of Andros lies amidst turquoise waters enclosing the second largest reef in the Northern Hemisphere," Corto explained. On the flybridge of the powerboat leased for that occasion, Corto entertained his guests when another voice saw it fit to provide details.

"Although it's the largest of the seven hundred islands of the Bahamas, it's also the least explored," Perry, the owner-operator of the boat volunteered.

In spite of the pleasurable ambiance, Jared had elected, ever since coming aboard, to remain aloof. Emilio, however, appeared grateful for such an opportunity. On perceiving this, Corto invited him inside the cabin where, on the wooden dining table, he unfolded the nautical chart of the Bahamas.

A unique lesson on navigation was to take place.

Standing beside Emilio, Corto did not just give a lesson. He promoted the lure of the sea. As Corto's fingers traced the many islands' contours, Emilio leaned over and succumbed to the chart's inviting whisper. With uncertain fingers, he touched it. Lines and numbers took forms of caves, fearless adventurers, naval battles and shipwrecks.

For Emilio, the chart offered more than mere latitudes or depths of waters. It was a gateway that evoked exotic visions to someone who, a week ago, had none. What was absolutely remarkable was that Corto had also felt it, sensing that Emilio's occasionally introverted and seemingly nonchalant behavior camouflaged a deep emotional resentment of some sort. But this spectacle held another meaning, for in Emilio I saw traces of Nicholas, who had withdrawn from me the day I had struck him in the face the third Sunday of June of last year—on Father's Day.

What followed this distressful thought was the first of many magical moments of this journey.

"By the way, do you know what they used to call Andros Island?" shouted Perry. "No? Well, they used to call it Espiritu Santos—the Holy Spirit!"

Then Michael seeped through the wall before me. Somber emotions rose from his eyes. Even the way he moved was accomplished with dreadful intent. He came at me, hazy hands outstretched. Although noticing my puzzled expression, his stare manifested a sort of grim resolve, combined with the sort of wisdom only achievable through the growth of one's soul.

Promptly he lunged forward. My incredulity had left me unguarded from the shock of Michael's touch. There was an instant of space travel. All sights and sounds vanished from my senses, when quite unexpectedly I found myself in the house where I had grown up, caught in some spell where I was but a spectator.

I watched in silence. Vivid images of my father's violence paraded before my eyes. Cries from my mother failed to stop my father's cruel hands. But wait! Other graphic beatings rolled before my eyes. One after another. Beatings I had blocked out. Sadly, I realized that my father's abuse lasted many years. Next to me, Michael winced and painfully trembled, seemingly forcing himself to look, as his stare travelled incessantly from the beatings rolling before him to the burning imprint I couldn't conceal from my eyes.

Then, all at once I found myself back inside the powerboat's cabin. But these accursed images had left their mark!

Words spoken gently captured my attention.

"Have you ever heard of Joshua Slocum, or Ellen MacArthur, for that matter?" Corto asked.

Emilio shook his head.

"Slocum was the first solitary sailor to circumnavigate the globe," Corto informed. "He did it aboard a sailboat of less than thirty-seven feet in length, from eighteen hundred and ninety-five to eighteen hundred and ninety-eight, after sailing through trials only the sea can lash at you, carrying his will beyond the oceans and into the dreams of countless of inspired souls. As for Ellen MacArthur, she successfully circumnavigated the globe in two thousand and five in less than seventy-two days. Now, if you pause to consider the elements she faced at sea, fixing up all the possible gear that breaks up in towering waves, the constant rigor and concentration demanded, this while navigating the best possible course between the few twenty minutes naps she allowed herself each day, then you understand how faith in oneself is imperative for such endeavors. For no craft, no matter how splendid, can cross oceans without the Captain's will."

Corto laid his hand atop Emilio's shoulder. "There is in this world, young man, no shortage of self-pity. Your journey can be made under the same applied principles as these great sea odysseys, one mile at a time. But you must be the one at the helm. You must!"

A short time later, the boat anchored. Masks, fins and neoprene suits appeared from storage cavities.

"Did you know that huge limestone blocks found near Bimini in nineteen hundred and sixty-eight fueled the lore of the famed lost city of Atlantis?" asked Corto. He threw a quick glance at Michael, winked, and talked of legendary birdlike creatures with red eyes, three toes, three fingers and a long tail that lived in the forest of Andros. "These creatures, called *chickcharnies*, are said to be very scary-looking."

Michael was amused by such stories.

Suiting up, Corto supplied Jared and Emilio with advices on the subtle art of spearfishing. "You must take advantage of a fish's curiosity, blend into their element," Corto instructed. "This means no sudden gestures, in order to limit the vibrations in the water. And if you find yourself facing a shark, listen attentively; don't panic, and face the shark head on until the appropriate moment presents itself to exit the water."

Jared's eyes widened unbelievingly.

Instructions on how to use a speargun were next. There was a perfected ease with which Corto manipulated the weapon, a detached easiness that confirmed suspicions I had harbored ever since spotting his scars. Here was a man, highly skilled in the instruments of blood. Minutes later, they dove into the water, followed by Michael and me.

All around us, brilliantly patterned inhabitants of the teeming reef scurried from the safety of one coral head to the next. Nearby, a moray eel with a gaping mouth full of scissors darted out of its refuge, eyes like yellow neon. It slithered along the bottom until it quickly dashed inside a crevice. A short distance away, a cloud puffed up from the white sandy bottom, when a big stingray opted to change neighborhoods. And above all of this, three spearfishermen prowled the hunting grounds, looking down, then left and right, their excitement well contained within the slow, deliberate intensity of each movement.

Moments later, Corto spotted a grouper. Despite his depleting air reserve, he prolonged his stay, leveled his speargun when, responding with its suspicious instinct, the grouper descended further down.

Seeing this, Corto swam in long, smooth strides and surfaced next to Jared and Emilio. They exchanged glances, synchronized their descent and dove to the bottom, powered by the thrusts of their black rubber fins, their bodies perfectly vertical.

The three divers descended in the deeper blue and gently circled the coral formation that sprouted from the sands. At that moment a dolphin swam towards Michael, who began glowing intensely. The dolphin behaved excitedly, swimming tight circles around him. Nearby, Corto paused above a crevice to see if a fish would risk its way out of hiding. Just then the grouper approached. Without hesitation, Corto took aim.

Suddenly a loud scream was heard. With outstretched arms, imitating the eerie 'Oooh' sound of a ghastly ghost, Michael flowed forward.

"I'm a *chickcharnie*!" he shouted. He waved his hands, and repeated the ghostly wail which had me burst out laughing.

Startled, the grouper, in a flurry of kicks, went to Michael and briskly darted through and through his luminous shell before swimming away.

I observed Michael for a while. He appeared intensely gifted. No doubt destined for something special. After all, he had been perceived by Jane, and only a few hours ago had unearthed my buried memories. And now, animals, to which he demonstrated an interest, fell under his charm. What else could he do?

That evening, with the boat anchored off the darkened coast of Andros and Michael back aboard Thairica so that he could spend time with his two little friends, Corto and I talked while alone on the foredeck.

"How is it neither you nor Paris ever talk about the brain?" I asked.

"Because the brain belongs to the body, whereas the mind belongs to the soul."

I nodded, then asked about the first of the five stages.

"The first stage strives to awaken the mind," he answered. "Think of the celebration displayed at the parade, the colors, the sounds, all necessary factors to increase one's sensitivity to their surroundings. That was the whole point of last evening, same as this spearfishing expedition. Properly stimulated, the mind proves to be capable of great leaps into the unknown."

Wishing his advice on a troubling matter, I decided to bear my soul.

"Last year, I hit my son Nicholas," I shamefully confided. "And earlier today, I was assailed by memories of beatings I suffered at the hands of my father. Beatings I had blocked out."

"The day you hit Nicholas was a manifestation," he answered in a voice filled with compassion. "In all likelihood, these events you selected to bury, because they were denied a proper grave, increased your sufferings and led you down a path of denial and self-destruction. Tranquility of mind is imperative for spiritual growth. To achieve this you will need to find not only the strength to confront your past, but also forgiveness."

I tried to remember, on my own, all of the beatings. But then, no matter how awful the memories, a more abominable thought suddenly emerged. Did I hit Nicholas only once? Were my father's beatings the only ones I had blocked out? A horrible feeling overcame me. I confessed this thought to Corto.

"Know this," he insisted. "Nothing is wasted in a soul's journey, neither joys nor pains. Our experiences define us. They help shape our ultimate design."

"Yet I fail to see the reason behind Michael's death," I retorted, curtly, "and how it fits into *my* Original Design."

Corto peered into my soul with curious eyes. He smiled strangely, and stared right through me—right where my heart would have been. Having perceived a danger such thoughts could bring to my journey, whatever was discernible in my ethereal core and mysteriously murmured to him was dutifully relayed.

"Sunshine alone will not breathe colors into a garden," he cautioned. "For this you need the rain, which dresses the flowers in magnificent robes. Man's faith must be greater than the range of his eyesight. My friend, you won't find answers by questioning God."

Adventurers of the Soul

Moments before setting sail for this great journey, Corto insisted on delivering a few words. He stared at the guests assembled on the foredeck, hands on hips, his voice as clear and fierce as his eyes. He spoke of the history of the Caribbean, of the Caribs, Tainos and Arawaks, and of course the Conquistadors. He spoke of meals seasoned with a thousand spices, the torrid rhythm of drumbeats, of savors and delights. He spoke of natives with intelligent limbs off the coast of Trinidad, cheating gravity by the way they skipped to the top of a tall palm tree in less than five hops. His voice carried more than words. It held gleaming gold doubloons. He nursed our spirits, filled them with visions lost through age or deception.

"The most valuable skill you'll learn is to become one with the environment," he stated. "That skill will force you to look, listen, smell and read signs of Mother Nature."

Hearing this I recognized at once the first stage, which stressed the mind's awakening.

"Some people go through life blind to their environment," he resumed. "But not you. Not after this voyage. And if you ever find yourself in some predicament, desperate or lost, look at nature for inspiration. In your hands you hold the power to shape your destiny, to live something few dream of and even fewer attempt."

The veritable journey finally began.

They sailed a few hours during the day, then dropped anchor in a secluded anchorage where some read novels while others captured lobsters for their dinner. But it was the sight of Paris and Corto, immersed regularly in silent meditation, which compelled all.

Seated cross-legged on the foredeck, through the magic of enhanced concentration, they became water, became mountains, became outer space. Freed from the restraint of their earthly bodies they wandered to places yet unseen from me.

"I want to learn!" Esmeralda declared one morning while Thairica was under sail. With a penetrating interest, she asked Paris about the benefits of yoga, having witnessed her expertise in that discipline.

With Thairica's pendulous motion eliciting some consideration, seduced by the challenge, Paris agreed to demonstrate forthwith the rewards that come with stern discipline. She squatted down, placed her palms on the deck, locked her elbows between her knees and lifted her feet. A sudden gust of wind puffed the sails and tilted Thairica. Under the heeling motion, Paris showed Esmeralda the excellence of her balance, with the vessel's slanted angle, now steeper and steeper, unable to alter her unshakable immobility. Thereafter, these two quickly formed a bond, with Esmeralda noticing Paris' every gesture with piqued curiosity.

For the first week of the journey, Thairica sailed a course which took them to the Berry islands, followed by the Exuma Cays. Aside these new islands rolling before me, what also caught my attention was Jared's moody and restless behavior.

One morning, he approached Corto at the navigation table. "How much did you pay for your boat?" he asked.

"How much?"

"Yes, how much, or, better still, since the boat is a few years old, how much is it worth?"

"How much is it worth," Corto repeated.

"In dollars, you know."

"Yeah, I know. Bling-bling."

"If you want. Now, how much?"

"I'll answer your question, but only after you give me some details about you."

"Like what?"

"Do you believe in the soul's immortality?"

"What does that have to do with the price?"

"Everything!" Corto laughed. "It has everything to do with it." Smiling, Corto waited for a reply.

"But I don't get the allusion," Jared argued.

"Answer my question, and I'll answer yours."

"Who can say for sure?"

"I want to know your beliefs."

"Why?"

"By God! Answer this simple question."

"But I still don't understand what this has to do with the price."

Having heard enough, Corto briskly headed for the foredeck, took off his shirt, and plunged into the turquoise waters.

Nonchalantly gazing at the peaceful wavelets of the sea, I tried piecing together Corto's words when Esmeralda approached Paris. "I want you to know that I believe in Spiritual Guides and of their subtle messages meant to help us on our earthly journey," she said. "Perhaps this comes from my unfulfilled romantic side . . . who knows? Anyways, there's something I want to ask you."

"Go on," Paris said, noticing her hesitation and swift coloring of cheeks.

"Do you think that, perhaps, something is supposed to happen between Jared and me?"

"You mean . . . romantically?"

Esmeralda's cheeks flushed to a redder shade. "Yes, romantically."

"It's a possibility," Paris said after a quiet moment of reflection. "Are you hoping that this is the case?"

Esmeralda grinned, then as if blown by the salty winds, the smile vanished.

"What am I saying, I'm no fool," Esmeralda muttered. "I'm probably not his type," she added, her hands unconsciously brushing her plump hips.

"Listen carefully," Paris cautioned. "Jared is also here because he has issues, same as you. Everybody needs help at some point in their lives, a fact some are too proud to acknowledge. But there's one thing I can assure you when it comes to men, and that's my lack of surprise for anything they can and will do."

"Why is that?"

"Because men are strange!" Paris exclaimed. "Why is it women see the potential in a man, the treasure underneath the sunken wreck in some cases, whereas men have to see gold at first glance?"

Esmeralda smiled, yet remained silent.

"I will introduce you to the five levels," Paris said. "Know that the meditation process aims at connecting Earth, which now hosts our soul's journey, and the Divine, which serves both as a point of origin and ultimate destination. In the first stage, we seek the awareness of our inner-self and strive to understand the connection with the universe."

Though Esmeralda had intently listened, she lowered her head and yet again touched her hips.

"You think you could help me lose this fat?" she uttered with disgust. "I mean, all of these meditations, can they actually help me lose weight?"

"Yes, if you attach the appropriate energy to your desires, unlike what you just did. But before pursuing this avenue, let's try something else instead."

* * *

The decision of only briefly exploring the Turks and Caicos confused me.

"That's because the human spirit strives when challenged," Paris told me before I even had a chance to ask her. "And so far," she added, "only Esmeralda is venturing out of her comfort zone."

From a once reserved and cloistered woman, Esmeralda intently pursued, under Paris' encouragements, a change of destiny which started to produce faint, but visible traces.

"What about the other two?" Paris asked me. "We shall substitute this prominent scenery for a more honorable exploration—that of their soul."

A few days later, having crossed over to the Dominican Republic, Thairica sailed the northern coast in search of adventures that would satisfy this purpose. Yes, the quiet anchorages and small villages possessed a beauty meant to encourage one's inner-exploration. Unfortunately, of the three guests, only Esmeralda followed a meditation routine.

"Forget your ego," Paris ordered at the beginning of each exercise. "What we seek while working on your emotional level is to infuse energy into your mind and body. Since most of the exercises deal with the elements, it is from their boundless energy that you shall extract this strength we seek."

These lessons I eagerly devoured.

"You have left your comfort zone," Paris told Esmeralda. "This showed tremendous courage. But you resist your Original Design and the entailed lessons when you ask, 'why?' And not, 'what lessons should I learn from this?' There's a reason behind every event. Have more faith in the purpose of things. Spiritual Guides are there to guide you. They have certain manners, obey strict rules, shadow their host's every travel, yet are seldom solicited. With an acute mind you'll learn to distinguish their messages, recognize their whispers, celebrate their touch. All of this mysterious and spectral activity takes place along the vaporous frontier between two worlds. The awareness of your design, of your Spiritual Guides, of a Higher Power guiding you alongside the path of spiritual growth can only be achieved through enhanced skills. Now, let's sit down, close our eyes, meditate, and work on those skills."

That week, I also spent interesting moments with Corto, who felt the secrets of the world could only be whispered to him while he was experiencing the extreme.

"You understand my fascination?" Corto asked me while sailing Thairica through a violent storm one day, alone and miles from shore.

Above him the clouds gathered, while all around the invisible winds whipped the ocean into a frenzy. He peered at the impalpable horizon unleashing a barrage of waves that glided and growled and lifted his ship so high it appeared ready to be launched into outer space.

Smiling, Corto trimmed the sails and soared, freed of his earthly shell.

The indomitable spirit, the Adventurer of the Soul, stretched the boundaries of his domain. And at that moment I knew that the storm had not surprised him. He had known all along, had expected it. In all certainty had even wished for it. Its ferocity sanitized his cruel and brutal past, soothed his spirit. For was it not a mirror image of himself?

The waves tossed the vessel, filled the cockpit, soaked his limbs, yet filled his eyes with stars.

"Look around at this purity which needs no glitter," he exulted. "Fear is what makes a man small, makes a man less than a man."

"But not everybody is comfortable on the water," I cried over the whistling winds.

"And not all waves are made of water," he replied. "Only in the presence of obstacles does the spirit seek to soar. But many wish never to be tested or opposed, and so they remain grounded. Don't they know that a tree will grow taller if next to another one and battling for sunlight?"

I then understood how a soul amassed wealth not from absence of failure, but through repeated attempts to conquer.

The waves roared. The winds hollered. Distant memories penetrated his mind with such vividness that nothing besides those recollections seemed to exist.

Then the deception of having lived in mankind's flawed code of honor escaped his lips, just as a dark cloud detached itself from the brooding sky and met up with his spirit in some accursed reunion.

"How many achieve career peaks with a hollowed core?" he asked. "The only thing worth conquering is your soul. Behold how the waves wash away every lie ever told, how they peel away one's false layers. The ocean sees right through you, demands everything you have, extracts all that you are, because the sea chastises the deceiver."

Blue and white rollers moved bluntly across the heaving ocean and bullied Thairica with frightening ease, while Corto, with a wide grin on his face, cried aloud that he was free!

I asked why instructions often came through storms, and if this paradox, of finding peace through wrath, angered him.

"Why should I be angry?" He looked at me with eyes holding the Truth. "The swells are summoned by the sea, and though foaming, the essence is pure. This day doesn't tarnish its nobleness. It is through the purity of water that I appraise its spirit. I know its heart. And the ocean, mighty, timeless, immortal, owes its power to its essence, not its name."

I then understood how one's nobility is linked to his spirit, not his title. I understood that Heaven rewarded the trials at sea, not the time spent on the soft sand of a quiet destination.

Thunder ripped the skies. The horizon vanished. Wave after wave the blue ocean displayed its ancestral appeal—a threatening frontier tinged with death and gold.

As Thairica dipped and rose he turned to me, shrugged his strong shoulders, his eyes fierce and dangerous.

"Where else does a man like me belong?" he asked sternly. "Where else can I go if I wish to stay away from the battlefields? I'm possessed by this fighting spirit. A man of war, addicted to danger. But the warrior has become uncertain, and that can prove fatal."

After years as an elite soldier and sailing a few times around the world, he knew the mild neighborhoods held neither adventure nor magic. All that to him was priceless and vital. He loved, fought, conquered and suffered. He was a true adventurer, a spiritual warrior. He was everything I had failed to become. No wonder I enjoyed his company so much!

With the storm behind him he headed for port. Once ashore, his knees buckled. It took him a moment to turn back into a land person, for his body to adjust to the ground's firmness. He smiled, his mind still riding waves, his spirit enhanced by another conquest.

"Every storm is a pillar upon which rests my temple," he declared. Comfortably seated in a restaurant, sipping his coffee, he found its flavor always richer on such days. And the exhaustion of his body alone betrayed the storms needed to appease his nature.

Ahead of him, daylight beckoned.

One night, while anchored near Cabo Rafael, on the Dominican Republic's north coast, I asked the Captain if he thought everything was going according to plan. This was his answer:

"My wife told you during your first sail, Thomas, that you possess intelligent and calculating eyes. Know that within each plan of the Universe lies thousands of others, ready to spring forth at the bat of an eyelid. Each of them holds a viable alternative, for the soul's mission is to conquer. And it doesn't matter if it's an ocean, a mountain, or in this case, more aptly, the oceans and mountains within all of us."

He looked at the night sky, or so I thought, and added in a faint whisper:

"This journey is in the early stage and will soon be handed a gift from above. I feel this from the sound of my blood rushing through my veins, from the pulse of stars light years away, but, mostly, from your son's core, which an hour ago began to glow even more."

I looked up at Michael, near the top of the mast. A dazzling beam of light, silently piercing the darkness, bearing a message, fell upon him, coating every atom of his core so magnificently that for an instant I believed him to be brighter than the ancient Pharos of Alexandria. I kept looking, speechless and in awe, at this mysterious communication taking place. At this light seeping into his very soul!

The next morning, with the sun above the tree line, the anchorage revealed a multitude of shallow reefs surrounding Thairica, leaving mere inches between hull and rugged coral heads.

Small wooden shacks with thatched roofs could be seen on the mountain's flanks, scattered along a path that snaked its way from the sandy shore all the way to the summit.

Thairica's crew ate breakfast in the cockpit and observed a large sloop motoring into the bay. Moments later a woman and two men proceeded with the anchoring maneuvers.

"Morning!" the woman said.

"Good morning," all replied.

After exchanging casual words about the weather, the woman and two men retired into the cabin, no doubt to satisfy their morning hunger. As everyone aboard Thairica talked about activities to be enjoyed at a nearby resort, I glanced at the sea, crystal clear, silent and still.

Suddenly a gleaming flash caught my eye and out of nowhere Michael appeared. Judging by his serious face, I knew something had been asked of him. I remembered how my deeply buried past had been unearthed and how, while watching its effect on me, Michael had suffered.

Perhaps such trials were designed to test his faith.

Hovering near the other sailboat, Michael seemed to be gathering forces. He looked at me and for a moment, the sunrays, lured by the purity of his essence, dashed and danced within his core. He appeared complete, like one coming into the possession of a gift granted by a Higher Power, then vanished inside the sailboat.

Shortly after the woman erupted into the cockpit. "Excuse me," she shouted, "but I have a big favor to ask. It's for a charitable cause." Her eyes shone from the seriousness of her plea. She spoke of her two brothers' stomach cramps, thus being unable to transport three crates of medicine to the isolated village at the top of the mountain.

Without a pause Corto offered his services.

As per their agreement, an hour later, on the white sand and under a beating sun, the three crates waited to be hauled to the village.

"You're certain that this will be no trouble," the woman asked Corto.

"Not at all," he replied. He turned around and faced Jared and Emilio, who contemplated the crates as if trying to guess their weight.

"Well then, men, ready for a little exercise?" Corto asked.

"Where exactly are we supposed to bring these?" asked Emilio, at times robbing quick glances at the resort which had been scheduled in the itinerary for leisure activities.

"The crates have to be brought to the village at the top of this mountain," Corto pointed.

"Whoa!" Emilio exclaimed. "All the way to that top?" He sighed profoundly.

"Yes, that top," replied Corto. "The one at the summit."

Both Jared and Emilio started to moan.

"I don't understand any of you," Corto said, his cheeks reddening. "You dream of adventures, yet when one arises, you prefer indulging in the kind of comfort you've known for weeks and shall benefit for many more."

"Well, John, it's just that . . ." Emilio started.

"Go on," interjected Corto.

"It's just that it's so high," Jared groaned.

The air stood still during a tense moment of silence.

"You know," Corto began, shaking his head, "we could go on talking until sunset, that won't change the reality of the moment, which is that we are here, able to provide assistance to people less fortunate and in need. However, I also said you were not obliged to do anything you didn't fancy. So, by all means, go to the resort and indulge in your dart game, pool ping pong, water bingo or whatever the hell you may find!"

Abruptly Corto bent down, picked up one crate, and walked away. A few minutes later, guilt having forged its way, Emilio and Jared followed.

The trail they used cut across a lush mountain, creased with numerous streams that snaked their way into the sea. Jared and Emilio walked without much enthusiasm, unmotivated and bored, their faces lacking excitement.

"Put some passion in your stride, Emilio!" Corto snapped. "Let out this bottled anger of yours. By God! Don't you know you can tell a man's character by his stride?"

The sun had reached its zenith. Their pace suffered. Using their elbows, they pushed aside the many branches which encroached here and there on the trail. Yet another hour had passed, when panting, they rested in a small clearing.

Corto observed the forest with admiration. He unrelentingly directed their attentions to the surrounding beauty. The bright red plumage of a bird, the many green shades of an iguana that, having sensed its detection, scurried away.

"Observe the cottonmouth snake over there," Corto indicated with lively eyes.

"Where?"

"The brown one with dark spots that looks like the branch you were about to walk under."

"Is it poisonous?" asked Jared, frightened.

"Only if you bother it."

Corto's stride was sure, as if inhabited by the forest itself. His ears picked up the feeblest trickle of a brook. Smiling, he parted the undergrowth, discovered the source, and drank from it. Having quenched his thirst, he stood up, deeply inhaled and exhaled, then turned to Jared and Emilio. "Now, at least your soul will have something to build upon," he said.

"I notice you like talking about the soul," Jared commented, breathing heavily.

"That's because I'm a seeker," Corto replied. "A seeker is an Adventurer of the Soul; one who strives to discover the essence of life."

"A lot of time spent debating issues which have been argued for thousands of years," Jared declared.

"The absence of clear answers neither disturbs nor discourages the seeker," replied Corto. "And there is a reality which you should come to terms with. We are spirits, and seekers strive for the awareness that shall bring them to the portal of the after life, for ultimately we will spend, in our eternity, more time roaming the spiritual plane than the earthly one."

"I'm not sure I'd like the attention that these endeavors would bring," Jared countered. "To have a lot of people snicker behind my back doesn't appeal to me."

"Ah! Fear of judgment," Corto remarked with a firm voice. "One of the fundamental qualities of the seeker is to cherish his marginality, his resolve to stray from the pack mentality. Assimilation floods the spirit. Look around and witness how Man closes his eyes to the mystical, all the while drowning his true nature with worthless objects and titles. For certain people, the attachment to their image proves greater than that of the growth of their soul. They live in a perfect order, their choices having undergone the silent, but very real approbation of others, be it their clothes, their cars, or their character. And that is why you, my friend, show no more character than a trained monkey who waits for his master's acknowledgement to jump for joy and peel his banana after performing some trick!"

The redness sweeping Jared's cheeks disclosed the fullness of the affront. His eyes glared as he bent to pick up his crate.

Up the hill they marched, when after pushing their way through thick branches they entered another clearing. Corto paused, drew deep breaths, and calmly put down his crate. Something had prompted his senses. Hands on his hips, his eyes incessantly swept from left to right. Abruptly his head stopped swiveling, and he stared straight ahead. Just then two men, concealed in the dense foliage with flawless stealth, stepped out.

"We will take those, amigos," one man said.

Both Emilio and Jared appeared relieved, but this only lasted for a brief moment.

"No thanks," Corto replied, curtly.

"But," Emilio interrupted.

"None of that from you, young man," Corto instructed. "Trust me. The General would hate to discover that you didn't make it to the top. He trusts that someday you will make a fine soldier, like your cousin in Santiago. You don't want your uncle to endlessly brag to your father, do you?"

Looking at the two men, Corto produced from his shirt pocket a cigarillo. "Now," he pronounced measurably, with that tone gleaned through countless of dangerous encounters. "I'd appreciate it if you got out of our way, unless one of you happens to have matches for my cigar. I seemed to have forgotten mine at the *commandancia*."

Seconds later, Corto tucked the unlit cigarillo in the corner of his lips, picked up the wooden crate, and lightly, but insistently, brushed past the two men.

Under no desire to be left alone and obeying Corto's lead, Jared and Emilio swiftly moved behind.

Startled by Corto's boldness, the two men shook their heads and headed the other way.

"What was that all about?" Jared whispered, with a hint of alarm not meant to travel outside the scope of a few feet.

"Scoundrels dealing in the black market," Corto informed.

Soon after this encounter, rain fell on them, hard, like a gray curtain.

"It looks like we might have to sleep ashore tonight," Corto pointed.

"It's just rain," Emilio said, surprised that a man who had just confronted two suspicious characters would seek shelter from a simple shower.

"Yes, it's just rain. Unfortunately this path will soon turn into a very nasty mud slide, so I suggest we hurry up. On the double!"

After another hour, the three men knew that the summit was close, and drew strength to complete the remaining stretch.

"Finally," both Emilio and Jared groaned. Tired, their clothes completely soaked, they were quickly met by running and giggling young Dominicans who, smiling and laughing, led them into a large cabin with a chimney.

We found ourselves in complete darkness. Moments later a bright spark pierced the darkness, and as elongated flames charged upwards, the whole interior came alive.

Around the central fireplace, the villagers sat silently, yet curious. It was then that Corto spoke of his quest, which once shared kindled the Dominicans' interest. The chilling stories mesmerized the listeners.

"Why pursue something that only death will validate?" Emilio asked.

"I told you before," answered Corto. "It's because I'm a seeker. It's in my blood. A man might question a lot of things, but he can't go against his own blood. Remember this; everything in life, you must do for your soul. A good clue as to what your purpose might be is by discovering your gift."

Throughout this oration, an appreciation of his words was felt by all.

All except one, that is.

"You speak of eternity and the Universe," interjected Jared in a loud voice. "Then tell me why I sense this lurking menace about you."

Corto sat, very still, as Jared's comment enticed recollections of fallen, bloodied bodies which rose from the grave.

"Yes," Jared eagerly pursued at the sight of Corto's hazy eyes. "Tell me what fate awaited the two men encountered earlier on the trail if they would have tried to steal the crates?"

"Yes, I do admit," Corto said, slightly disturbed, "that it could have turned badly."

"What exactly do you mean by—turned badly?"

"I think the answer doesn't warrant more explanation."

"But it would have turned badly for THEM," Jared persisted, his voice tainted with arrogance and triumph.

"Yes, for them," Corto acknowledged, preserving his calm. His face showed neither displeasure nor remorse when Jared, seeking revenge for the monkey comment, pressed him to explain.

"I have this troubling vision of you," Jared taunted, "of you fighting." Tightening his fists, he mimicked a flurry of punches:

"Fighting, fighting, fighting!"

"You haven't been paying attention," retorted Corto, in a joyless tone. "I do these things because I have a gift for this type of encounters, and to such a gift I commit myself entirely. However, my search aims at discovering the extent of what's permissible to both the Universe and my conscience. That's why I cherish the belief that our task is to leave this planet a better soul, which is where you'll find the answer to your question of a few weeks ago."

"Which one is that?"

"The one about Thairica's worth." Saying that name, Corto's eyes sparkled. "Thairica will bring me to the ultimate shore. It is a place not of this Earth. As such, compared to the boundless experiences and prodigious step forward my soul will achieve while at the helm, Thairica has no price!"

* * *

The following morning, with the mountainous coast of the Dominican Republic rolling by, Corto, at the helm, studied the landscape, the rocky cliffs here and there giving way to stretches of white sands. Suddenly a couple of galloping horses appeared into view. This vision proved irresistible for the Captain. Sails were furled, the anchor was dropped, and the group went ashore.

On the outskirts of the beach there was a wooden shack. In it a man waited, while further away the horses nibbled on the scarce patches of grass.

"I want a good horse, amigo," Corto told the Dominican man.

"I give you the black stallion," replied the man, who seemed confused when Corto removed the saddle.

"You have ridden horses before, amigo?" asked the man.

"It's in my blood," Corto said. He paid the man handsomely and hopped in one bound onto the horse's back. Pockets of sand flew out of rapid hooves, as Corto dropped out of sight. Later that day, Paris and Corto indulged in kite-surfing. Wave after wave, the adventurous couple surfed, aided by persistent winds which remained vibrant yet not over-zealous.

Then as the sunset splashed its colorful presence, Corto handed out glasses filled with red wine. He emptied his own in two swills, danced barefoot on the sand the way of the Greeks, and sang Sinatra songs, just like an Italian.

During the following weeks, Esmeralda honed her sailing techniques, and when at anchor spent her time either reading, meditating, or taking private guitar lessons from Paris. A romantic at heart, Esmeralda still believed, to my horror, in a possible relationship with Jared—a trait she owed, no doubt, to her avid reading of adventure books!

Esmeralda's nautical skills had far surpassed those of Jared. When asked about weather conditions, Jared would immediately run to the radio, whereas Esmeralda would first stick out her head and study the sky.

Jared, on the other hand, had brought his bureaucratic attitude to the sea. Though he sometimes demonstrated a learning desire, he remained deaf to the voice of the ocean and, even worse, treated Esmeralda with disrespect. Indeed, for weeks, he remained insensitive to any acts of kindness Esmeralda attempted. At times, though illogical, since both had never met prior to this voyage, Jared's attitude appeared as the settling of a distant grudge.

Although continuously subjected to Jared's gloomy impulses, this did not diminish Esmeralda's learning progress. For those few weeks when Thairica was under sail she never retreated to her cabin, even on rainy days. Rather, she observed the magical way with which a light breeze of very few knots propelled a seventy tons sailing vessel. Her son, however, had also noticed the changes. Feeling more and more neglected, he measured, with great concern, the prodigious skills captured under Paris' private tutelage.

On her many visits ashore, Esmeralda demonstrated the proficiency of her dealings. There she bought the best fruits and vegetables, prepared recipes in the galley which consisted of grilled snapper, wahoo or bonito, which they caught while sailing, complimented with fried plantains that had everyone raving.

Paris and Corto, on their part, devoutly secured the peacefulness procured by the sunsets. Afterwards, they would dance on the foredeck without music, 'just to keep the flame ablaze', as they would say. They never preached, yet their faith and wisdom attracted a following. Many sailors, whom I called 'Spiritual Sailors,' knew of their travels and arranged their itineraries accordingly.

During this period Michael witnessed every action of benevolence performed by our hosts and became a devout admirer of Paris. To my delight, I was present during many of the talks held between Paris and Esmeralda and one morning, while privately retreated on the foredeck when sailing across the Mona Passage to Puerto Rico, the intricacies of the second stage unraveled.

"Though you have yet to fully master the first stage," Paris told Esmeralda, "which is to seek the awareness of our surrounding elements and inner-selves, I will introduce you to the second stage, which introduces you to the mind's power. Close your eyes. Feel the cooling breeze tickle your skin, the gentle sway of Thairica, as your body rises and sinks in harmony with the sea. Feel the sun's beating rays as it heats your face. Picture those rays entering your body, and warming your heart. There is a fabulous gift you will develop with these meditations. The gift of warming people's hearts! Since nature is pure, a union with its essence is primordial to transform you from a five sensory being to a multi-sensory being. Now, rise above the deck, then slowly descend into the water, not to sink in it, but to become water."

At the end of this exercise, Paris resumed the lesson by saying, "Once capable of being absorbed in a tree's bark, or in water, or even by becoming a ray of sunlight, what I hope for is that nature will impress upon you the notion that *you are energy*. This in turn will help you when comforting others, which is an important part in your spiritual journey. You will notice that living on a boat does have its advantages when doing these meditations with water. And that's one of the main reason sailors were chosen to pioneer experiments with energy."

"You're talking about this elusive fraternity I noticed in various ports and anchorages," Esmeralda commented.

"Yes," Paris replied, pleased by Esmeralda's awareness. "Being at one with nature is paramount to some of the research. What's important in the second stage is to cut out feelings of self-gratification when performing a good deed. Once you've achieved this, a higher awareness will come, and on the third level you'll be able to command pockets of positive energies, which you'll transfer to someone in need, this with a simple wish."

That afternoon, after taking Esmeralda to a Puerto Rican village, Paris intended to show the second stage's practical application.

Soon they observed a twenty-year-old woman joylessly minding the market's fruits and vegetables stall, all the while faced with a pressing clientele.

"Can you feel that woman's distress?" Paris asked.

"How can you tell?"

"I can read her aura, which is one of the gifts you'll acquire as you ascend the stages. For now, let's observe the ones who come into contact with her, and see if they show any concern."

We observed the multitude of customers she served, and how not one dared to prod her melancholic sphere. Worse. Most even seemed annoyed by it.

"Follow me," Paris said, "and witness how quickly her sadness will be swept away."

With Michael suddenly by my side, we invisibly escorted Paris and Esmeralda as they moved towards the market.

"Tell me why a face of such beauty doesn't smile?" Paris asked the young woman.

"Thank you for asking," the young woman replied, "but it's nothing."

"Ah! I see," Paris retorted. "Matters of the heart."

The girl somberly shook her head, her eyes showing disconsolation, which was to be expected when young love is devastated.

"Dear sister", Paris kindly said. "You should focus on all the qualities you undoubtedly possess to feel better about yourself. Just consider the strength you demonstrate, silencing your anguish so that you can bring home your livelihood."

She extended her hand and brushed her shoulder.

"There are many who do not possess such will," Paris assured.

Though these words appeared to alleviate the woman's concerns, what was most amazing was Paris' intense, yet gentle gaze. There she stood, green eyes filled with strength, and the pockets of energy flowing out of them carried the supportive whispers meant to shatter one's self-enclosed barriers. Ever so slowly the charge of this invisible force took over. The young woman's composure altered, and it became quite obvious that her mind had welcomed this unexpected burst of freshness.

A short silence ensued, before Paris, pleased by the awakening, asked for her name."

"My name?"

"Yes, your name. Why do you seem so startled?"

"Excuse me; it's just that no client has ever asked me that question."

"Ah! But my dear sister, I'm not just a client, am I?"

"It's Yanira."

"Yanira, such a beautiful name," Paris complimented. Following this encounter, both Paris and Esmeralda took a taxi back.

"We're all connected," Paris told Esmeralda. "When helping others, you also enrich your own soul. Never forget the healing power of a simple smile, and always strive to do something from the graciousness of your heart, for the Universe senses everything and the soul will not reap the same reward. What you have witnessed here today is the power of energy-transfer—a power you'll develop as you progress."

Having witnessed the practical application, confident in her nautical abilities, abilities that complemented her harmony with nature, Esmeralda beamed for the next few days.

But just as the whole world began to smile at Esmeralda, Emilio's behavior turned it cloudy. Quite simply put, this was a period when Emilio' every gesture uttered a silent cry of rebellion, ultimately bringing his mother's prospects to a halt. Astutely aware and gifted, Paris had, for quite awhile, noticed, through color changes of his aura, she later confided to me, a discernible reversal in Emilio's emotions.

"Emilio fears a second abandonment," Paris told me. "And I think more trouble lays ahead for his mother."

The following day, seeing that he had failed to stop his mother's inner quest, Emilio harbored suspicions of his own worth. These suspicions had plunged him into such confusion that, when at the helm for what was to be an easy approach in a wide and unoccupied channel of Culebra, in the Spanish Virgin Islands, he deliberately strayed off course and ran Tharica aground on a sandbank.

This small occurrence had a devastating impact on Esmeralda. Having tenderly reassured her son in the cabin, she went into the cockpit and, her eyes filled with tears, contemplated the sea under countless stars. At the sight of her shaking her head, I knew all too well the source of her torment. Doubt, the natural enemy of serenity, dark like the night, and slippery like smoke, was extending its grasp.

She listened to the peaceful lapping of wavelets against the hull, and studied the faintly disturbed mirror of the sea, concluding shortly after that a tranquil surface, at times, conceals greater dangers.

Then all that she had lived these past few weeks appeared as a dream never to be dreamt again. She whispered, "Emilio." In the cooling breeze, she added her own wisdom. "When a woman becomes a mother, she becomes the family."

Nothing could rival those words. A formidable statement she murmured again and again. For the thought of Emilio healed the pains of doubt. Her son! She could never relinquish the inviolable significance of motherhood, shirk its demanding duty, betray nature's mightiest bond. Instantly she appeared solemnly resigned. The splendor of her role sparked the new glimmer in her dark eyes.

"This isn't even a choice," she murmured, obedient to her heart's command, though I did detect faint inflections of sorrow in her voice.

She walked to the pulpit, leaned over the railing, looked at the life force which had stirred her core, and with tears gently falling into the sea, she expressed her gratitude.

Spiritual Sailors

Thairica, ever faithful, journeyed forward.

"I hear Esmeralda's silent plea," Paris told me one night. "Sadly, it will never vanish, especially not under this forced exile."

Earlier that day, Paris had asked Emilio to support his mother's inner quest. But Paris had failed to sway his reasoning, for Emilio had been abandoned by his father and anticipated the same consequence if his mother kept blossoming.

"Standing rigidly behind every fear is a barricade," Paris confided. "One only made fragile through the persistence of love, and that emotion alone may break its hold."

"What could be Jared's fears?" I asked.

"His emotions," she said after pondering, "may have taken roots long before today."

"You mean since childhood," I countered.

"No, I mean before that. A lot of people carry experiences from their previous lives."

"And a lot more people don't share those beliefs," I replied.

"You must understand that traumatizing episodes, sometimes, traverse the ages and remain concealed, like a grave deprived of a tombstone, only disclosing its existence when stumbling on its massed earth."

* * *

The sight of Cooper Island, in the British Virgin Islands, shimmered before us. Shielding their eyes from the late morning sun, all hands on deck marveled at the succeeding islands of Sir Francis Drake Channel. Norman Island. Peter Island. Dead Chest.

After anchoring in Manchioneel Bay, Corto informed the guests that a private appointment forced him and Paris to go ashore. Minutes later, having tied the dinghy to a dock, they walked a short distance until finding themselves near a cottage. Coming down the stairs of the verandah, a man moved towards them. One whose name had been mentioned more than once in these past few weeks.

The man extended both hands in a greeting gesture.

"There you are," Senator Williams said. "I have been expecting you. Come in, please! It's so refreshing to have you!" He escorted us to his house and opened the door.

"We brought along a friend," Corto informed.

"How marvelous!" exclaimed Senator Williams. He had a stately face, dignified and confident, with clear blue eyes, a light complexion, and thick silvery hair. He showed us around his large, rustically furnished home, then led us to the garden where the three of them sat down on rattan chairs. Since Senator Williams could neither see nor hear me, Paris dutifully acted as interpreter.

"You no doubt are acquainted with some of Einstein's work?" Senator Williams asked me. Paris relayed to him my acknowledgement, and he proceeded. "Einstein considered matter as frozen light, hence underlining how everything in this universe consists of energy. Well, in nineteen thirteen, Einstein discovered a source of energy he called the Zero Point Energy. You may find references to it in some ancient texts and even the Bible under other appellations, namely God's energy, or The Eternal Energy. We know that samples of this energy are already used in quantum applications, by yogis who stop their breathing for weeks, or levitating monks. All of these individuals have a high degree of fulfillment, perhaps on their way of becoming Ascended Masters. As for the finer details of the recent discoveries, I would never dream of cheating Saul from telling you."

"You mean we are to go there?" Corto asked, genuinely surprised.

"Of course," he replied. "I know you sailed to that island last year."

"Yes," Corto acknowledged.

Senator Williams leaned towards Paris, his eyes expressing great hopes. "This trip would mean so much to Saul, who expressly asked for you," he said. "Of course, you are to sail there after completing your present assignment."

"What about the latest results we've been hearing?" Corto inquired. Slight frowns creased his forehead.

"You mean Leticia," Williams said. He stared at Paris, and though his eyes were compassionate, there seemed a slight trepidation behind them. "Although her gifts greatly contributed to further advance the research concerning the curing of minor injuries," he informed, "the advanced stages of the fourth level, which I believe she found overwhelming, may have caused her some instability before being denied to her."

Suddenly Michael appeared. Moving closer to Paris, possessed with that enchantment which lures into obedience, he smiled. His presence had a profound effect. A message seemed to form itself in the space between them. Returning the smile, Paris nodded. What was happening? Or, more importantly, what was about to happen?

"Where is Leticia now?" Corto asked, very seriously, for the thought of that uncharted power, of Paris delving in its mysterious depths, impressed upon his rugged features a trace even Michael's magic could not erase.

"In Antigua," Senator Williams answered. "Near a quiet village on Monks Hill."

* * *

With Thairica on the east side of the Anegada passage, Paris and Corto's presence attracted the Spiritual Sailors exploring the Leeward Islands.

"You still haven't disclosed the name of this fraternity," I told Corto in a voice meant to show him my exasperation.

"The silence I observe is not meant to frustrate you," he insisted. "This riddle is an important step in your path to awareness. Pay close attention to what will happen tonight."

As he said this, Thairica was moored near Saba Island, situated some twenty-eight miles south of St. Maarten, next to four other sailboats whose crews were set to participate in a unique meditation session.

I hovered near the top of the mast, next to Michael.

"Fantastic, isn't it?" I said, pointing at the moon's reflection dancing on the sea's dark surface.

Lying on the foredeck, Paris and Corto quietly watched the sky, while Matthew and Danny, tightly nudged between them, searched for falling stars and satellites.

"Are you ready for the session?" Corto shouted. "This will demand a higher degree of awareness from you."

"I believe so," I answered back. "Although I still can't move an object, I have perfected my skills."

One of the most mysterious qualities of an ethereal being is the varying intensity of our energy field. The ability to vanish through walls, yet at times to move solid objects. This phenomenon is solved through the persuasive force one is capable of projecting. And since the proposed experiment demanded that we lie down on our backs, my mind had to ensure that my wispy shell *feel* Thairica's deck while avoiding any distraction that would either send me high into the air, or, through the deck and into the ocean.

All at once the four sailboats approached. Like the sea they roamed, these sailors of quiet might and serene character moved with aquatic elegance.

"Here, put a fender right here!" one sailor exclaimed.

"Watch the spreaders!" shouted another.

After binding together all five vessels, the fellowship of sailors admired their labor. Floating on the sea, the assembly of vessels looked like a space station.

A faint breeze played with the structure, its axis pivoting, as if invisibly tweaked by an invisible giant. Finally, once completed, the sailors put out the lights aboard their craft. The stars winked, and the whole celestial vault appeared with such vividness that everybody impulsively extended their arms. This was the exercise we needed to perform. To connect with the sky while embraced by the ocean—to join our two worlds.

Eyes closed, we listened to Paris' entrancing voice and were quickly transported into outer space. To Saturn we first traveled, like wanderers seeking life's mysteries.

We had stepped out of our bodies (although this was fairly easy for me) and took the form of the ringed planet. Around the sun we revolved, bathing in its brilliance while Earth appeared into view. How full of life and blue were its oceans. Following Paris' command, we individually pictured the sun's golden rays.

"You will now extend the same courtesy to the moon," she commanded. "Visualize every ray exiting the craters and polishing Earth with their silvery magic."

She beseeched us to discern the tiniest detail of the moon's furrowed surface, every inch of this celestial sphere. I summoned my will and in a moment of intense visualization saw the smallest piece of rubble, the narrowest fissure, the most delicate variation of its soil.

Then Paris instructed us to build a temple, stone by stone, pillar by pillar, silvery rays piled atop golden ones. A sublime oasis which was to become our shrine. Quite unexpectedly a flash of purple seeped into my mind. All of the world's problems had been purged. The suffering, the torment, the famines and useless wars. Every distasteful act Man is capable of, at once erased, for we had claimed the essence of the Creator.

I wanted more.

I eagerly awaited Paris' next instructions, when once again her voice pierced the quiet darkness. She instructed us to feel our planet's liquid curvature, to seek the sky's infinity, and harmoniously synchronize our two worlds.

"You have left your body," she said, her words bringing us closer to the Kingdom, "yet your mind and soul remain, for they are but one. The ascending path is near. But suspicion, distrust and uncertainty in your Original Design will rob you of this enlightenment. Only faith can restore your happiness. Only love can guard you against the many perils blocking the path. You have become celestial voyagers and shall forever strive to enrich other people's lives."

Suddenly lightning swept across the horizon. Some nearing Force held me in its grasp. In what land did I roam? Towards me the Force floated, or, I towards it.

"What are you?" I asked, unable to restrain myself.

"To those in presence of a Force," Paris said, no doubt conscious of what we were experiencing, "I entreat you to enter your shrine."

I entered my shrine and noticed a magnificent yellow and purple Light. There, I knew at once, loomed the Almighty. Startled, I opened my eyes, and witnessed the astonishment of all.

Later that evening, Ivan, a husky Swedish sailor whose vessel was part of the orbital station, asked Paris to share more of her wisdom.

With a flowing, graceful ease, Paris stood up, and leaned against the mast. "I carry the sound of waves and glorious twilights at sea wherever I am," she said. "These sounds, sights and scents constitute the essence of my wandering estate. To the anchored wealth, I'd rather ride the winds."

Applauses rang throughout the orbital station, followed by a deep silence.

"I detect some anxiety in your eyes," Paris told me. She rose, took a few steps, and settled down to a spot where she began her yoga routine.

"These are remarkable times," I confided. I had experienced such emotions lately. In this world in chaos, with governments guarded by religious extremists, what future awaited these sailors searching for this mystical energy, all the while striving to ascend the spiritual path? Was such an awakening even possible? Would the men of power ever allow this?

"They can't control our thoughts," Paris said, ardently.

My anger had been so intense that its frequencies had been picked up by her kabalistic wizardry.

She looked at me. "You can't stop the signal, Thomas. You can't. Our thoughts are formed where the beam of their searchlight doesn't shine. No shackles can restrain what they can't grasp."

She talked like one endowed with a mission.

"Once a signal is launched," she continued, "it goes everywhere, and forms a consciousness, ready to be harvested. And it doesn't matter if bodies are kept apart. No, absolutely not! In the end, the men of power shall not be defeated, but rather enlightened. Yes, it's true that many know of us. They have branded us as outcasts, even crackpots. But it's them I pity. People only obsessed with money, blind to the stars and living in a state nothing touches unless pressed hard against their skin."

The conviction of her voice was fierce.

Curious about her level of awareness, I made the observation that of the five proposed stages, I had yet to learn on which one either she or Corto belonged.

"If you ask my husband," she answered, cautiously, "he will tell you that he belongs to the second level, whereas I belong to the third."

"And if I ask you?"

She shook her head. "I truly don't know."

She exhaled deeply, squatted down, placed her palms on the deck, locked her elbows between her knees, and leaned forward, supporting her weight solely with her arms.

She remained perfectly balanced, mentioned that this posture was called the Crow, and said that she would next perform the Bow.

Lying face down on the deck, holding both ankles, she raised her head while arching backwards. Her grace was admirable! Her execution flawless! Before my eyes her body infused me with images of various creatures, and I remember thinking that should Heaven ever approve of one embodying both the sprightliness of the lioness and swiftness of the eagle, then, no doubt was she endowed with the specimen's necessary attributes.

The Staircase of Energy

I found no enhancement in Corto's words when he had earlier commented on Antigua's beauty. Behind English harbor, which showcased numerous large yachts, elegant clippers and other anchored vessels, could be seen a rolling canopy of smooth hills that surrounded the anchorage.

"Was this island part of the original itinerary?" I asked Corto who, at the helm, negotiated the channel's many buoys.

"Not quite," he answered, in a discreet whisper. He looked at me gravely. "I just want to see for myself, make sure Paris knows what she could be getting herself into."

"Will it make a difference?"

He remained silent, obviously distraught.

"Perhaps if her powers included the foretelling of the future, then you would be spared such anguish," I added.

"Yeah, right," he muttered. He nodded slightly. "Wouldn't that be great," he added. Seeing that some of the passengers looked at him, he restrained from further explanation. Then, once satisfied that he could again secretly confide, he murmured:

"Long ago I would have agreed, but last year, during one of my travels in the lands of The Great Spirit, I came across a sorcerer whose powers shone as much as the sun. 'Spells and enchantment only go as far as the Heavens allow,' he had then told me. And because we are to dwell in a power directly linked to God, the decisions we must take must be taken solely out of faith."

Minutes later Thairica was securely tied to the dock. After clearing the Customs formalities, they all went to a restaurant perched atop one of the hills overlooking the harbor. There, while Corto talked to Emilio, I listened to Paris discreetly explaining to Esmeralda the benefits of the second stage meditation.

"With practice," she whispered, careful not to attract Emilio's attention, "you should be able to hear the sunrise, feel the moon's attraction, even sense the blood rushing through your veins. By acquiring such senses . . . senses other than those meant to experience the material world, you will be able to reach the proper conclusions about the causes and effects of important events in your life."

Needless to say, these words held a particular appeal for me. To discover what events had shaped *my* present state, I naturally felt the necessity to revisit Jane and Nicholas. In order to accomplish this, I moved next to Michael who, after reading my thoughts, promptly brushed my hand.

Instantly a sinking sensation took hold of me, as space travel wielded its wizardry. I found myself floating inside my home's living room, feeling hesitant, yet thrilled. Just then, the sight of Michael, his core burning with an unknown yet decisive purpose, caught my attention.

"Michael, be careful!" I cautioned. "Watch your powers, so you don't scare them." Instantly his core grew paler and paler. I marveled at his expertise, well aware that his lofty design would soon unravel. There could be no other conclusion.

Sounds of voices from the kitchen increased my anticipation. Through the closed door we passed, and once on the other side we saw Jane and Nicholas sitting at the kitchen table. Mary, Jane's sister, was also there, and all of them were immersed in old family albums. Jane, obviously moved, was cautious not to burst into tears, for that would affect Nicholas. This was her role—to be strong and brave and support him through this crisis.

"You remember that Christmas, Nicholas?" Jane asked. Her fingers directed his attention towards the intended picture. "This was taken years ago, before we moved into this house. Ah, what joys we shared in those days, before . . ."

"Before what?" I furiously screamed.

It was in the suffering of that recollection that Jane had abruptly stopped. "We had such good times before moving here," she resumed. She pondered with a dutiful, heavy stare, and frequent nods of her head.

"We did, we really did," Nicholas murmured sadly. Jane, aware of Nicholas' pain, pressed his hand, and lightly smiled.

And that smile lit Michael's eyes like a Christmas tree. There was nothing I could do to stop him. Michael approached the table, and the message he intended to convey captivated my very soul. With his mischievous blue eyes set afire, he stretched out his wispy hand towards his mother. Just then, at the *point of contact*, I saw the heavenly twinkle.

Jane froze at once! Her face turned as white as a ghost! She lifted her head and searched all around, hopeful that her secretive longings could have been answered.

"What's wrong?" Mary gasped, in a worried voice. Jane's startled look only frightened her more.

"Sister, what's the matter?" Mary insisted.

Nicholas, alarmed, intensely studied his mother's eyes. Then, as Jane's face brightened, her eyes suddenly sparkled from a thought that seemed to cross over the few feet separating them. He knew! Nicholas began to rise when Jane seized his arm.

"Sit! Sit down!" Jane ordered, fearful any sudden gesture would scare us away. Nodding, Nicholas leaned back, while Michael repeated the loving gesture.

Over and over, time and time again, Michael stroked his mother's cheeks, mindful, as his nature vanished into hers, not to arouse the specter of death.

Legions of tiny spikes marched from Jane's arms to her shoulders, from shoulders to torso, and from torso to her throat. Just then Jane enticed the others to hold her hands while staring into this enigmatic emptiness filled with hushed thunder, and unseen lightning.

"Hello Michael! Hello Thomas!" Jane shouted, in a rejoicing tone. "We want to tell you that we love you, will love you always and forever. We miss you tremendously, will always miss you, but ease your worries, we are doing better."

"Jane!" Mary abruptly interrupted. "I know your loss is great, yet I implore you, for Nicholas' sake as well as your own, to break free from these voluntary hallucinations."

A shadow swept across Jane's face. Slowly but surely, her convictions evaporated.

"I'm your sister," Mary continued in a low, resolute tone. "I know what's best for you. And these beliefs you entertain . . . these illusions of departed ones coming back as spirits are unhealthy."

Jane lowered her eyes, hesitantly, and shook her head.

All these denials Michael absorbed with loud giggles. He turned to me so that I could witness his exuberance, then moved towards the counter where, with a gentle sweep of his hand, he brought life to a tea cup. The cup trembled. Three gasps were heard when the cup warmed up and began to glide.

Of the long and smooth surface of the counter, five feet separated the cup from the edge, while the cup, inexorably, maintained its course.

"There can be no other explanation than what I've been telling you!" Jane shouted. "My beloved Michael is doing this. He is doing this to show me that he is well and to give me hope."

Jane wiped her ongoing tears, for at this moment her doubts had vanished to the beat of a moving cup. Mary's disbelief suffered. She rubbed her eyes and stared open-mouthed at the scene played out before her.

"This can't be happening," Mary whispered. To everyone's expectation the cup reached the end of its course, tipped over and crashed. Rising from her chair, made stronger by the new hope filling her heart, Jane outstretched both hands, wishing to enter the land where Michael and I roamed. Relentlessly, she searched the emptiness, trying to connect with the impalpable entities standing so close.

"I always hoped of receiving such visits," Jane confessed. "Although you have proclaimed that too much hope taints the mind and promotes illusions, you cannot deny the only possible explanation for what just happened here."

Happy at what he had done, ecstatic in fact, Michael quickly moved towards me and whisked me away. Thankfully I had, at the very least, been afforded a clue as to where I needed to seek the source of my misfortunes.

I found myself back in Antigua, in a quaint restaurant with Corto and his joyous band of sailors finishing their meals. Moments later the group crammed into two taxis. One hour sufficed to bring them to a small village near Monks Hill. There they were informed by an old lady to visit the hospital if they wished to see Leticia.

"She's there every night," the old lady explained.

With the intention of pursuing Leticia's trace, we reached the hospital, and entered. There we ventured down a corridor and saw a woman dressed in a white sari with charts in her hands.

Promptly the woman made her way over. "I am Doctor Gardner," she said with a polite nod. "May I help you?" She took a few steps forward, her lips curled with a gentleness that brought comfort.

"We came here hoping to find a friend of ours," Paris said. "Her name is Leticia."

"You mean the sorceress!" Doctor Gardner exclaimed.

"The sorceress?" Paris queried.

"Yes, well, that's what everybody around here called her," Doctor Gardner volunteered.

"Why this nickname?" asked Paris.

The doctor smiled, and took a few moments to gather her thoughts. "Leticia visited us a few months ago," she informed. "She entered one morning and asked if she could see some of my patients. Naturally, I thought of those with no relatives, who are thus deprived of human contact outside the medical assistance we provide. I therefore agreed that she may visit two patients, one of them being a dying man. Strangely enough, after her visit, that patient lived a few months longer than expected. It was the most amazing thing."

Wishing to discuss these matters privately, Corto asked the group to wait outside, and once everyone, including Michael, had left, Paris asked if Leticia still performed such treatments.

The doctor shook her head. "No," she said, somberly, "because since the patient eventually died, she felt that she had only prolonged the man's agony."

She touched her chin with her thumb and forefinger.

"I remember her saying that soon there would be a majestic event," she confided. "Wait a minute. Let me think. A coming! Yes! That's what she called it. A coming! And that the whole world would rejoice. It was the strangest thing, the way she had said it."

"We were told she was here every night," Paris pursued.

"That's because a lot of people claim to see her at night, floating above the hospital grounds in a white gown, like some ghost. And that's why she came to be known as the sorceress."

She again shook her head. Her eyes became moist, and biting her lips, she looked upward, as if seeking answers from a place outside her grasp.

"I never believed in forces greater than our own," she whispered. "Until the day I met her."

"Perhaps there's a deeper purpose you should seek from all of this," Paris stated.

As the scope of that reply registered in Doctor Gardner's mind, she stared at the woman before her. Could there be, in the gleam of those emerald eyes, another being of the same mettle as the one who had stirred such confusion?

"Come with me," Doctor Gardner entreated, leading Paris and Corto in front of a closed door, which she slowly opened.

When we entered, the room was plunged in such a dusky atmosphere that it took a few seconds to distinguish the patient from the bed.

"Here she is," the doctor indicated with a deliberate movement of the hand towards a young, devastated woman. She approached the patient, wondering perhaps if the woman's sunken cheeks and opaque texture of her ashen gray skin could ever be reversed.

Same as everyone I observed how that silenced existence trapped inside a decaying body had already lost its personality, its musical animation, its spark to enjoy the gift of life.

Doctor Gardner took her patient's pulse. What she felt turned her face grim.

Slowly approaching, Paris stared at that withering life just as a beam of sunlight streamed through the window. Inaccessible and in the advanced stages of the disease, the young woman lay on the bed, her soul trapped inside this depleted carcass, awaiting God knows what to cross over to the other side.

Mere inches from her face, a thin shaft of sunlight danced and worked its way closer as Earth complied with its ageless rotation.

"This is the other patient Leticia visited a few months ago," Doctor Gardner confirmed. "Leticia came here, put both hands above her and seemed to draw energy from a place none other but her could access. After the patient's awakening many hoped for that miracle to endure. But as you can see the cells in her body continued to degenerate and the outcome is what you now behold—a ravaged body sheltering a tormented soul."

"Why do you say that?" asked Paris.

The doctor, under the toil of a very grave confession, shook her head somberly. "Because this young woman was disavowed by her family long before AIDS shamelessly tore her flesh. Seems her way of life was disapproved by many. Sadly, before falling into a coma, her last words spoke of her soul's damnation, since many associate this disease with the wrath of God. It's a grave thing, to harbor such thoughts before departing."

The thought of a soul entering the after life burdened with guilt had a profound impact upon Paris. The sight of her lower lip quivering and afflicted eyes betrayed Paris' emotions to such an extent that I truly believed she had made this patient's suffering her own.

"Strangely enough, I sense your presence here is anything but a coincidence," Doctor Gardner remarked. "Confidently, I tried administering the same treatment as Leticia, but as you can imagine, I couldn't. I mean, I just couldn't. But you, I must say, strike me as very different from anybody. As a personal favor, for me and for this young woman, could you try and put her soul to rest?"

Looking intensely at the patient, Paris approached.

This was the kind of moment I enjoyed the most; the gifted soul solicited for a supernatural application. There were discernable vibrations coming out of Paris' outstretched hands, and sparks extending beyond her fingernails. Her eyes shone. Images were perceived. Mysteries were revealed.

Struck by this, deep whispers repeatedly glided outside the doctor's lips, barely audible, all with the Lord's name.

"Leticia stood on this side of the bed," Paris affirmed with unmistakable certainty. As she said this, I noticed that her silhouette had fallen under the trembling beam of sunlight.

"Yes!" the doctor loudly exclaimed. Her forehead deeply furrowed, she excitedly asked how Paris had found out.

"I feel her energies," Paris replied. Hands penetrating the unknown, fingers fluttering the air like a butterfly's wings, she observed the patient.

Suddenly Michael crossed into the room. With a vivid interest he contemplated Paris, and judging from the animated beacon within his core, I knew he had detected the seed of a kindred spirit. A kindred sprit he swiftly entered!

A deep gasp escaped Paris' lips. After exiting Paris' body, Michael hovered close to her, and the intensity of his stare possessed a potency—a potency that could never wither.

Paris nodded, and joined her hands. Then, from her hands emerged a thin shaft of light that plunged inside the woman's ribcage.

"Oh . . . my God!" the doctor muttered. "I can hardly believe this. You share the same gift. This is the same kind of light I once witnessed, except, perhaps, this time it appears more intense, more potent! What comes next? Can you sustain this energy?"

Paris looked at Michael. Something in his eyes spoke of a role that was destined for her. It was then that a disturbing moan rose from the patient's body. Heightening sharply, it rushed frantically all around and resonated time and time again against all four walls. I hastily turned to Paris. As her eyes fixated Michael, who answered her stare with one of profound wisdom, once again resonated against the walls the same horrific wail.

Inspired by her duties, Paris lowered her hands, and the distorted light spilled over both sides of the bed to form a shell of vibrations.

All of a sudden, through the young patient's sealed lips arose the confessions of her soul. I listened to this voice that spoke of despair and suffering, lamenting how certain religious leaders had wished her skin scorched by the flames of hell. Eyes firmly closed, the young woman winced and frowned as those words of distress and agony resonated across the room, disclosing the fullness of the discrimination done to her.

"I wish to leave, yet I'm afraid," the voice confessed. "Is it right for someone who never hated, someone never contaminated by the poison of malice to fear the after life?"

Paris bowed her head, her teary eyes inches above those of the patient.

"Everything is fine," Paris whispered. "You have nothing to fear. God loves you and awaits your arrival with great joy. Seek the Light, my beloved sister. Rest assured, as you prepare for this great journey, that the way you endured ruin, agony and prejudice will be seen favorably in Heaven."

With tears trickling down her cheeks, Paris kneeled and repeated the consoling plea until she detected the faint ripple sealing the young woman's last smile. Expressed in that smile I recognized peace, deliverance, and as the energy field vanished, she exhaled her final breath.

But then, just as I gazed at the body, the young woman's ethereal soul rose above it! I quickly looked all around and noticed that this spectacle was invisible to the human eye.

Completely absorbed, I stared.

Life had fled the body, yet life stared and smiled at me. It was as if the young woman knew how the very essence of her soul, made more mysterious by her tormented fate and smoothed by the love of a woman now belonging to another world, had been restored.

With newly found serenity, that soul beamed a smile to Michael and disappeared into a world I knew would be welcoming. For her judgment lay within herself and in the hands of God—not in the sometimes twisted and unjust workings of mankind.

* * *

Later that day, sitting next to her husband and children in the back of a pick-up truck while the guests in the forward cabin kept company with the courteous driver taking them to the eastern side of Monks Hill, Paris somberly reviewed the deed she had just performed.

It was only when seeing Michael, floating high above in some aerial ballet, that her eyes lit up. Michael twirled and laughed aloud. A blessed soul on an ultimate calling, and Paris, like a most devout disciple, lovingly contemplated him. I had noticed, for quite awhile, something unique between the two of them. Moving closer, I asked Paris about the stages.

"Ah, very well," she gladly answered. "Let's resume what you have witnessed so far. You remember that the first stage was the awareness, the discovery that we are one with nature and by consequence, one with all of creation."

"Yes," I replied. "This is to be followed by the awareness of our journey into the Divine, for spiritual growth can only happen with the acceptance of the Original Design."

Her eyes beamed upon noticing how well I had understood her teachings.

"The second stage aims at developing the tools of our mind," she resumed. "This can only be done by vanquishing the ego. You see, there's something very destructive in the way the ego reacts to criticism. What we perceive as a negative comment is often blocked out. Now, how are we going to better ourselves if we obstinately refuse to hear anything we don't like?

"You mean there's a stage just to deal with the ego?"

"There is more to this stage than simply adopting some objectivity when facing criticism," she countered. "A soul engaged in the path of spiritual elevation will perform gestures of pure benevolence, and this by banishing any sense of self-gratification. As for the third stage, this one introduces you to samples of The Eternal Energy and ultimately paves the way to larger ones. These are the goals of our meditations; to awaken and harmonize our inner-selves with all of creation. We all, to a certain degree, feel other people's energies. Haven't you ever entered a house where moments before a violent discussion had taken place, and felt this odd sensation? The third level also strives to develop the intuition, and this is accomplished through an acute insight. We go about our days without doubts, without shame, fear or envy, for all these emotions come from the ego, which has been vanquished when understanding that all of us are linked and share the same fate, which again is . . ."

"Spiritual growth," I completed.

"Exactly! The third level enables one to accomplish healing gestures, like those I provide to my children on occasion, or even energy-transfer, like I did to

Yanira. It's a quantum application acquired through our mind's empowerment. In this level we begin to feel the energy flowing deep inside of us. During our meditations, we hear the blood rushing through our veins, this because we are so attuned to our inner-selves."

"What's the fourth level?"

"Samples of The Eternal Energy, the one binding us all, can be wielded in many ways once one reaches the fourth level. Yogis, able to live while buried for weeks. Thought reading, monks creating objects out of thin air known as 'Tulpas.' All of these are but some of the applications of this power. Different masters possess different gifts, yet all share a common goal—to serve the Divine. The woman we are set to meet, Leticia, is believed to be in the early stages of the fourth level. It has been said that those at the fourth level cherish a deep connection to the skies, that they can foretell the future, so long as the Universe allows it, and even enter other people's dreams."

"Have you ever met her?"

Paris shook her head. "No, we've never met, and although she wasn't informed of our visit, I have a feeling she is expecting us. You see, those at the fourth level have command of nearly all of the mind's faculties, having reached the level of a near ascending master, for the Ascended Master belongs to the fifth level, that of messenger of God."

I looked at her with deep fascination.

"As you've said weeks ago," I commented, "that's the level that enables one to accomplish miracles. But how does one reach this level?"

She took time to reflect. "The fifth level," she began, cautiously, "the one we believe to be the full harnessing of The Eternal Energy may only be accessed by one endowed with the highest level of fulfillment—the Kingdom of Heaven. It's a stage achieved by someone with unbounded faith, with no inkling of self-gratification and who strives at bettering the world."

I thought about all that Paris had put forth. She could, and this I had witnessed not long ago, send pockets of positive energies to someone, like she had done to Yanira. She had also demonstrated on more than one occasion her acute intuition when reading my thoughts. What had taken place in the hospital room brought up new questions. I inquired about this alliance between her and Michael, about what she had felt, about how much of the energy she had wielded belonged to her, and how much belonged to Michael.

"I wish I could answer," she replied. "For that would mean that I know. But I don't."

The rumbling of the engine ebbed, and the pickup truck came to a stop.

"Take this dirt road," said the driver to the group, "and have fun with the witch!"

They walked awhile though the dense foliage and stopped at the edge of a large clearing. Tropical darkness rapidly invaded. Thankfully, up ahead a large campfire flickered, emitting a dim, though much appreciated glow.

"After you," Emilio said to Jared, tauntingly. "Or perhaps, are you too scared? Ooooohhhh!"

"Nonsense!" Jared declared. "It takes more than the mention of a witch to scare me."

Paris and Corto stepped forward, carrying their children in their arms. They entered the clearing, and glanced at a small house situated next to a large circle of rocks in which wooden logs burned and crackled. Casually, their eyes wandered around the premises. The whole clearing seemed serene and tranquil, yet somehow agitated with hidden secrets, with concealed dangers.

Then, just as we thought ourselves alone, a soothing chant broke the silence. It began like a murmur; faint, enticing, charmed with the spirit of the occult, the one that shines yet pulls you into a somber place.

Curious eyes searched for the singer, undoubtedly female, but to no avail. Standing motionless, they listened to the melodious voice—one possessed with beauty, and drama, a voice dappled with love, with despair.

Out there, beneath the depths of darkness, the voice rose, purposely signaling its location. As if on cue a shadow promptly passed through the clearing, going from one side to the other. Aghast, everyone stared at the small house and, in front of it, at a woman.

She sat on the earth, her legs crossed, in the middle of this jungle, conscious of her impact. In fact, so compelling was her presence that everything around me faded. All sounds and sights at once muffled and darkened but for the vision of this Latino woman.

She waved a welcoming gesture. It was then that we entered into her grasp. Her palms were hennaed. She wore many silver rings, and her eyes, black as coal, lively and smoldering, displayed the mastery of the occult. Her lips, voluptuous and bright red, smiled at her visitors.

"Welcome, welcome," she said. "I am Leticia, the one you seek. Please, come closer."

She rose to her feet, and placed little stools around the campfire while learning their names. She gazed at Matthew and Danny, asleep in their parents' arms. "Beautiful children," she told Paris, her slender fingers buried in their hair. She escorted Paris and Corto inside her house so that their children could lie down.

"I'll go inside," Michael told me. "I like watching over them while they sleep." I nodded, and watched him fly inside the house just as Leticia, Paris and Corto came out.

"Let's sit down," Leticia insisted, throwing a few logs into the fire.

Through her daunting, fiery eyes, she stared at her guests. Unexpectedly, Leticia's eyes settled upon Esmeralda.

"I'm sorry your life suffered from intoxicating male dominance," Leticia offered in the most casual tone of voice, bringing forth a look of shock from Esmeralda.

Leticia let out a wild laugh. "You wonder how I knew of the pain inflicted by your ex-husband?" she asked, beaming. "And also by the man you came to know following him?"

At once Esmeralda's cheeks colored correspondingly to the expanse of her remorse and humiliation.

"No need for those emotions, my lovely," Leticia assured in a comforting tone. "It wasn't your fault, or, was it?"

Esmeralda, curious, whispered her astonishment. "How did you know?"

"My lovely. I can feel your thoughts' vibrations."

Willfully or not, Leticia's words carved their way into Esmeralda's refuge.

"Women," the sorceress resumed. "We suffer in silence, or do we? Men think that because no words are spoken we cannot communicate. They forget that each thought is branded with a magnetic code, and that those born with the aptitude of creating life stand united, out there, nurturing the gift, anxious for the signal."

Again she let out a wild laugh.

"Don't worry," she assured Esmeralda, her eyes suddenly very intense. "I had a vision. Soon, we shall stop congregating in secrecy. The corridors of power are trembling with fear. Men wish to stop us. But there's an angel watching over us, and we shall prevail. Can you fathom such a vision?"

"Y-y-es," answered Esmeralda, hesitantly. Her eyes traveled left to right. She searched for allies in the darkness, and though conscious of others by her side, felt unprotected.

Aware of her distress, Leticia approached Esmeralda, and took her hands. "I don't wish to change you," she said. "I only wish for your true-self to emerge. For this, you must surrender to your calling, and cast away those trying to enslave you."

In an enigmatic fashion, Leticia appeared to all. There was no escaping this mistress of nightfall. She inserted her hands into a pouch slung around her waist and, after dabbing her fingers in black powder, touched Esmeralda's forehead.

"Do you believe I can make things better for you?" Leticia asked Esmeralda.

"Yes."

"Good. Do you believe that Paris can make things better for you?"

"Yes."

"Excellent! Now, all that is left is for you to believe in yourself." Leticia sat down, crossed her legs, and observed the faint smile curving Esmeralda's lips.

After suffering years with a wife beater, her resilience fortified by having raised her son alone, Esmeralda discovered her will mightier than previously imagined.

"I *am* strong," Esmeralda whispered to herself.

"Never stop repeating it," Leticia entreated. "Rituals insure your spirit's progression. Savee?"

Leticia then spoke of the importance of settling matters before the after life when suddenly Emilio jumped to his feet.

"Again with this Mumbo Jumbo!" he shouted. "You're the reason why some look down on Blacks and Latinos!"

"Emilio!" Esmeralda cried.

"No, Esmeralda," Leticia reassured. "I welcome all comments. Let him speak."

"All I've been hearing on this trip is about doing things for the after life," Emilio groaned. "What if there is no after life? Don't you get it? If there isn't one, then we should just enjoy ourselves! Now! And if there is an after life and we're sure of coming back anyways, then why not enjoy ourselves just the same. This is bullshit!"

Through Emilio's anger, I recognized the fear of abandonment which had stirred confusion in his mind.

"This Voodoo, Mumbo Jumbo, abracadabra, after life is crap!" he cried. "A pure waste of time! Whether we're sure of coming back or not!"

"Ah, I see," Leticia countered. "So, based on your reasoning, if there is no after life, then your life pursuit should be one of bodily pleasures, of endless partying."

"Exactly!"

"Same as if there is?" she actively pursued.

"Yes!" he exclaimed, his frustration showing.

"Forget the future, since it's uncertain."

"Yes!"

"Live now, since life is eternal."

"Yes!"

"Live now, since life is not eternal."

"Yes! Yes!"

"I see."

Leticia briskly rose to her feet, closed her eyes and, with outstretched hands inches away from Emilio's head, she took deep and profound breaths.

Leticia wielded her craft, and so great was her power that some minute air disturbance stirred the darkness between her wavering hands. Struck by the phenomenon, all who witnessed this occurrence, who stared intently at the bent waves of energy, knew themselves faced with a priestess in the process of thought-reading.

Seconds later, just as the air disturbance vanished, Leticia opened her eyes.

"Tell me how it felt to deliver the medicine to the poor and sick people in the Dominican Republic?" she asked. "And please, let your heart speak, as it did now, not your ego."

She had baited Emilio with shrewdness. What cunning!

Startled, Emilio stared, eyes wide and incredulous.

"Oh! You wonder how I knew," Leticia said, obviously pleased. "My dear Emilio, the world of thoughts is a mystical realm I enter at will."

Emilio nodded. Layers of his disguise were being peeled away, this as he felt the heat of Leticia's stare bearing down on him.

"Now tell me what your heart feels knowing of such misery, especially when so few are willing to act?"

"Enraged!"

"Enraged, yes, yet all you do is talk. Is this right? You would like to do something about this, yes? It tears your heart, this injustice, yes?"

"Yes!"

"Yet you intend to do nothing but talk, thump your chest and point an accusing finger. Are you of the weak kind or of the strong?"

He pondered.

"You hesitate!" Leticia exclaimed. "That is good. I have you thinking now. So, there is a chance that you would do something about it, say, procure more help to those in need?"

"Yes."

"Well, young man, you're very far away from a life whose sole pursuit is one of mindless pleasures. You know what to do with your two hands, but that ability is silenced by an inept mind, one you need to cultivate. This is done through the rituals of meditation, of prayers, of reaffirming yourself constantly of your true-self. Tell me what you felt when Corto took you away from your afternoon volleyball game for an arduous trek in the mountains?"

"Anger."

"And now, when the smiles of those little children slip gently into your sleep?"

"Pride!" Emilio exclaimed with conviction.

Leticia moved closer, and took his hands. "Since we speak of helping those whose names remain unknown to us, do you want to know how you can help the one who raised you alone while juggling two jobs?"

Emilio nodded.

"By simply allowing your mother to blossom. Savee?"

Suddenly the fire's glow lessened.

"I did something for Esmeralda, for Emilio," Leticia said. She stared at Jared. "Aha! Yes, I see. Young, and vibrant. You think the world belongs to you, but fail to see that it's you, who belong to it. No wonder you're such a pitiless sailor!"

Jared's breathing quickened. He squirmed on his stool, and turned away.

"Jaaarrred!" the sorceress teasingly murmured. Her chilled modulation and sanguine eyes commanded a spectral effect.

"Jaaarrred." She took pleasure in whispering his name. "Do not worry, O' brave one. I will not dip my fingers in a goat's blood and draw a pentagram on your forehead."

She burst out laughing.

"I don't want to hear this," Jared blurted.

"Oh! You don't want to hear this," she teased. "Jared, I shall take you on a journey and tell you about people obsessed with their egos."

Leticia briefly looked around her, pleased that everyone paid attention, and resumed. "These self-centered people, with important titles, come out of the elevator at the end of their day. They unhurriedly head for the revolving door, knowing that once outside their status fades away, as their steps bring them to the anonymous crowd, which swallows them in its austere conformity. Dark suits and brightly polished shoes. Not one honest smile. Such a person is a master without domain."

Jared shut his eyes for a moment, bothered by the comparison. Aware of this, the sorceress nonetheless went on. "They breathe the stale air without taking time to live. They have conquered the world, or so they think, having suppressed everything that had once stirred their hearts, be it music or poetry, honesty or love. But what else can we expect from people trying to change what they can't understand!"

"Such as?" Jared inquired.

"Well, a quick look at the way some people cheat their appearances through surgery comes to mind. The body was created perfectly by God, yet many are slaves to their egos. Old age is a time meant to bring us closer to a true introspection of our life. Closer to the truth within. Closer to God, not closer to a plastic surgeon. Savee?"

Very slowly the sorceress approached Jared, stood in front of him, and touched his shoulder. "In conclusion, Jared, I do believe that your heart is pure, yet you need to do the first step."

The prospect of a cure kindled an interest. "Which is?" Jared asked, arching his back and lifting his chin. "That is, in case I choose to trust your assessment."

"Ah, but of course. The curse of the false unbeliever, accepting only what doesn't scare you. The first necessary step is to recognize that the ownership of objects only serves an image you wish to project towards others. Breaking the admiration for what cannot cross over should be your first goal."

Leticia took a stick, and stirred the burning, crackling logs. "Look at this campfire. The hearts warmed by its flames define its existence, not the wood it devours."

With slow footsteps shuffling the sand, Leticia went back towards the pile of dried wood, picked up a few more logs which she threw into the fire, then sat down. "I have a story to tell," she announced while staring deeply at Corto. "A story I learned from a Navajo tribal chief. One you may recall told to you by your grandmother, Corto."

Decidedly, this woman possessed remarkable skills, for was it not the first time any of them had met?

After adding that the story would also benefit another listener, Leticia began. "There was, a long time ago, a young warrior whose father was the village's chief. Having won many battles, the young warrior believed himself invincible and beyond the grasp of the local witch doctor. This saddened the chief, for he knew that a self-centered man would never make a good leader. One day, the chief ordered the witch doctor to devise a way to show his only son the glory of what lies above the skies, and thus illuminate his path. During that private meeting, the chief asked the witch doctor to recite the sacred incantations and have the spirits of passed warriors manifest themselves in order to awaken his son's awareness to The Great Spirit. The witch doctor refused, and told the chief that no outside manifestations would sway his son's arrogant beliefs. Furious, the chief banished the witch doctor. As the witch doctor left the village, the chief's son sneered at him. Glaring, the witch doctor shouted, 'May your father be struck by such an illness that he will die in six moons, unless you find a way to fill this vase with water.' As he unleashed this dreaded curse, the witch doctor produced a small vase from under his robe."

Here Leticia paused and pointed to a vase next to her feet. "It was a vase like this one," she indicated. Everyone glanced at the vase, before the sorceress resumed her story.

"As prophesized, following the witch doctor's departure, the chief became seriously ill. Quite naturally, everyone in the village expected the young warrior to fulfill the healing destiny, this by filling the vase with water. The warrior rushed to the nearest well, put down the vase, took the bucket full of water and, having tilted it, noticed, to his great dismay, that no water entered the vase. 'What is this madness?' the warrior cried. He quickly rushed to another well, then another, and every time experienced the same horrific conclusions—that no water entered the vase. One moon passed, then two, and then three. The chief grew sicker and sicker, while his son grew more and more discouraged. Then, one night, as he sat next to his dying father's bed, the warrior looked at the visitors—the same ones who had paraded before the chief since the illness had struck. Only on this night, the warrior noticed, for the first time, how genuine was their grief. He began to realize that, in some way we're all connected, born from the same strand of life. A strand that is never ending. As this illuminating conclusion fathomed its way into his mind, tears began forming in the corners of his dark eyes. Tears that gently rolled down his cheeks and fell right into the vase he held between his knees. Water had broken the vase's impenetrable seal. His heart pounded. He leaped to his feet, rushed outside the tent towards the nearest well and hurriedly filled the vase. At once his father's illness disappeared, and the warrior soon realized that by saving his father's life, he had, in fact, saved his own."

Here Leticia observed another short pause. "Like I said, it was a simple vase," she resumed, eyes lowered to the spot next to her feet, inviting the others to do the same. But wait. The vase was gone. Vanished! Everyone searched under their stools. This whole charade brought laughs and dismayed frustration.

"It's not me!" Emilio said aloud, upon noticing how some looked at him.

"Of course it's not him," Leticia confirmed. "How could his hands grab something intangible?"

"You mean we all imagined the vase?" asked Esmeralda.

"No, you all saw it. In this case, I used my powers of thought and created an object which emitted a frequency you all perceived."

"Fantastic!"

"Stop it!" Leticia cried. "I'm only a vessel."

There was a pause, and in the lit and silent clearing a great premonition compelled Leticia to stare at Corto.

"They know about Senator Williams' endeavor," she cautioned, "yet they ignore where Saul conducts his research, which for now has to remain a well guarded secret. Be careful who you meet."

She quickly turned to Paris, and narrowed her eyes. "Tell me if the words spoken here tonight reflect the wisdom of the skies?" she asked.

"You speak of enlightenment," Paris replied, "which lives even in the midst of darkness, and strives when nourished from the inside."

"Excellent! What's the biggest crime against oneself?"

"The biggest crime is not considering our soul's evolution as life's prime objective. We are taught to react immediately to events. To associate emotions with results, whether good or bad, if pleasurable or to be avoided, all of these while only considering the impact on our earthly personality."

"What about the research being conducted?" Leticia asked, beaming.

"Soon the research will help someone harness The Eternal Energy. Then, from a heightened awareness we shall be purified and celebrate the coming of a universal empire."

"Marvelous! And what is your mission?" Leticia demanded, her dark and enigmatic eyes irresistibly lighted.

"My mission is to show the way. To deliver people from the cause of their suffering."

"And what could you say to someone who puts the satisfaction of his appearance and personality above that of his soul to change his mind?"

"I would say that the inevitable death of the body buries both the appearance and personality, and that the soul's evolution should guide every action."

"Well said! And how can one change the way he or she feels? How can we master our emotions, which at times generate impulsive and harmful actions?"

"Mastering our emotions can only be achieved by mastering our thoughts. Strict and unrelenting vigilance insures we remain in control of the thoughts emerging from our mind. It is through this self-scrutiny that we can best eliminate impulses of negativity."

Obviously pleased, Leticia smiled and tilted her head, gracefully. In that position she remained, for a few seconds, until her dark eyes considered Paris through the fire's dancing flames.

"Your eyes," said Leticia, hesitantly. "Your wonderful eyes reflect nothing less than exquisite purity. But there's something else about you. Something . . . more."

Leticia rose from her seat, and stood immobile for a while, as though she had picked up the vibrations of a secret prophecy. With great humility she approached Paris, hands filtering the air for something, when abruptly she stopped.

All at once Leticia appeared nervously excited. Between magical hands that during the course of this evening had appropriately detected unspoken secrets, there surged a formidable revelation.

"I knew it!" Leticia said, in a trembling voice. "People have been looking only in one half of this world while the one we await belongs to the other!"

Leticia delicately touched Paris' cheeks, and in a voice barely audible, murmured:

"You're the one!"

Above the flames of the campfire, those words seemed to float and linger, while Leticia appeared lost in the wonders of an astounding vision. She was staring at Paris with gleaming eyes.

"Listen to me," Leticia said, decisively. "It's within your grasp!"

Around the fire where everybody sat there passed a sudden breath of wind. One seemingly inhabited by some surreal entity, I faintly perceived. One that got Leticia's immediate attention.

Flames rose and embers flew. The crackling of logs increased, darkness retreated, while the wind's furious hands shook everything in sight.

Eyes lowered, drawing a deep breath, Leticia ever so slightly bowed, with the deferential air of one acknowledging a superior. Countless secrets seemed to exist between Leticia and the wind. And as the wind faded, so too did Leticia's impulse to volunteer any of her abilities.

But who could forget those few words, made more impressive by the power of the voice behind them?

"Now, I am tired and shall retire," Leticia said. "You will forgive my old fashioned manners, but ladies and children will sleep with a roof over their heads, while the men enjoy the comfort of sleeping bags under the canopy of stars. There is no appeal. This is my home, and my decision is sacred."

Leticia stared at Corto. "You have known worse conditions, yes?"

She disappeared inside her house, only to emerge moments later, her hands wrapped around something she secretly pushed into Corto's idle hands.

"I beg you one favor," she murmured, making certain that her words did not transgress their tight seclusion. "You are to open this little box only if greatly confused." With a discreet smile, she added, "In it you will find the persuasion that your heart seeks."

She walked towards her house, then abruptly stopped and turned around. "Please convey my greetings to Saul and Esther, when sailing to the island, into the mystique. You are to go there, very soon, yes?"

"Where is this island?" I asked Corto.

He turned to me. "Sail south-east from Trinidad, embrace the eastward current, and find the lone, roaming albatross."

Part Three

Sharpening my Perception

Seeds of Triumph

The next few weeks brought me hope. At last, I had gained a point of reference, when Jane had confided that she had been happier in our old home. Of course, spending precious moments with Michael also filled me with delight.

"Did you see the dolphins swimming around today?" my son asked me one night, as both of us hovered next to Thairica's mast.

We talked about a million other things that we had witnessed while at sea: the creatures, the waves and colorful sunsets. I found myself bewildered that a few square yards of cloth was all that was required to travel to the far corners of the world. The joy my son brought me during these simple emotional moments emphasized that it mattered not what father and son did, so long as they were together. And those endearing moments spent talking together shall live on forever.

Unfortunately, although exposed to concepts that, if applied, favored one's spiritual growth, my powers did not augment.

Furthermore, of the questions which puzzled me, one proved particularly enigmatic. Why would people wish to halt a global spiritual enlightenment? Leticia had warned Corto on the necessity of keeping Saul's retreat a well guarded secret.

"It's all about desires," Paris told me one night while Thairica gently swung on her anchor, in Guadeloupe. "Some wish for spiritual elevation, and some wish to dominate others. In both cases, the desires within each of us and the corresponding actions determine the conquering spirit. The Creator acknowledges these tests so that one can prove his or her worthiness."

"But aren't the ones distracting others from their paths, in a sense, counter the Creator's plan?"

"Not at all. They're part of the necessary obstacles one must overcome."

"And what do you think of Leticia?" I inquired.

"Leticia exemplifies the devotion to the Creator. For this she is allowed spiritual elevation. You no doubt noticed that she grew quite testy when hearing people applaud her triumphant use of The Eternal Energy. That is a perfect example of how she denies any credits for having produced a vase out of thin air. The same power enables her to leave her body and float freely above the hospital grounds at night, no doubt searching for ways to offer help and transmit some of her energy. She knows herself to be a 'channeler,' someone used by Higher Forces. The pleasure she derives from her powers is in her devotion to the Divine, whereas the powers used and wielded by those who wish to control others take their source in the pleasures they derive for themselves."

One of the changes I had observed these last few days was Emilio's openness to let his mother prosper, though traces of concern, at times, crept across his face.

"One's bitter emotions cannot be sweetened by lessening the aspirations of others," Corto told me one morning. "Emilio almost fully understands this. Luckily for us, a total understanding can be performed in harmony with the sea. There is something enclosed in the water, a healing potency so intense and striking that any undertaking, even if done with restrained moderation, summons from your core a kinship and mastery."

That afternoon, while sailing along the coast of Guadeloupe, as everyone admired the luxuriant mountains palpitating under the sun, the silence was abruptly broken.

"Take down all sails!" Corto loudly ordered. "And you, Emilio, grab the helm. You see that stretch of sand over there? That's where you're taking us. On the double!"

Corto started the engine. "This approach might prove a bit tricky," he cautioned Emilio. With a playful smile, somewhat tainted in a devious sort of way, he rested a comforting hand on the youth's shoulder. "It's now time for you to leave the realm of the electronic mariner. Tell me how one is supposed to enter the heart of the ocean if only able to read luminous dials? Knowing how to read a tidal chart is fine, but it's the understanding of the moon's cycles that connects you to all of creation."

I became intensely interested in Corto's words when the sight of a growling line of foam came into view. Loud gasps were heard when the guests noticed how large waves, after completing a mounting charge during which they blocked, if only for a few seconds, the horizon, broke heavily at the exact spot Corto intended to go.

As Thairica inexorably motored forward, I saw other approaching sailboats trying their best to coordinate their maneuvers, while preying rollers were spewed from the unseen, unfriendly seabed. One by one, the sailboats went forward. Hulls cringed, teeth were clenched, as sailors tempted their fate over the sandbar which marked the waves' crashing point.

"You can't expect me to steer!" exclaimed Emilio.

Corto moved closer, pressed his body against Emilio, thereby blocking his retreat. The two of them looked at each other. There would be no turning around. With quick calculation, Corto appraised the approach and laughed aloud as the ocean's spray stung his face. With a forceful gesture he pushed the throttle all the way forward.

The engine roared. Thairica leaped forward. "Stay focused!" Corto urged. "Keep it steady!"

The rocky motion increased. Nearer and nearer came the breaking line of foam and spray. For Emilio, these few seconds contained the wealth of the world. His breathing stopped. He had become the moment. His hands tightened around the helm, his eyes as wide as the expanding swell beneath them. In awe, he stared at the liquid barrier just ahead and saw much, much more. Suddenly a savage burst of emotions was heard as they surfed past the brightly shattered barricade.

Leaping forward, everyone crowded around Emilio, whose gaze excitedly traveled from the jubilant smiles inches away from his face, shining, wet and sincere, to the vanquished sandbar.

"I had a lot of problems with the waves," Emilio finally managed to say. "I just wished they wouldn't have been so strong."

"Don't ever say that!" Corto remonstrated. "Don't you see that the waves that tossed the ship also forged your character? Nothing glorious arises from inertia. Nothing! If you try to contain the waves, wish them smaller, then you are left facing ripples. And what kind of man faces ripples? Now go and get ready! We're going ashore! This calls for a celebration!"

Once on the beach, I joyfully observed Matthew and Danny running alongside the rushing fringe of bubbly froth, as they eagerly scanned the wet sand for seashells, polished stones and other collectables. They bounced and giggled upon noticing their vanishing small footprints, then jumped higher and higher to stamp deeper, more lasting ones. How delightful to see Michael join them, and as he jumped I noticed, with a fair degree of surprise, how much the wet sand caved under his invisible presence, eliciting cheers from his two friends.

Shortly after the whole group strolled along a path that led to a small village. Coming towards us, two ten-year-old boys were pulling a buggy filled with wooden statuettes.

Finally we arrived at a restaurant. I was immediately charmed by this place. Like an old town tavern, the constant clinking of toasted glasses mingled gaily with the vibrant colors of different flags pinned against the walls. Above us, a large ceiling fan drew lazy circles, while to the right a massive wooden counter ran the length of the wall, with rows of glasses and bottles arrayed behind it. As Corto entreated his party to sit at a table near the dance floor, a strong voice was heard.

"Welcome!" a dark, thin, yet energetic man I guessed to be the owner shouted. "Welcome! Come in, come in!" He approached the group, gave out menus, and ordered his staff to join three tables together.

After taking their orders, the owner left, just as a man and woman entered the restaurant.

"Josh and Barbara," cried Paris, pleasantly surprised. She leaped to her feet and insisted that they joined them. For some reason, I immediately knew that they were Spiritual Sailors.

"When we heard you were sailing these waters," Josh said, sitting down, "we decided track you down." Josh and Barbara were in their early thirties, on a round-the-world voyage.

"Is this your new crew?" Josh asked.

"Yes," replied Corto, his lips curled in a faint, revealing smile.

"Ah! I see," Josh acknowledged. "How many invisible deckhands?"

"Two," Corto answered. Then he turned towards the owner. "We'll need more wine!" he ordered.

Shortly after the owner came by, put drinks on the table, and took more orders.

"To chasing sunsets," Corto toasted, lifting his glass of red wine.

"To sunset chasers," replied Josh who, after a few sips, proposed to share a few stories about Corto.

Noticing the group's enthusiasm, Josh told them of the time Corto had to let go of a fish he had speared off the coast of Yucatan to satisfy the appetite of a very tenacious great white shark.

"And what about that time in Egypt," he continued, "five years ago, when you faced an angry mob threatening to lynch a woman suspected of being unfaithful?"

That statement provoked an immediate silence from the group.

"What is this strange disgust you hold against crowds?" Josh pursued.

"That time in Egypt," Corto began, "it was not so much my boldness that afforded me victory, but rather, the silent void made by clouds without thunder."

Corto's eyes shone. Leaning back, he felt Paris' hand on his arm, and realized that everybody was staring at him. He glanced at the unused jukebox, fished some coins from his pockets, and stuffed them into Emilio's hands.

"I want a party!" he shouted.

Within seconds the place was alive with music and dance.

"You want to dance?" Esmeralda asked Jared.

"My legs hurt," he replied, moments before he rose from his seat to order a drink at the counter.

Paris rose from her chair. "Come and dance," she said, grasping Esmeralda's hand.

Eyes lowered, Esmeralda refused.

"I think it's for the better," Esmeralda said. "I'm not very graceful."

With that special something emanating from his gaze, his core endowed with the faculty to awaken wonders in people he touched, Michael approached. He looked at Esmeralda, narrowed his eyes, and seemed to guess her shame, her pain.

Michael stretched out his hand.

Instantly Esmeralda shuddered, and the next second she appeared as someone completely different. Her eyes exuded a strange wildness. With fluid ease she sprang to her feet.

"Flamenco!" she cried.

Corto didn't let the roaring command go unanswered. He went to the jukebox, searched his pockets for coins, and smiled as he pressed the button.

Amused, I watched Esmeralda take off her shoes and gracefully glide to the middle of the dance floor. With the clapping of her hands, the stomping of her feet, she appeared as a Gypsy woman.

Obeying the bold rhythm, Esmeralda grabbed her skirt with both hands and whirled it higher, revealing brown thighs that gave off a soft, creamy glow.

An outburst of applauses filled the air.

Curious as to the extent of her charms, I glanced at the counter and immediately noticed Jared secretly measuring the elusive passion which the dancer had, until then, concealed, yet at this moment feverishly unleashed. Even in the short span of a fleeting glimpse, his trained eye, in cunning habit, had favorably soaked images of moving hips, and inviting lips.

All around me, the patrons' glaring eyes devoured the dancer.

"Look at this, Alphonse!"

"I'm looking! I'm looking!"

Loud pounding noises followed Esmeralda's every move. Shouts rang throughout the place.

"Yiiahhh!" shouted one man. "I feel the Souffrière raging!"

Barefoot locals crammed inside the restaurant, spellbound, as Esmeralda stomped her feet and rolled her wrists above her head. Jared, with his mouth wide open and fidgeting hands, appeared greatly impressed.

Then, as the song came to an end, Esmeralda stood, motionless and defiant.

A loud clamor sounded. It was as though the Souffrière had erupted and vibrated throughout the butterfly-shaped country. People leaped from their seats, followed by sounds of trampling feet mingled with chants of "Bravo! Bravo!"

In a matter of seconds, the patrons had completely surrounded Esmeralda.

As the atmosphere inside the restaurant settled down, Esmeralda trotted back, all smiles, and sat down to put her shoes while catching her breath. Her eyes discreetly glided towards Jared. A glance aimed at invitation, not intimidation. Then Jared abruptly turned away.

A few hours later, it was time to leave.

"My dearest friends," Corto told Josh and Barbara, "we shall meet yet again, when the winds agree to such renewals."

Moments later the group strolled back towards Thairica, when a persistent gesture by Matthew, a constant tugging of his father's arm caught my attention.

"Daddy! Look!" Matthew said, his tiny hand pointed at one of the two boys I had earlier seen pulling a buggy. "The little boy is crying!"

Having rushed over and inspected the boy's limbs, Paris seemed relieved by the absence of injury. Then the sight of Corto walking to a spot where a few men were assembled was quickly followed by Paris' sharp cries:

"John, stand down!"

Ten yards away from us there was a group of three men surrounding a young boy who kept jumping up to grab a carved statuette, which the men teasingly kept out of his reach. A separate group of onlookers, having sensed the growing excitement, gathered around, and just watched.

"Give it back!" the young boy cried.

The man holding the statuette ignored the plea and looked at the crowd of onlookers. "We did pay the boy," he said.

"Menteur, you paid half!" was the boy's reply.

"Why not pay the boy what you owe?" Corto said aloud, in a tone that neither enticed nor provoked. There was, though, a subtle defiance in the way he stood, with legs spread apart, knees slightly bent, like the coiled springs of a leopard, ready to pounce.

"This is none of your business," one of the men snapped.

"Right now, it is," Corto replied, stubbornly, although I did detect some gladness to his tone. As I saw the three men move towards Corto, Paris suddenly rushed over.

"You need her to fight your battles?" one of the men asked.

"She's here to fix your injuries," Corto taunted.

Through the charged atmosphere of conflict, Paris appeared as the only hope for a peaceful resolve. She insistently pushed herself into the middle. No words were exchanged, anger faded, and the pockets of energy flowing outside of Paris' eyes lessened the men's aggressiveness. Then, just as peace seemed to have been reached, unexpectedly another man came over and vigorously shoved Corto. That gesture seemed to draw the three men out of their spell, as they too, moved towards Corto.

What followed were actions I had suspected Corto capable of, ever since noticing his scars. In the blink of an eye he leaped forward, and through a series of kicks and punches powerfully delivered, disabled three of the men.

Fists clenched, chin tucked in, Corto faced the remaining foe, when Paris yet again, stepped into the middle. They remained close to each other. The three of them, silent and thinking of their next move.

"No more," Paris pleaded. She looked at Corto, told him to remain behind her, and tried to convince the other man to unclench his fists.

"Move aside or you'll get hurt," the man said.

"There's no need for any of this," Paris calmly suggested. She stared deeper into the man's eyes and seemed to yet again convey peaceful and becalming instructions. Suddenly a flicker exited Paris' eyes and, as it intensified, it appeased the man's heaving chest while seemingly draining the hostility from his limbs.

Dutifully following these proceedings, Corto remained tense. And though the man's aggressiveness vanished, what began as a slight twitch of fingertips being raised near Paris' face, proved too risky for Corto to ignore.

At once Corto pounced forward and, affiliating combativeness to the uncertainty perceived, he erased doubts with a flurry of blows, this while ignoring Paris' horrified shrieks.

Two hours later, after being assured by the local authorities that no formal charges would be pressed against him, Corto sat on Thairica's foredeck, with Paris by his side.

"I know you enjoyed that," Paris murmured after some time.

Corto's eyes flashed a look of surprise.

"Perhaps you could tell me what course of action would have best suited you?" he argued.

Silence fell between them, as Paris stirred her thoughts. "You didn't have to strike the last one," she finally mentioned.

"He could have attacked you," Corto vehemently replied.

"You don't know that for sure. I believe he was just mesmerized."

"I couldn't afford any doubt. You can't torment my conscience with this. It's as clear as crystal."

"What I see, clear as crystal, is how easily you rely on your lethal arsenal."

"By that, do you imply the skills that assured retribution against the idiots trying to cheat an innocent boy?"

"Oh, that's it! Yes! Those very skills, forged from actions that wake you up at night, covered in sweat and screaming!"

These words forced a short-lived, yet profound silence.

"Listen, John," Paris resumed, taking his rugged hands into hers. "Not only do I know of your pain, I share it. If you wish to master your eagerness for combat, as you've told me in the past, this is done through renunciation."

Corto looked at his knuckles, and exhaled profoundly. "I loath the use of force, yet find it unavoidable and, at times, compelling."

"These burning souvenirs of yours will take time to vanish," Paris insisted. "I know this because I have traveled to the distant lands of your mind. I know of your nights in the icy forests of the Balkans, crossing frozen streams and chewing worms while eluding capture from an enemy platoon. I know of your many battles on the scorching sand dunes of the Middle East, of the time your air tanks malfunctioned at three hundred feet below the ocean's surface, all alone in the dark with God knows what continuously bumping against you. Wandering your nightmares feels like being whisked by a hurricane into a bottomless pit! What you lived is unforgettable. But the path to inner peace will reveal itself only when you begin to show trust in human nature. I prefer to give people a chance and assume that goodness will prevail in them."

"You mean give them a chance HOPING that goodness will prevail."

"Yes, hope!" Paris impatiently said. "Hope, John. Listen to me, I said listen to me. Don't you roll your eyes at me! I am talking to you!"

"Forgive my reflexes," he objected sarcastically. "I was taught to react to my enemy's intention, not his words. Gentleness is not the virtue that protects us. Entire civilizations were eradicated from the face of the Earth because they lacked strength! Only the sword could have saved the Incas and Aztecs from the Conquistadors. Building pyramids in perfect alignment with the sun did nothing for them!" He clenched his fists. "Strength, Paris, is the only virtue that insures our survival. The evil we are fighting is too dark to be vanquished by a flicker! It's my curse, I know it full well, and I will always bring force when needed."

"The Universe takes care of this," she retorted.

"That's it! I'm part of the Universe, and I took care of it. Thoughts aren't enough to secure peace. Even prayers are sometimes answered by actions done by men like me."

She shook her head. "I don't get you. You preach peace, yet all the while yield so easily to violence."

"This path is not without its paradox," he commented with traces of irony.

"There is no paradox. Emotions are the offspring of thoughts, thoughts you train to control through meditation."

She stared at her husband, saddened by his absence of remorse.

"Well delivered words are a great incentive," she convincingly declared.

She wrapped her arms around his neck. "You could have disarmed them by the sheer weight of your eloquence, like that time in Egypt, when a mob wanted to lynch a woman suspected of being unfaithful. You're not a soldier anymore."

"Bah! I'll remember that next time. Hopefully, the ones I'll face will only be armed with good intentions."

"You promised me." She loosened her arms, and just as they dropped to her sides he quickly recovered her wrists to renew her embrace.

Later that night, alone on the foredeck, Corto turned to me. "Now you know what obstacles obstruct my path," he confided. "This is what I have to resolve, my instinct of violence and its ensuing burden on my conscience. I hate possessing it, yet not enough to wish its banishment. I loath the trials that crafted this deadly art to perfection, yet feel emboldened by its availability and effectiveness. It's that burden of doubts that impedes my growth, for the Universe sees into one's heart."

His eyes were obscure, his breathing irregular. His mind had suffered more than his body. Exhausted and confused, he first looked at his hands, then at the sky, and asked in a tormented voice:

"Will the men that died by my hands or by my side ever get out of my head?"

Building my Temple

During the few weeks it took to sail from Guadeloupe to St-Vincent, Emilio appeared less threatened by his mother's endeavor.

"When will Jared demonstrate a more opened-minded attitude?" I asked Paris. "He seems to wander a planet of his own creation."

"That's because his eyes haven't yet perceived the secret nature of all events, which finds its purpose in the elevation of our soul. He hasn't yet assessed the tools of observation and rejects all deliberation hurtful to his ego."

This was also a time when I closely observed every Spiritual Sailors crossing our path. From the air, the Islands of the Caribbean appear like riders of a great caravan scattered across a desert whose arc stretches a vast empire three thousand miles long, from the Bahamas to South America. It is this very geographical characteristic that distinguishes these sailors. They are nomads who speak a language honed by countless of nautical miles. They seek the knowledge beyond this planet. They embrace a path between Heaven and Earth. Dozens of men and women sailing the oceans, attuned to their inner-selves, pursuing their destinies.

"We test our spirit in the wild," Corto told me one morning. "There are no lies in the wind. We enter darkness welcoming the unknown."

Later that day, as Paris and Corto ate lunch on the island of St-Vincent, a man entered the restaurant.

"Please, won't you join us?" Paris said to that man. "We could use some fresh discussion."

The man gladly pulled a chair and sat down. "I've learned never to refuse such impromptu invitations," he said.

After brief introductions, the man, whose name was Tony Menos, spoke of his work for a non-governmental agency specializing in the building of schools. Dark hair, slimly built and in his early forties, he possessed a stare which showed the enthusiasm and romantic peculiarity of his mission. After a few minutes, however, sighing and shaking his head, Menos revealed the unreasonable difficulties that plagued the project he strived to accomplish.

"It feels like a conspiracy," he confessed. "None of the villagers wish to help anymore."

"Why is that?" Corto asked.

"I haven't yet stirred a positive interest among the population," he replied. "Well, not enough to have them challenge the one impeding my efforts. You see, some people here wish to make a profit out of a non-profit organization and have control over everything from manpower to the price of lumber. I haven't even been able to unload the last shipment of equipment because of the special tax they wish to coerce from me."

Paris and Corto's stunned faces enticed Menos, who seemed genuinely relieved of having found a receptive audience, to volunteer more information.

"What I am faced with," Menos said, "is a certain individual by the name of Jorge, who exerts an influence difficult to counter."

"What motivates this Jorge to obstruct the project?" Paris inquired, in a concerned voice.

Menos offered a frown, indicating the perplexities of the matter discussed. "Oh, well, I guess I could resume it in a single word—money. With every dollar given to the workers he undoubtedly would perceive his share."

"And what if we offered our help?" Paris asked.

The next morning, the three of them met at the construction site, which comprised a settlement of tents for workers living far away, a cement foundation (which the villagers had managed to complete before being coerced by Jorge) and an old, abandoned wooden house with a verandah that offered a plunging view of the harbor. From above the ground, Michael and I observed the dozen villagers who had showed up under Menos' persistent appeals.

"Listen to me, my friends," Menos began, looking at the villagers with a hopeful smile. "Isn't there anyone here who wishes to help? Yes, you are asked to do this as volunteers, because the money received from our organization went to purchase the materials."

He made another plea and tried dangling a vision before their eyes, one of hope for the future.

But there was another man on the premises called Jorge, whose presence I felt as troubling as the emergence of a frightful premonition. With arms crossed over his muscular chest, this man factored every little detail taking place, staring as if to impose his will from a distance, until his eyes caught sight of Corto. Then Jorge's eyes gleamed, and he smiled like a reptile. Having decided that Menos had said enough, Jorge walked towards the villagers as if the world belonged to him.

"Don't listen to him," Jorge blurted, forcing Menos to be silent. "There's no reason to work for free, when in fact there's money available for salaries."

His oration, however, was interrupted by a short chuckle.

"You have something to say?" Jorge growled at Corto, who stared back with equal dislike. The two men moved ever so slightly towards each other, then stopped.

"I fail to see how the building of a school endangers you in any way," Corto said, provocatively. He put his hands on his hips. "You're nothing but a coward!"

"John-"

Abruptly, Paris' hand shot out and seized her husband's forearm.

There was a moment of unquestionable animosity, restrained fists and imminent violence. It was then that the battle between two warriors from opposing sides began its course towards a bloody conclusion.

Jorge's fingers twitched uncontrollably, as he surveyed Corto's rigid posture.

Suddenly Michael approached the crowd. Curiously, something peculiar interfered with the soft lines of his face. Without the silky exuberance preceding so many of his flights, he awkwardly glided forward, head lowered, eyes afflicted. These flagrant and heartbreaking signs outlined an immense inner battle.

At length Michael, no doubt under a command that shook his very core, looked at a man whose feet quietly scraped the uneven ground. Then, with what I believed a great displeasure, my son brushed through him.

Instantly the man lifted his eyes and looked all around. Then he started to move. Amid the crowd of villagers, a faint shuffle of shoulders tremulously made its way from back to front.

Seeing this, Jorge turned his attention away from Corto.

"Oliver!" he called out sharply.

But the man whose lively eyes did not coexist anymore with the agreeing crowd, whose rebellious thoughts had stirred the inertia of his limbs, walked on. For a few steps. Then he staggered. He would have fallen if not for some invisible force reluctantly wielded by Michael, which against all laws of gravity supported him mere inches above the ground. This force swiftly helped him back on his feet so that he could pursue his defiant stride.

"Oliver!" Jorge screamed. "Stop right there!"

The man stopped.

"What are you doing?" Jorge cried, furiously.

"I just want my children to be educated."

"You wish them educated so that they can flush toilets for tourists in three languages?"

"That will be up to them," Oliver replied. "I just want to make sure that the choice is theirs."

There was a moment Michael seemed troubled when looking either at me, Paris or Corto, but mostly at Jorge, whose sight he wished to avoid at all costs!

Another man then made his way towards Corto. Then another. And another. The crowd uneasily swung, like some malfunctioning pendulum in search of its rhythm in the fog of confused ideals.

Jorge took a few steps forward, tightening his fists. "If another one of you crosses to the other side, I swear I'll make his life a living hell!"

For a while, nothing moved, until Paris stepped forward, standing with prominent grace, eyes clear and truthful. "Mister Jorge," she calmly said. "Could you not prove your great compassion for their children by letting them decide for themselves?"

Within a few seconds the magic of Paris' eyes had enveloped the villagers. Fear melted away into the air. And throughout the crowd visions of children attending the school flourished.

"I'm helping," a man said, as he moved forward.

"So am I," another quickly added. "Are you coming, Wilbur?"

"I'm right behind you."

"What do you think you're all doing?" Jorge raged.

"Building a school," a man retorted.

Soon, all but a few had joined the ranks.

Humiliated, Jorge remained silent, yet I could tell that vengeance tantalized his wild mind.

* * *

That night, sitting on the abandoned house's verandah, a preoccupied Corto contemplated the construction site with disturbed eyes. An earlier argument with Paris had greatly affected him. This was heartbreaking. Though I kept him company, I didn't press him into a conversation and continued, as he did, to mentally replay the heated exchange.

"One must react when seeing injustice," he had strongly affirmed. "If no action follows your outrage, then your outrage is no more useful than compliance."

Her eyes had flashed with genuine surprise.

"So Ghandi was compliant?" she had vehemently replied. "He helped free millions by his compliance? Same as Martin Luther King?"

"If I can resolve a conflict, then why shouldn't I?"

"How? By provoking that crazy maniac? By insulting him?"

"If a confrontation is going to take place, then Jorge should have a worthy adversary."

"You?"

"Me!"

"So a peaceful solution is impossible?"

"Highly unlikely."

"And this you know from experience?"

"From my experience of dealing with men such as him, yes," he had snapped, impatiently. His past battles had taken full possession of his being. "Death is a constant companion of men like Jorge."

"How can you be so sure?"

"A man of war recognizes another one at first glance."

"But how can you be so certain? How can one striving for light recognize darkness so easily?"

"Through my constant battle awareness. It has served me well in the past."

"And you're sure you're not being a bit paranoid?"

No! This isn't paranoia, Paris. Darkness is everywhere. Even between two suns."

"And this pending confrontation doesn't worry you?"

"Not at all. And like I said, I am more than willing to meet Jorge anytime and anywhere."

"How often have I told you that the only two things to be found inside a raging volcano are fire and ashes? You're a man of the sea. Be like water. Flow around the points of impact. Circle them. Isolate them with your love, your might, your peacefulness. Water always finds a way to seep through."

"You know there's a good chance that Jorge comes back and torches the whole place to the ground. To prevent this, I must stay here. And if he comes, what do you suggest I do? Give him a hug? Sing Kumbaya?"

* * *

They worked at the construction site all week long. Everything seemed to converge towards an undeniable success. The villagers worked in complete harmony, while Tharica's guests reveled in the enchantment cherished by the village. Even Jared helped on the construction site, although he kept his distance from Esmeralda when he did so.

"All that is given with love is added to the soul," Paris told me one day. "Witness how the villagers forget themselves at the construction site, striving for a goal that shall benefit others. Observe and learn from this. Perhaps your hope of salvation lies in the fate of alleviating someone else's torment."

That afternoon, dark clouds rolled across the sky one after another, and turned day into night. Soon the sky unleashed a violent storm. The raging winds convinced everybody to seek the shelter of the wooden house where, huddled together, they watched the school's newly erected walls crumble.

The site had a feel of desolation the next morning. Jared, discouraged, watched a few villagers pick up the scattered tents.

"All this for nothing," he muttered.

"You know about the laws of physics?" Corto asked. "Specifically about inertia?"

Jared frowned, and asked Corto to share his insight.

"Well," Corto began, "did you know that once vanquished it gives way to motion, which in turn requires but a fraction of its original application to sustain momentum? If you wish to translate these forces into human emotions, then fear exemplifies inertia. Fear is what prevents people from initiating new beginnings."

The villagers, upon hearing those words, vowed to work until the school's completion.

As we talked on the verandah that night, this because Corto had decided to once again sleep at the abandoned house, sounds of discontent pierced through the tents.

"Come with me," he whispered. Like a great jungle cat, he delicately jumped from the verandah onto the ground, and deftly neared the campsite. As we moved closer, a silhouette disclosed its presence when struck by the moonlight.

Corto crouched behind a tent, where he remained perfectly still for a few seconds before raising his head. The silhouette, by that time, had left. Right then, something came to my mind. With me by his side, such covert tactics appeared quite useless, for I could easily report to Corto what I heard or saw. All of a sudden a force took hold of me and forbade any interference.

We entered the campsite. Corto squatted down, waiting, listening. Muffled sounds pierced the darkness. Then the murmurs grew louder.

"We have to leave or else severe hurt may come!" a man said.

"You think so?" another man replied.

"Yes! Go to your homes tomorrow and never come back!"

Seconds later liquid shadows exited the tent and glided without a sound.

"Looks like a mutiny in the making," I commented.

Corto nodded. He had heard enough.

Back on the verandah, I confided to Corto that some unknown force had maintained me in a state of inertia, fearful that he would conclude otherwise. But such explanations were superfluous.

"I'm aware that spirits navigate a narrow river," he said. "This was communicated to me years ago when I ventured in the lands of The Great Spirit. I know about the limited actions allowed to circumvent events that would impair the Original Design. Sadly, I don't think you could be of any help . . . for now."

I felt the power of his words. Words given added weight considering the source. The realm of the after-world and whispers of invisible entities were to Corto a sacred breath of life.

Resting in a hammock, he seemed assailed by an obscure memory. One that had turned to a wild fascination. One that persistently begged to be heard.

"Like those entities that use their powers to protect the Original Design," he declared, "I always thought of myself as an earthly version. This was revealed to me during one of my travels in the lands of The Great Spirit. But lately, all of these conflicts with Paris have shed doubts. Perhaps my interpretation has been wrong for all these years."

He appeared utterly drained. I knew by his hollow eyes and voice turned into a whisper that this dilemma provoked a great confusion.

"My body and spirit come with all of the deadly skills impressed upon me," he confided, perplexed. "To obey such a disposition is in my nature. And yet, the Universe saw it fit for Paris and me to meet, to fall in love, and from this love to create a family."

Through the fine mist in his eyes he contemplated his predicament. "What should I do?" he murmured in a weary tone. "What should I do?"

He buried one hand in the folds of a towel that served as a pillow and produced a weapon.

"You have a gun?" I exclaimed.

"A flare gun," he corrected, smiling with appreciation as all of the object's finer details comforted his tactile sense. He became so absorbed that I suspected little else mattered to him at this point, save for the cold feel of the weapon in his hand, a sensation that had infused energy in his exhausted body.

"Do you mean to use it to signal for help?"

"No," he chuckled. "To shoot at one of the gallons of gasoline I tied to the trees. It's just in case Jorge comes back."

"Why not a real one?"

"They would like that, Jorge and his men," he said, laughing. "Can you imagine? Looking for a weapon in a town where the hired hands work for Jorge. No, the prisons here will not have me as a guest."

Nonchalantly, his fingertips stroked the length of his scars. It was then that his will wandered far away. Gone were the philosophies and talks of spirits and the after life. He now spoke of warfare, with a troubling and nostalgic anguish. Though he winced from the grisly memories, he nonetheless went on. He confided in me, trusted me, because he felt it important I understood his trials and sufferings.

The military had gotten a hold of him, and in the process had invaded every fiber of his being. He spoke in a voice strangled with emotions, a gifted warrior lost to dark episodes. The memories clung to him, in effulgence of gunpowder, in cries uttered by amputated men. He roamed the battlefields, his mind re-enacting the gunfights, his hands mimicking the weapon's recoil, his eyes darting everywhere. How many were out there? How many would he kill tonight?

"Years ago," he said in a voice no louder than a whisper, "while racing through the sand dunes of Somalia aboard a stolen jeep, I desperately tried to stop the flow of blood gushing from a colleague's severed arteries, this while shooting at our pursuers. I would love to live in a world where the telling of such stories did not exist. But can it truly be?"

Just then, on the verandah, from this great and yet troubled spirit emerged the somber gravity of that dueling paradox. Like most soldiers, the fire which had forged him could, in time, relent some of its hold and fade into embers. But never into ashes.

He looked towards the bay, searching. Through the shapeless obscurity he recognized Thairica. He marveled at the sight. He breathed deeply, his heart passionate, though shielded by a scarred torso.

* * *

A few days later, while walking around the construction site, Paris and Corto noticed the villagers' nervousness. It was then that Oliver, the gentle soul who, through Michael's nudge, had been the first to brave Jorge's rule of obedience, privately went to them and informed of the reasons for their meager performances.

"We are being spied on."

"By who?"

"Ian. He sneaks out every night and reports to Jorge. And all of us still fear that demon."

Minutes later, everybody witnessed Ian's forceful eviction. The sight of his clothes carelessly tossed into a duffel bag and repeatedly kicked down the field as if it was a soccer ball infuriated the informant.

"And don't forget to tell your master who it was that threw you out!" Corto shouted, as his last kick sent the bag flying thirty feet into the air.

A few hours later, Ian was heard saying all over town that the man responsible would pay dearly, because Jorge now wanted to meet with him—in private.

Informed of this, Corto, his irritation simmering and ignoring Paris' pleas, wasted no time. Having promptly left the settlement, he anxiously marched into town and took a seat on a terrace.

He chose a busy restaurant where the numerous prying, hypocritical eyes of hired hands would have little trouble recognizing the man wearing the straw Stetson.

He ordered a plate of fish and fries, devoured the meal, presumably oblivious to any danger, yet I sensed all through his being a state of constant attentiveness.

Shortly after his roving eyes picked up two men exchanging quick words in the street, glancing surreptitiously in his direction before one furtively took leave of the other.

Minutes later a man entered the terrace and, having turned the wooden chair so that his forearms rested on the backrest, sat down without asking permission.

"You're late," Corto taunted. "I was expecting you during the main course, not at coffee."

"It might be a small town, but there's so much to do," Jorge replied with equal pleasantry.

After an exchange of very few words, Jorge, his aggravation already high, drummed his fingers on the wooden table and interrogated Corto on his true motives for helping.

"You wouldn't understand," Corto replied with certain traces of gladness upon noticing his adversary's shaken composure.

"This is ridiculous," Jorge snapped. "You have no gain here, and will soon leave. It makes no sense." He shook his head. "And yet, you're still here."

"Yes, I am."

"I'll be dammed."

"You probably are."

Unfettered by that comment, Jorge buried one hand in his shirt pocket and retrieved a cigarette, which he lit. He inhaled deeply, then blew the smoke in Corto's face. Seconds later, Corto, having reached inside his shirt pocket, produced a cigar. Under playful eyes he lit it, and blew, measurably, in Jorge's face, for what must have been half a minute!

A sneer etched its way across Jorge's lips. "You will leave here, before some misfortune falls upon you," he said, his eyes showing no emotion aside cruelty. He inched himself closer to the table. "You have a nice sailboat, and I find someone granted with such mobility and refusing to leave very annoying. Tell me why you won't ride the trade winds out of here?"

"I live by a Code outside your reach."

Jorge's natural malicious character appeared unable to intimidate Corto. He pumped his biceps and rolled his shoulders, which were big and powerful, without any effect. His eagerness to convince a man unimpressed by this show of strength at last made him lose control.

"Get the fuck out of here!" Jorge screamed.

Very quickly, the few villagers who ate and drank on the terrace, amid shuffling of chairs and hurried footsteps, exited the premises.

Jorge again expressed his rage. "What are you looking for?"

"How I came here, is by a force of wind, and what I'm doing here is by a force of faith."

"You're a courageous man," Jorge said, trying to regain his composure. "But you're just one man, and not so different than me."

"I'm nothing like you."

Jorge produced an exaggerated grin, displaying white and dangerous teeth. "You think I don't know the secret of your eyes? Confrontations like these are a blessing for you."

"You know nothing about me," Corto insisted. "You're just a soul for hire."

"Perhaps. Yet whenever I killed, it was for my own satisfaction, whereas you, my friend, whenever you killed men, and killed men you did, you did so under orders. So, which one of us is the soul for hire?"

For a while, none of them spoke.

"That's exactly the kind of answer expected from a twisted, sadistic beast," Corto finally said.

"An assessment I'm perfectly at ease with," replied Jorge without a pause. "You see, I've heard of you and of that quaint little brotherhood of sailors and find myself in total accordance with your beliefs concerning the soul's immortality. Strangely enough, I think both our spirits have traveled thus far a path charged with suffering, torment and confusion. And now, as human nature encodes yet again many of its flaws when crossing over into the material world, as our body embraces our much affected spirit, *I am* the one who seem most at ease with the combined effect."

He leaned forward, and asked with a sneer that both ridiculed and provoked, "Why aren't you?"

With a quick motion of his hand, Corto shook off the curled ashes of his cigar. He resumed his position, forearms on the table, ready to fend off an attack, or strike first, should he desire. There could be no truce between these two species. They were natural enemies.

With the intention of exploring Jorge's wicked path, Corto's eyes plunged deeper into those of the man not two feet away from him. A unique power invested Corto's stare, one with unbounded intuition. I had never fathomed such a possibility.

For a moment, Corto seemed possessed by a sorcerer from the lands of The Great Spirit. His eyes expanded. A great inner distance was traveled.

A journey through the ages. A spiritual exploration to unearth the source of Jorge's murderous character.

Corto shuddered from that voyage, with eyes instantly filled with a strong repugnance.

"There can be no peace between the cobra and the mongoose," Corto finally said.

"Interesting," Jorge countered, "since none of them behave like a domesticated dog. Stop kidding yourself. You're not the type whose nature is satisfied by hammering nails. And if there's one thing I know how to do, it's how to hammer nails. No, there has to be another reason for your stubbornness."

"I don't know what you mean."

"You know exactly what I mean!" Jorge protested. "Your eyes say it all. Familiarities are often found in exact opposites."

"Perhaps."

"Yes, perhaps. And perhaps I AM the one representing what it is you seek."

Corto arched his eyebrows.

"Aha!" exclaimed Jorge. "I'm getting to you!" Intent on rattling his adversary some more, Jorge added, in a threatening tone, "This wife of yours, for having put these poor peasants into some sort of a trance, will pay. I will torture her to death, and you'll be there to watch me."

A flash of anger swept across Corto's face. "Speak about her once more, and you die. Right here, right now."

No words were spoken for a while. Instincts were tamed. No sense in fighting today. The swords had been drawn on their first meeting. Soon, blood would be spilled. Both of them knew this. It was written.

"This goodwill mission of yours won't last," Jorge calmly resumed. "The ordinary man, who suffers in silence and carries his burden until he dies, exhausted and unhappy, that one will always outnumber the daring ones, such as yourself. You might regard me as an evil man, but I'm just a man. And there are many like me, many more than there are like you. As for the ones caught in the middle? So long as they live and die with a fluffy pillow under their head, they don't care. Now, if you had any brains under that cowboy hat of yours, you would sail away with the morning tide."

"We will leave only once the school is built."

"All of this will lead to a very unpleasant conclusion," Jorge warned. "One you'll surely regret. There are many dangers that can plague a sea voyage, such as storms, sharks, pirates—but none are deadlier than me."

"My only disappointment is that you lack the will to finish this right now," Corto replied. He looked ferociously at Jorge, and with much rage leaped to his feet and left.

Following this confrontation, security had become Corto's main concern. Everyday he would scrutinize the workers to see if any of them harbored secret intentions behind their friendly smiles. He would then relay the details by phone to Menos, who had travelled to the north of the island for business meetings.

Three days later, two walls had been erected. This was also the time when Jared insisted on staying at the abandoned house, afraid that a fever he had caught might contaminate Matthew and Danny. It was there that I witnessed a delightful scene, when having awakened from a deep sleep, Jared noticed Esmeralda seated on a wooden stool, reading. Guilt took hold of him. As he tried to get up, no doubt to apologize for his behavior, his limp body collapsed. Rushing over, Esmeralda wrapped her arms around his sweaty body and tucked him back into his sleeping bag.

"How long have I been sick?" he asked, looking around the room.

"Two days."

"How's the construction going along?"

She felt pleased by his question. "We have encountered some delays, but progress is being made."

"I must get up and help."

"You will do no such thing," she insisted. "Not only is a sick man of little use on a construction site, but he poses a threat to others and to himself."

"Well excuse me, Mr. Trump!" Jared snapped, then realizing how inopportune his tone of voice had been, he bit his lips. He looked at her strangely. "What else can I do?"

"You tell me."

Jared shrugged his shoulders.

"Haven't you learned about this new concept called conversation?" she demanded.

She stared intensely at him. "How come you never talk to me?" she bluntly asked. "Is it because of me?" Her voice resonated across the room. She stared at him, waiting for an answer. "Is it because of me?" she repeated, in a louder tone.

"No!" he exclaimed. "It's not because of you." He nervously squirmed inside his sleeping bag.

"I know this isn't the best time to confront you, here, while you're sick," Esmeralda explained, "but there are things I need to know. So, is it my race? My size? Because I know it's not my gender, just by the way you looked at the Gypsy woman in Freeport."

In spite of her insisting stare, Jared evaded the question. "I told you before; you have nothing to do with my feelings."

"Listen, I came here to help you."

"I noticed, and I wish to thank you for watching over me while I slept."

"I don't mean that," she hastily retorted. "I mean to help you figure out why you're a part of this voyage. If you won't listen to anybody's advice, then perhaps you should pay close attention to the changes happening in me."

"Ah yes! You've become a true Joan of Ark!"

"For someone whose beliefs stretch only as far as his eyesight, I find your obstinacy quite unreasonable."

He looked at the ceiling, exasperated. "Whatever," he gasped, rolling his eyes before gazing outside the window.

"So this is your defense mechanism?" she pursued.

"What?"

"Being cynical. That's your defense mechanism. It's okay, mine used to be self-pity."

"And you changed all that in a few months? I find it hard to believe."

"You're hoping to make me angry, aren't you? That's just another thing I learned. Anger is really against yourself, for if you dominate your thoughts, then the others have no control over you. And, my friend, you have before you a woman who knows absolutely everything about being controlled and dominated."

"Listen, I agreed to help out and build this school," he replied, shaking his head. "But don't you question why we even bother?"

"What do you mean?"

"Come on. As soon as we leave, Jorge's men will burn the whole building to the ground."

"Nothing great is produced easily."

"I agree, but all it takes is a few to wield an unwanted influence."

"For once, I also agree with you. All it does take is a few to wield an influence. But what if those few were the ones ready to rebuild the school? Savee?"

"Oh, no, not you too!" he cried. He flung his arms high into the air.

"What?"

"Talking like that sorceress. I must be having a nightmare!"

"Well, you have to admit that she did perceive quite a bit of your character."

With forced restraint, Jared listened. Who did this woman think she was? A few months aboard a ship, a meeting with a sorceress, private tutelage, and voila! Did a few lessons suffice to instill such brashness?

"Are you telling me that you found your purpose by building this school?"

"No," she corrected. "I say I prefer to build my inner temple. It matters not where I came from, only where I want to go."

Jared absently gazed at the sunset through the window.

"Think about what you're living now," she beseeched.

"Mosquitoes and diarrhea, thank you very much."

"I'm saddened by your lack of vision," she retorted, shaking her head. "It's as John always says—change your thoughts, this is going to be fun."

He narrowed his eyes. "You're really enjoying all of this," he said, genuinely surprised.

"I always dreamed of adventures. Even saw all of the movie adaptations of Mutiny on the Bounty, from the one with Clark Gable, to Marlon Brando, to Mel Gibson."

He smiled.

Instantly, Esmeralda's face seemed relieved. "Ever since I was a young girl, I absolutely devoured novels filled with exotic names that whisked me away to faraway lands," she resumed, enthusiastically. "I always dreamt of a life of adventures and romance."

He grinned.

No sooner had she realized the implied double meaning that her cheeks swiftly colored, and hastily she added, "Romance for life, that is."

She sighed profoundly, and regained her composure. "I absolutely loved the hours spent reading," she resumed. "There, in my bedroom, the magic of those words transported me to remote corners of the world, establishing trading posts up some unexplored river, cutting a path through the jungle with a machete. I think I inherited my mother's romantic appeal."

"No doubt, with a name like Esmeralda," he replied, laughing.

She reached for a pitcher on the floor, poured fresh water into a glass, and handed it to him.

"Thank you." He drank a few gulps, then handed it back. "So what happened to your dreams, between having them as a little girl and now?"

"I married someone who—"

She stopped her confession, fought back tears dampening her eyes. "All I ever wanted was to know that I belonged somewhere, that my life had a purpose," she finally said. "Yet the only people that encouraged such a self-discovery were met on this voyage. It might seem silly to you, but I know I have a purpose in this life, that God only made one Esmeralda, and that my uniqueness should not be cursed, but glorified."

He tried consoling her as best he could. "Some people never fulfill any of their dreams," he offered. "But not you. Here you stand, years later, on a tropical island, sailing like some pirate queen, facing bandits, building a better tomorrow for people and dancing the Macarena while baking coconut pies."

She burst out laughing. "Now, why can't you be more like that?"

"Like what?" he answered, his lips curiously curled.

"Like you are now; genuine, authentic, without this stern wall around you."

"What if I answered that this is the true me," he retorted.

"Then I would say that you are lying, because the sorceress saw right through you and said that your heart was pure."

"Whatever," he muttered.

"Whatever?" she replied, in a louder tone. "Listen carefully," she said, disappointed that he had chosen to once again hide behind his facade. "Since you insist in flaunting this image of an indestructible leader of men, the Big Kahuna, I have a challenge for you."

"You can't be serious," he gasped.

"Absolutely! Since you're so convinced you're this dominant force of the business world, I challenge you to go outside tomorrow and have the men do more work for you than for me. We will each take five men, set the same goals, and at the end of the day we shall see who the winner is."

"You can't be serious," he repeated.

"Yes I am. You should be so anxious for this kind of challenge."

"Why is that?"

"Let me shed some light on myself." She stood up, hands on her hips, eyes wide and breathing deeply. "I come from a family of six, have never completed high school, and two of my brothers are in jail. My father, a wife-beater, deserted my mother when I was eleven, and I repeated the pattern by hooking up with a wife-beater of my own. That was the only thing I knew. The only reality I had been exposed to. Not wishing the same fate as my mother only served as a magnet. Mind you, I landed a real pearl. My ex-husband, not only content on physical abuse also managed to inflict extreme suffering with his insults. In front of our son, he used to call me fat whore! 'Fat whore where's my dinner? Fat whore bring me my beer!' Thereafter, I upgraded on my relationships. I actually replaced him by one that *only* beat me. But you see, none of this matters. I know where I'm going. Do you?"

"I'm sorry," he offered sincerely.

"Sorry for what?" she snapped.

He hesitated slightly. "Sorry for your environment."

"No," she rejected. "There's no need, and furthermore, let me tell you that I don't question my upbringing, or any of my choices, since they made me the woman I am today."

She took a short pause, collected her thoughts, and resumed. "Normally, taking into consideration your business education and prolific career, wouldn't you say you hold a slight advantage over me? Shouldn't you be anxious to accept this challenge and shut me up for the rest of this voyage?"

Her pressing words and insistent manner disconcerted him. She had gained an outlook on life which still eluded him.

"Is that the prize?" he asked.

"If it's what you wish for, I'll remain on the foredeck whenever you lounge in the cockpit. Not only do my eyes see all too well, but my heart is no fool either. And I don't care if it is my size, or color, or both of them that blocks you. My main concern when coming on this voyage was my son. Not some useless search for a boyfriend."

She opened the door, and turned around. "Get some rest," she advised sternly. "You'll need it tomorrow."

The next morning, after making his way to the campsite, Jared smilingly appraised Esmeralda's attire. Tool belt around her waist and Corto's straw Stetson shading her eyes.

"You can still back away from this wager," he said.

Esmeralda politely declined. With nobody backing down, the event would take place.

After assembling her team, Esmeralda stood in front them, silent. Close by, sensing her protégée's hesitation, Paris asked the workers to huddle closer.

Under Paris' instructions, the men formed a circle, closed their eyes, and listened. "I want you to imagine yourselves on graduation day," she began. "Feel the pride and love as your wife combs your little girl's hair, or when you fix the tie on your little boy's outfit. Immerse yourselves in their emotions, as their tiny fingers joyfully grab their diplomas and scream with joy. Hold that picture in your mind. Be sensitive to the energy you send out in the universe as you curl your fingers around your children's diplomas. Now, open your eyes and curl those same fingers around your tools. Hella! Time for work."

The men sang while they worked, and whispered their admiration as Esmeralda extracted every effort through kindness and smiles. The sight of her wearing Corto's Stetson, tool belt around her plump waist, and striving under the hot tropical sun while handling the construction site, was priceless.

Jared stood in awe. How could she have developed so fast? Her way with men surprised him, giving out orders that carried the strictness of the task and warmth of human relations. She hammered the nails with them, whistled their soft ballads, labored side by side and embraced with love everything she did.

Jared's howling voice, however, did not gain him any support. Furthermore, the workers of his team jokingly designated him as 'sak van,' which I later learned was English Creole for 'air bag'. He repeated his orders obsessively, instructing them on the next task before the one in progress was completed.

"What's that you said? Not finished yet? Of course I know you're not finished. You see these two things above my nose? They're called eyes. That's how I know you're not finished!"

The louder he shouted, the slower the rhythm of his team.

"Come on! Let's go. I'll pay you out of my own pocket if you hurry."

"I would pay to see him lose," one murmured.

They all laughed.

"Oh, I'm so glad you find this funny," Jared blurted sarcastically. After this outburst, there was little he could do to inspire his team. The men walked without haste, eyes fixated on the ground, arms lacking the precision and exactness of purpose. All of this smelled like defeat. Something Jared would never allow. Insensitive to the possibility of injury, he carelessly held up a sheet of plywood with one hand and proceeded to hammer it to one of the thick wooden beams. Seconds later he found himself lying on the ground.

This and other gaffes culminated in a disastrous performance. Not surprisingly, when five o'clock came, Esmeralda was crowned the winner.

Frustrated by his failure, Jared threw the hammer violently to the ground, and so as to avoid congratulating the winner, put some distance between them by promptly sitting under a tree, hands under his chin. Over several long agonizing minutes, this prince of concrete, stripped of any influence over men when not sheltered by his title, contemplated the reasons of his defeat.

Seeing this, Corto went to him.

"I don't understand," Jared mumbled. "I studied at Harvard, earned hundreds of thousands of dollars last year. I own a Ferrari, for fuck's sake! What did I do wrong?"

"Nothing," Corto assured. "Absolutely nothing. She only did it better."

That night, as a means of celebration, a great bonfire was organized. There, in the middle of the compound, under a full moon, the villagers got together. They carried wooden debris and other flammable objects, poured gasoline, threw matches and stared at the flames leaping towards the sky. Music joined the bonfire's crackling sounds. And the villagers, who sang, danced and shrieked with delight, whipped the celebration into a frenzy.

A slight distance away, Paris sat. Lured by her smile, I moved towards her and noticed the manner with which she observed Esmeralda, the winner of the contest who performed, to everyone's delight, a flamenco dance.

"Can you see the purity of her flowing limbs?" Paris asked me. "Just look at her."

She observed Esmeralda's shackles of past domination loosening with every thump of her feet, every clap of her hands, every arc of her dark, wild hair.

"One's self-esteem can be affected by doubts, by uncertainty, by thinking that we are forever captive of a cruel upbringing," Paris revealed. "Consider what Esmeralda has accomplished. By not questioning her past, by not asking '*why did this happen*?' but instead, '*what should I learn from it?*' she concentrates on her spiritual growth, and not on finding excuses. You see, Thomas, though conceived by Light, we all experience darkness. And darkness has a purpose. Through faith and mental vigilance, your higherself rises out of the shadows. The way we seek to return to the Light is what defines us."

As the clapping sounds of Esmeralda's hands lingered above the fire, Paris turned to me, and said:

"I build empires."

The Riddles of Fate

Defeat had turned Jared into an insufferable pest! He obstinately refused to help himself and basically did little else than mope all day long. He often accompanied Corto to the local restaurant, only to sit on the terrace with that blank stare of disbelief.

His refusal to perform any of his designated maintenance tasks aboard Thairica had also become a serious concern.

"He's seriously getting under my skin, this one," Corto snarled. "I know my emotions belong to me, that he has little to do with them, but what little he has to do, is enough to . . ."

"What he needs is time," interjected Paris. "Just give him time to absorb the fact that his personality was but a mere illusion. Only by dropping his fears and emptying his oldself can the light of his higherself enter. Then, once ready to visualize what it is he wants, with our help, God willing, it will materialize."

"What I'd like to give that Metro Man is a swift kick in the—"

"Stop it!"

* * *

One morning, as I floated around the village I surprised Jared and Menos having a friendly dialogue. After debating whether or not to intrude on their privacy, some slight change in Menos' eyes put aside such reservations.

Standing under a palm tree, Menos, who had just returned from his trip to the north of the island, showed genuine concern for Jared's defeat at the hands of Esmeralda. But it was during talks of Leticia however, that Jared extorted a greater interest from Menos.

"And you say that she produced an image out of thin air?" Menos asked.

"Unbelievable, wouldn't you say?" replied Jared. "What if I told you that, perhaps, this vase was more than an image? That it was the real thing! And that, just as suddenly, it disappeared?"

"What do you mean, it disappeared?" Menos inquired in a strange voice, for stranger than his voice was what I believed to be the manner with which he tried to conceal his amazement.

"I mean, *disappeared*," Jared repeated, his voice very low, like someone uncertain as to the veracity of his own words. "I tell you, at times, I feel on the verge of some great discovery, for myself, even for mankind. Leticia predicted such an event. There is something quite amazing in the way Corto and Paris live their lives. Especially Paris. Do you know that I secretly observed her one night while my cabin door was slightly ajar? Lighting candles without any fire? Moving a spoon without touching it? Keeping a needle vertical on its tiny pointed edge? I've tried such maneuvers. I can't! How can I? How can anybody?"

He stopped, and searched Menos' eyes for traces of belief.

"They're special people of some kind," Jared resumed, "helped by Spiritual Guides and other heavenly messengers, or so they claim. Coming from a man like me, all of this must seem like pure lunacy."

"Not at all," Menos anxiously replied. "In fact, I heard stories about them while I was away and would love to hear more. Perhaps we could do it on my sloop, which I keep anchored not far from here. Yes, that's a good idea. Let's go sailing and talk about all of this. What do you say?"

Two days later, as if to satisfy his curiosity about Paris' power of influence, Menos asked her to persuade the owner of the lumberyard supplying the school project to reduce his prices. She agreed. Aboard Thairica, Paris and Esmeralda sailed north and anchored near a small town. There they met Hector, the owner of the lumberyard, and talked while two other men lazily sat in the shed-like office.

Quite naturally, before attempting any negotiations, Paris underlined the school's importance. It was then that her pleas for lower prices were met by laughs, sneers, then finally sharp and repetitive refusals.

"Many of this island's children will attend," Paris persisted. "A lot of people have thus far donated time, effort and money into this. Perhaps a small contribution—"

"I already told you the final price," Hector interrupted.

"Yes you did," she retorted. "In a manner that is expected of you, it seems."

"Listen carefully," Hector said. "I won't lower my prices. I barely make enough to survive."

"I'm not surprised!" Esmeralda promptly interjected.

"What exactly do you mean by that?" Hector blurted.

"That if you showed more compassion to others, then some of the goodness would be returned to you."

"Ha! Listen to her," Hector grunted. "She comes here, tells me how to run my business, and—"

"Perhaps someone should!" Esmeralda interrupted.

Paris tried to intervene, but it was too late. The provocation had been too strong.

Hands on her hips, eyes wide with passion, Esmeralda bluntly continued. "I mean, look at this place. The ghettos in my home town look like mansions compared to this."

"Is that so?"

"Yes, it is so!"

The slamming of doors followed Esmeralda's outburst. They left the lumber yard dissatisfied. Esmeralda shook her head, shocked, for the last few weeks had her believe in the impossible.

"No sense in feeling weary," Paris comforted. "Somehow," she added, in a cautious tone, "I feel nothing could have changed Hector's decision."

This statement, however peculiar, was to be followed by an even stranger one from Corto, a few hours later, when he explained to Paris that he had surprised Menos and Jorge having a friendly discussion.

Receiving such news, Paris replied that both could have been peacefully sorting out their disagreements.

Corto leveled his eyes into hers. "Emilio was with them," he announced.

Paris sighed heavily. Obviously touched, she narrowed her eyes, and asked what possible conclusion could be drawn from all of this.

"Maybe I *am* just a bit paranoid," he admitted, trying to ease her concerns. "With me at the construction site, watching over the children, Jared moping around somewhere, you and Esmeralda gone for the day, perhaps Emilio just happened to be walking by when Menos and Jorge met."

* * *

How come intense misery so often follows spectacular exaltation? Such was the depth of my reflection when news of Oliver's murder shook the entire island. The macabre discovery of Oliver's bloodied body, found half-buried on the path linking the village to the campsite, sent shockwaves across the little community. Everywhere in town, people asked, "Did you hear what happened to Oliver?" Up and down main street, the villagers walked, confused.

"This can't be!" a woman said. "Not Oliver! Who could do such a thing?"

"You know very well who committed this atrocity!" one man exclaimed. "Stabbed through the back, was he? Only one monster could commit such—"

"Enough!" another woman interrupted. "You want to be next?"

"All of this would not have happened if —" the man stopped, and stared at Corto and Jared walking by. Others refused to remain silent, and blatantly cursed and sneered at Corto and Jared.

The next day, Ivan, the Swedish sailor, anchored in the bay. Once ashore, his giant strides shook the ground. "Tell me where he is, that son of a bitch, so I can ram my fist down his throat!"

"I'm happy you came, dear friend," Corto said. "The one we seek has left the island."

"Look," Ivan shouted, as he directed a mighty arm towards the sea. "The Frenchman is coming. And over there, that little dot that grazes the horizon, that's Victor, your American comrade. I tell you right now, Corto, many more are coming to show their support. Whoever did this may escape the laws of Man, but in the end, his soul belongs to God!"

The next two days passed in excruciating agony. The little town mourned, having lost one of theirs under incomprehensible conditions.

I dared not approach the subject with Michael, whose tormented eyes made me want to curse God, again. I observed the weight of his agony, his ethereal shell wearied and of a shade less brilliant.

Inside destiny's embrace, in that unavoidable path of the Original Design, he abandoned himself. That path, cloaked in the secrecy of clouds rolling high above him, was one he felt compelled to understand.

As I reexamined Michael's behavior on that fateful day, moments before charming Oliver's mind, I understood, from his then joyless face and hesitant manner, how much he had dreaded that possibility.

As for the reason for this tragedy? Though shielded by the mysteries of the future, there emerged something in Michael's eyes, so perfect and limpid and nourished by his love of Heaven that I felt him on the verge of unlocking a message I could not decipher.

I therefore searched for an explanation. The most logical explanation to any problem is often the most obvious one. Somehow, from the ruin's ashes, something great would emerge. There could be nothing else!

For a short while, I experienced a deep fascination. The sight of something mighty blossoming from Oliver's grave erased the knowledge of the manner with which the seed had been planted. But this vision darkened under the sounds of church bells. Then the sight of mourners pulled it under the ground.

Later in church, several villagers openly displayed their anger towards the small group of visiting sailors. And when the priest asked Paris to come to the altar to say a few words, the villagers looked at each other in awe. None of them had expected this. Somehow, it fueled their indignation.

Paris waited for the whispers to fade, closed her eyes, collected her thoughts, then addressed the gathered crowd. "There are people who, even though they live next to you for years, will never leave an imprint on your life. Then there are people like Oliver; quiet, peaceful, and yet of such a magnificent character that they remain with you forever, even if you only spend a few minutes with them. A few, glorious minutes."

She then told the silent crowd how Oliver, through his decisive step forward, had laid the ground for educating countless of children. "The boys and girls who will attend the school shall be known as the everlasting testament of that brave soul. They shall grow under the shadow of his courage, as Oliver will live on in all of their smiles."

At the end of the service, people held hands and bowed. With discreet nods, the villagers acknowledged all of the visiting sailors, before congregating by themselves.

The next morning, Thairica set sail.

* * *

The vessel sailed under a mournful silence. Alone in the cockpit, Corto steered south, his eyes looking farther than the horizon.

"Paranoid," he muttered, in a disgusted manner. "Paranoid, my ass! I should have known better. Paranoia can be a soldier's best friend. A paranoid soldier always outlives a naïve one." He looked at the sky, overwhelmed with guilt. "I should have known better."

"You can't choose the days to cherish faith," Paris told me later that day when I asked her to explain the purpose behind Oliver's death.

"When confronted by someone's death," she resumed, "some are introduced to the riddles of fate, and give their appreciation to people of Oliver's mettle. Should the daring ones embrace idleness because death looms over them? Death looms over all of us, whether out there, experiencing life, or in hiding."

That night, anchored in Bequia's Admiralty Bay, I approached Michael. He stared at the ocean, at the moon's reflection, dancing upon this liquid mirror.

Abruptly the desire to pursue the clue put forth by Jane during our last visit emerged from deep within my core. Michael looked at me, delighted by my wish, anxious to perform once again his extraordinary gifts, for there was no question in my mind that such readily available abilities would very soon be wielded.

His ethereal shell gleamed. He moved towards me, extended his hand, and as soon as *contact* was made a myriad of rays hurled me into the sea, transporting me six years back in time.

Instantly I found myself in my old neighborhood, having recognized with ease the apartment where Jane and I had spent a few, but memorable years together. Tons of souvenirs blossomed, most of them about our 'battling years', the designation given for the period of time when Jane, Nicholas, a newborn Michael and I had shared a three-room apartment. We were a family of tranquil means and abundant love.

Then something happened. Other images of those years crossed into my mind. It was winter, and the heating had been malfunctioning for weeks. Still, the colder the nights, the closer the four of us bundled under one blanket. This vision was filled with the joy of living. Even the hot meals tasted better.

One recollection, however, was not as tender. I was reading a book when the doorbell announced a visitor. It was my father who, a few minutes after walking in, wondered aloud how I dared to support my family like this. We argued. Words became shouts. My outlook darkened after his departure. I made a vow. "I shall secure his blessings. This, I swear."

Thus had I been despoiled of my treasure. Initially, for harboring an oath born of contempt and fuelled by my ego and subsequently, for striving for artificial gold, when true wealth had already been mine. Having seen more than I could bear, I wanted to return to Thairica, yet was denied the luxury.

Experiencing the scope of another space travel, I suddenly found myself at home, right in the middle of a fight. Nicholas proved to be extremely difficult. He reminded me of Emilio, of myself at that fragile age. Unsure of which path to take. A time when a good father is such a necessity. He was brash, angry and recalcitrant. Jane tried to reason, and felt overwhelmed.

How could I ever forgive myself?

This was the reward of my greed. This sight was unbearable. I turned away, ashamed that I had unknowingly began to dig my grave while still alive.

* * *

The next morning, inside Thairica's cabin, Paris was giving a math lesson to Matthew and Danny. Of course, as soon as an opportunity presented itself I confided to Paris what I had experienced during my recent space travel.

"Don't despair," she encouraged. "Your resilience will soon bring rewards." She observed a short silence. "Abdication proves to be a necessary ally of growth, she added. "Just observe Jared's rejection of Esmeralda's triumph. The same release will prove imperative for Oliver's village. Most recognize such a necessity, yet how many truly apply it when personally touched?"

She stared at me in a strange way. Then quickly she arched her back and feverishly looked all around. When she saw Jared, barely out of his cabin with his snorkeling gear in hand, her eyes widened.

"Wait, Jared!" she cried.

She took a few steps in his direction. "I don't think it's wise for you to go into the water," she cautioned.

"Ah? And why is that?"

"I'm not certain," she countered, hesitantly, as she lightly grabbed his wrist. "My intuition tells me that you shouldn't."

He smiled. "All of this attention is very nice, but I don't quite believe in those superstitious inclinations of yours."

She took a step forward, and tightened her grip. "I don't get many of those," she insisted, "yet those that do come should not be ignored. There is serenity in their command, and peace of mind if you obey."

"I've heard your theories before," Jared retorted, curtly, "perhaps even compared your apparent gifts to those of Leticia at some point. But most of these concepts were buried last week in a graveyard in St-Vincent, wouldn't you say?"

With a brisk movement he freed his wrist, then ascended the companionway. Seconds later, on hearing the splash of water, an outburst of furor flashed across Paris' face. She leaped into the cockpit, spoke to Corto, and anxiously watched him dive into the water. Seconds later a dreaded word was heard.

"Shark!" Emilio shouted. He agitatedly pointed to the large, unmistakable triangle slicing the aquamarine water.

The deadly predator swam towards the two bodies, and briefly drew a few circling patterns before weaving its way towards the vessel. Instinctively, everybody backed off. As the striped features on the twelve foot-long beast indicated it to be a tiger shark, we nervously watched this predator, supreme and unchallenged in the ocean, kick its powerful tail and briskly sprint towards Corto and Jared.

"Stop splashing like that!" Corto ordered, but to no avail. Unable to free his mind from the fear, Jared splashed the water, sending out the vibrations of a distressed fish—vibrations too inviting for the sinister predator to ignore.

And as if this wasn't enough to drive me mad, to this sight now merged the emotional cries, screams and shouts of two children; "Daddy! Daddy!"

Forcefully grabbing her two boys, Paris rushed them down the companionway and into their cabin. Then she hurried back into the cockpit, reached inside a storage space under the seats, and retrieved a long speargun.

"Back off everybody!" she shouted. She loaded the spear and pulled the rubber band with all her might, though I knew full well the limited damage such a thin spear could inflict against the rough skin of a tiger shark, especially from thirty feet away.

Near the two endangered men the shark's tail thrashed, churned and sliced the foaming waters. With the unrelenting determination that its specie had honed over four hundred million years, the tiger shark probed for an opportunity to strike.

Fearing the worst, I looked at Michael near the top of the mast, and saw him summoning from his core powers undoubtedly magical. His lips constantly moved, as he scrutinized the vaporous blue horizon where ocean and sky met. He looked so inspiring. Beams of light exited his waving, spectral hands, and his persistent stare penetrated a sea stirring with awakening creatures.

"Look! Over there! Emilio shouted. His trembling hand pointed towards another dark shape moving underwater. Seeing this, Esmeralda tried to scream, but the sound never made it past her parched throat.

With quick eyes Paris tracked the other fluid assassin, her steady hands leveling the speargun at the sinuous creature.

"That's it," she murmured to herself. "Come closer."

Instantly the dark creature vanished.

Seconds later it reappeared, circling so as to build up speed before clearing the ocean's surface. It was then we realized that this one posed no threat. The dolphin built an invisible fortress. It sprinted and taunted the shark, leaving the slower maneater in confusion, enabling the two men to escape and be heaved aboard Thairica.

Tears filled everybody's eyes when the dolphin leaped high into the air. Water streaked off its sides and glistened like precious pearls in the sun's golden exposure. Following its reentry, the dolphin continued to swim around the shark, baiting the disarrayed maneater into the open ocean. I looked up at Michael, content, eyes closed, his translucent hands held high above.

After this episode I remained on deck, anxious to once again witness Paris' abilities.

"Just lie still and welcome the healing energies inside you," she told Corto while touching his head. At once his face soothed under the application, anguish escaped, and strength flooded every part of his exhausted body. Then it was Jared's turn. I stared at the distorted light that hopped and circled around Paris' two hands, and could not help but notice how much more powerful she appeared.

With this in mind I pondered. Surely, aside from materializing an object (something she had never performed before me) she demonstrated the same abilities as Leticia. And the sorceress, Paris had said, belonged to the fourth level.

With great care I collected my thoughts. Paris, though having mentioned to me that Corto thought of her at the third stage, undeniably belonged to a higher one. After all, didn't she wander the lands of Corto's nightmares? Didn't she move objects and light candles simply by using her mind? The potency of Paris' hands, confirmed by the wavering columns of light, this time without being countenanced by Michael—like that time with the dying patient, strengthened my conclusion of a great destiny in store for this priestess.

Paris eased Jared's distress. Minutes later, seeing that the foredeck was unoccupied, she discreetly entreated him to go and meet her there. But before going, she kissed her husband, asleep with his sons bunched over him inside the cockpit.

"Jared will now receive a small dosage of what should have been dispensed to him a long time ago," she murmured.

Shuffling his feet, Jared humbly stood. Unable to withstand Paris' gaze, he inquired, in what I believed a genuine, concerned voice, "How are Matthew and Danny? Such terrible spectacles should never be witnessed by children."

"They were slightly traumatized, but will improve. Thank you for inquiring."

"Thank goodness for that."

"Yes, thank God for that!" she snapped, her eyes red with anger. "Now, stand still, if you please, I wish your full attention, so that there are no misunderstandings."

It took her a moment to quiet her incubated uproar, for her eyes to return to their emerald color.

"Flesh forgives easier than the heart," she said. "My husband will, in all likeliness, not hold a grudge against you. But that does not subtract you from *my* sentiments. Ever since your arrival you have approached all matters with the utmost stubbornness. Now, you may sneer at what we do—those emotions belong to you and have no impact upon me. Conscious that only *you* may open the gates to your spiritual path, we even silenced our objections, back on St-Vincent, when you shirked your duties. But if you wish to remain as you are, you *will* be disembarked at the nearest airport. Have I made myself perfectly clear on this matter?"

Jared lowered his eyes.

"No, no, no!" Paris admonished. "Don't look at the deck. Look at me. Yes. Like that! Like someone facing what he should have faced a long time ago. Now, do we have an understanding? Or, as my husband would say—are we clear?"

Breathing heavily, Jared finally opened his lips. "Yes," he simply, yet firmly answered.

After this discussion, Jared remained on the foredeck by himself. His eyes wandered towards shore. The sight of curved palm trees—trees that because of their flexibility are able to withstand hurricanes, exhibited both the calling of the wild and the lure of the spiritual path he now yearned to embrace. He raised his head, observed the falling sun, and seemed to perceive in it a little more than the natural rotation of the Earth. This appeared to strike him. Tears rolled down his cheeks. The most formidable appeal is always the one that stands the farthest from us. With this in mind he pondered. Suddenly, a new thought emerged. Of course! Faith, the giver of life, of love, but mostly, the remover of illusions! Wasn't this the only path leading to one's inner temple? Wasn't the acceptance of the Original Design and unity with nature part of the meditations? Meditations which had contributed to Esmeralda's spiritual development? Clever woman!

He peeked into the cockpit and observed Corto, eyes closed, his wife and sons next to him.

He admired this man of conquering will. His courage, his strength of character. Jared's passionate eyes shifted over to Paris. How could one possibly begin to imagine the strain of events which had shaped her devotion and healing abilities? Turning around, he plunged his eyes into the turquoise waters, those that had nearly claimed his life and yet, had truly given it back to him.

He entered the cockpit and gazed at what Thairica's breast cherished—that group of people committed in helping others. He cleared his throat, begged for their attention, and vowed to be open-minded.

Upon hearing those words, Corto got up, careful not to disturb his children's sleep. "Meet me on the foredeck," he whispered. He momentarily observed Matthew and Danny, mouths slightly opened, breathing heavily, their bellies slowly distending from each intake of the searing air. Small beads of sweat appeared on their upper lips. Once in a while, one of them would moan, or jerk a leg, an arm—tremors that displayed the silent horrors stranded in their fragile minds. I suspected a few sessions at the hands of their mother would be necessary to completely remove any trauma from the morning's incident.

After preparing two drinks, Corto joined Jared on the foredeck where, once seated, they admired a most promising sight.

"Sunset," Corto whispered.

The sun's magic reflected off the sea, travelled across the waves and touched their hearts. I knew Corto viewed the elements as extensions of the Creator and that he favored, above all others, the sunsets. For there he was, joyful, serene, as the wind's tender fingers playfully teased his disheveled hair while mocking the surface of the sea. He murmured secret incantations at the orange disk slowly sinking out of view, and then sighed. That's when I knew this Adventurer of the Soul was in the final phase of rekindling his spirit. Observing this, at long last, I finally understood his fascination for sunsets. Soaking the sun's energy constituted a ritual aimed at bringing him closer to the Heavens. As for the time of such worship, he preferred his communion at sunset, when the sacred radiance mellowed just enough to allow an enduring eye contact.

For the next minutes I imprinted this image of him, as he gazed and rejuvenated. A spiritual warrior torn between the spirits of the Dove and the Eagle, watching the sun's last glimmers fighting off darkness.

* * *

They spent the next week sailing the Grenadines. During that time, Jared, true to his pledge, began a meditation routine, although his manners towards Esmeralda remained unchanged. All of this made little sense to me, to the point that I seriously wondered if Jared even knew the source of his own emotions.

But that was soon to change.

One night, Paris and Corto threw a party on one of the islands of the Tobago Cays, near Horseshoe Reef, a place that routinely hosts many gatherings of sailors and vacationers. Loosely scattered on the beach glowed dozens of fires. Dressed in a red blouse, Esmeralda complimented the final touch of her attire with a white gardenia weaved in her hair. Seated next to Paris, she searched the night and noticed Jared, slumped against a palm tree. She and Paris exchanged smiles, their eyes covertly spilling some devilish plan.

"He hasn't looked at me all day," Esmeralda confessed, looking very much perplexed.

"That's because he's interested," Paris reassured. "Trust me. He hasn't looked at you the same way since the flamenco dance."

"So you're telling me he's not talking to me because he's interested."

"Men are strange," Paris said. She handed her guitar over to Esmeralda.

"There are so many people," Esmeralda observed, uneasily.

"Don't worry, everything will be fine."

"I still don't know if I'm ready," Esmeralda persisted. "I only know a few chords."

"Do your best! Send out good vibrations to the Universe! The rest shall be made easy by your golden voice!"

Paris rose to her feet.

"John, I have a surprise for you," she announced, bringing the small chatter to a halt.

Esmeralda's unsure fingers stroked a few chords. "Its okay," she mumbled to herself. Just then Michael, eyes filled with the language of the stars and laughing tremendously, popped into view. After a short moment spent looking at Esmeralda, he extended his hand and *brushed* her fingers.

At once Esmeralda quivered, chills spiked her arms, and her wild eyes gazed at the unexplained eruption taking over her skin. She recomposed herself in the short pause which followed. Facing the anxious audience, she cradled the instrument, her eyes intensely riveted on her fingers.

Next moment a melodious sound rose from deep within her dreams, of strings expertly stroked, of moving lips that produced the loftiest of voices as she sang the song 'Into the Mystic.'

Pure ecstasy promptly filled the air. Esmeralda's baffled eyes looked at her possessed fingers, seemingly stroking chords not yet learned. Such a sight took me back to the Bahamas, a few months ago, to the guitar-playing Gypsy woman. And judging from Jared's eyes, I knew his mind had travelled to the same place. A place inhabited by palm readers and crystal balls, bazaars and violins, by flamenco dancers with flowery ornaments in their hair. As the last note lingered above the still audience, with great deference, Corto walked over and knelt before Esmeralda.

"That's one of my favorite songs," he said, very moved.

Just then, unexpectedly, Esmeralda conceived a rainbow in darkness, as she absentmindedly began to sing 'Let it be,' by the Beatles.

The surprised eyes of the singer, with her talented fingers and elegant delivery of the lyrics polarized the crowd.

Sailors and tourists, who, on this night, sat under the same moon, from all surrounding islets of fires, immediately came together. With silent footsteps shuffling the powdered sand, they approached, and once near the singer, united their voices to the festive night.

To show their support, many tried, unsuccessfully, to ignite their lighters amid a persistent breeze. But the winds knew nothing of Michael's affection for the Gypsy woman.

Looking amusingly in my direction, my darling Michael pointed a finger towards the sky.

"Watch this, daddy!" he cheerfully shouted.

With a grand sweep of his hand he charged the air with mystery. Logic and physics were voided. Dozens of lights defiantly ignited despite the overzealous winds. From the air I beheld Esmeralda, seated on the ground yet elevated to a state of bliss by the applauses. She believed their honesty. She rose to her feet, took a few steps forward and bowed her head. As the silence overtook the dying applauses, the huddled crowd, however, remained.

"May I take over?" Paris asked, arms extended, having sensed the anticipation. With the instrument in her hands, she rapidly engaged the rhythm of Bouzouki music.

"Hella!" Corto shouted, both of his strong arms held parallel to the sand, snapping his fingers, pleasurably transfigured in a cheerful imitation of Anthony Quinn from Zorba the Greek.

"Hella!" he roared. It was a fascinating sight! Men and women dancing, united not by touch, but by spirit. Eyelids half-closed, teeth flashing, the dancers abandoned themselves to the improvised richness and provocative movements of the Greek dance.

"Come!" Corto shouted. "The best day to live is always today!" He joyfully watched Esmeralda dancing her way into the circle of revelers. As for Jared, the only one not dancing, he observed the gypsy-like vision, arms and feet possessed, her mocha-coffee colored skin bathed by the fire's weeping glow. Wide-eyed he remained, and for quite long, I must say.

Next, with the music reaching its climax, everybody looked at Paris furiously striking the last chords before ending the song on a high note.

Seconds later, sweaty and exhausted, the crowd scattered back to their respective fire. Shortly after, Paris handed out a multitude of drawings from a leather folder. "Esmeralda drew those," she indicated. They cheered. One of the drawings attracted a lot of attention. It depicted Jared, hands tightly clasped around a rope while casting a bold look over his right shoulder, crimson sweat trickling down his forehead, his eyes expressing commitment and purpose.

Holding the portrait near the fire, Jared beheld the flattering richness of character, which overshadowed the lively colors used and revealed the impalpable emotions poured into each wavering line.

Deeper into the portrait his eyes sank.

Then, same as Jared, I pondered on the source of such details. Was Esmeralda's craft molded by her desires? Or, had the Universe bestowed upon her some miraculous brush, which once put to work removed the crust, thus enabling her skillful fingers to reveal, without distortions, one's true-self?

Esmeralda, having pleaded for Paris' help, mostly on the subject of her appearance, had undoubtedly inherited much, much more. For though Paris had acknowledged Esmeralda's desire to change, she had favored changes from the inside-out, not the reverse.

Music and paintings speak their own language. From emotions to hands, then hands to seduction. As for Esmeralda and Jared, what had been captured in her mind and converted by her hands would endure in his heart. Through the strength of creation, skilled hands and a passionate soul, Esmeralda had modeled a portrait of femininity Jared had never fathomed. In essence, the strength of this portrait not only underlined the artist's perception of the subject, but, mostly, encouraged the subject to discover the artist.

Unsteadily at first, Jared approached Esmeralda. With each step taken, his ribcage heaved a little bit more, for what he desired had been in front of him all along—as it sometimes happens in affairs of the heart.

"I'm . . . ah . . . I'm going to get myself a . . . drink. Anybody want one . . . Esmeralda?"

It was the first time he had offered anybody anything. Just a few words. No more than a dozen, really. And tinged by a fair hesitation, I might add. All of which was spilled through the transparent display of body signals.

That's how spiritual consciousness enters one's mind. Emerging from the shadows it creeps up on someone, soundlessly, without fanfares or ribbons. It kindles and conquers your core. And like the North Star it lights the way.

Floating next to me, Michael looked beyond the constellations, and smiled. From the other side of infinity, the Heavens had blessed his intervention. An invisible intervention which had made this night an unforgettable one. For the night had been sprinkled with magic. A night that had inspired more than a fragrance, color or vision. It had aroused a taste. As for Jared, it had aroused the taste of coffee.

The Answers Within

Later that night, Jared, eager to understand his emotions, requested a private audience with Paris. The two of them quietly retreated on Thairica's foredeck, as the surrounding waters reflected the melted outline of the Tobago Cays.

Intent on discovering the secrets of his soul, Jared inquired if Paris' gifts included the extractions of buried memories.

"To understand your predicament," she said, "I need to discover the period that preceded your moral decline. To appreciate your fears, I must first examine your loves."

Paris listened to Jared's life, to all his affections, his confused demonstrations of love, his need to artificially please others.

"Am I beyond salvation?" he asked, tears rolling down his cheeks.

"Fear not," assured Paris. "There's always hope."

She approached him, her hands about to be pressed against his head. Columns of light flowing from the tip of her fingers were put to work when coming into contact with Jared. Closing her eyes, she surrendered to the power, as if penetrating some distant land for a long-buried artifact.

Just then Michael moved by my side. Through his magic, I was shown the images Paris perceived—those of a conflict between two men of different races.

By some mysterious insight, I knew these images revealed a reality lived a long time ago, in Louisiana, in eighteen fifty-nine, to be precise. A time and place of slavery. African-Americans on one side and plantation owners, like Jared, on the other.

This persisted for a few seconds, when with Michael's disappearance the familiar sight of Thairica emerged all around me.

Jared, eyes wide and breathing heavily, eagerly awaited Paris' interpretation.

"You need to know that souls have no gender or race," she said. "Still, at times, they carry baggage from their previous lives. In your case, the events lived by you as a white man owning a plantation have left a permanent and negative imprint in your mind. Making you aware of this is only part of the cure. The rest is up to you."

As Jared returned to his cabin, she remained on deck, exhausted. Sitting cross-legged on the undulating vessel, her path appeared clearer. Like some antique oracle, all who came to her anxiously awaited her teachings, her beliefs. And that's what scared me. Within this troubled world she would have to be cautious.

True, new spiritual teachings have always been part of the world. But imprisonment, suffering or death, often greeted those who brought them.

* * *

Thairica's hosts and crew woke up to an unusual sight the next morning. A sloop captained by Menos, a man unseen since leaving St-Vincent.

"Permission to come aboard," he cheered, after anchoring next to Thairica. He then took his dinghy, rowed his way over and communicated to Thairica's hosts and crew his intention on tagging along for a while.

"My work in St-Vincent is done," he indicated. "The school is finished. Many children attend, and I have indicated to my employers my desire to sail around the Caribbean for a few months. Naturally, having learned of your whereabouts from other sailors, I thought that perhaps you wouldn't mind an extra pupil."

Menos wrapped his hands around Corto's shoulders. "Great things are said about you," he added with a touch of deference.

Corto observed Menos' face, as if trying to read behind each fold some unspoken word.

"I will be most discreet," Menos insisted, "tag along from far behind, should this be your wish."

That afternoon, both vessels sailed to Mayreau. Once anchored in Saline Bay, everyone except Esmeralda and Jared went ashore for a dinner marking this reunion.

Meanwhile I was surprised by Emilio's sudden melancholia. Curiously, there had been no recent incident to explain his drastic change. Then I thought of his mother, left alone with Jared aboard Thairica, as a possible source for his concerns.

Immediately I returned to Thairica, in time to discover the foredeck occupied by two beings wrapped in a pleasant silence, with Esmeralda gifted with the winning disposition that one exudes with self-assurance.

Her smile sparkled in the moonlight and invited parley.

"Have you figured out that you now embody one of the characters you so dearly cherished years ago in your novels?" Jared enthusiastically asked.

"So long as it's not Mutiny on the Bounty," she answered, laughing.

"I was thinking more along the lines of Treasure Island."

Moving around the foredeck, she minutely inspected Thairica. The excitement of new horizons invaded her eyes. That ship, caressed by the invisible tide, invited the contemplation of the impossible. She stopped, and remained very still, her eyes lively, waiting, for a word, his touch, perhaps. Since none came, she turned around and caught sight of his hands, motionless, yet eager to touch her where she had once feared he disliked.

A fresh breeze came from land, and enveloped in each lapping wavelet was the allure of distant travels striving to be satisfied.

"The land breeze proves quite refreshing, doesn't it?" he asked.

"Oh? Please, tell me more," she murmured, with a subtle, yet unmistakable hint of passion.

"Well, this happens when the air mass over the water becomes warmer than the one over land." He motioned to a patch of foam gliding pass the hull. "And here, you can see the tide has turned and now drifts from shore to sea."

She leaned against the mast, obviously pleased.

Jared looked at the sky. "Do you see those three dazzling stars in a row?" He held out his hand to the sky. "That's Orion, the mighty hunter of the sky, sitting on the celestial equator and admired throughout the world, unlike Polaris, which is only visible in the northern hemisphere."

Esmeralda was smiling wholeheartedly now. But as Jared pointed to the different constellations, his enthusiasm unexpectedly began to cloud Esmeralda's dreams.

She searched his eyes. "Who—are—you?" she muttered in a tone of voice filled with broken desires. Ghosts from the past, from both of their pasts, wished to be heard.

She lightly pressed her hand on his chest. "Listen to me," she said, gently. "If you truly are the man who sees Thairica not as a ship, but as a spacecraft, ready to whisk us away to the far corners of the universe, ready to provide a beacon for our spirits, for such is the potency of this vessel, then speak now."

A short silence followed, in which Esmeralda's dark and glimmering eyes prompted Jared to reply.

"I know there are mystical forces at work here," he acknowledged. "This ship, heaving under our feet, and breathing, yes, breathing, I just know it, dangles before me the fascination of a great life!"

Esmeralda stared at him, briefly, before looking at the many anchored sailboats appearing here and there like silver shadows in the night.

"Tell me again who you are," she demanded. Thairica's description had struck a chord.

Sensing Esmeralda's excitement, Jared proceeded to unveil his secrets. He spoke of his many conquests and absence of love, of a successful career achieved through shady maneuvers, of hardships in Louisiana long ago.

"All of us are living something incredible," he convincingly declared. "You know who I am," he assured. "But most importantly, I think I finally know *who* I am."

"Think?" she suddenly cried. "Think? What do you mean, think?"

An expert at reading emotions, he cleared his throat and, with a wide stretch of his lips, tried to reassure her. He appeared weary, yet honest, and declared that hasty words were often misunderstood.

Esmeralda shook her head. "Doubts about you also imply doubts about me, about us. Knowing who you are comes before anything else."

As her hand brushed his cheek, her touch explored the man before her and, I sensed, even more so the spirit beyond the frontier of his skin, which appeared at once mighty and vulnerable.

She broke her touch, turned around, and climbed down the companionway, leaving Jared, with his face a shade paler, alone on Thairica's foredeck.

The prey had become the hunter.

Part Four

Revelations of your True-Self

Surrendering to the Original Design

A few days later, Thairica and her hosts and crew, accompanied by Menos aboard his sloop, sailed into St-George's harbor, in Grenada. Once in the city, the group strolled around the cobblestone square, where many horse-pulled carriages offered the opportunity to delve into the charm of the old town.

"Magnificent creatures," whispered Corto. His admiration for horses, which appeared boundless, was interrupted by Esmeralda.

"Poor animals," she observed thoughtfully. "Caught in this heat pulling tourists."

"Trust me," Corto interjected. "Their magnificence remains unaltered. Just look at them! No task can ever spoil their royal bloodline."

"It's been weeks since you last indulged yourself," Paris remarked. "Why don't you go for a ride while I tour the island with the group?"

Having paid the owner of the carriage, Corto removed the harness and hopped onto the horse's back.

For two hours Corto wandered around town.

"You can always join Michael and the rest of the group if you wish," he told me, as he ordered his horse to a halt. "Escorting me through a maze of narrow alleys may not necessarily appeal to you." He tapped the horse's strong neck. I answered that somehow, some strange feeling compelled me to stay with him. Moments later, thinking that perhaps he wished to be by himself, I flew back to the cobblestone square.

I wandered around when something caught my attention. A muffled, distressful cry that came from the outer rim of the square. Eager to satisfy my curiosity, I swiftly flew through air and crowd. Having reached the end of the square, I hovered, and there before me stood a woman in tears, her hands held up like someone begging for help.

At first I didn't know the source of her distress. A few seconds later, however, the sight of a strongly built man with a light complexion and a ponytail swiftly moving towards her, offered the explanation. With great force he brought her to her knees. The grin on his face showed how little he cared for the crowd's outrage.

His hands, buried deep inside her hair, shook wildly, so much so that the woman's body heaved and plunged according to his will.

A bigger crowd began to form. However, if ever Corto's contempt for crowds proved to be true, it was here. Now. For the woman's many cries fell on lethargic limbs.

I felt outraged. The man's cynical grin and crowd's inertia combined to drive me mad. But at that moment, sounds of hooves travelling above the crowd gave me hope.

There was no hesitation in Corto's manners. He kicked the horse's flanks and neared the center of the square, caring little, if at all, for the people purposely and vigorously shoved aside by the strong animal he commanded. The horse marched on, snorting heavily, while Corto only slightly pulled the reins. Baffled, the crowd parted, just as the woman was dragged into a side street.

With a vibrant kick of one leg, Corto dismounted.

"Who's that woman?" he urgently asked the horse's owner.

"She's just a prostitute," the man answered, nonchalantly. He took a stained handkerchief from his pocket, and wiped his sweaty forehead. "And besides," he added with a tone of indifference, "she isn't even from this island."

Corto had heard enough. He ran down the side street and quickly located a narrow, seedy alley, which he entered. Dozens of bulging garbage bags were piled on each side, and as Corto ventured further three sniffing stray dogs scattered away. Corto stopped, listened, advanced slowly again, alert and cautious. Then we heard the unmistakable sounds of slaps, a man cursing, a woman's pleading cries for help, which stopped when the slaps grew louder. I tried to pinpoint the location. Unable to do so, I turned towards Corto, and saw him crouching low. Suddenly he bounced to his feet and headed straight for a door which thunderously opened under a fierce kick.

As Corto paused for a moment on the threshold he watched the man with the ponytail slightly release the hold he had on the woman's throat. This sight incensed Corto.

Instincts born from avoiding death, from dispensing death, came to life!

Corto ran forward, threw himself on the ground and with both of his heels, violently struck the man in one knee. The blow was devastating, and the man crumbled in intense pain.

Very gently Corto helped the woman to a chair—the only piece of furniture aside the soiled mattress.

"You must go!" she urgently stated.

"You're dead!" the injured man snapped. "Both of you are dead."

"Shut up!" Corto shouted furiously.

"He speaks the truth," interjected the woman in a panic-stricken tone. "This man is just a lackey, but the others coming for me . . . they are ten times worse! They are the ones running this slavery ring. Please, stranger, you must go. Now!"

The fright on the woman's face, her words of caution and the threats from the man combined to raise within me concerns for Corto's safety.

Sounds of fierce barking rose from the alley. Someone was coming. Beyond the exploded doorway and into the alley, Corto's eyes travelled. More than one, he knew. More than one person was waiting for him.

After a quick glance around the room, one which helped him locate a broom near the mattress, Corto immediately went to work. He broke the broomstick's end, then pressed the penetrating tip against his palm. The sharp sensation seemed to offer some assurance.

Again, same as when he had fought in Guadeloupe, a subtle glimmer emerged from his eyes. Although outnumbered he seemed fearless. Lured to the battle, no doubt, and seduced by a world he wished to forsake.

Then, in the brief pause his eyes took to examine the improvised weapon, the injured man's shouts alerted whoever prowled outside.

Corto placed a comforting hand on the woman's shoulder, and mustered a faint smile. "On my honor," he vowed, "I have never left anybody behind. Stay here, I will come back for you."

Promptly Corto leaped into the alley, stick in hand, finding himself face to face with two other men. But this time, unlike in Guadeloupe, both had knives.

The narrow alley, which until then had solely witnessed the flow of flesh-hounding men and defecating dogs, gave way to a furious battle. Wishing themselves further from this scene, the pack of dogs scattered away.

Corto's strategy rested on his ability to disable the advantage their superior weapons posed. He accomplished this with quick thrusts to their faces. Using his cunning, Corto feigned backing down when, suddenly, he pounced forward, like a boxed jaguar, and dastardly poked one man's cheek. The man fell to the ground, and checked his wound. The battle raged. The two men tried their best to corner Corto, but Corto had guessed their fiendish plan and constantly avoided, much to their dismay, their attacks. He wielded his stick like an expert swordsman, and tirelessly lunged at his assailants. This appeared to work magnificently, as one opponent, inheriting a sudden charge, would backtrack ever so briefly, yet sufficiently, to allow Corto to dash towards the other man.

The whole combat had been waged for a few minutes when, emerging from the room's exploded threshold, the woman's screams for help rang through the alley.

Their projected echoes escaped the grasp of all. This sudden distraction proved to be the necessary ally Corto needed, as one of the men, having turned around to investigate the cries, fell to the ground when Corto slashed open his face.

Corto vigorously rushed towards the other opponent. Abruptly he stopped and, in the blink of an eye, returned to the fallen adversary, whose senses and instincts had enticed him into a costly, inopportune examination of his wound. With the sharp edge of Corto's stick pressed against his throat, the hatred in the man's eyes turned to panic. He looked at his accomplice who, growling and cursing, reluctantly threw his knife on the ground. Dutifully Corto picked up the two knives, then bent over the man on the ground and ruthlessly punched him until he became unconscious. Then quickly Corto turned around, ran, caught the remaining foe, and proceeded to hit him. Hard. Repeatedly.

Only one detail prevented a clean getaway. One Corto took care of by returning inside the house where he relentlessly pounded ponytail man into the land of nightmares.

* * *

Two hours later, Paris, at the helm, steered Thairica away from Grenada. Progressively, with distance came relief. Down below, Melina—the one Corto had rescued, was being tended to by Esmeralda.

Strong winds favored a hasty course. The sails, puffed and filled, briskly crackled, as Thairica journeyed south. After relinquishing the helm to Jared, Paris joined Corto on the foredeck.

There they sat, Paris remaining silent, waiting for further explanations, for the need to flee the island had only been briefly explained. As Corto related the series of events, his confession seemed to transport Paris to the narrow alley. Through his words, she envisioned the exploitation, the misery, the room's hostile stench.

A slight upward curving of her lips betrayed her emotions. She stared at her husband. True, some of his actions in the past had not warranted her appreciation. His path was laced with blood. This time, however, it seemed that she unconditionally gave her approval. The evil done to a sister. The ruined hopes and murmurs of love never to be spoken or heard . . . all of these rolled before Paris like the vast expanse of the sea she wished could facilitate their getaway.

"I tell you this," Corto declared. "I know there was a purpose for my presence back there, yet I fear you might think that I'm responsible." He paused momentarily, then slapped his knee. "I know about the Laws of Attraction, but I swear to you, on the souls of our children, that I don't wish for any of this. It just happens."

"You don't need to swear. Your word is more than enough."

Corto let his head drop on Paris' legs. "You're absolutely priceless," he said. He looked up at her. Her green eyes were truthful, and her approval carried such a soothing effect that he let out a deep sigh.

With a gentle hand, Paris caressed his face. Next she winked at him, and with that sign conveyed more than acknowledgment, but rather a blessed endorsement.

Still, Corto appeared too preoccupied to enjoy Paris' support. His face darkened. "Ever since the start of this voyage," he related, "we've been plagued. First, the trouble encountered with the building of the school. Then, Oliver's death, followed by the shark attack." He shook his head. "And now this," he muttered.

"You know the Universe doesn't throw anything at you that you can't handle," assured Paris.

Thoughts of Emilio leaped into Corto's mind. "I thought he was doing extremely well until a week ago," he remarked. "Somehow, I feel he's carrying a great guilt."

Later that day I was granted an unexpected glimpse of Melina's life. One obtained through Michael's help. One he no doubt thought favorable for my pilgrimage.

Gliding towards me with that idea firmly in mind, Michael noticed the anticipation his magic stirred in my soul. Suddenly I floated around Melina's home, years ago, in a quiet village of her native Trinidad. Her face exhibited the enchantment of youth, a glow reflecting the romance of life one could expect in their late teens. More images came to me. Thanks to Michael, I saw Melina's most cherished dream, that of three children running on the grass. An eight-year-old girl played with her two-year-old sister, while a one-year-old brother watched while nestled in his mother's arms.

The beauty of her island, the constant laughter of children, the tender kiss of life, the love of one man—this was Melina's ideal future.

More images came. Images of Melina waiting for her boyfriend. She looked at the path that linked her house to the road, anxious for his presence, hoping for a mystic night in which she would spill her secrets. She closed her eyes and felt safe.

Then her boyfriend turned into a snake.

Gone were the nights filled with magic and dreams. Lured by false promises, that honest and trusting smile followed the forked-tongue impostor who loved only money. A furious storm swallowed her smile, same as the stars, which faded from the sky, one by one, to the beat of vulgar hip thrusts with depraved strangers.

Years of brutal inhumanity with twisted men, their oily bodies and the taste of poison from their mouths had pulled her into a lightless void. She had given her heart to this viper, having her soul impaled and diseased in return.

How could Paris not approve of Corto's actions?

During the next few days the sun never touched Melina's face. She lacked in her own mind the right to stare at people in the eyes, for such a privilege could only be gained through trust in others, but, mostly, pride in herself.

Meanwhile, Esmeralda spent as much time as she could with her son, hoping he would reveal what was troubling him. Such a confession, however, never came.

It was, therefore, a most unusual sail along the shores of Trinidad. One made more curious when Melina, seated next to Paris, confided:

"Joyful scenes of you with your two children bring memories of similar dreams I once dared to dream."

"Two girls and one boy," said Paris, nodding her head.

"How did you know?" Melina countered, astonished. That question also popped into my mind. Then I remembered Paris' particular kinship with Michael and, if not from him, concluded that her keen abilities in these matters had greatly improved.

"These can still happen," assured Paris.

"You don't understand," Melina whispered. "I can't have any children!" She sobbed, as she declared that her womb had been ravaged. She thought about her broken future. Looking up at the cloudless tropical night sky, the stars, devoured by guilt and shame, had melted into the darkness. No hope lived up there, or around, or anywhere. That night, Melina cried herself to sleep.

The following day Thairica anchored near the town of Paria, though Menos chose to stay aboard his sloop in an anchorage further down the coast.

"We need to go ashore and buy some provisions," Paris told the group. On her part, Melina asked to remain aboard. Observing that she seemed of a more cheerful mood, it was agreed that she could stay by herself, although Paris and Corto entrusted upon me the task of frequent visits.

"What for?" I asked. "Whenever I try to help, this is met by a powerful decree forbidding I utter a single word. Even the softest sand doesn't show any of my footsteps."

The sight of Melina, with a slight glitter in her eyes, alleviated everybody's concerns.

Next we made our way into town, where soon after entering the marketplace there came upon me a sudden premonition. Images of Thairica, images impossible to dismiss, floated before me. Thairica, cradled by the invisible tide, appeared to be hosting an event I was to uncover. I whisked over. There I found Melina, seated at the salon table, enjoying a cup of freshly brewed coffee, smiling, as if relieved of a terrible burden. She grabbed a pen, a piece of paper, and began to write. Reassured, I rejoined Paris and Corto, where my ability to relay my findings offered perhaps the first step to greater achievements.

In awe and wishing to communicate this to Michael, I searched everywhere for him. I rose above the ground, looked all around, but his sight, his very vibrations, had vanished from my senses.

Suddenly a flash of light. A quick thought surged up in me. Something *felt* wrong. Something *was* wrong. Very wrong! Melina's calmness, the letter—these were totally incompatible with the way she had behaved these last few days! At once I returned aboard Thairica. Although seeing Melina calmly writing, the accuracy of her fingers, the care she took with each letter and punctuation, gave this simple task a ceremonious characteristic that begged to be investigated.

Immediately I made my way over her shoulder, and read the content.

To my dearest friends

The spark of life has disappeared, and deep within I feel the coming of utter darkness. It is a grave decision I have taken, but feel certain that your presence, although brief, did make my life a little better, even though my life was lost years ago.

Thank you for your kindness.

Melina.

"Oh, my God!" I whispered. "Not her."

Those words foretold something grave and forbidden. Her flesh had been ravaged and plundered, but her spirit, assailed by ghosts rising from the turmoil of a bed, had suffered even more.

The harshest punishment one can endure is the constant delaying of the sentence. These ghosts had haunted her sleep, soiled her heart, cut to pieces her hopes and beliefs.

Putting down the pen, Melina deeply exhaled. She placed the note in the middle of the dining table, rose to her feet, moved towards the galley where she washed her cup, headed into her cabin, and closed the door behind her.

I immediately joined her, and saw her staring at herself in a small mirror.

"You're nothing and don't deserve to live!" she whispered in an icy voice that would have frozen the blood of any mortal.

She squatted down, inserted her hands into the closet, and behind a bounty of clothes and sailing shoes, she retrieved a rope. Then she moved towards the bed and proceeded to tie a hangman's noose with a precision undoubtedly acquired through many rehearsals. With brisk movements, she tested the sliding knot and, once satisfied, slipped the noose around her neck.

This abomination I would never permit! There was no time to lose. I swiftly flew to the market. Once next to Paris and Corto, I felt immensely relieved that I could relay what was happening. A look of horror flashed across their faces.

"John, take the dinghy and hurry!" urged Paris.

Just then the group's puzzlement turned to alarm when seeing the manner with which Corto rushed to the dinghy-dock and Paris, holding the hands of Matthew and Danny, trailing behind him.

Uncertain as to the cause of such a frantic behavior, everybody sprinted behind, only to helplessly witness Corto hop into the dinghy and relentlessly pull the engine's start cord.

"Start!" screamed Corto, his face red with frustration.

"What's going on?" Esmeralda asked, slightly out of breath from the run.

"We fear something terrible is happening to Melina," Paris replied.

Suddenly, two hundreds yards away, Corto saw another dinghy anchored in a few feet of water. He covered that distance in no time, hopped into the dinghy, and tried to start the engine.

"Aw! Come on! he yelled.

"May I help you?" asked a man making his way towards him.

"Yes," Corto answered. His right arm repeatedly pulled on the start cord. "Is this your dinghy?" he asked, panting.

"It is."

"I need it to get to my ship, the one over there. It's an emergency." Not waiting for a reply, Corto continued his efforts to start the engine.

"Strange," the owner commented. "It's never this difficult."

Corto stopped, and nervously searched. With no other dinghy in sight, he dove into the water and swam, arms flying high. Unbelievingly, more misfortunes were about to strike when, not even thirty feet into his course, Corto abandoned, barely making it back to shore.

There could be no doubt that some great force was at work. This I knew by the way Corto painfully limped his way out of the water. Harsh lines sculpted his face, as his wide eyes stared incredulously at his right knee.

Again I willed myself aboard Thairica, and noticed that Melina had just begun to tie the rope to a fixture on the wall. I screamed in horror. It then struck me. Perhaps the Universe had extended my newly acquired powers. Perhaps the task of saving her had been destined for me!

Awakened to that possibility, I madly swung my airy limbs through and through Melina. From another dimension, another world, I struggled for a touch. An impact. A shiver. Anything! But, as I contemplated Melina pursuing her dreadful scheme, my hopes crumbled.

I flew back to shore. As I neared Corto, I detected fear in the corner of his eyes. That emotion, never before displayed before me, further enhanced my despair.

With Melina's fate drifting towards the unavoidable, the sight of Jared and Emilio rushing towards Corto rekindled my hopes.

"Melina is in trouble!" Corto screamed. "Go! Now!"

This dramatic appeal travelled across the sand, not only reaching Jared, but the one standing just behind.

The ocean. For a few seconds, Jared stared into its mysterious depths. The thought of deadly, triangular fins raised both concerns and hesitation. He winced, looked at Thairica, and dove into the water.

"I'm faster than you," Emilio shouted, seconds before his body charged through the surf.

With powerful strokes, Emilio glided across the surface, making remarkable progress with his piston-like arms. Truly, his speed proved inspiring. Stimulated by this, I rushed back to Thairica and found Melina tightening the noose around her neck and about to let herself drop to the floor.

Unable to look anymore, I rose to the top of the mast, and observed the exploding foam nearing Thairica. And Emilio was the source of it—a determined and splendid swimmer. His efforts had brought him very near when, out of nowhere, gale force winds whipped up white-crested waves. Brought to a stop by the sea's unexpected unruliness, Emilio gathered his bearings. Eyes made blurry from the flying, salted spray, limbs straining to keep his head above the charge of five foot waves, he stared at Thairica.

A secret message seemed concealed in the folds of these waves, like a threshold meant to be crossed, free from the shades of impenetrable doubts. Three hundred feet separated Thairica from the swimmer. A formidable trial under such conditions.

Emilio fought his way, up and down and under this liquid barrage. Finally, with a loud cry he climbed the transom ladder, leaped into the cockpit, rushed through the companionway and vigorously crushed open the cabin door.

* * *

Hours later, Emilio, by himself on the foredeck, stared at the sea, perplexed, in need of an answer. The sounds of Paris' steps made him turn around. With eyes filled with tears, he looked at her. A look of hope, tinged with uncertainty, like one on the verge of solving a complicated problem. Minutes went by when unable to grasp the event's full significance, he finally shook his head.

"Is Melina all right?" he inquired.

"Yes, thanks to you."

"You really think that this was a sign?"

"Yes," assured Paris. "One which stresses your importance in this world. One showing the healing you can bring to others. It's a complex sign for a youth to fully grasp, yet even you can't deny Corto's sudden knee injury, which has miraculously disappeared, or the sea's sudden irruption, which could only be vanquished by someone with incredible determination. Through opportunities aimed at helping others, the Universe reveals one's nature."

Having thought of himself of no special purpose until then, Emilio stared once again at the shimmering ripples of the sea, too emblazoned to entice further gloom, too mysterious to surrender the unexplainable.

"We all see this cloud hanging over you," Jared said, once close to him. "Rest assured that should it break, then as one, we will stand in the rain with you."

"Thank you, Jared," Emilio replied. He rose to his feet, and moved towards the mast, confused as to whether or not to retreat to his cabin.

Just then Michael, whom I had not seen since Melina's suicide attempt, popped into view. With burning rays coming out of his eyes, he stared at the ocean. Curved fins quickly travelled across the quiet waters, and Thairica, gently floating, was besieged by peeking blowholes. The dolphins swam and jumped, their dark eyes filled with light and hope. From where I hovered, their liquid maneuvers resembled a well orchestrated plan and soon emphasized another sight just as formidable, seized by Esmeralda who, having discerned a unique spark, exclaimed, "Look at my son's eyes!"

Nature, perhaps because of its wholesomeness, entices the purity within us all. Serving as messengers, the aquatic monarchs of the sea, through playful eyes and giant leaps, conveyed this appeal.

"When caught in some predicament, feeling desperate," Emilio whispered, "look at nature for inspiration."

He nodded, entered the cockpit, and invited everyone to listen.

The next hour unraveled at an unbelievable speed. Repentant and honest, Emilio confessed his part on stowing two kilos of cocaine aboard Thairica.

"Please tell us why you did this?" his mother asked. "You must tell everything, Emilio. This is a grave matter. Don't protect anyone."

"It was Menos," Emilio admitted, his voice a barely audible murmur. "It was Menos," he repeated. "He told me it was the only way Jorge would allow the school to be built."

Corto immediately rushed into Emilio's cabin. Seconds later, with two packs of white powder in one hand and a diving knife in the other, he pierced the bags and dispersed the contents into the sea.

* * *

A string of curses. A string of low, menacing curses blurted through Corto's clenched jaw greeted Menos once aboard Thairica.

"Why the hell did you do this?" Corto asked. His fingers twitched, longing for an excuse to wring the man's neck. "What exactly were you thinking of when you entrusted Emilio with two kilos of cocaine?"

"You may recall that at one point, Jorge could have ruined the whole construction project," answered Menos. "Unless I accepted his proposal, things could have escalated for the worse."

"What could possibly be worse than a man's death?"

"Oliver was alive when I accepted to move the drugs," Menos countered. "After his death, I foresaw even more trouble for all of us if I would have gone to the authorities with that story. One of theirs had just died. You think they would have shown compassion towards us?"

"And where were you supposed to deliver this drug?"

"I'm not sure," answered Menos. He shrugged his shoulders. "All I know is that Jorge is supposed to call me on the radio to fix a rendezvous."

"Which radio?" Corto pressed. "The SSB or VHF?"

"VHF."

"The one suited for short-distance communications?"

"Um, I see your point."

"You see my point? With Jorge so near?" Instinctively Corto looked around and tried to guess his foe's whereabouts.

"I would never subject any of you to any danger," assured Menos. "I would have taken the merchandise when no one would have been aboard and gone alone to meet him."

"That's not the point!" Corto snapped. "Do you have any idea what Emilio endured for you?"

Every possible option seemed considered by Corto. He gently pulled Paris aside. "We need to recollect our thoughts," he whispered. "Thairica was involved in drug smuggling, and I don't want her to be seized by the authorities." He shook his head. "Even if *I'm* the one who destroyed the drugs, I fear Jorge's vengeance could include collateral damages."

"By that you mean to say everybody's at risk?" she murmured.

He looked into her eyes. "That's what I mean."

Paris quivered, cleared her throat, and asked about the alternatives—if they were any.

Immediately Corto looked all around. But the horizon, though smooth and noiseless, failed to alleviate his worries. Across the empty blue miles before him, nestled in the unknown, danger lurked.

"We're sailing without a compass here," Corto said. "But there's a place which could offer both the security and time to gather our bearings. Although we had planned on sailing there after dropping our guests, it's best we go there now."

"You mean Saul's Island?"

"I mean Saul's Island," he confirmed. "We shall set sail for it after taking Melina to her village."

Paris considered his proposal. Through faint nods of her head, she assented, finding herself overpowered by his sense of command.

* * *

The next day, with everyone aware of the new course of action, Melina sat alone on the foredeck, as Thairica sailed inexorably towards her village. Silent and self-absorbed, Melina wondered; had her covert activities reached her village?

Sensitive to Melina's preoccupations, Paris moved next to her.

"Why am I haunted by visions of a stone-throwing crowd?" Melina asked.

"With the Lord in your heart, stones thrown at His shield wither into dust," Paris replied.

"Let's just hope that they turn to dust before hitting my body, and not after."

"I understand," Paris said. She placed a gentle hand on Melina's shoulder, and lightly pressed on it with a touch that, though timid in appearance, applied a soothing balm. "The only answer I can offer is to surrender to the fate that the Universe has set for you. Only then will you be free of such questions."

"I don't get it," countered Melina. "I was dragged, beaten, and locked up inside a sex-dungeon for years. Why am I the one afraid of being demonized?"

"Are you to live the remainder of your life with the weight of these devious acts pulling you underwater until you drown?" Paris asked.

"What does it matter?" replied Melina. "If you only knew."

Paris deeply exhaled. "But I do know," she said in a voice no louder than a murmur. Her fingers dug deep into Melina's shoulder. For a second, Paris looked at me. And what a stare! The stare grew fiercer, then suddenly became peaceful.

"I beg your forgiveness," Paris hastily and sincerely said. "Only a few things get on my nerves. And women condemned for man's sins, enslaved for man's passions, and degraded for man's weaknesses rank at the very summit."

"I'm scared," Melina said. "All my family died in my absence and I have nowhere to go."

"I too have fears," Paris confided, sullenly.

Three hours later they arrived in Manzanilla. As Menos stayed behind and watched over the vessels, Thairica's entire group hitched a ride aboard a truck which ventured further inland. They travelled across the mountainous landscape, through countless hairpin bends and below intertwined branches arched high across the road.

Soon the truck came to a stop. As the truck driver sped away, the group was abruptly greeted by an outburst of shouts, as they observed Melina's deepest fear. Word of her coming had indeed reached these boundaries. A dozen people standing at the bottom of the road leading to the village shouted their opposition to Melina's return.

In front of these people stood a man with a severe face, dark suit and tie. In one hand he held a Bible, and a silver cross hung around his neck.

"Where are you going?" the man asked in a harsh and deep voice.

A chorus of voices rang through the barricade.

"Leave this village," one ordered.

"Whores are not welcomed," blurted another.

To the consternation of the crowd, Paris moved closer, unperturbed by their number, and asked why they felt imperiled by Melina.

Standing rigidly, the man in the dark suit, whom people called Reverend Raymond, glared at Paris. "We heard of this woman's sins, and don't want to be infected," he said.

A bright redness swept across Paris' face. "Shouldn't your compassion sparkle with the same intensity as that of your cross?" she asked.

Raymond took a few steps forward. For several minutes, he recited a monologue on the importance of preserving virtue.

"Even at the risk of committing an assault?" Paris shouted.

Raymond took a few more steps forward.

"Shall I recite the passages condemning sinners?" he shouted. "What could you possibly say that would rival the wisdom of the Sacred Bible?" He brandished the Bible he held, and smiled as the crowd rousingly approved.

I looked at Melina. Head bowed and feeling dirty, she achingly endured the crowd's insults. The ghosts of Grenada had made it here. And they had found a voice.

As her wound widened, I wondered if anyone could stop this blasphemy. Instinctively I looked at Michael, who was following the scene with a deep, probing gaze, his youthful face looking quite dignified.

The sight of a man atop the hill riding a horse-pulled carriage mobilized Michael's attention. That man, after getting off the carriage, joined a small gathering of people who observed the scene from a distance.

The loud intolerant crowd brought my attention back to the blockade. No parading troops could possess more orderly ranks.

"When I came here," Raymond said, methodically, "and heard the people wondering why so many had left their village, I knew that the closures of nearby factories had nothing to do with it. It was the lack of morals that favored this exile."

"You may have swayed these people's hearts with the eloquence of your spite," retorted Paris, "but my will is unconquerable from the likes of your kind."

Raymond's eyes turned somber. Meanwhile, I noticed that the sunrays were bouncing off Raymond's silver cross in a myriad of sparkling lasers. Aware of this, Raymond felt ennobled.

"The sign speaks for itself," he declared.

This was followed by another denunciation from Paris. Her words spoke of compassion, of reason, of letting God's judgment in God's hands.

To this Raymond replied, "Perhaps you lack the wisdom to hand down a judgment."

"Wisdom comes with love," Paris countered. "I don't see any in your eyes right now."

"Woman, how quick is your tongue, how sharp is your mind, and yet the Bible says . . ."

"Quoting the Bible by heart is an easy way to avoid a true discussion," Paris interrupted. "Why don't you use your own words to debate? Furthermore, what did you do to Melina's abductors? Surely, there must be some conspirators living on this island? Perhaps this village? Did you cast stones at them? Are Man's sins submitted to a different scale? Perhaps you should be reminded that an Enlightened One is a soul, first and foremost, without gender or race, and that, God willing, when Christ comes back, it could very well be in the body of a woman!"

Raymond turned pale. "I . . . I . . . have . . . the . . . light," he mumbled, blinking excessively.

At that moment Michael, displeased by Raymond's behavior, waved his glorious hands. Immediately, from as far as I could see, clouds rolled across the sky and quickly blocked the sun—this in the absence of any wind. Raymond's cross had lost its sparkle.

I had then supposed this to be the last of Michael's influence that day, yet could not have been more wrong. As the crowd stood united, with Paris never considering a withdrawal, Michael's core greatly intensified. There was something previously unseen about his essence, which now possessed a different hue of purple. Believing that something great would very soon sway the crowd I braced myself for Michael's magic when, to my surprise, something spooked the horse atop the hill. Then without warning the horse and carriage wildly charged down the hill, just as a little six-year-old girl ran across the road . . . and was horrifically trampled by hooves and wheels. The girl bounced, rolled, was dragged several feet before settling on the ground, her limbs spread out awkwardly. Screams echoed throughout the road, immediately followed by the deep gasps of terror-stricken villagers flooding the scene. Lying on her back, perfectly motionless, her ripped clothing covered in blood, the young girl's eyes, although opened, remained silent as a grave.

I hovered above the turmoil. The cries were horrific, especially after the failed attempts to revive her. This scene deeply offended me. But it was the sight of the dead girl's father, rushing down the hill and kneeling by her side, face twisted with pain and holding his daughter's hand, that simply proved unbearable.

How could this death fashion itself in the Universe's Original Design?

I swiftly turned around and threw Michael a vicious glare! Though I knew he hadn't done this, he nonetheless had known about it. Yet my son hovered there, simply hovered, having witnessed all of this without lifting a magical finger. He who summoned dolphins at will, ignited candles in the wind, commanded clouds according to his mood, and infused music and dance into people. How in God's name could he have allowed this?

This senseless death shook my very core. Concepts elaborated over the course of the past months withered away. Faith? The Original Design? NONSENSE!!!

All at once the villagers eagerly looked upon Raymond to do something. But, searching for a culprit, Raymond quickly recognized the perverse course that would favor the preservation of his throne.

"This village is dammed!" Raymond shouted. "Little Maria is dead. God has forsaken us. Do you see what happens with the arrival of sinners?"

Resolutely, Paris urged forward, pushing aside all who stood in her way. Having reached the father, she rested a hand on his shoulder, stared deep into his eyes, and enjoined him to pray. Kneeling down, she grasped the little girl's hands, brought them to her face, and pressed her lips upon them. A sliver of light appeared between Paris' fingers. She pursued the treatment with a heightened degree of green in her eyes. But little by little, as Maria's limp body refused to stir, this failed attempt only strengthened my faith's repudiation. As I reluctantly observed this scene, I noticed that some in the crowd knelt down and prayed, while others stood, silent.

"I implore you, Almighty God," cried the father. "Please don't take my little Maria. She's all I've got in this world."

Angry, I sheltered my soul from further sorrows by turning away. Just then a Force stirred the air. A Force unlike any I had ever seen before. A Force filled with greatness and purity. Instantly the clouds vanished. The sky awoke, and under the endorsement of the sun commanded that all life offer proof of their devotion. Trees tilted their heads. Blades of grass giggled under the teasing breeze. And even the moon, the silver lover of mysterious nights, sparkled against the blue canopy.

Into the Force's spell I plunged. The certitude of an upcoming, formidable event shook me, as Michael hovered ten feet above the ground. He stared at the sun, and sought to appropriate its force, until his core embodied that blissful power.

The sun lived in his eyes. The sun, eternal, inexhaustible, and giver of life. Then Michael playfully directed his beaming eyes over each of his airy limbs, which upon reception, proceeded to ignite, leaving his wispy shell the color of miracles.

Finally he glided towards little Maria, and I thought, could what I desire and crave for really take place here? Now? Was I to witness a phenomenon which has puzzled mankind ever since its first breath?

Time and time again Michael *brushed* Maria's face, his smile foretelling an upcoming victory. Then midway through a stroke, with his hand inches beneath the girl's brown skin, which rendered more surreal the whole process, Michael waited for a ripple.

But unexpected immobility caused Michael to shake his head. His touch, the product of Heaven, had failed to stir the slightest tremor. Uncertain, Michael frowned, yet his disappointment by no means carried the same disavowal my spirit had earlier embraced. Quite the contrary. He approached it like a formula to be concocted. An enigma that needed to be solved. To this Michael committed himself entirely.

Just then, the riddle revealed itself in his whole, dignified, wonderful smile. There was a tense silence as Paris tremulously searched Michael's eyes, sensitive to any signs my son would volunteer.

Gently laying down Maria's hands, Paris stared into Michael's soul, intently, until her face brightened. Very solemnly Paris clasped Maria's hands and pulled them once more to her lips, this as Michael applied, yet again, his transparent touch. Only this time, Michael leaned over and whispered something into Maria's ear.

Beneath flesh, over the boundaries of this world, life still appeared within reach when a distorted stream of light erupted from Michael and Paris' touch.

No quivers, unfortunately, rose from Maria's body. Although this maneuver proved unsuccessful, there seemed hope in Michael's eyes. He looked at Paris, this time with something that was both mystical and singularly commanding.

At once Paris searched the crowd.

"Come!" Paris called out to Melina. "This will only work with your help."

Some of the onlookers tried to block Melina, but were brutally shoved aside by Corto. Yielding to Paris' entreaty, Melina knelt down, took Maria's dead hand, and raised it to her heart.

"Give me your other hand," beckoned Paris, thus ensuring the sisterhood's unbreakable triangle. "Now, transfer your love into this soul."

Searching Maria's face for bursts of life, Melina prayed, at times appearing quite perplexed. Dutifully, Michael inserted his hands inside Maria's body.

"Sacrilege!" Raymond shouted vehemently. With wild movements he shoved aside the people pressed against him. "How dare you touch her? What purpose does this prostitute serve? Look at her! Soiling little Maria's soul!"

"Enough!" Maria's father cried. His flaring nostrils successfully convinced Raymond to be silent. He then put his hand on Melina's shoulder. "Please, do what you can to save my little girl. She is my world."

Melina nodded, and pursued her task.

Fortunately, Paris had detected Melina's troubled concentration. Through the cold vastness where death wandered, life yet seemed within reach. "Commit your devoutness to God," Paris told her. "While thoughts of Him flourish, visualize and absorb the love which will then fill all of your being. It is that love, that purest and mightiest of energy that we seek. Such a power may only be achieved through purity of heart. I beg you, Melina. Let go of any thoughts of hatred, be it towards others, yourself, or God."

The haunting souvenirs of cruelty and desecration disappeared in the echo of those words.

A few feet above the dead girl's body, purple and yellow sparks appeared, raising deep gasps from the crowd. Again Michael murmured into Maria's ear. The sparks grew stronger, and seeped into Paris and Melina's arms. This was magnificent! Sweat rolled down both of their faces. Holding hands, they withstood this crashing waterfall of radiance.

The spell strengthened, and as the circle of limbs endured, wavering flutes of energy entered Maria's body.

Suddenly . . . oh, my God! The twitch of a finger! Such a faint sign. But life was in that sign! A sign stirred within Maria's core, achieved through her own means. Under the force of a struggling soul, throbbing fingers sought the excitement of every limb. And what a struggling spirit this little girl proved to be when, at long last, at the sound of Maria's cough, at the sight of her moving her head, I had witnessed the birth of all life!

A thunderous applause swept the air as Maria found herself being tightly squeezed in her father's arms.

"I will praise you, Lord, with all my heart," said Paris. "I will tell of all your wonderful deeds."

Touched by such a miraculous scene, ashamed of having renounced God earlier, I swore to never again question any events.

A joyful scene, however, turned the crowd's mood from loud exclamations of wonder to that of anger. Scornful stares struck Raymond and drained his vitality. Having lost his credibility, the false messenger stood before them, vulnerable.

"It's your fault that some people have left this village," a man accused. Under vile chants, shouts and insults, the crowd circled around Raymond.

"He's the one we should banish," shouted one man.

"Not before receiving a serious beating," voiced another.

"None of this!" exclaimed Maria's father. He rushed forward and pitted himself and his daughter in front of them. Next he asked for silence, so that he could speak.

"Rage is unnecessary," he insisted, looking sternly at the crowd. "Hatred will only damn our souls, same as the silence we observed when we knew that Raymond preached malicious interpretations from the darkness of his soul, and not the Light of the Sacred Book. No, my friends; knowledge, reason, faith in the meaning of God and open debate are the tools that will guard us against the accursed coming of a false messenger."

With Maria gently sleeping in his arms, he stood in the middle of the dusty, uneven path, and waited for the crowd to disperse. Then he walked towards Melina, still on her knees, her initial fear not yet dispelled.

He looked at her.

"A million thanks could not express my gratitude," he declared honestly.

"I ask for none, but would settle for one," she replied, eyes lowered, as if unused that a man could be so polite towards her.

He gazed at her with sincere, admiring eyes. "Then I thank you," he said. "From the bottom of my heart."

These few words struck Melina, and she finally lifted her head.

With care and elegance, he offered his hand so that she could rise, which she did. Facing her, he said that she could go to his house for the necessary time to get organized, if she decided to stay in the village, and lastly, that he was a widower. The compassion of his gaze heightened, as I detected in his brown eyes the glimmer that precedes declarations of the heart.

"Like I said, you can stay with us," he repeated. "Rest assured, nobody will ever hurt you. I promise."

Melina bowed her head, then without any signs or warnings whatsoever she promptly walked away.

It was only when Paris ran and caught up with her that she stopped.

"What is it?" Paris quickly inquired.

"You know I can never have any children," answered Melina.

A beam of light raced across Paris' smile. Sparks appeared in her eyes, and I expected soothing gestures to follow. A hug, a friendly embrace, perhaps. But with the enlivened conviction of a messenger bringing a gift, Paris stroked Melina's stomach and let quivering fingers paint vibrant colors upon a blank canvas.

"Miracles do happen!" Paris said, convincingly.

Meanwhile, not far from this scene, Maria, awake in her father's arms, began to describe the incredible journey her mind had witnessed while briefly wandering the after life.

"Daddy," she confided. "I dreamt of the cutest little boy with blue eyes. Both of his arms were stretched out, and he kept repeating the same thing."

"What did he tell you this little boy?"

"Well, I was holding on to a ledge, and he kept telling me to let go. Yes! Those were his exact words, 'Let go, let go, I will take care of you.' Daddy, do you think he's the little brother I always wished for?"

"I thought you wanted a little sister."

"Now, I want both!"

Unlocking the Power

On a sea filled with white-crested waves, Thairica glided inexorably towards an island unknown to tourists. One forgotten by governments. As for Michael, flying high above in the sky, he dazzled us with a whirlwind of twirls. Now and then he giggled at the sight of his airy limbs, which he now could kindle at will when staring at them in a certain manner. Wishing to know exactly what had happened in Trinidad, I asked Paris for her opinion.

"Although Michael was clearly the beacon that polarized the will of a Higher Force," she said, "the assistance of two mortals confuses me. Perhaps Saul can provide the answer."

With Paris observing a deep silence, unable to reach a conclusion as to the powers used to revive Maria, I decided to examine the endeavors of the Spiritual Sailors. Let me share with you an experience that happened while sailing along the coast of Martinique.

That day, the whole ocean appeared like a stirring mass of nervous mountains. As Thairica left the coast behind we caught sight of an object—dark brown, undulating in the blue and white waves.

Corto probed the sea, and moments later located that same object. Seconds later, it vanished. As Corto changed course, everybody in the cockpit speculated about what had been seen. That gleaming dark pearl the ocean tried to smother under a foamy blanket. Taking position at the mast, Paris steadied herself with one hand, while looking through the binoculars.

"It's a boy!" she cried. "A wonderful little boy! And he's spearfishing!"

"In this weather?" replied Corto.

As we approached, murmurs of astonishment spread across Thairica's cockpit. How could that dark pearl, like some struggling coconut, brave such choppy waters? At his age? Alone and with God knows what, swimming around him? How incredible! Here was the displaced spirit of the Masai warrior, spearing fishes instead of lions. Here was the spirit of the hunter from thousands of years ago. Tales of his great adventures invaded my mind. Now, what also caught our attention, aside from his obvious swimming skills, was his speargun. Constructed out of a straight piece of wood, this primitive weapon had been grooved in the middle to accommodate a rudimentary spear made from a shirt hanger. Rubber bands made from a worn out bicycle tire ensured the necessary thrust. As the young boy repeatedly plunged into the deep blue water, we also noticed a floating device consisting of a dozen wine corks wired together. To that floating device the young boy had tied the only fish he had speared, plus a meager sandwich wrapped in a plastic bag.

Ever so gently, Corto maneuvered closer to the young boy. "What's your name?" he asked.

"Joseph," the boy panted. He collected the fish he had speared, swam towards Thairica, stretched out his arms and was pulled aboard as if someone had picked up a wet penny from the street. His short curly hair glittered and looked decorated with diamonds.

"What are you doing?" Corto asked.

"Spearfishing, of course," the boy answered between gasps of air.

"I can see that, but in this weather?"

"I come here twice a week. No matter what!"

"No matter what?"

"I have to, so that my brothers and sisters can eat."

Hearing this, Paris paid generously for Joseph's bounty. Corto, on his part, retrieved from a storage space a small speargun, one he knew Joseph could use.

"This is for you," he said.

Joseph accepted these offerings with polite smiles and inquisitive stares, as if to say; 'yes, here I am, Joseph, armed with this crude instrument and a sad story, forced to take risks to feed my family. But don't you dare feel sorry for me. For I am not just fishing . . . I am building my temple, and my family's affection proves to be the only treasure I desire.'

He looked at the speargun, lightly smiled as he caressed its length, then brandished it above his head. They all cheered. He bade them goodbye, turned around, and swiftly plunged head first into the sea.

What you give belongs to you . . . what you keep is lost forever.

Like Corto had once told me, "A revelation can come in a thousand disguises. And a lot of times revelations come under the appearances of a child. Your path will become clear when you can recognize the revelations that the Universe displays before you."

As for Joseph? Well, let's just say that Martinique had ceased to exist that day. This is what happens when you recognize a revelation. The places you visit give up their common names. They become thresholds. St-Vincent becomes the island of Oliver, and Trinidad becomes the island of Maria. You may leave those islands, but the revelations last forever.

As we caught sight of Joseph hopping on the sand, we knew of a new name for the island known as Martinique. This boy had casted a spell. From then on this island carried the fragrance of an intrepid and lofty little soul diving unruly seas to nourish his loved ones.

It was the island of Joseph, the brave little spearfisherman.

* * *

Paris steered Thairica through the waves at great speed. Alone in the cockpit, she looked at the late afternoon sun, knowing all too well how quickly it would sink below the horizon now that they sailed close to the equator.

"Do you wish to review the stages while we're alone?" she asked me.

I welcomed her suggestion. "The first stage," I began, taking my time and weighing each word, "entices the acceptance of a Higher Power, which for me is easy to fathom."

She nodded, obviously pleased, and bade me to go on.

"The second stage," I continued, "stresses the development of the mind and removal of the ego."

"And the third?" asked Paris, her smile growing wider.

"The third stage introduces us to samples of The Eternal Energy. We seek to harmonize our inner-selves with all of creation, and this leads to the fourth stage, when, with a pure mind we seek to merge with the Divine."

"Marvelous," exclaimed Paris. "Please continue."

"Then there's the final stage, the Ascended Master, accessible to one having reached the Kingdom of Heaven."

As I shared my recollections, I wondered about the teacher standing before me. What possible stage could be hers?

Turning around, Paris observed Menos' sloop way behind, like a tiny white speck at times swallowed by the hopping horizon.

Moments later, I contemplated little Maria's revival, particularly when it was initially performed by Michael and Paris. What obstacle had caused such an alliance to fail? Could the boiling stare that Paris had given me when she was trying to comfort Melina hold the key? A stare unlike any I had ever witnessed before?

A few hours later I heard an unexpected confession. That night, the stars twinkled like never before, as if to encourage those under the sky to confide their darkest secrets.

Corto, having relieved Paris at the helm, stared at the radar screen, and sighed with relief when a luminous dot which he knew to be Menos' sloop blinked momentarily. Moments later he contacted Menos by radio, gave some instructions, and adjusted his course a few degrees to the east. Although sailing near the South American continent, there was not the faintest trace of that great land mass. Its presence, I knew, grew smaller and smaller.

Alone on the foredeck, Paris quivered in the crisp air. She clipped her harness, and remained seated, solidly gripping the handhold, her eyes searching the night.

Suddenly, a bright spark appeared in the middle of the thousands of stars hung high above, as if that light had travelled an incredible distance for a special purpose. Overwhelmed by this magic, Paris surrendered.

"There's something you must know, Thomas," she whispered to me, as if afraid that the blowing winds would carry her words towards Corto. "Years ago," she resumed, her eyes filled with tears, "something abominable happened to me."

"You're talking about what you told Melina when on your way to her village, aren't you?" I was honored that she found in me someone worthy to share her secret.

"Yes," she replied, not without tremendous difficulty. "I was working in a camp in northern Thailand, in a town called Mai Sai, near the Myanmar border, when—"

She paused, and fought to stop the tears rushing out of her eyes, and tremors shaking her limbs.

"Oh, I wish to make you understand," she murmured. "For it's beneficial for YOUR journey that you learn from my trials and believe in the virtue of forgiveness. I implore you, Thomas . . . listen, so that you may benefit from my weakness."

I nodded.

"At the camp I provided medical care to Burmese girls who had been forced into prostitution and had managed to escape." She stopped, breathed deeply, and resumed. "There had been rumors of corrupt Burmese soldiers planning on crossing into Thailand to destroy our camp." Again she broke the conversation. But this time her body horrifically writhed and convulsed, as if assailed by invisible hands, groping at her like an unforgiving disease. She clasped her hands together, and looked into the cockpit. Satisfied that Corto seemed outside the reach of her words, she bowed her head, and said:

"I was raped!"

She winced as if a spear had been driven through her heart. There was a silence. The great spark in the sky reappeared. Paris let out a muffled astonishment. Although her body trembled tremendously, she went on. "Tortured and raped by three repulsive bastards!"

She looked at me with eyes of a strange luster, her voice tinged with the distant echoes of that day.

"After the attack," she resumed, "I fell unconscious. Three days later I opened my eyes and saw John for the first time, there inside the hospital room, watching over me. I lied to him, and made up a story about a horseback accident. You see, Thomas, I recognized John immediately. I knew that in front of me stood my soul mate, the one that most assuredly had been with me in previous earthly lives. I never told him about the attack. I didn't think he could have handled it. And I still believe I made the right decision, for knowing him as I do, he would have raided the region and unleashed his wrath. Never pausing or resting. Never! Until death would have claimed him."

She paused, and shook her head. "I wanted neither death nor vengeance. I wanted *him*. So I kept silent."

Her eyes swept the dark horizon. Beyond the obscurity, the memories were making their way back. That's when Michael appeared. He brushed his hand through me, and at once I was whisked away from Thairica's deck and flung into the jungles of the Orient.

Through lush foliage, I advanced, and moments later entered a campsite. I ventured deeper, and saw Paris. She tended to a young pregnant Asian girl, and made sure that she ate well enough to feed the added life inside of her. Moments later Paris exited the tent, entered the next one, took the pulse of another girl, dabbed her forehead with a white cloth, and silently prayed. Other images appeared, of Paris carrying heavy bags of food, exhausted from the tropical heat, painfully loading them into a buggy. But then, other images rushed through my mind. Three Burmese soldiers silently crossed the narrow Mae Sai River, then ventured inside the campsite, and set tents on fire. Paris stood in their way, adamantly blocking their path. She was instantly slapped for her resistance.

Undaunted, she looked into the men's eyes, and searched for the minute clue that reveals the secret of one's soul. Her examination took her deep inside the soldiers' hearts. She asked herself, 'How can such unholy thoughts even exist?'

"Stand aside," one soldier ordered.

Aware of her upcoming fate if she resisted, Paris breathed heavily, and nonetheless refused to move. A portion of the violence that would be unleashed upon her quickly followed. The soldier ran forward and swung his rifle in her face. Bones cracked, blood spurted high into the air. Moments later, bloodied and lying on the ground, Paris was dragged to a concealed location in the jungle.

I remember the torment of these images, of Paris lying on her back, arms pinned down by two maniacs, with the third one heavily pressed against her. His slithering wickedness first perforated her flesh, then worked its way into her soul. Screams for mercy were ignored, as one of the soldiers holding her arms sniffed white powder. That gave him the character of the devil. And the devil went to work!

"So, Farang, me think you're ready to go home, yes?"

"No yet." The savagery exploded, and the last animal, after zipping up his pants, viciously kicked her face over and over again, all the while cursing at the green lights he wished to extinguish.

This sight was so unbearable that I willed with all my might for these images to stop. But they kept rolling before me.

Finally, worn out by his fury, the beast grunted, "Now, you can go home."

The soldiers marched away, howling and barking. Naked and bleeding, face down in the mud, it took hours for Paris to regain consciousness. Incredibly, she managed to crawl towards the campsite, where she collapsed. Suddenly the torment of these images stopped.

Michael's wispy shell shimmered, as if that episode had stirred his very core. He squirmed, as his eyes detected in Paris' crisp lips, furrowed forehead and heaving chest the pain swelling inside of her. He pouted, and murmured words in a language neither Paris nor I understood—like an old dialect.

Such a dreadful entrance inside Paris' heart had afforded me a glance at all the trapped ghosts who, from the darkness of their cage, tried to drag Paris into a lightless void. But this episode, in fact, had truly revealed the brilliance of her soul.

Next to me, Michael was visibly under great pain. His feelings for Paris knew no bounds. Kindred spirits attract kindred spirits. And often, I was soon to discover, the light you see is really the reflection of another source.

I stared at Michael. My son. An old soul. Back on Earth for a purpose. Undoubtedly a glorious one!

Hesitant at first, he took a step towards Paris, waited for her smile to take another, then another. He slipped inside of her, and listened to her racing pulse as she closed her eyes and nursed the ghosts back to sleep. Then suddenly he bolted to the top of the mast.

That display was so moving that the only question I could think of was, "What became of those men?"

She let out a deep sigh. "They were never identified and brought to Court, if that's what you mean. They, of course, will have to answer to God, although I did hear, a few weeks later, that three soldiers fitting their descriptions had their throats slashed by a total stranger appearing out of nowhere, this just as they were raiding a campsite run by the Red Cross in northern Thailand."

Here she paused, and looked at the stars, longingly.

"What about the revelation you had at the temples? I asked.

"A revelation that promoted the virtue of forgiveness," she answered. "A forgiveness I have not yet wholeheartedly embraced, since I still wonder, at times, why this happened to me. And though I long to embrace a total forgiveness, what happened in the jungles of Thailand must forever remain a secret from John. It took years for the Universe to join us. I don't wish for his prompt instinct to ruin everything."

At last I perceived a subtle change in our conversation, and I wished to know more about her. "Did you possess your gifts before being initiated to the five stages?" I asked.

"To a certain degree, yes, but I always kept them in the privacy of my heart. These gifts are not to be selfishly paraded, which is why you'll never see a monk levitate in front of an audience."

Paris gazed at the pin-points of fire spread across the sky. The love she felt for God seemed limitless. Then she looked at Michael.

"Look at your son!" she urged me. "Notice how faithfully he performs his tasks! How he feared for Oliver's fate and yet still touched him. It is his faith that inspires me to seek total forgiveness. A soul on the ascending path cherishes all struggles. Would Jared have developed without Esmeralda? Would Emilio enjoy clarity of purpose without Melina's failed suicide attempt? Would a false messenger hold dominion over a village if not for Melina's intervention? Or, again, would I seek total forgiveness without Michael's luminous example?"

She was beautifully animated now, and inhaled and exhaled with obvious delight.

"We travel a path where certainty is willfully concealed," she said. "I have given you all of the required tools, Thomas, and though Spiritual Guides wield signs that may invade our dreams and conscience, it is you who must seek the perfection of your soul, unlock your mind's power, and commit yourself on becoming a man of wisdom."

* * *

Four days at sea had brought Thairica close to Saul's island. Beyond the darkness, somewhere, land lurked, near and unseen. So anticipated.

Finally, dawn awakened the dark sky. Corto glanced behind, and distinguished Menos' craft on the horizon. Beyond Thairica's pulpit, Saul's island rose and sank, lingering before our eyes in broken sequences like a mischievous mirage. At the next moment the sea unleashed impressive blue and white rollers. The foamy crests roared under Thairica, causing many to flash distraught looks between one another. A few minutes later, a swift eastward current was felt.

Michael, high above the mast, smiled at me. Gliding higher, a lone albatross graced the air currents, while a few feet beneath the choppy surface, dozens of coral reefs streamed by on both sides of Thairica. These pillars surrounded the whole island, ready to seal the fate of anyone unfamiliar to their formation. Turning around to entice Menos to follow their course, Corto and Paris stared at each other, perplexed by his absence. Their distress was reinforced when numerous radio calls went unanswered.

"There's nothing we can do to change this," Corto said. "Let's keep our mind on the present."

After tense minutes spent sailing around the underwater sentries, the current brought us between two rocky cliffs and into a secret gorge.

Deeper inside this narrow passage Thairica glided. Sporadically, slender beams of light bounced off the polished rock and showered everything, from top to bottom, with kaleidoscopic colors.

"Magnificent!" exclaimed Jared, unable to restrain his emotions. "Where's Menos?" he asked, realizing his absence.

"He'll come later," Corto answered, grimly.

Near the farthest wall, a sailboat, neatly tied to boulders, partially concealed the bottom of a carved staircase that linked the sea to the cliff's summit.

"D'Artagnan," murmured Jared, upon reading the name on the transom.

"And there's the captain," Corto said, waving his hand at a grey-haired man climbing down the hundreds of steps.

* * *

Guided by Saul, the man who had greeted them, the group walked along a path that snaked across the island's smooth hills.

"This island has no natural resources, no strategic significance," Saul confided. "This is why the government of France never bothered doing anything with this place, unlike the prison colonies it built on Devil's Island, twenty miles to the west."

Having reached the house, I was struck by the monumental size of the front door, seemingly conceived to entice those who had braved the sea to enter, which they did.

For a moment, the crew lingered on the threshold.

"Come in!" urged a woman making her way to the front door. "Welcome to our home. I'm Esther. Come! You must be tired after such a long voyage."

She opened her arms.

"Don't make me beg you to come in, because I will," she added, her cheeks delightfully reddening.

She was a woman of medium complexion, same as her husband, about sixty years of age, with intelligent eyes and a plump figure.

"John and Paris," Esther said. "It's been too long. How long has it been Saul?"

"Too long," he agreed.

They sat at the enormous table covered with cauldrons of fish, vegetables and fruits. Time and time again Esther jumped to her feet and poured water in their glasses, discussed various subjects with everyone around the table, leaving after each interjection the impression of great knowledge and wisdom.

Later that day, with lunchtime over, I followed Saul, Corto and Paris into a study. It was there that I was finally introduced to Saul, and heard firsthand of his work.

"It's not only amazing, it's absolutely glorious!" This proclamation astonished Paris and Corto who, having just sat down, had never witnessed Saul exhibit such excitement. The promise of triumph hung on Saul's curbed lips, lending an air of genius to the man.

"Hear this!" Saul said, his eyes beaming. "We know that cells always regenerate themselves. Some organs take a few months to be fully composed of entirely new cells, whereas others take years. This natural process insures an organ's wellbeing. Unfortunately, if that organ is afflicted by a disease, its cells not only become infected but also contaminate newly created ones, since those come from the same source. What I'm exploring is a way to maintain the level of purity of a particular organ. To have the newly regenerated cells escape the grasp of infection simply by appropriating another subject's energy, one free of infected cells."

"And this energy will always prevent a newly created cell from becoming infected?" asked Paris.

"Preliminary experiments are encouraging," replied Saul. "To be certain, research scaled through years of observation is needed. Yet I believe that these newly regenerated cells, even after mingling with the infected ones, will preserve their immunity for a longer period."

"How exactly is the energy transferred from one body to the next?" Corto pursued.

"For this," Saul explained, "we need someone with a gifted mind to meditate in harmony with the one afflicted with a disease—one also with a gifted mind, of course. Such treatments take time . . . weeks . . . perhaps months, and can only cure an illness which is not yet alarming, for the curing of a grave disease, I suspect, needs the help of a third party. Let me explain. For the past few years I have been studying a book dating back thousands of years and which details the use of The Eternal Energy. Nobody knows where this book was written, but I do know that it found its way in Europe during the Middle Ages. Aware of this, the Church ordered it to be burned. As you can imagine, the owner buried it, until many years later it ended up in my study. Then one day, as I was examining a drawing, a beam of light struck the page. Not knowing if I was dreaming or not I examined the drawing more closely and noticed, for the very first time, a detail which had previously escaped my scrutiny. Follow me, I will show you."

He rose from his chair and led the way into another room. In it, rows upon rows of books adorned the many shelves. The light of day had slowly dimmed, and Saul, intent on showing the drawing, lit a lantern and set it on the large wooden table. He walked towards the shelves, lifted the heavy, ancient tome, and placed it on the table. The sheer sight of it felt like I was traveling back centuries in time.

"Ah! Let's see now," Saul said, turning the pages. With a deep sigh, he gazed at a drawing of a man lying in bed, who was staring at another man standing before him and whose hands, inches apart, seemed to be handling some sort of energy mass.

"Look, there," Saul insisted. "Next to the one lying in bed, notice the brightness in the drawing, and how the man standing up peers in that direction, and not towards the sick one. Of course, there's a faint sparkle between the man's hands, but that sparkle pales in comparison to the brightness in the room's corner."

Saul took a step back so that Paris and Corto could examine the drawing more thoroughly. With the deep furrows of mental exertion, Saul very slowly paced around the room.

"At first I thought this detail was nothing more than a glossy smudge," he explained, "which is a natural assumption considering the volume's age. Then I focused on the Sanskrit text next to the drawing, which was added by the twelfth century Buddhist Saint Milarepa and which mentions a Being of Light in the room. Until now, I had always believed the man standing up to be the Being of Light. But what if the Being of Light is the glossy spot we see here?"

Nodding and sighing, Saul recollected his thoughts.

"I'm onto something," he said, calmly. "I know I am. There has to be a connection between the sparkle between the man's hands and the brightness in the room's corner."

Having listened intently to each word, Paris seemed to wake up from a dream.

"The sparkle between the man's hands is the reflection of another light," she whispered.

Saul looked intently at Paris, and asked her to repeat, which she did:

"The sparkle you see is the reflection of another light."

"Yes!" Saul said, excitedly. "A light I feel shares a close destiny with the reflection. My dear Paris, if you possess any information pertaining to our subject, please, I beg you to share it."

Not sparing any details, Paris first spoke of the liberation of a soul, then about the miracle in Trinidad.

Saul deeply pondered. "Hmmm! I see," he said, endlessly nodding his head. "I understand the predicament more clearly now, although this also offers more hypothesis to consider. How is it that Michael, after enhancing your powers, accompanies you everywhere you go?"

"I have a question," Corto said. "One which has been puzzling me. Why were Michael and Paris' powers insufficient for Maria's revival?"

"By that you are referring to the help provided by Melina, the woman you rescued?"

Paris and Corto nodded.

"Perhaps her role with Maria was to supply a missing morsel," Saul volunteered. "A morsel Paris may in the near future possess. One she will need to earn through an upcoming trial. Then again, perhaps that morsel was denied so that the Universe could realign Melina with the Original Design that had been altered when she had been forcefully taken away from her village."

Rubbing his chin, Saul fell silent, as if becoming aware of another consideration. "You know, Paris," he said, in a calm voice, "I have this premonition about you."

His quick eyes revolved around the room. He walked over to a table and, in one swift motion, grabbed a knife which served as a letter opener and sliced his left forearm before Paris or Corto had time to react.

Blood spurted from the wound, in pulsating gushes that dripped on the tiles. Paris and Corto stood speechless for a few seconds.

"I'll go get a towel," Corto said, rushing towards the door.

"No!" Saul cried out. He searched his pocket and took out a handkerchief, which he pressed on the gash, under the very eyes of Paris, who winced and contemplated achingly the line of blood trickling down the length of his arm.

"I have not gone crazy," Saul insisted, his eyes limpid. "Do not be afraid, dear Paris . . . and let me come close to you." Hesitant and panting, he moved towards her. "Please, put your hand on my wound, and let us both meditate on its healing. Though this is a slight variation of the regeneration process I spoke of earlier, it's one I must conduct."

Paris contemplated the bleeding arm coming closer and closer.

"While I seek the energy sent from your mind," Saul said, "I beg you to only entertain thoughts of the Divine, as you no doubt often do."

Obeying Saul's command, Paris clasped her fingers around the blood-soaked handkerchief.

"Yes, no need to apply great pressure," Saul encouraged. Moments later, Saul instructed Paris to quit her meditation. He removed the handkerchief, and stared with meticulous care at his arm.

"This is far better than expected!" he exclaimed. "To have cells instantly regenerate. This is absolutely remarkable!"

Corto leaned over, and gasped upon seeing the dark red healing tissues that indicated that the scarring process was well under way.

"Can you imagine what would happen if we spent hours on it?" Saul excitedly cried. "No doubt, the scar would be lighter and flatter. Perhaps even gone."

Paris, trying to ascertain all of the implications, exhaled deeply.

"If my abilities are greater," Paris said, "then, as you pointed out earlier, why is Michael still around?"

"This is what I believe is happening," Saul replied. "What if the Being of Light's mission consists of locating a kindred spirit? A being endowed with a gifted mind and able to reflect, a little perhaps, but reflect nonetheless? A being able to one day shine from within?"

"You mean . . ." Paris hesitated.

"Undoubtedly, my dear Paris, you were already capable of harnessing, to a certain degree, The Eternal Energy. But what Michael did when entering your body in the hospital room was to authorize your access to bigger samples. This was the reason behind my self-inflicted wound; to see how potent your mind had become!"

Saul looked at his scar, amazed. "That you had already reached the fourth level is something I had suspected last year. Still, what you just did even Leticia could not achieve. No doubt, you have reached a more advanced stage. To me, it appears you are on the very brink of the fifth level. And the only conclusion as to why Michael continuously follows you around is because there's more to come! Don't you see? What I believe is that Michael, under a great command from High Above, was sent to witness the virtues you possess before approving your final passage into the Kingdom of Heaven!"

Here Saul walked yet again towards the volume lying on the table. He stared profoundly at the drawing, and smiled, as if he had uncovered mankind's greatest secret.

"That's what we all aim for," he murmured. "The Kingdom of Heaven."

"What exactly is Michael looking for prior to this confirmation?" Corto asked.

"Well," Saul began, clearing his throat. "I believe the virtues of faith, love, charity, sacrifice and forgiveness are all virtues that lead to the ultimate level of purity. Look at the lessons bequeathed by Jesus Christ, forgiving mankind as he was being nailed to the cross. The people who witnessed this wrote about it. Those people who had followed him and relayed his message beyond the shadow of his departure, making sure that this tragic moment in humanity survives the ages. That message is there for inspiration. Yes, forgiving your worst enemies for an abominable crime most assuredly demonstrates the soul's utmost purity."

Saul briskly paced all around the room, unable to contain his growing excitement, then abruptly stopped.

"My dear Paris," he said. "I believe you are but a step away from mastering by yourself The Eternal Energy. This is what this Being of Light is here to confirm. He's on a mission from God to make sure that the next Ascended Master is pure and worthy. Mankind has been waiting two thousand years for someone to lead it out of the shadows. I ignore what trial you will face, but one thing is for sure, if you succeed, a great role awaits you!"

They left the study shortly after, while I stared at the drawing for much of the evening, churning everything I had seen and heard. Both Saul and Paris had spoken about the reflection's destiny. But what about the light's destiny? Throughout this journey, I had witnessed Michael and Paris' increasing powers. Then it struck me. The soul's evolution in both worlds—that's what this journey was all about! I began to see a mysterious design in the works, yet unable to grasp its full significance, I exited the room.

* * *

Early next morning, Corto endlessly paced the length of the verandah, staring, as a sailor always does, at the stretch of sea before him. This time, however, I detected an unusual trepidation in his composure when, in fact, the sight of deep blue waters always brought him peacefulness. Believing this to be linked to the unspecified trial awaiting the one he loved so dearly, I approached, hoping to offer comfort when a powerboat came into view.

Corto leaped forward, grabbed the railing with both hands, and narrowed his eyes. Menos, at the bow, was clearing a path around the underwater sentinels. On the boat's flybridge, two muscular men, unknown to Corto, could also be seen. So this was the reason behind Corto's uneasiness. I wanted to tell him that perhaps some logical reason had compelled Menos to head back to the continent the previous morning and make it here accompanied, but stopped, for the sight of Jorge at the helm filled me with disgust.

Corto ran up and down the hills, towards the carved staircase. It was there that he met up with Menos, who confessed how a discussion with Jared in St-Vincent had prompted him to conduct a bit of research.

"A lot of people," Menos said, as he jumped out of the boat onto the narrow path, "are wondering about this island. Wondering what will be discovered."

"Is that right?" replied Corto. His eyes travelled over to Jorge and the two men, still aboard the boat, before settling on Menos, who was securing the lines around the boulders.

"A lot of wealthy people," Menos added, "who wish to know firsthand about some research."

I looked all around, tried to feel Michael's energies, yet curiously he remained absent.

Then Jorge, satisfied that he could disembark, leaped over the railing and landed next to Corto.

"Finally," he boasted. "I have the pleasure of meeting you again, John Corto. Your wife and you are known throughout the Caribbean, thanks to your charitable work. Unfortunately for you, you dispersed into the ocean something of great value to me."

"As expected, I'm sure."

"Of course," he laughed. "When Menos suggested this trap to discover the location of this so-called famed island, promising the drug's weight in gold if I went along, quite naturally I valued his offer, though I now wonder if the offer was not a bit light."

At those words Menos' face turned inquisitive, and he asked Jorge to clarify what he meant.

"Ah! The bliss of ignorance," Jorge teased. "So priceless!" He put his hand on Menos' shoulder, and closed his grip forcefully. "What I meant," Jorge resumed in a subdued, threatening manner, "is that whoever hired you must surely be capable of doubling the original offer. Why do you think I insisted on coming to this isolated piece of rock in the Atlantic?"

A few feet away, Corto, his hands perfectly still, keeping his breathing deep and measured, examined the scene with studious eyes.

"I want more money," Jorge whispered into Menos' ears.

Menos' face became very pale. At length he recovered some color, and looked sheepishly at Jorge. "You'll get your money as soon as we return to the continent," he promised, his eyelids blinking erratically.

"Remember," Jorge hissed, "I want double!"

"Yes . . . yes . . . of course," Menos mumbled.

Jorge released his strong grip, and approached Corto.

"Now, maybe it's time I go upstairs," Jorge said. He looked at the carved staircase. "There's another person I'm anxious to see—your wife! Yes, the one with the magical eyes. I haven't forgotten her."

Corto's hands moved slightly.

"Never mind going upstairs." Corto blurted, his fingers twitching. "Do you think they'll agree on doubling the price? Think about it. With Menos surely in touch with whoever hired him every step of the way, how many islands are there in this corner of the world? Pinpointing this island and identifying the researcher is a question of time, this without Menos' help. But there's a surer way to get your money."

Surprised, it took a few seconds for Jorge's widened eyes to return to their normal size. "Go on," he said, with a smirch.

"There's a man who'll pay your ransom, an American politician I can summon on the continent. But there's a condition."

"I'm listening."

"You and your men stay in the gorge, and tomorrow at first light I'll go with you to Kourou, in French Guyana, to settle this matter. Only there will the ransom be paid. Once done, you may even try to kill me, as I suppose you will, but the deal goes down on the continent."

Hearing Corto's proposal, thoughts of a covert plan entered my mind. One which involved the secret evacuation of the island's inhabitants while Jorge was away on the continent. Looking at Jorge's devilish sneer, I perceived that he, also, had guessed Corto's plan.

They remained close to one another, their eyes locked in a prolonged stare. A tense, impenetrable silence followed. The hatred between them intensified. Then Corto, wishing to bait Jorge to accept his proposition and unable to restrain the war cries in his heart, said:

"My spirit and body, as of now, have united and become one. Men of action who have tasted combat, feel their spirit suppressed when away from the battlefields. The outcome has already been decided. All that is needed is for us to enter the arena. By the glitter in your eyes, I see that you agree. You and I were meant to die in battle!"

* * *

Later that evening, Paris and Corto strolled around the house, barefoot, their feet sinking in the pleasant grass. Earlier in the day Corto had relayed to her, in great details, the meeting held with Jorge and Menos. It had been a demanding task. He had stressed the importance of him leaving alone while the rest evacuated aboard D'artagnan.

Holding her hand, he looked at her with eyes concealing the fate he felt most assuredly awaited him. A week ago, they had sought protection. A safe haven. An isolated place where they could have conceived of alternate arrangements.

Corto cleared his throat, and reiterated his plea. "I have to do this." He needed to convey the urgency of the situation without raising panic, although his speech clearly demonstrated a warrior's ruthless insight. This came not only from his nature and training but from a deep conviction of his unique role to serve the Universe with gestures only he could execute.

"I need time to think about all of this," Paris said, her eyes moist, her composure rattled. She shook her head, troubled by the disclosure, then went inside the house.

Moments later, Jared approached Corto. Having been briefed, like everyone else, on the meeting with Jorge, he looked at Corto—at the flames burning in his eyes.

"You're going to wage a battle of some sort, aren't you?" he exclaimed.

Corto turned away, and walked towards the cliff.

"I want to come with you," Jared proposed, pitting his body next to Corto.

Though Corto remained silent, the imminence of war intensified. Wave by wave it seemed that the mighty Atlantic was chipping away at the cliff.

"I'm coming with you!" Jared insisted.

"Drop it!"

"Never!" Jared said in a louder voice. "You can't deprive me of this. I'll fight you, if that's what it takes!"

The steadfast outburst shocked Corto. He stared deeply into Jared's eyes, which under a clear moon reflected a silvery resilience.

"This isn't your fight," Corto bluntly said.

"Not my fight?" Jared shouted, indignantly. "How do you know this isn't my fight? You, who always says that the battles choose the knight, and not vice versa! What about the rituals encouraged all along this journey? Weren't those aimed at developing one's noble potential?"

Jared paused, his eyes alive with the certainty of his purpose. He stared at Corto, and explained that his whole life had been marred with illusions. "How can I better the world, better my soul if I'm not allowed to pursue my destiny?"

Corto tried silencing him.

Promptly Jared lifted his tightened fists in a daring boxing stance, a further proof of the undiminished ferocity framing his intentions. Resolutely he vowed he could never return to his previous life, not after witnessing what he had been allowed to see. He talked of little Maria's miracle, of how vibrant life felt through the spray-filled air, of how strong the spirit becomes when at sea.

His voice trembled, tears filled his eyes.

"I can't go back, not anymore," he cried. "What good are any of my trophies if I lose my soul in the process? I know now that to strive for something you can't bring over to the other side is useless!"

Memories of his former life haunted him. Dreams of his true destiny inspired his rage. "No wealth amassed over handshakes equals the sensation of charging through the waves under thousands of stars," Jared said. "You, above anyone else, know that life is self-denied to many of the living. For the first time I know why I came into this life. Let me have this moment. This moment which contains the treasures of my destiny!"

With no more words escaping Jared's lips, his stern features softened, albeit they still bore a grim firmness, one I knew could not be totally erased. As the sound of the raging ocean grew stronger and stronger, Jared turned around and closely observed the seething waters. He, who at the beginning of the journey had behaved so ineffectively at any of the nautical skills.

He shook his head, and grinned when recalling aloud that distant epoch. Then he smiled, for these savage waves that had unsettled his stomach, a long time ago, presently proved to be his most prized argument.

With a wide sweep of his hand he gestured at the brewing tumult of the sea.

"Captain Corto!" he shouted. "You know you'll need me. Just look at those waves. By God! You, with all your sea experience should recognize the necessity to bring me aboard."

"Sailors brave these conditions all the time when crossing oceans alone," replied Corto. I couldn't help but notice how the winds had picked up and snatched away the foamy crest from each wave, creating a sustained curtain of mist.

"Yes, perhaps, but they do so without trained killers after them, don't they?" Jared replied. "Please, tell me how you intend to defeat Jorge by yourself. Let me guess. You probably thought of drawing them into shallow waters, though because of Thairica's draft you would in all probability run aground first. And then what? Turn yourself into some sea-creature and surprise all four of them? Did you consider that they most certainly carry weapons and will shoot you as soon as you swerve from their plan?"

As the implications of that last question sank into Corto's mind, his eyes considered the man before him under a new light.

"If this happens," Jared hastily pursued, "you know they'll come back here. And you know what will happen then, don't you?"

"You know I can't afford to have Jorge or any of his minions come back to this island," Corto replied, in a concerned voice. "For that, I'll do whatever it takes."

"For that, you'll need a partner," Jared remarked. "True, I don't have your skills but, what I do have, my will, my desire to win, is all yours. I may not be a soldier, but I am a soul on a mission. Take me!"

Far away, the dark horizon devoured one by one the stars that had ventured too low. And only high above did light seem everlasting.

Corto pondered, haunted by visions of Jorge and his minions out there, within the vast inscrutable expanse of sea and sky.

"What you say is true," Corto admitted, thoughtfully.

* * *

After this discussion, Corto wandered around the house.

"My fate is not what worries me," he told me. "A warrior must never worry about his time of death. But what about Paris? Why did the cosmic forces ever conspire for our union?" He shook his head pensively, and retrieved from his shirt pocket the small box given to him by Leticia. He examined it, as if undecided on which course of action to take. He stared, deeply, wearily, wondering if the box contained the answer. Wondering if that answer would suit his purpose. Wondering if opening it constituted a betrayal of some kind. It was a hard decision. He held the box, unsure of what to do.

The sight of Paris exiting the house halted his examination. With a swift movement he quickly inserted it back inside his pocket. Rushing alongside her, he encountered difficulties maintaining the rhythm of her very decisive strides. They stopped, lied down on the grass, and a few seconds later Corto was struck by her request. With loud gasps of protestation he voiced stern objections to her plea that they summon help from the outside.

"We are relatively close to Les Iles du Salut," Paris insisted. "The continent is near enough for a navy frigate to be here in a matter of hours. Why don't we call the authorities with the satellite phone?"

"Because in all probability, Jorge would be freed sooner than expected and he would come at us with a vengeance. This is a risk I must take, for the sake of all."

"Then I'll come with you," she snapped.

Promptly Corto propped himself up.

"No you won't," he vehemently protested. "This isn't your fight."

"Don't you dare suggest that you know my destiny better than me," she voiced in a tone at once subdued yet commanding. Raising her upper torso so that she rested on one elbow, she faced him. "You would like it to be so clear, wouldn't you?"

"What do you mean?"

"I know you all too well," she said, testily. "You relish this dilemma. This situation inserts itself so well in your quest to learn what course of action is permissible by the Creator, for at long last your eyes and not your faith, will erase any doubts. You proclaim that faith is the absence of confirmation from the eyes. Yet here you are, eyes burning with this lust for combat. This lust which secretly appeals to your heart, happy to wage an unwinnable war!"

He looked at her gravely.

"You have never doubted me before," he said, visibly shaken. "I've lived through all sorts of warfare, from ambushes in the deserts to clashes in rainforests, and never have I encountered an opponent crafty enough to surprise me."

His prompt response forced her to momentarily look away. Their long standing divergence had succeeded, over time, to wedge them apart.

"Life is not a fairy tale," he said, solemnly.

She looked into his blue eyes, and slightly shook her head. "Too bad," she whispered. "The ending is always so beautiful."

She turned away.

"Look at me," he said. With gentle fingers stroking her cheek he forced her eyes to look into his.

"If I wasn't a man of faith," he suggested, "I would have slit Jorge's throat and buried his carcass where Oliver's body was found instead. I had feared such a possibility, yet did nothing to prevent it."

"You can't always act on possibilities. Not when your actions can burden your soul. Remember, murder is never part of the Original Design."

"We've had this discussion many times," he said. "You wish for me to deny my instincts. But at times like these, perhaps the blossoming of YOUR Original Design is what matters most. A design which can only be achieved through my nature."

She gazed into his feverish blue eyes and seemed to detect a distant sparkle that he tried to conceal. Again she made a plea to go with him.

"No, no, and no," was the answer. "Your place is with the children, with the research. And though this advice comes from a man of war, it's the only one that makes any sense. We are justified in defending ourselves. It's legitimate."

"I'm not talking about being legitimate," she retorted, her cheeks reddening. "I'm not even talking about being right. I'm talking about what's good, about what's true. You think death holds the meaning of life, but it doesn't. Faith holds the meaning of life."

"Faith and beliefs, I agree. But YOU are the one called upon from High Above. YOU are the one chosen to shape mankind. This I deeply feel. And if I must die in the process, then so be it. Nobody else can face this threat. Nobody! There's no need for you to join this expedition. All that matters is that you stay alive."

"How can you even say that? How can you even believe yourself of lesser importance than me?"

There was a long silence spent looking into each other's eyes. He gently curled his arm around her neck. In need of closeness, she quietly let her head drop onto his chest, and both reverently stared at the stars . . . for a few seconds.

"Something else is troubling you," she murmured.

"What makes you say that?" He shrugged his strong shoulders, and feigned not knowing what she meant. But when she repeated her concern, insisting that he came forth on a night of such importance, he appeared caught off guard. He shifted on the ground.

Observing his uneasiness, Paris resolutely pursued her intuition. "There's something else lurking in your heart besides the desire to solve this riddle, isn't there?"

The moon's silvery rays shone in her eyes, touched his heart, and enticed a confession.

"Paris, I can't do what you do," he confessed, passionately.

His emotions surged forth, and the next moment, in a louder voice, he sought the justification of his skills. "Give me a battle. Pit me against Evil, so that Good may triumph. This proves simple, easy. Easier, in fact, than helping others the way you do."

"And you think that sacrificing life and limbs will compensate for this?"

He lifted his eyes and beheld the sky.

"Fighting is what I know," he admitted. "It's what I do best. I thought that by virtue of sacrifice I justified all of the years spent honing my skills, this while insuring a proper karma."

"Unbelievable!" she exclaimed, amazed.

"You heard Saul," replied Corto, adamantly. "Faith, charity, forgiveness, all virtues I strive to attain. Sacrifice, on the other hand, is right up my alley. To die for a good cause is perfect for me."

"Are you serious?"

"Yes!"

"My love," she said, calmly. "I, who know you best, can testify for the purity of your beliefs."

A waterfall of fingers stroked his chest, and put doubts to rest. "Your heart is magnificent," she complimented. Her embrace brought back souvenirs of their union. Exquisite souvenirs which made the urgency of the situation seem distant and quiet. After kissing, they looked up at the thousands of prickling jewels spread across the great sky.

"You're beautiful," he whispered. "Because of you, I've learned to love myself, and that's a miracle."

"Shhh! Don't say that."

"And yet, I feel that now is the moment to bear my soul. You've always been the only one for me. Do you remember our first meeting?"

"Yes," she said, after hesitating. Then she looked at him with a forced smile.

"You looked absolutely splendid," he declared. "Even after the nasty horseback accident you suffered days before." He stroked her hair, touched her cheeks, felt her breath on his neck—that breath which had given him life.

"I love you," he said. "Always have, always will. It's your love that binds all of us together."

He turned away, sighed heavily, seemingly confused and uncertain about what to say next. And though he had spoken from the heart, Paris felt his strength scurry away to a secluded arena. All through her passionate embrace, his spirit had left his body and gone to faraway battlefields. He tasted Paris' lips, yet did not quiver from their exquisiteness. In silence, he devised combat strategies. Such vital moments spent fighting windmills.

She embraced the shadow of her husband, absorbed his ghosts in silence, all the while choosing not to share hers, knowing all too well that distractions kill soldiers faster than bullets. She didn't care about what was justified, or right. She cared about what was good for him. But grave thoughts surged from within, and this time her shivers proved too compelling not to be felt. There was some drama behind those green eyes, too overwhelming not to be prodded.

"Do you recognize Aldebaran?" he asked.

She didn't answer.

"Right there," he said, pointing his finger. He tried piercing her silence and searched the confines of her eyes, until her smile halted his examination.

"Yes, Aldebaran," she acknowledged. "The first star we spotted together."

"You scared me. I thought you had forgotten."

"I haven't forgotten that evening," she reminisced.

"Seems like just yesterday," he said. "We had left the Mai Sai hospital to visit the nearby temples, where you wanted to watch our first sunset together. You looked at the sky with a pensive expression, hoping, perhaps, that the Heavens would surrender some sought and undiscovered mystery. It was a fantastic sight! Moments later it appeared that Aldebaran's grand appearance finally answered your prayers, found its way into your heart, and overwhelmed your liquid eyes. I have asked myself many times what possible instructions had been enclosed in this revelation. But I never intended to pry your privacy. For I was already in love with you, had been before you ever saw me."

Paris quivered, muffled a faint groan and turned her head slightly away.

"What is it?" he asked, the tip of his fingers caressing her face. The ghastly past had awakened her innermost chambers, with the closeness of their bodies enabling Corto to detect the feeblest shiver, to feel her heart's minutest disturbance.

She held her breath, bit her lips. "It's nothing, my love," she whispered. "Just promise me you'll return."

She struggled not to burst into tears.

"I will," he vowed. "I promise. No matter where I end up in the universe, I will never cease searching for you. Never!"

"Now," she cried, "make this night ageless and forever, and hold me . . . just . . . hold me."

* * *

I flew to the other side of the island. Near the cliff, Jared held Esmeralda's face between his hands. Delicately, he kissed her, as the mighty sea raged below.

"You're absolutely priceless," he told her. Her presence brought forth a desire to sail to the edge of the world. To experience an incredible journey, one within the reach of the daring spirit. Somehow that thought had a profound effect. All that they had shared flashed before him. The dance. Her towering personality on the construction site. The way she had perceived him on canvas—heroic, bold, victorious. By then the joy, the elation of having found a soul mate had stirred Jared's emotions. Tears formed in the corner of his eyes.

"Tell me why this is happening now?" she asked.

Jared, enthralled by her dark eyes, appeared unable to answer. Confused thoughts charged through his mind. But then the waves, thundering below, brought him back to his senses. The spray, rising high into the air and whipped by howling winds, stung their faces. Once again, the wild ocean had spoken. Reminded of his commitment, Jared willingly suppressed the regrets of leaving her.

He leaned forward, and held her hands. "You remember telling me that knowing who we are comes before anything else?" he asked.

"Knowing our true destiny is the greatest treasure."

"My destiny will unravel tomorrow, and God willing, I'll see you again, now that I understand the meaning of Thairica."

"Tell me."

The glimmer of victories emerged from his eyes. "The exhilaration of new horizons, of new lands and blissful sunsets. The people we help as we sail from latitude to latitude. The meditations under a star-filled sky which bring us closer to a higher consciousness. The flame for high adventure which once ignited, launches our spirit beyond the Milky Way. That's Thairica!"

She absorbed his interpretation, pulled him closely, and observed that he had reached the level the Universe had set for him. He had acquired an immense wealth—his purpose, his destiny.

Two thoughts came to me upon hearing Jared's interpretation of Thairica.

First, life, because of its mysteries and seductive origins, had gilded his spirit through a series of encounters. Like the all-powerful sea, life, captivating in its form, dignified in its might, created solely for the purpose of sustaining other lives, cherished him in its embrace.

The second thought pertained to the name given to those sailors roaming the oceans while building their inner temples.

They were Celestial Sailors.

Meeting our Destiny

It was the middle of the night. Corto and Jared, standing on the verandah, were discussing strategy when Paris noiselessly opened the door and insisted on seeing her husband alone. Then, once Jared had gone inside the house, she informed Corto of her decision.

"That's the way it's going to be," she decisively concluded, after telling Corto that she was coming along.

"This is madness!" Corto shouted, in an astonished tone. "We had an agreement. What happened in the last few hours for you to change your mind?" Her decision had put his protective instincts in turmoil. Corto gasped, threw his arms up in the air, and grumbled a few words.

A short distance away, I perceived an ethereal jewel that glimmered in the darkness. A soul not seen since coming on this island.

"No, daddy!" Michael pleaded upon seeing me approaching. Just then he vanished. Only once, and this prior to brushing against Oliver, had I seen my son with such a starless stare!

Right then I knew. Death would come to one, perhaps many.

For a few minutes, Paris tried to soften Corto's resilience. She spoke of a look given to her earlier by Michael.

"What did the look mean?" Corto asked, narrowing his eyes.

"To follow my intuition," she answered, delicately.

"That's it?"

"That's enough!"

Corto shuddered from her proposition. Their children's fate and threats uttered against Paris the previous day accounted for the pain in his eyes.

"We will leave them in good company on this island," she volunteered, as if reading his thoughts. "If you sweep aside my proposal, you willfully reject the stages of development from which you draw much inspiration. There is no alternative to one's inner voice, the one we train to recognize the murmurs of Spiritual Guides and other Heavenly Beings, the one we know leads us to fulfill our destiny."

He considered her words.

"One's calling must never be denied," she resumed. "We live by a Code and must abide by it, especially in confusing times." She beamed with such might and conviction that Corto's resistance vanished.

"You speak the truth," he finally replied. "Still, you must understand why this brings hesitation and uncertainty."

Reaching out for his waist, she pulled him closer, at once sensing, through the indistinct whisper of his loose embrace, his suppressed objections. Though the delight normally associated with her body seemed absent, as if his arms were enclosed around thin air, her soothing voice and gentle words progressively gave her form.

"I'll go along with your decision," he said, brushing her hair away from her eyes. "But I must ask, and this for the sake of our children. What will become of us?"

He trusted the purity of her eyes, looked deep into her soul, very deep, and knew the answer before it was spoken.

"Truly, that's something even Michael ignores," she answered. "He follows his faith, and so shall I. I don't know what will happen, only know it must happen."

* * *

"Remember, Paris," Corto cautioned, a few hours later. "You must come down the steps only when Jorge is out of view. I want to make sure that he doesn't see you."

She nodded, and gently took his arm by the elbow. In silence, Paris, Corto and Jared moved along the obscure path that took them through the hill's swells and crests towards the gorge.

Shortly before dawn they arrived at the top of the carved staircase. Nervously, they peered at the vague shape of Jorge's powerboat, hundreds of steps below.

With a subtle gesture, Corto pointed to a spot near the staircase. Moments later all of us discerned a few silhouettes that broke the darkness. Abruptly shouts rang throughout the gorge.

"Bunch of incompetents," Jorge raged. "Stuck here and forced to watch over complete idiots instead of going up and making sure that they're not up to something."

"But your eyes saw the same thing we did, Jorge," one of the muscular men answered, baffled. "The tide! An unbelievable tide! The way the gorge filled up with rushing waters only to retreat seconds later, lifting the boat and pulling the lines almost to the point of snapping them—it was complete madness. All of us had to remain here to protect the boat."

"Then how come those two sailboats were never threatened?" Jorge shouted suspiciously, pointing an angry finger at Thairica and D'artagnan. "How is it they are tied to the same boulders, in the same fashion, while their lines never tightened nor slacked? And don't you dare tell me again that it was something surreal, some *divine act* as you put it, or I'll stab you in the eyes with your own knife, you moron!"

Joyful thoughts of Michael entered my mind. Though I still remembered his tragic eyes, the force that had compelled Jorge and his men to stay in the gorge instead of invading the island had been of his doings. I just knew it.

Finally, it was time to go. Accompanied by Jared, Corto descended the precipitous staircase, leaving Paris concealed, following their every movement. There she waited. Her nervousness betrayed by irregular breaths.

Next the sound of engines reverberated throughout the gorge. Moments later, anxiously gripping the powerboat's helm, Jorge waited to exit the gorge.

"Why aren't you coming?" he asked, irritated. Thairica's engine was running, but the vessel still remained tied to the boulders.

"It's a tight squeeze," Corto answered. "I'll turn around and come out only when you're in the open ocean."

Growling angrily, Jorge slowly motored out of the gorge, casting repeated glances at Corto and Jared.

With Jorge and his men out into the open ocean, Paris allowed herself a deep sigh of relief. She climbed down the steep steps, grabbed Thairica's lines, turned the bow to face the exit, jumped aboard, and quickly went down the companionway.

Out of the gorge and around the lurking sentinels the voyage to the continent started, with a fresh December breeze and following seas. Two hours later, Les Iles du Salut stirred the eastern horizon. They came and went, and as we pursued the voyage to the continent, Michael appeared. Above the top of the mast he hovered, his tranquil eyes watching Jorge's boat motoring behind Thairica.

I wondered what possible activities had kept Michael away. I flew to him, expecting to hear that he had visited his mother and brother.

"Your daddy wants to know if he can visit you," he said.

I was speechless. That thought had never crossed my mind. Unable to think clearly, I decided to take my time before giving my father an answer. I started to relay my decision to Michael, when promptly he vanished. Not knowing what to make of this, I entered the cockpit. Jared, at the helm, stared at the continent severing the horizon. Next to him, studying a nautical chart, Corto weighed his options.

"What are your plans?" I asked Corto.

He discreetly shook his head. "Paris coming with us changes everything," he whispered. "I have to make sure she's safe. That's my only concern."

"How?" I pressed.

He shrugged his shoulders. "God only knows."

Suddenly Paris emerged from the companionway and swiftly made her way over to the aft deck. There was a methodical way with which she had done so.

"Paris!"

Instantly Corto jumped from his seat and grabbed her arm.

"Paris, get back inside!" he ordered.

She ignored his command, and remained in plain view.

"You've given me your love, and for this may you be blessed," she said, tears running down her face. "Now it's your trust I need. And no matter what happens here today, know that I, too, will never cease searching for you throughout the vastness of the universe."

Progressively fear made its way into Corto's eyes. He looked behind to see if the others had caught sight of her. Again he tried convincing Paris to go inside the cabin. Inexplicably, as she stood there, she seemed to beckon some attention, which she won when Jorge's sick grin traveled across the sea.

Corto looked at her. Her eyes were decided. Moreover, she touched his cheek, and smiled, as emotions at once joyful and dramatic rose from within.

"A supreme power instructed me," she said. "This power must be followed. You must understand."

A spark of light racing towards the top of the mast caught my attention.

"Michael!" I cried. "What have you done?"

I looked back, and saw Jorge producing a pistol from under his shirt. Judging by the way he angrily hit the helm, I knew that murdering Paris had become his sole obsession.

On seeing this, the concern visible in Corto's eyes vanished. The grim resolve expected from the soldier prior to an attack took over. Forcefully he took Paris by the arm, commanded her to take place inside the cockpit, then nudged Jared aside and took the helm.

The strong breeze had so far enabled Thairica, sailing under full canvas, to maintain a speed of sixteen knots, admittedly no match for a dangerously gaining powerboat. Horrible thoughts entered my mind as Jorge, after getting replaced at the helm, jumped on the foredeck. What fury that man possessed, as he exhorted the helmsman to go closer. Uninitiated as I was to criminals, it was hard for me to fathom the existence of a more despicable being.

I looked at Michael. Sparks exited his eyes. Suddenly a freak wave rose from the heaving ocean and crashed against the powerboat, undermining Jorge's balance.

For a second all of us believed Jorge was going to tumble into the sea. But Jorge regained his balance and swiftly jumped back inside the cockpit.

Twenty miles away, the coast beckoned. A possible refuge, unfortunately beyond their reach because the winds had suddenly died. The ocean lifted and lowered Thairica in its pulsating embrace as Jorge, back at the powerboat's helm, circled around like a shark with its prey. Unable to start the engine, Corto stared at the hoisted sails, uselessly fluttering.

Again I looked at Michael, whose beaming eyes answered my silent appeal. Suddenly a milky veil rolled across the water. Nearer and nearer the fog came, stretching out its vastness, tugging everything effortlessly into its misty breast until Thairica's mast, sails and hull vanished without any protest.

Rumbling sounds of Jorge's boat came closer before growing distant. Wishing a joyful ending, I moved next to Michael.

"Please," I begged, "favor a destiny in which Paris, Corto and Jared survive, and not Jorge."

Michael stared at me. Flickers of a jeweled sunrise beamed out of his eyes. All at once I felt ashamed. How dare I harbor such thoughts, when but a short while ago I had sworn allegiance to God, promising never to question any events after witnessing Maria's revival.

Resolutely, I turned my attention to the actions to come.

As expected, Corto's combat instincts took over. He closed the radio, conscious that any sound could betray their position, and examined the many luminous screens, where nothing but irrelevant readings emerged. Next he lowered the dinghy into the sea so that it could provide an instant alternative, for all knew the perils of coastal navigation. Especially in fog!

"Make sure you hold on to something at all times," Corto cautioned in a low voice, should they suddenly run aground. With his index finger pressed upon his lips, he commanded silence, while his eyes darted all around. Then he crossed over to the foredeck, listened for a while, before reentering the cockpit. He shuffled tensely. Once more he jumped and crossed over to the pulpit, leaned forward with both hands holding the rail, his eyes and ears attentive to a fog filled with concealed men relentlessly searching for an opportunity to kill them. He tip-toed back to the cockpit.

"Why not use the dinghy?" Jared whispered.

"The engine would give away our position," Corto replied. For the next few minutes Corto extracted from many storage spaces all kinds of objects. A vast array of knives, flares, jugs of fuel and spearguns. Then, with the serious will of a soldier planning battle, he again consulted the nautical chart of these waters.

As if by magic a gust of wind filled the sails. At once Thairica heeled at a slight angle, its bow slicing the waters as if aware of the destination. Amazed, Corto beheld the mysterious peculiarity with which the vessel sailed. Taking the helm, he followed a course he believed ran alongside the reef-strewed coast.

The chase persisted.

On occasion, Jared's deep and intense breaths seemed to puncture holes in the heavy fog, awakening the pursuers to their position. Every time this happened, the sounds of the powerboat's engines surged on one side and crossed over to the other, tracing some unknown and wild course.

There was sheer madness in these maneuvers.

"They're circling around, hoping to ram us," Corto informed. The knowledge of enemies close by had expanded his eyes and deepened his murmurs.

Tense moments passed before Jared broke the silence. "I fail to understand his obsession," he whispered. "Jorge risks hitting the same reefs as us, only at a greater speed, and possibly be killed in the collision."

The eagle eyes of Corto intensely searched all around, and he raised his head and smelled the air like an animal longing for a scent. "Jorge follows his heart," Corto replied seconds later. "No matter how insane or dark the pursuit."

"But he's human," Jared protested, "and as such should be ruled by the instinct of self-preservation."

"Trust me," Corto admitted, gravely. "I've seen the likes of him many times. Although he is at the present time a human traveler, he cannot contradict his essence, which in this particular case is nothing less than pure evil."

Jared nodded. "Pure evil," he murmured, with a touch of disdain. After a short moment which gave him the time to reflect, he asked about Jorge's seething hatred towards Paris.

"Jorge recognizes in Paris the exact opposite of himself," Corto explained, his eyes leveled into the one he loved. "Since Paris represents the splendor of Light, one who strives to deliver beings from suffering, one who teaches and shows the way, what Jorge amounts to is that destructive and wicked speck wandering the fringe of the universe. The one that scorches with his touch, cursed and forever damned. An unholy spirit caught in a diabolical cycle, materializing from one body to another. I understand the beast quite well, considering that in St-Vincent he praised his hammering skills!"

They listened attentively. Again Corto deftly jumped out of the cockpit, walked all around, unable to remain motionless for more than a few seconds, in search of answers the fog would not disclose.

"What about their radar?" Jared whispered.

"I've been keeping my attention on all the instruments. I'm guessing that, same as us, all they're getting is incoherent readings."

That the equipment was incapacitated by mystic forces at work seemed natural to Paris, whose face had remained passive upon hearing this. Jared's eyes, however, widened unbelievably at every bird cry he mistook for a nearing enemy voice. Many times I tried summoning enough will to provide help, to relay Jorge's position, to allow Corto to stretch their safety zone. But I couldn't, since the specter of my limitations prohibited any unmerited influence.

Suddenly a shrieking noise came from the front. It grew, tore the silence apart, and sounded like the suffering of metal. Fear consumed everyone's eyes just as a prodigious jerking motion rose from beneath their feet. Abruptly everything stopped. Bodies crashed into one another. Corto got back on his feet, ran up and down the deck, then reentered the cockpit and informed that Thairica had hit a reef.

"Everybody in the dinghy!" Corto ordered. They moved to the aft deck just as the boom crashed through the awning, slightly cutting Jared's forehead before hitting Corto behind the neck, pinning the unconscious Captain under its weight. Horror could be seen in Paris and Jared's eyes. Very thoroughly I searched everywhere for Jorge's boat when I noticed that the fog was thinning.

"Quick!" Jared said. "Let's get him inside the dinghy."

Paris and Jared fought their way amid collapsed sails, torn canvas, tangled lines and twisted metal. The winds grew. Murky sights of land appeared. Paris and Jared pulled and pushed and lifted the wreckage pressed against Corto's body. Then the noon sun, poised on making an appearance, shot through the lifting fog a polished light that reflected shiny dimples on the surface of the sea. The faint rumbling of engines added to the terror and merged with the waves crashing over the reefs that were holding Thairica captive. Of the protective fog, only a thin veil remained, one I knew would soon completely fade away. The rumbling rose. The sounds slipped past on both sides and circled around when in a sudden flash of light the fog dissipated and exposed the closing range of the pursuers.

With hands under the fallen boom, the weight of which crushed Corto's body, Jared tried to lift it. Nothing happened. However, as he did so, by sheer destiny, Jorge's powerboat also ran aground. But this relief was short-lived, for Corto's body appeared impossibly trapped. With great resolve, Jared struggled to free Corto. Under his hands, feet planted on both sides, the boom rested like an immovable object.

Repeatedly he and Paris tried lifting the heavy obstacle, and seeing how difficult this proved to be, I expectantly looked at Michael. His eyes gleamed brighter than ever before, and he appeared detached from everything outside the range of these individuals below him. I remember thinking of his powers, uncertain if he could handle the design entrusted upon him. I also remember thinking how surreal this all seemed—the ageless battle of Good versus Evil.

Then a strange sense took hold of me. One which spoke of a blessed little soul having undergone strict examination since joining the realm of the after life. My core throbbed with excitement. Having witnessed the birth of miracles, another great privilege was given to me, as I observed four souls, through the virtues of faith, forgiveness, sacrifice and hope of salvation, meeting each of their fate. Here I beheld beings of different stages, each pursuing their destiny while battling the forces of Evil.

With all of his strength, forehead gleaming with blood that streamed out of his cut, Jared exhausted himself completely. Struck by this sight, I looked intently. Then I remembered. No wonder I was experiencing *déjà vu*, for this sight had already been immortalized on canvas. How incredible. Jared's posture—the one Esmeralda had re-enacted on canvas, was relived. Here. Now. Only instead of crimson sweat dripping down his forehead, it was blood that was trickling out of his wound.

Seeing this, Paris appeared dazzled. Choosing to remain silent, she combined her strength to that of Jared. At last their efforts were compensated and, once having cleared the object, Jared shouted:

"On your feet, soldier!"

That command stirred Corto, who looked up, rose to his feet, staggered briefly, disoriented, then jumped inside the dinghy. Twenty yards away from them, Jorge and his men also embarked in a dinghy of their own.

"No time to lose," Jared said. He vigorously pulled the start cord, and beheld helplessly how his many attempts had failed to breathe life into the engine.

"We have to row," Corto ordered.

They paddled their way to shore, encountering very tricky conditions created by the surf. Luckily, Jorge's attempts at starting the engine had also failed. He hit the engine violently, swearing and kicking it. Just then rushing waters coming at Corto's dinghy from many directions combined to overturn the rubber craft. Exhausted and pale, they desperately tried to reach the bank some fifty yards away.

At length their efforts were rewarded. Gradually supported by the flood tide, they walked in waist-deep waters until the bottom rose from under their feet. With cold clothes clinging to their chilled bodies, they cleared the water, their feet hungrily swallowed by the wet sand. Then they trudged their way towards a lone road that appeared before a line of palm trees, in turn guarding a lush forest that stretched high and wide.

"What now?" Jared asked, panting excessively.

"Now we look for help," Corto answered. He breathed heavily and rubbed his hands over Paris' shoulders.

Unaware of where they had landed, they walked along the deserted road, and stopped. A signpost nearby indicated the town's name—Sinnamary.

"Look!" Corto shouted, his finger directed at Jorge's craft gliding at great speed across the waters.

Down the road they ran. Sights of a church appeared at a distance. Jorge and his men were just behind. Moments later a gunshot was heard. Corto searched all around and located a demolition site, which they entered. It took but a few seconds for Corto to realize his mistake, as this maze of dilapidated walls on the verge of collapsing over broken bricks, pieces of glass and refuse of all sorts offered little protection from Jorge's crew, now entering the site.

Suddenly the winds picked up. Red dust instantly filled the air. Watching Jorge breach the distance, Corto, unable to suppress his feelings, turned to Paris. "I don't understand why you insisted on coming," he said. "All I ever wanted was to protect you."

He had failed her. Still, uncertain as she was of her own fate, Paris looked unafraid. Briefly, her eyes sank into those of her husband, obeying a sudden urge to seal, in that precious stare, the entire world that they had built.

Corto went to her, opened his arms for her embrace, and violently fell to the ground when hit behind the head by Jorge's pistol.

"That's for opposing me in the first place," Jorge growled. "Finish him off!"

Immediately the two muscular men, Menos opting not to participate, rushed over and repeatedly kicked Corto's prone body.

Meanwhile, having struck Jared on the head and kicked him into unconsciousness, Jorge turned towards Paris. He dangerously moved in her direction, eyes red with anger.

"I've been dreaming of this longer than you've lived!" he shouted. Once within striking distance, giving in to his savage fury, he delivered a powerful blow to her face. Blood flew in the air, as Paris crumbled to the ground . . . for the first time.

"Stop!" Menos pleaded. "There's no need for any of this."

"Then you're a fool," Jorge replied, undisturbed, "to think you can only go a certain distance when following people you know nothing about."

Jorge forcefully grabbed Paris by the hair, and pleasurably slammed her face on the bloodied ground. Time and time again.

Unexpectedly a great cry rose from the piled bodies and supplied Corto with added might. Precise and powerful blows dished by Corto interrupted Jorge's brutal treatment. As the hits multiplied, I fathomed a victory for the man overturning the odds and unleashing his rage on his opponents' faces. Incredulous to such a prospect, Jorge followed the fight with an amused expression when, pushing away the two men's limp bodies, Corto lunged forward and brought him down.

For the next seconds a ruthless battle for control of the pistol held in Jorge's hand took place. They rolled and twisted on the ground like two savage animals locked in mortal combat. Corto tried prying the pistol from Jorge's fingers. He saw it as the key to their survival. Seeing how difficult this proved to be, Corto tried to drill his fingers in Jorge's eyes. But when Jorge turned his head away, Corto switched back his attention on Jorge's hand, sinking his teeth into it. This was immediately followed by the two men who, having shaken off their blurry vision, charged and pinned Corto to the ground.

My hopes plummeted. With a primitive growl, blood flowing from his mouth and nose, Jorge grabbed Paris by the hair and yanked her back to her knees.

I could not let this abomination last any longer, even if it meant the implosion of my soul and complete disappearance from everlasting existence!

I summoned all of the atoms of my being and channeled them for a single purpose; kill Jorge! With a wild cry I plunged inside his ribcage and, seeking to inflict the worst possible agony, I clasped my hands around his heart. Driven by hatred, my eyes fastened on a pulsating organ of the darkest kind, I tried ripping and tearing it apart! To my great distress, nothing happened. Again I looked at Michael to implore his intervention, and knew immediately by the beams of light racing out of his eyes that the horror taking place below him had already galvanized his soul.

He hovered above the ground, too magnificent to have come from anywhere else but Heaven. He had its allure, its splendor, and also the power over everything under the sky.

The torture taking place had increased his radiance. He intensely observed Paris, on her knees, repeatedly hammered in the face until she crumbled . . . for the second time. A few feet away, Corto fought one man, when another sneaked behind and pounded him on the head, rendering him unconscious.

"Enough playing," that man said, as he produced a knife from under his shirt.

Suddenly, from as far as the eye could see an avalanche of lightning poured from the sky. Clouds menacingly rolled across the horizon, dark and thunderous. Crude gusts of wind shook the palm trees, snatched the foam right out of the white crests raging in the Atlantic, and where Michael hovered there surged a flash of blinding light.

I could not turn away from this sight. Through the light's gleam, a faceless vortex appeared. One I believed embodied a power of infinite might. One charged with a harsh and profound task. One I also knew to be Michael.

Under some formidable amendment, Michael's present form hovered on the outskirts of the after life. Charmed with the gift of visibility to mortals. Uncertain as to what they were faced with, the men looked at each other, confused. And I must confess of the joy I felt, for I knew that concealed in this light awaited an unforgiving scale ready to weigh each of their sins.

"What the . . ." the man holding the knife gasped. He winced, dropped the weapon, and achingly looked at his scorched hand. "What is this sorcery?" he yelled, turning to the others who, same as him, could not formulate an answer.

"Let's get out of here," Menos shouted, fearfully taking a few steps back.

"Stand your ground!" Jorge blurted, dangerously raising his pistol. "Or I swear I'll kill on the spot."

Down below, I perceived movement on the ground. Did I really see a brick moving by itself? I looked at a piece of glass nearby and detected at once the same faint tremor.

Suddenly a great rumble pierced the air, and the horrible clouds rolling across the sky appeared packed with a wrath ready to rip Earth into pieces! Abruptly the ground trembled, and the hundreds of trembling sticks and shaking bricks seemed to eagerly await further instructions.

Realizing that the rising tumult was somehow linked to the luminous entity hovering before them, the men hurriedly bunched closer together and tried to fit behind Jorge who, with one hand, savagely lifted Paris to her feet.

Ever so slowly, Menos and the two men opted to step back, careful to avoid any of the items fiercely pounding the ground. Yet as they moved, the blazing light followed, ten feet above the ground, dreadful and terrifying. They looked into that light, when amid this brilliant vortex progressively ignited until becoming a white fire, a face started to take shape.

Aghast, I stared, unwillingly. For though hovering close to such an entity, trying to pierce the revolving, burning layers, though I vaguely recognized the features taking form, I experienced anguish at the thought that this moving white fire was, in fact, Michael.

They retreated a few more feet, when the hundreds of bricks and sticks and pieces of glass froze the blood in their veins and compelled them to stop.

"Cowards!" Jorge screamed. "Afraid of a little sunburn?" He laughed wildly, his cheeks retaining the exaggerated stretch of his sinister madness. Then as if to prove his bravery he angrily struck Paris. With a fiendish grin he contemptuously stared at the ground, which trembled and roared.

"I've been waiting for this day all my life!" he shouted with insulting mockery. He angrily shook his fist, spat at the white fire, at the sky, his eyes blazing like the flames of hell.

Torturing a woman in front of this heavenly manifestation did not bother him at all. His hostage was his guarantee. The weapon clasped in his hand procured insurance. Furthermore, because of his nature, thoughts of his death did not scare him—so long as he brought along the one he so terribly despised.

"You're coming with me," he hissed. He tucked the pistol in his waistband, bent over to pick up the knife from the ground, and stabbed Paris on the right side of her chest. Blood gushed from the deep wound. There are no words to describe what I felt when she crumbled for the third time.

I turned around.

"Michael!" I screamed. "What are you waiting for? Kill that monster! NOW!"

A long and piercing wail escaped Paris' lips. Regaining his senses, Corto lifted his head. Struck by the horror of Paris lying next to him, blood gushing from her stab wound, somewhere in the deep confines of his soul emerged the necessary strength to mount an attack. He leaped towards Jorge who, with a trace of delight, raised the knife and stabbed him in the abdomen. With an arrogant sneer, Jorge watched Corto fall.

Bleeding and helpless, Corto looked at Michael with deep, poignant, and provocative eyes. As the seconds passed by, Corto's grim features gradually softened, as if Michael's eyes had somehow answered his silent plea. Corto smiled faintly, yet he smiled nonetheless.

"So valiant the way you fight until your dying breath," Jorge whispered in his ear. He grabbed Corto by the back of his hair. "For these are your dying breaths."

Despite Corto's precarious fate, there seemed a peaceful comfort in his half-closed eyes, something Jorge found very annoying.

"Your eyes seem so at peace, my friend," Jorge inquired. "How can this be?"

"I'm not afraid of you," Corto muttered. "I know where I'm going, and that's fine with me."

A look of spiteful animosity swept across Jorge's face. "Really?" he taunted. "Very well. If death doesn't scare you, then you won't mind me slashing your whore here in front of you and sending her along, won't you?" He shoved Corto's face to the ground, and laughed when seeing the blood pouring out of his stomach. Again Jorge's steel fingers grabbed Paris and lifted her to her feet like a rag doll. Unable to rise, Corto stretched out a bloodied hand, and cried out:

"Paris!"

Jorge grinned.

"Don't you touch her!" Corto screamed.

Jorge slightly leaned towards Corto. "You see how accurate I was that day, at the restaurant? I was right all along—your kind exists only through mine. We come from the same source."

He savagely yanked Paris' head backwards.

"Ugh!"

"Yes!" Jorge exulted, savoring her agony with blood-shot eyes. "Cry if you must, for this magic of yours will not save you." He relished her sufferings, and grotesquely licked his lips while inching the knife next to her eyes. With a sickening delight he twirled the blade.

This was too much for me to bear. Wishing to once again plead for Michael's intervention, I turned around and saw him suspended in the air, wrapped up in the revolving folds of this white purifying fire.

Michael gravely stared at the squirming ground. Objects hopped and dropped and bumped into each other when one in particular, a sharp-edged brick, rose effortlessly higher than the others and remained motionless, waiting.

Then came the moment I had wished for, when before my eyes the brick flew forward with an unbelievable precision, and severed Jorge's hand from his wrist.

When Jorge realized what had happened, he raised a horrible cry. That sound quickly spread around, attracting all eyes to the foot of the furthest wall where Jorge's hand lay, fingers senselessly wriggling around the knife's handle. But that was not the end of Jorge, who quickly buried his stump under his armpit to stem the thick sprouting of blood.

"You think this will stop me?" he screamed. He stretched out his good hand and forcefully grabbed Paris by the throat until she coughed out blood and fragments of broken teeth.

"You now see how alike we are," Jorge growled. He contemptuously spat in her face. "Good or Evil, we share the same color of blood."

Progressively he released his grip, made certain that she could stand on her own, then inched his good hand towards his waistband, towards the pistol he had tucked there.

Unexpectedly, pleas for pity arose from Paris' mouth.

"Haven't you filled your thirst for blood?" she muttered, painfully.

Jorge looked surprised, although the cruelty of his face did not abandon him.

Perceiving that Jorge had rejected her appeal for mercy, Paris invoked, yet again, through words barely audible exiting her badly battered lips, his redemption:

"I beg of you, let us go, for your sake."

She stared at the shaking ground, lifted her head, and gazed at Jorge, unblinkingly, with eyes free of anger.

Jorge's fiendish laugh answered her supplication.

Again Paris implored mercy, convincingly, only this time, she looked at Michael:

"Please, forgive him."

These few words had an immediate impact. But instead of gratitude, Jorge's eyes bore, if possible, an even greater hatred. Like a panicked animal he struck her face, clawed at her eyes.

"Take that back!" he furiously protested. "Take it back! Take it back!"

He pulled her face closer. Stronger and stronger grew his rage, as he choked Paris with the insane viciousness of a devil.

Paris felt his tightening grip. She summoned all of her strength, looked him in the eyes, and said:

"I forgive you."

"Oh, no you don't!" he shouted, his eyes consumed with fear. "Trying to save me? No, no, that won't work. No, today is the day you die! The day you all die! And after I'm done here, you can watch from the after life the way I'll strangle your children one after the other!"

As Jorge's incendiary remarks were met by a look of deep pity from Paris, I quickly turned towards Michael. A being composed of white fire, in appearance somewhat like a child, but not innocent, with eyes like golden meteors. For a few seconds, nothing aside those golden meteors seemed to exist, as the fury of a formidable storm began to form and grow until impossible to contain.

Then the wrath of Michael thundered!

Out of the hundreds of pulsating objects, one of them, the biggest square brick around, rose higher than the others and remained suspended, for a fraction of a second. Suddenly it flashed forward and decapitated Jorge—his head rolling twenty feet away from his body!

After striking Jorge, the brick ferociously exploded against the wall and made a large imprint. Just then an old black woman entered the site. Amazed, she watched the spectacle raging before her, and with her right hand repeatedly crossed herself.

Turning around I saw Corto, kneeling next to Jared, who had just regained consciousness, while Menos and the two men exchanged frightful looks between one another. Here and there the bricks, once picked up by this invisible force wielded by Michael, were hurled forward, slicing the air before grooving upon the wall an ever growing imprint. And at the crossroads of this storm, through the dust-filled air, Paris' face showed a mosaic of emotions.

One after another the sharp objects flew dangerously close to her. She steadied her legs, raised her arms parallel to the ground, and remained perfectly motionless. Deadly projectiles, at times flying in tight formations, relentlessly outlined her body. Fearing for their safety, Menos and the two muscular men cowered behind Paris.

High above, through thick and dark clouds, a light of golden and purple shades beamed down and struck Paris. This luminous blessing crowned her head. Ever so slowly Paris rose two feet above the ground, while the projectiles hurled by Michael poured like a waterfall all around her body, which she kept rigid even if hovering, her arms still held parallel to the ground. Down below, Corto hugged the ground, and felt the bricks and sticks wreak havoc. Worried for her safety because the objects flew so close to her, he cried:

"Paris! Paris!"

He carefully observed those beams of light plunging into her head, and seemed fearful of her fate. She was all that mattered to him. Would she leave? Had her time come?

"Stay with me, Paris!"

The lashing winds screamed. The sky raged.

"Stay with me, Paris!" The appeal came from the deepest part of his soul. The sight of Menos about to flee the shelter her body provided interrupted his pleas.

"Stay behind!" Corto ordered.

"I can't stay here!"

"If you try leaving, you'll be buried here!"

Ignoring the advice, the two muscular men dashed towards the road, each of them completing but a few steps before being struck and killed.

With great devotion, Corto stared at Paris. He knew of her faith, knew the weight of her decision, and wondered if earthly life even stood a chance. A powerful struggle took place opposing the realms of two different worlds. Heaven appeared to her, dangling colorful and magical images before her captured mind. They made her smile, they made her cry, and by the way she looked at Michael, she revealed her choice.

She had reached her treasured level, as did Michael, whose revolving folds of fire, in the most surreal fashion, magnificently expanded at the top of his shoulders. He flew to Paris, smiled, touched the side of her chest to halt the bleeding, then dissolved into thin air. Abruptly the objects stopped their assault and resumed their normal inertia. With the clouds above us dissipating, the light crowning Paris' head dimmed progressively, just as her feet regained contact with the ground.

Many people, alerted by what was to be known as The Great Storm, rushed onto the scene. Mouths opened, eyes filled with tears, they walked towards the wall.

"Do you see what I see?" a man asked. Uncertain, he lifted a shaky hand, and lightly touched the sign which had been grooved by the flying bricks.

"Do you see what I see?" he repeated.

"I see it!" the old black woman exulted. "I witnessed the whole thing," she added, beneath her breath, and with her right hand she again obsequiously crossed herself. Her eyes widened. She spoke to all that came, eager for her testimony.

"I saw the whole thing," she repeated. "I saw the flying lady. I saw the white fire with the golden eyes. I saw the judgment for those three dead men, and I saw . . ." Here she sobbed. Words failed her when trying to explain what she had seen last.

Several gasps of wonder were heard. More people came. They crowded around her and repeatedly asked about the imprint.

"I saw the birth of this emblem," the old woman declared, tearfully. She wiped her eyes with a handkerchief, and added:

"This is the mark of Christ!"

A greater crowd assembled, anxious to hear the old woman's testimony, which she gave.

"All my life," she confided, "I waited for such a sign from God. God does animate every sunray, reside in every raindrop, awake every sunrise, and reveal Himself in every smile you arouse. Always have I cherished the conviction that what turns a simple musical note into a symphony is not linked to the stage, but to the inspiration."

She told everyone what had taken place, finally able to describe Michael's shape at the end of the encounter—a shape I will divulge to you later . . .

Having heard her testimony, the crowd walked timidly to the wall where already dozens of men and women were praying under the geometrical figure consisting of two lines perfectly intersecting one another.

"If I were you, Menos," Corto advised, "I'd forget about the little trip to the island."

"But I have to tell what happened," replied Menos. "It would be wrong not to tell."

"It's not a question of right or wrong," Corto gasped. "It's a question of doing what's good. Now, if you'll excuse me, I would like to be alone with my wife."

Corto staggered, his shirt drenched with blood, towards Paris who, observing that his hands applied pressure to his abdomen, rushed to him.

"Allow me," she said. She pressed her hands on his stomach. "Everything is fine," she declared a few seconds later.

Seeing that everybody seemed involved with things of their own, I searched for the co-author of the signature on the wall. The more I searched, the more I saw people struck by the majesty of the seal left upon the wall, the more I realized the achievement of Michael's design. This led to the possible conclusion that Michael was gone. Surely, he would return, I told myself . . . hopefully.

Just then, loud and persistent shouting filled the air. Insults quickly rose within the commotion. Though love had been present at this sight mere moments ago, anger had chased it away. Why? Looking closely, I noticed that the place thronged with people divided into two sides, engaged in some fruitless argument. It was a sight like so many others, built by beliefs, but quickly corrupted by skepticism. Then blind pride took the colors of different flags. That's when violence erupted. Relentlessly, men and women shoved and pushed, debating at the top of their lungs the significance of the imprint. What did it matter? For whether it was a disavowal or a deep conviction of the imprint that fuelled this mob, the clenched fists of one side and bruised flesh of the other were set to wander the same after life. Sadly, such a conclusion never entered their preoccupied minds.

Saddened by the unrest, Paris promptly made her way near the source of their dispute. Her mere presence silenced the crowd. Trembling fingers wished to touch her. Some, at the sight of her injuries, shrieked in horror before fainting.

She was the bloodied voice Evil had wished to extinguish. A mass of butchered flesh and broken bones limping before them. Bruises and deep lacerations covered her body, while her cheeks, atrociously deformed, had swollen to such a degree that it covered the nose, which had totally caved in. Her eyes, barely discernible behind bulging eyelids, appeared drained of their emerald magic.

Tortured yet indomitable, Paris pointed at the imprint.

"Please, do not claim ownership of neither events, nor diagram indented before you," she began. "For I entreat you to see in this symbol the mark of love, with no particular denomination. This should never become a shrine under a particular banner."

She paused, and sighed with relief as she gazed at the imprint shaped for rejoicing and hope, experiencing none of the suffering associated with the encounter. Already, a serene expression worked its way across her face, influenced by the source of the imprint more than the contour. Addressing the expectant crowd, Paris said:

"Struggles are meant to inspire the ascension of your immortal soul, and that path resides between your soul and God. The Kingdom is within you. Different denominations should not argue this symbol. No one should claim ownership of Heaven, notwithstanding how devout they are. For such a conduct brings neither privileges nor blessings in the after life. Your temple will be great when you seek your soul's purification, when you seek to return to God with the highest level of consciousness, enhanced by your deeds and forged by all that you love."

* * *

Prior to these memorable events, the town of Sinnamary had been of little interest for tourists. Most of the people traveling to French Guyana, which is an oversea department of France, choose to visit Kourou, where one can visit the Space Agency, or Cayenne, the capital. Since Christianity is predominant in this country and since, according to the calendar, the events at the wall had occurred on the twenty-third day of December, you can appreciate the interest sparked by the testimony of an old devout woman.

News of the event instantly travelled around the globe.

Scores of networks urgently came and knocked on her door the same day. Letting them into her home, the old woman passionately explained to the news crews how, on her way to church, she had witnessed The Great Storm—a battle of Good versus Evil.

"Hundreds and hundreds of bricks flew by themselves," she excitedly related. "They missed the flying lady by a hair! By a hair, I tell you, before crashing against the wall and grooving the sign where the people go to pray."

"And can you tell us once again what force lifted those bricks?" asked a reporter.

"The bricks, the sticks, the pieces of glass—all of these were commanded by Heaven's most powerful sentinel!"

You remember I told you that when fearful for their safety the men had sought refuge behind Paris, her body rigid even if hovering, her arms held parallel to the ground? Such was the shape presented to Michael who, upon returning his tempestuous acknowledgment, had carved the unmistakable imprint of a cross!

Those who cherished faith saw in this imprint the undisputable mark of God and since Christmas was but two days away, the fervor rose. Others, however, thought that the sign was nothing else than a vague shape of indistinct features, thought that The Great Storm was nothing but a ploy.

How uninterested and uninspired some people become under their tedious, bleak, and regulated lives. Have the sunsets forever lost their splendor and amount to no more than the inevitable coloring of the skies due to the ageless rotation of the Earth?

The next day, Paris, lying in a hospital bed, observed how two French doctors intensely stared at her. Through the windows facing the Atlantic Ocean, an inspiring sunrise plunged inside the room. Corto, standing next to Paris and lovingly holding her hand, amusingly observed the doctors' bewilderment. Clearly, their hushed voices did not approve their machine's diagnosis.

"What do you mean no broken bones?" one doctor asked.

"The X-rays show that—"

"Never mind the machine!" the doctor interrupted. "The machine is wrong! It must be wrong. Look at the pictures taken when she was admitted yesterday."

Stares travelled incessantly from pictures to patient.

"*Mais, c'est incroyable!*"

Her injuries had healed remarkably, so much so that only faint traces of Jorge's brutal treatment appeared discernible.

"*Mais, c'est absolument impossible!*" the French doctor insisted. "*Ce n'est rien de moins qu'un miracle!*"

His colleague's open-mouthed expression only validated that deduction. On the left side of the folder a doctor held were stapled several pictures of Paris taken the previous day. The laceration on her abdomen, the broken cheekbones and pulverized nose, the enormous swellings and cuts on her battered face, all of these betrayed an encounter of unparalleled savagery.

The doctors intently stared at the pictures, then at Paris, and no matter how often they performed this ritual it always failed to produce a logical explanation. Some accelerated molecular process, unheard-of, unthought-of as of yet, was working its magic before their very eyes!

Uncertain, with a serious but polite tone, one doctor turned to Corto. "You, sir! he cried. "Are you not her husband? Can you explain this recovery?"

Corto shrugged his shoulders. He narrowed his eyes, and guessed, from the doctors' insistence and skepticism, that they intended to keep Paris under observation for an unspecified period of time.

"God knows," he simply said.

"But you were with her when all of this happened," the doctor insisted. "You walked beside the gurney, held her hand. And did you not sleep here overnight?"

"Yes, that I did," Corto acknowledged. "In this very bed, and not for a minute did my hand let go of hers."

"But wait a second," the other one interjected. "Did you not come here with a fresh and hideous scar on your stomach? Are you not the one some say was stabbed by the knife found in an amputated hand? Are you not the one some say miraculously recuperated after a brief touch of this woman's hands?"

The doctor quickly crossed the close distance separating them and lifted Corto's shirt. His cheeks reddened. "Forgive me," he said, embarrassed by the absence of any scar.

Corto stood still, stared at them, and yawned.

"Come," the other doctor suggested. They exited the room, their quick eyes stealing a last peek at Paris before the sounds of their footsteps echoed down the corridor.

"How come they never inquired about Jared?" Paris immediately asked in a faint voice.

"Simple, he was never admitted," Corto answered. "His injuries didn't present any danger, and as we speak he's taking care of retrieving Thairica from the reefs."

"How's Thairica?" she asked.

"She's afloat."

"That's all we need."

He kissed her hand.

"Please, John, I know that complete madness will follow us hereafter. I just wish to board Thairica and sail to Saul's island to continue the research. There's still so much to discover."

"You really think it's wise, after what happened?"

"It's my destiny."

"Yes, I agree, although you might consider a short rest before returning."

She smiled. "Ah, my love, I can't begin to describe this Force which flows through my veins. Now that we know the path to The Eternal Energy, more will join us, and we will finally be able to rid the Earth of disease, war, hatred and domination."

He looked at her admiringly, attentive to her words. She had made known her purpose of bettering mankind.

"Is there still a place for me near you?" he asked, uncertain.

She brought his hand to her lips, kissed it, and quickly consoled his sensibilities. "You think all of the cosmic forces which conspired for our union would have done so if it wasn't forever? The Universe is not that cruel."

For the first time since her admittance he let go of her hand, which I knew had been used for joint meditation. He leaned over and held her. She felt vulnerable in his arms, and that pleased him. But that embrace had stirred his very core. An inner voice spoke to him.

'Soon, the day will come to reveal this diamond to the whole of humanity,' the voice said.

He shuddered. This was something many religious leaders would never accept. That the Chosen One, The Prophet of God, was a woman!

"You need to rest," he said. He kissed her, tenderly, and as soon as he closed the door behind him his eyes precipitately took a grim expression. Trembling, he leaned against the wall to recuperate from a sudden weakness in legs that had always been invested with steady power.

"You seem troubled," I remarked.

Eyes filled with mist, he looked at me, confused. "No doubt, like Paris once said, the Universe doesn't throw at you what you can't handle."

These words, he had uttered in a voice filled with doubts. He shook his head, pensively. "Her purpose was revealed from High Above," he said. "And though she insists that there's a place for me by her side, I wonder. I mean, I really wonder. What help could an Ascended Master require?"

He seemed lost. Reluctantly, he produced from his shirt pocket the small box given to him by Leticia. He held it up in the palm of his hand, dreading a prophecy he did not wish: that of a future without Paris. His strength seemed to pour out of him in a steady stream.

This sight proved quite uneasy for me. I felt like a boy losing his hero.

Like a lost spirit, he opened the box, and like a revived spirit, he closed it. Instantly he recovered the fullness of his might. I was freshened once again by his sight, and before I could ask what magic the box carried, he shouted in the exalted voice of one discovering a sought treasure, “I shall fulfill my destiny!”

Wishing to satisfy my curiosity on another matter, I inquired about the particular stare given to him by Michael.

“For a long time,” he answered, weighing each word, “I was uncertain of my journey, this because of what I did and what my nature enables me to do. But no more! Light is the soul’s best friend. I know now why my path was drenched with blood.” His certitude reflected in the tightened muscles of his body. He raised the box to the level of his eyes. “And this, on top of the silent instructions given to me by your son, confirms it. In front of you stands a man liberated from a distressful paradox.”

An ultimate mission enlivened his eyes. His soul had been created solely for that task. Already he had a presentiment of upcoming dangers. Corto wasn’t afraid, but he needed to prepare. His blue eyes seemed to have grown bluer. Now that his skills had reconciled with his spirit, he had reached the mastery of himself. He embodied the ultimate warrior. He had the wisdom, the might, and he knew exactly which road to take.

He turned to me and said:

“I must sit down, meditate, and journey to the lands of The Great Spirit for guidance. There, I will meet up with many of God’s sentinels and gain valuable insight for the upcoming battle.”

In the middle of the corridor he sat down and crossed his legs.

“I know my role,” he declared in a most convincing voice. “There is a message that needs to be delivered! Inner temples to be built! But many will try to stop us. Luckily, there are sentinels everywhere.” He smiled, closed his eyes, and added, “Even in the jungles of northern Thailand.”

Celestial Sailors

The next day, after leaving the hospital, Paris and Corto went to a restaurant near the mouth of the Sinnamary River, where they joined Jared, already seated at the terrace.

"I can't thank you enough for what both of you did," Jared declared, "and allow me to vow fidelity to the Celestial Sailors."

"Are we to believe that you no longer care about what others think of you?" asked Corto.

"Precisely," replied Jared. "I no longer belong to their world."

As his words were met with smiles, he said:

"Perhaps you can also provide details as to the entity at the center of The Great Storm."

The inquisitive glimmer in his eyes was intense. "You see," he resumed, "I was often told of such entities during my youth, and was absolutely astonished to see one just a few feet away from me."

"Ah," Paris gaily replied. "That soul, like all of us, was engaged in a path of spiritual elevation of its own, this until becoming one of God's most powerful sentinels."

Moving closer, I noticed a lofty glitter wavering above Paris' raven hair, like a golden halo, and knew immediately of her lasting coronation.

"And what about the other entities you spoke of when I first set foot on Thairica?" Jared pursued. "About Spiritual Guides responsible for the ad I answered?"

Here Paris smiled, and her widened eyes exuded a mystical gleam. "Spiritual Guides are uncanny beings. They are the hesitation you feel before dangers. They are the tingling that precedes desires. It's your intuition that brings you into contact with them. Modern psychology designates such beings as your conscience, yet fails to explain its origin. It's quite sad, really, this need to erase all of life's enchantment. To view sunsets as the natural rotations of the

Earth. To believe that loose floorboards and dampness are solely responsible for a house's creaking noises. Our soul is not an illusion, it's magical."

"Speaking of magic," Corto interjected. "Would you say that the potency of a spell is conditional on the skill used, or, mind of the beholder?"

"I guess both," she answered. "Why do you ask?"

Here Corto pointed towards a sloop that lightly swayed on the gentle swells in the harbor, its bow pointed towards the open sea suggesting a predisposition to swiftly sail away.

She looked intently at the smooth lines of the sloop. "That's D'artagnan!" she exclaimed, just as Saul, Esther, Esmeralda and Emilio entered the terrace.

With much joy Paris asked aloud where her children might be. Then, as everybody casually retreated, Corto pulled Paris close to him. There seemed some sort of agitation behind his eyes, like a lingering secret he wished to share.

"Everything of value I owe to you," he began, taking her hands. "You came to me like a fresh breeze, gave life to my existence, a destination to my journey. I've learned, from my travels and quests, that you don't divide the summit from the mountain, the waves from the sea. These come together, joined for the pleasures, as well as for the trials."

He wrapped his mighty arms around her, and whispered that he loved her, again and again, with the ambitious voice of one endowed with a mission. Her eyes sparkled as though she was about to cry. Words failed her. Then the excited giggles of two young boys travelled across the terrace. Paris swiftly turned around and saw Matthew and Danny rushing forward, each of them carrying in their small hands a gold pillow with something shiny in the middle.

"I trust you'll approve my choice of ring boys," Corto said.

"What?"

"Ring boys!" Corto exclaimed. "To renew our vows!"

For a long moment, all I saw was a tight assembly of bodies. Then Corto picked up one ring and slipped it on her finger.

Paris, deeply moved, raised her hand above her eyes and admired the sunrays striking the ring. It meant everything! A renewed commitment, the love of the only man she ever loved. But what was this strange emotion rising from the depths of her heart? Her intense breathing betrayed a mysterious awakening. She closed her eyes and felt her body assaulted by the ghosts of the Orient. Resolutely, she abandoned herself and was able to detect another message. Paris listened to that voice, at last faintly nodding as if to say, "This is it."

Hesitantly, she opened her eyes just as the voice of her heart heightened its insistence. "There is, my love, something you should know," she said. "Something I wish to confide to you."

"Something that happened along the Mai Sai River?" Corto asked.

"You knew!" she whispered. The swift coloring of her cheeks spoke of her sudden amazement.

"Of course I knew," he declared. "Why do you think I acted so strange on our last night together on Saul's island? All I ever wished was for you to tell me."

"And," she said, hesitantly, as thoughts of another attack at a Red Cross campsite came to mind. "What did you do when you found out?"

He kissed her gently. "You have nothing to worry about. Everything I did was approved by the Universe. This I know from a little boy's stare. Now, I have an important question to ask. Do you accept to spend the rest of your life with me?"

"Our destinies are forever linked," she said. She took his hand and slipped the other ring on his finger.

"Where did you get those?" she asked.

"In Antigua. They were gifts from a very wise person." He felt secure and at home. The strong were conceived to protect, and he would not concede an inch—not one, damn, miserable inch to anyone wishing to alter the Original Design bestowed upon her by the Universe. He knew his destiny. Like a faithful husband, he would love and support her. And like a sentinel, he would guard her.

Mankind was in desperate need for Paris. She had been called upon through the mutilation of her soul, appraised by the purity of her faith, elevated through her unconditional love, and confirmed by the splendor of her forgiveness.

A forgiveness Jorge had desperately tried to invalidate. Evil, the inseparable shadow of Light, had recognized Paris. Ever-present and relentless, personified by the likes of Jorge in this case, Evil had sought to prevent the birth of an Ascended Master. That was why Jorge had panicked upon hearing Paris' forgiveness, for that emotion, displayed truly and without reservation, had sealed her achievement. And this only underlined Michael's formidable challenge, having to witness Paris' agonizing torture, all the while suffering because he was uncertain if she would ever reach the treasured level.

* * *

I shared one last conversation with Corto prior to my departure. This took place while Thairica sailed back to Saul's island. There he was, alone in the cockpit, grinning like a child on this Christmas Day. Winds and spray danced on his face. In the vast expanse of blue and white water in front of him, every rolling wave left its mark on his immortal soul.

"People tend to complicate everything that comes to them, when everything of value is free," he told me. "The love of your spouse, that of your children, and especially the sunsets."

Corto stared at the distant horizon rising and falling beyond the pulpit, then turned to me. "My dearest friend," he said, smiling, obviously intent on insuring I receive his message. "I was told your father wishes to see you, and beg you to consider how easy and fluid the momentum becomes once inertia is vanquished. Hope only requires thoughts. In utter darkness, a single spark is all that's needed to supply a bearing."

He touched the compass, tightened his grip on the helm. An astronaut of the sea. His eyes sparkled from a thought he wished to share:

"Deep within we're all Celestial Sailors, spirits navigating through space towards the Almighty Light."

There was an atmosphere of exhilaration as Corto's family, plus the Celestial Sailors' three newest members, crowded the deck for the approach to Saul's island.

In a loud voice, Corto said:

"Strive to cross oceans. Your spiritual growth commands it. Inner exploration alone will prepare your expedition to the outer shores of the cosmos. Learn not to think in minutes and years, but in lifetimes. For the stars you see in the night sky, light years away, were ignited long ago."

Suddenly a force tugged at all of my senses, took a short pause so that I could bid farewell to Paris and Corto, and wrapped a thick fog around me.

Then in a flash, I was gone.

* * *

I was propelled into the whitest clouds imaginable, yet nothing could outshine Michael who, having achieved his blessed level, hovered before me, more magnificent than ever. In his eyes shone a fabulous glimmer, like the splendor of freshly created stars.

It was the beginning of a new life, his final destination. Everything stopped, as if the dawn of Time and twilight of Space had forever united.

I looked at him for what I believed would be the last time, sad at such a moment, proud I had been chosen to be his father. A faint trace of regret, perhaps because leaving me, was discernible in his voice and composure.

"I must go," he said.

"I know," I replied, longing to hold him, longing to cry, longing for gestures not becoming my nature.

"Will I ever see you again?" I asked.

"More of what I did must be done, but time is like our essence, infinite."

"Then I shall always cherish hope."

He smiled, tilted his head, and with love in his eyes asked in a voice filled with the music of Cathedrals, "Can you do something for me, daddy?"

"Anything! Anything!"

"After visiting your father, can you visit mommy and Nicholas?"

"I will," I answered, sensing I only had a few more seconds with him.

"Can I ask you one final thing?"

My smile answered him.

"Can you influence Nicholas to sail?"

Pure little soul that you are, even as you cross the final threshold you think of others.

"I promise. And you know what sound daddy cannot stand. The sound of your heart breaking. That is worse than all the volcanoes in the world erupting at once."

My beloved Michael. We looked at each other until his eyes dimmed in the sparkling light. A light ready to absorb, ready to enlighten. The clouds began whirling all around me. The brilliance intensified, and the next moment he was gone.

Farewell, my sweet little soul.

* * *

I remained motionless for a while, hoping and praying that he would reappear in all his glory.

Fate decided otherwise.

Needless to say, a meeting with my father did take place, orchestrated by the Master who had greeted me following my suicide, held on the plane I must dwell, since I'm unable to ascend to a higher one until acquiring some form of spiritual growth.

There is a price for one's life, even your own.

During that meeting, my father informed me that he and my Spiritual Guide had been the source of all the creaking noises I had heard prior to my suicide, this to halt my down-spiraling fate.

"When I saw you becoming what I had been, I had to act," my father explained.

"I'm sorry my actions didn't meet up with your expectations," I answered, dryly.

"Therefore you must commit yourself entirely to restore the good humor my other grandson seems to have forever forsaken since that dreadful day. He suffers from the ills of abandonment and Jane, though caring and loving, needs the intervention of the Divine. You know full well even Spiritual Guides are sometimes incapable of mustering the necessary encouragement when their signs are ignored, and invisible voices muted by the skeptical mind. When this happens, it is sanctioned that we intervene and act accordingly towards the alignment of the Original Design. Your knowledge has grown immensely from the events experienced these past months. Use it wisely."

Chasing Sunsets

Now that the reunion with my father had taken place, freed of obligations, I committed myself to help Nicholas. In order to get one's attention, a mortal's that is, there is a way favored by us spirits. Days with meanings are prized allies, for it's easier to reach a mind already thinking of us. Sadly, in my case, though I toiled persistently, no creaking noises, electrical interference, sudden ringing of alarm clocks or phones ever accompanied my efforts.

As expected when met by such failures, my stay at my old home only filled me with more sorrows, as I witnessed how unruly and rebellious Nicholas was becoming.

"I'm going out," he told his mother one evening.

"When will you be back?"

"If I come back tonight, you mean? I might decide to sleep at a friend's house."

"Will you phone me?"

"You mean, if there's a phone at his house?"

Mere words cannot relate to you my anguish. My persistent incapacity disconcerted me. Yet the plight of Nicholas remained my sole concern. I was committed to this endeavor with the greatest of care, having expunged, during another brief reunion with my father, all of his trespasses by telling him that I forgave him.

As I strived to unearth the secret that would favor my son's fate, I wandered through all the ports visited by Thairica. Perhaps the answer to my predicament had been obvious all along.

Then one day I visited the wall in French Guyana. Approaching Sinnamary from the air, I beheld an overwhelming mass of people. The main boulevard pulsated with activities. Vendors punctuated the streets every couple of feet. Stalls filled with fruits, produce, clothing, souvenirs and candles were lined next to one another. Although the traffic was horrendous, the absence of impatient horns baffled me. Men and women of all ages and colors inched along through street intersections and between trapped cars until they met up with the first of three cordons of gendarmes aimed to regulate the unrelenting flow.

I vaporized into this thick, moving mass and made my way over to the revered wall with the indented cross.

There, the ambiance was very different. A black man wearing a white suit, Panama hat and golden tie was engaged in a heated debate with an old black woman I recognized at once as being the one who had witnessed The Great Storm. Close by, there was a bulldozer, and inside, behind the console of instruments, sat its operator, waiting.

The old black woman pleaded with the man. "Monsieur, surely you are aware of these troubling times we live in. Preserving this shrine so that people from all over the world can come and pray would restore hope to those who feel God has deserted them."

"Oh, please," the man scoffed. "Don't turn this into a bigger circus than it already is."

"Circus?" asked the woman, surprised. "Why do you talk to me like this? Don't you recognize me? I'm the one who sat next to your mother in church for nearly ten years! God bless her soul."

"No, Madame," the man replied, with a scornful look. "I did not forget that my mother sat next to you in church for all those years, surely in hope of invoking God to stop my father's abuse, because she sure as hell never tried herself. And just yesterday she—"

Slowly he raised one hand to his eyes and seemed to wipe away tears. "The matter is closed," he sternly resumed. "And don't you dare bring up my mother again."

"I'm so sorry, Monsieur," the woman said. She opened the purse slung around her shoulder and retrieved a newspaper clipping. "But before destroying this wall, perhaps you should read this. Here you have the article about the two latest pilgrims cured by miracle, about a young boy who has recovered his sight, one which had been denied to him at birth, and about a woman who suddenly recovered the use of her legs. Look at this picture! Surely you can feel the joy she demonstrates as she takes her first steps in fifteen years."

Though she suffered from the heat, the old woman stood proudly, brought dignity to the opposition, while the man stared at her repulsively.

"And if this picture fails to sway your heart," she pursued, "perhaps the sight of people from different religions coming here will melt away your resistance. Already, around the world, there are some religious leaders who take this wall as an inspiration to sit and talk and work at erasing barriers between religions. And all of this thanks to the flying lady who, moments after The Great Storm, quieted all arguments and wrapped Sinnamary in a single sphere of love, of beliefs. This shrine is vital! For mankind can be cruel, Monsieur, it can be so cruel."

"There's nothing more to say," the man snapped. He dangled a large manila envelope. "This is the Court's decision. You have used up all of your legal recourses and, be advised, you will all be considered trespassers." As he said this he pointed towards two uniformed gendarmes.

Then very briskly he brushed the old lady aside.

"Look at all of this! the man said to the gendarmes. Hundreds of people waited patiently to pray at this shrine, many of them carrying umbrellas to shelter the elderly and crippled from the blazing heat.

"We are infested by garbage from all over the world, flocking to this spot like blind dogs to a scent," the man furiously added. "All of this will scare away those who would seek the tranquility and intimacy of my future hotel. Their pockets filled with real money, not the meager scraps collected from the few souvenirs shops littering the streets."

He took off his straw hat, wiped his sweaty forehead with an impeccable white handkerchief, and glared at those he considered with no more esteem than vermin.

Then he nodded to the bulldozer operator. The delays had come to an end. Behind the bulldozer's console, the operator, having received the go ahead, anxiously waited for the old black woman to stand aside. Throngs of pilgrims, hands joined together, prayed for a last minute postponement.

Suddenly, faint distortions taking place near the man in the white suit caught my attention. These distortions were followed by a blurry vortex, which with the passing seconds became keener and clearer until finally an old black woman appeared.

Aghast, I beheld this spirit who, by magic, conveyed to me that the man in the white suit was her son. Somehow, my intuition also grasped the dreadful reason why I was able to see her. Tormented by her son's cold handling of the matter at hand, she tried brushing him, endlessly reaching out her hand through and through, all the while moaning terribly. Having perceived her failure, the old woman sobbed uncontrollably, and when realizing that no tears escaped her vaporous eyes, cried hideously. Truly, she appeared doomed to carry a heavy burden. Oh, how I wished to console her. I could not permit that neither the burden she carried nor the anger her son felt be the cause of turning this wall of hope into useless rubble.

Then I realized how her predicament paralleled my own, and vowed to release my self-imposed burden, forgiving myself for my suicide, which lately, because of Nicholas' plight, had proven impossible. My resolve was augmented when I remembered the reunion with my father and of how cold and distant I had then behaved, treating such a privileged moment as an obligation, rather than a healing step for *him*. I realized one cannot feign forgiveness, for total forgiveness comes from the heart. A sort of immense releasing of energies meant to be perceived by the Universe.

I remembered the clue put forth during the visit at my first apartment, when I had sworn an oath born of contempt following my father's comments. We all strive for affection, for appreciation. But what are we to do when faced with a lack of support? What are we to do if we sense that we are denied that wealth of love and compassion? It was then I realized, at long last, how such a gap can only be filled from the inside.

Emotions are a product of thoughts. And thoughts, through proper meditation, can be mastered. Trials do for us what comfort cannot do. By realizing the importance of the struggle, armed with the proper mindset, hardships provide a most promising arena for growth. In essence, what we lack, offers greater opportunities for spiritual elevation than what we have.

I looked at the ground. The same ground Michael had brought to life. If only I could get one small object to move.

Just then, an astonishing and unnatural movement caught my attention. Near the man's feet, on the mound of dirt, debris and rocks upon which he rigidly stood, a small pebble began to tremble.

"Am I the cause of this faint movement?" I whispered. For the next seconds, I observed how this inert mass vibrated, and concluded thereafter that the prospect of such movement was indeed coming from me!

I focused my energy on a piece of glass that shimmered under the scorching sun. It, too, quickly began a tremulous dance. I felt elated, and encouraged, and instantly recollected my entire memorable journey.

I remembered the sorceress' story about the Navajo warrior's quest to fill a vase with water. I also remembered Paris' rape, and why unbreakable chains had forced upon me the sight of her ultimate ordeal. As she had so splendidly demonstrated, there is no victory like the conquering of oneself.

Once again I dwelled in a land of magic. And though the feeble dance performed by that little pebble and piece of glass amounted to the puff of a light wind, wasn't it that same force that had carried Thairica over thousands of miles?

I had vanquished inertia. I had broken the spell of my vase.

The sudden awareness of my powers increased the nervous pulsations on the ground. The man gazed, open-mouthed and confused, at the sustained impossibility to which I now added my gloomy voice, which stormed in his ears like Divine Intervention.

"How is it people's tears are denied access to your heart?" I sternly demanded.

He frantically looked all around, and quickly confirmed, through his isolated position, the impossibility of another person standing next to him. I repeated the question, and watched his increasing amazement.

"No, no! This can't be!" he murmured. His inflated eyes searched everywhere for some clue, some reasonable explanation, one that would dispel his haunting thoughts.

"Who is this?" he softly whispered.

"I am your mother's friend."

"This can't be," he repeated.

"Yes it can!" I hastily replied. "And let me add that your mother is here, with me, and grieves immensely for your soul."

"Mama!" he murmured, astonishingly. It was evident that thoughts of spirits startled him, his mind surely imagining tormenting phantoms rattling chains. I dispelled the turmoil of such thoughts, this with remarkable effect, for his eyes returned to normal size.

"I mean you no harm," I assured. "I speak on behalf of someone carrying a burden so great it prevents direct conversation."

"Prove to me you are what you say you are," he voiced suspiciously, like one expecting validation. "Yes," he pursued, in a stronger tone of voice. "Prove to me you are more than the echo of my wishes."

The man's mother looked at me, spoke through her eyes, and I relayed to him how she grieved for not halting his father's hands. But her confession didn't end there. She expressed great sorrows for taking her own life, yet rejoiced when recollecting tender mother-and-son moments. These thoughts I also conveyed, and it appeared that the man's mind immediately filled with memories of delicate meanings, as all of the banished specters of happiness refreshingly reclaimed their throne.

"Your mother's guilt is her curse," I resumed. "Don't let resentment become yours."

"What am I to do?" he asked, nervously. "How can I protect myself from evil?"

"You must do as your conscience commands you to," I advised. "Of course, you can always silence that inner voice by following those who operate outside moral boundaries. But I must warn you. There are consequences to everything in the after life. Everything!"

Panic struck the man's eyes. He rushed over to the bulldozer operator and ordered a halt to his project. Although the sight of pilgrims loudly cheering warmed my soul, other pressing considerations had me leave these premises immediately.

I returned home. I had not been there more than a few seconds that a dispute erupted in the living room. In front of me stood Nicholas, loudly shouting and wishing to leave for a few days. Seated on the couch in front of him was Jane, shoulders slumped, totally exasperated. Tears filled her eyes. Unable to look I turned around. Just then, on the front cover of a magazine lying on the table, I noticed the picture of a sailboat. Words printed next to the picture advertised a journey at sea!

It was the obvious sign I had ignored, displayed this time to realign Nicholas towards *his* Original Design, the one I had altered.

This sight underlined a unique sense of duty, with Nicholas intent on leaving the house, and the unnoticed magazine begging for a glimpse. I knew full well that the Universe indulged those committed to action, remembering my fruitless search for the ad once I had discarded it. Determined to help I searched for a way to get Nicholas' attention, when his set of keys provided the opportunity. Dutifully, I extended my hand, used all of my will, and succeeded to move the keys a few inches towards the magazine, slightly behind the telephone.

I watched Nicholas pace all around the living room, wondering aloud where he had put his keys. Seeing how his eyes seemed to wander everywhere but on the table, I went to the window and, using my newfound magical powers, I managed a tiny breach in the curtains. Sunrays immediately streamed into the living room and struck the magazine cover, which glowed for just a second! I looked back. Catching the draft coming through the window, the curtains gently fluttered. A discreet dance played out between sunlight and curtains, with the picture at times turning from coal to diamond, and back to coal again.

I peeked outside. Dozens of clouds glided across the sky one after another, threatening to permanently hide the sun and turn a diamond into ashes. I willed with all my might for the clouds to vanish, for the phone to ring. Although endowed with some powers, these did not extend to stopping clouds.

I applied myself and focused even more. But the winds raged, and swiftly pushed the clouds filing across the sky.

Just then Nicholas' Spiritual Guide, through the collaboration of my growth, progressively emerged out of his invisible shelter. And though his sight translated to an even greater spiritual growth on my part, it failed to entice the slightest elation, for other pressing events voided any sense of self-gratification.

The winds blew harder. Again I stared outside, and noticed how the clouds almost obstructed the sun. Distressed, I remembered having encountered only one Being of Light capable of influencing clouds and winds and knew full well, from the level of enlightenment achieved that day at the wall, that such a lofty state was neither mine, nor that of the Spiritual Guide.

And just as I thought of him, a spark lighted my intuition. Immediately I gazed outside. With great joy I saw the clouds coming to a complete stop, even as the wind furiously shook the treetops.

But with Nicholas intent on leaving without his keys, the situation became even more urgent. I summoned all of my essence into one, mystical, sublime impulse.

From deep within I experienced the rising of a Force. A wave swept across my core, and kindled my hope. Beyond my transparent fingers, an electrical current went to work.

There was a short confrontation, with my skills matched against the fleeing seconds. Finally the phone rang. On picking it up and listening to the dead tone, Nicholas appeared puzzled.

"Hello?" he said, before hanging up. His eyes suddenly narrowed. Something had caught his attention. Then a fierce stare fell upon the gleaming picture of a sailboat. The prolonged radiance enticed his dazzled eyes to read the article.

And when those words inspired images of adventures and mysteries, of treasures and discoveries, when the light inside him, made opaque by the shades of uncertainty, energized his spirit, he reached out for the telephone. Close by, his mother cherished hope. From Nicholas' lips there was first a formal inquiry, then faint gasps, followed by a loud exclamation of wonder. His smile grew wider, and quickly turned into a thunderous laugh just as Jane, wildly leaping in the air, madly rushed with open arms to embrace our son. Then, from that blissful moment, the Original Design whispered its secrets. I knew his heart would no longer nourish despair, but also, I knew exactly who had helped me with the clouds!

* * *

The sun, sinking to the West, extends its grasp and taints the horizon. This is my favorite moment of the day, so lively and vibrant, full of hope and promise. Little by little the golden eye falls into the sea. Above the masts of the sailboats anchored here and there in the Grenadines, distant stars begin to appear.

Sounds of laughter travel across the warm Caribbean waters. Nicholas, refreshed from his late afternoon swim, climbs aboard Thairica. He pauses on the aft deck, smiles, then looks to his right at Freedom, a sloop captained by Esmeralda, Emilio and Jared.

"Don't forget our dive tomorrow morning," he tells Emilio, before entering the cockpit. He warmly embraces his mother, his spirit the way it was intended, only stronger because of a long exposure to the sea and true friendships. Then in a firm voice he says to the family of four sitting on the foredeck:

"To chasing sunsets."

"To sunset chasers," they happily reply.

This triumphant sight warms the immortal soul. Spiritual growth is not achieved by skimming along the surface of our planet. For that you must journey deep into its oceans, deep inside people's hearts.

We flow towards wholeness, expanding while giving. Ahead of us, the horizon beckons. Our soul ventures forth, the seed of our existence, our link to God.

Only temporarily submitted to gravity, our essence belongs to the stars.

Although I wish could spend all my time with Nicholas, this cannot be. Now, I belong to another realm, although I often accompany his Spiritual Guide. Just in case . . .

There is something profoundly sacred between a father and his son. A bond that is unique.

I rejoice each time I think of the day Nicholas answered the ad, when his brother came to my rescue.

Someone forever unique to me.

God's newest angel. My little boy Michael.